LOUISE MANGOS writes novels, short stories and flash fiction, which have won prizes, been placed on shortlists and read out on BBC radio. *The Art of Deception* is her second novel. Her debut novel, *Strangers on a Bridge*, was a finalist in the Exeter Novel Prize and long-listed for the Bath Novel Award. You can connect with Louise on Facebook and Twitter @LouiseMangos, or visit her website, www.louisemangos.com, where there are links to some of her short fiction. She lives on a Swiss Alp with her Kiwi husband and two sons.

Also by Louise Mangos

Strangers on a Bridge

The Art of Deception

LOUISE MANGOS

ONE PLACE. MANY STORIES

HQ
An imprint of HarperCollins*Publishers* Ltd
1 London Bridge Street
London SE1 9GF

This paperback edition 2019

First published in Great Britain by
HQ, an imprint of HarperCollins*Publishers* Ltd 2019

ISBN: 9780008330989

Typeset by Palimpsest Book Production Ltd, Falkirk, Stirlingshire
Printed and bound in Great Britain by
CPI Group (UK) Ltd, Melksham, SN12 6TR

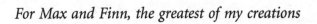

For Max and Finn, the greatest of my creations

Prologue

The vice of his fingers tightened on my wrist, and tendons crunched as they slid over each other inside my forearm. As he twisted harder, I turned my body in the direction of his grip to try and relieve the pain. His other hand appeared from behind him and the heel of his palm hit the side of my head. As it made contact with my ear, a siren rang in my brain, blocking all other sound.

I kicked out, my foot slamming into his shins. His forward momentum increased as he was caught off balance, and his upper body folded. His shoulder glanced off the picture frame on the wall and it fell to the floor with a clatter. The rebound flung him away from me. As he let go of my arm, we fell apart like a tree struck down the middle by lightning. I staggered backwards, calves ramming against the coffee table, pushing it towards the sofa.

Terror now ruling my fear, I grabbed the ceramic vase toppling from the table. I swung it ineffectually at his head. I was briefly surprised it didn't break, and the resistance of the vase meeting something solid tipped me further backwards. I let it go and it shattered at our feet. As I fell, my hips and back splintered the glass table top with a rifle-like explosion. Wedged into the frame of the table, head thrown back against the seat of the sofa, I stared at the ceiling in a moment of silence.

Chapter 1

'Stop! Stop it!' I yell, with my hands pressed over my ears.

My voice rasps in my throat and fills my head. The thudding on the wall ceases abruptly, and I take my palms slowly away. The ensuing roar of silence is tuned perfectly to the blood pumping through my veins.

My gaze is fixed on a pencil-drawn sketch taped to the mottled plaster, a child's portrayal of a chalet. The house is perched on top of a mountain with stick people skiing down one side of the hill. As my concentration wavers, I blink away a tear of frustration, and rub my temple. I was expecting to see the picture tremble with the thumping. But these partitions are solid brick; raging fists will not move them.

The subsequent stillness is painful, and I try to imagine Fatima in her two-by-four-metre space on the other side of the wall. The expectation of what might replace her anger increases the tension like the static of an impending lightning strike.

They have taken away her son, and won't let her see him even briefly for a feed. One of the female guards simply marched in and picked the little thing up from his crib, right in front of Fatima's eyes. We all came out to the corridor to watch in horror as the head security officer gathered Fatima's flailing arms and held her while the guard walked away with the baby. Then they locked her in. Who knows how long they'll keep the baby this time. An hour. A morning. A day? I suck in the musty air of my cell. Annoyance has prevailed over my sympathy. I want to scream and shout too.

Someone has also taken away my son, but I have to keep a lid on my emotions or it may backfire. Losing control would do me no favours in this place, especially as my son is far away, and I don't know when we will be together again.

I hope they don't keep Fatima's baby for long. She stole three packets of *Zigis* from the new Polish girl who came in last week. The one whose name no one can pronounce. Lots of z's and c's. Who the hell risks solitary for a handful of cigarettes? I guess the nicotine-deprived are desperate. They haven't seen fresh Marlboros for weeks. I don't even think Fatima intended to smoke them herself. She merely wanted something to trade. The theft led to a fight in the canteen, a messy affair resulting in tufts of hair on the floor and bite marks on various limbs.

I can't believe Fatima was caught so easily, especially after all the other stuff she helped steal, the stuff she didn't get nabbed for in her previous life. It turns out she was only the driver when she was arrested.

We all have previous lives. I still find it hard to talk about mine, so I choose to silently observe everyone else's.

That fight clinched Fatima's punishment. No solitary, simply take the little boy.

Her baby is called Adnan, and he's a sweet little thing. The guards periodically use him as a bribe to try to control her anger, but I think it makes her worse. How can they take this woman's child away? There's an irony to it, with the tainted history of this place. All they're doing is building a seething resentment that will eventually rise like the stopper on the top of a pressure cooker. Fatima is close to breaking point.

I know how she feels.

4

Adnan reminds me of Jean-Philippe, or JP as we called him within days of his birth. Maybe Adnan's Balkan roots have a vague link to JP's part-Russian ones. The same penetrating Slavic eyes, a strong squarish head, an almost simian brow. My baby is much older than Adnan, and no longer an infant. But I still think of him as a baby. The name JP stuck when he started *l'école maternelle* last year. His friends at school even adopted the soft 'Shay-Pee' in French.

I've noticed he tries to sign his full name, Jean-Philippe, on the bottom of his little notes and drawings to me now, a challenge for one so young. I hope he's proud he can spell such a complicated name. More likely his grandmother, Natasha, or Mimi as JP calls her, has insisted he practises his full title. She has always hated the acronym we use for his nickname, and is undoubtedly dragging him back to a more conservative tradition. Her whole philosophy seems so formal, so remote. Since I've been here, she's removed the strings connecting mother and child like a heavily glued sticking plaster, painfully tearing him from his Anglo roots.

He was 6 years old last week, and I haven't seen him this month. I have had to be content with sending cards and my own drawings and talking to him on the phone. To think he had a birthday without me, his mother. The court has obliged his grandparents to let me see him once a month. It's the most I could engineer for the moment. His father's family is trying to keep him from me as much as possible. It's a punishment far harsher than my imprisonment, and my heart aches for him constantly.

Fatima knows and respects this, but cannot contain her rage, despite being aware I can hear her, somewhat muffled, behind the wall. Motherhood for her is still fresh. The fear of separation has become a raw terror that something will happen to Adnan in her absence. I understand that, and can identify with it.

It's a love like no other.

* * *

Seven years ago

Settling on a high stool, I nursed a glass of cheap draft beer, watching the bustle of the après-ski crowd reflected in the mirror behind the bar. A figure in a red ski-school jacket, a folded ten-franc note clasped between his fingers, pushed his way between me and the customer at my side. The young man rested his hand on the polished wood. I bit back a retort as his elbow pressed against my shoulder. He leaned in, and I drew back, expecting him to address the barman.

'We are all vagabonds, you know.' His silky deep voice spoke English, almost a whisper at my temple, his breath warm on the shell of my ear. The hint of a French lilt sent a tingle down my spine. I turned, and instead of delivering admonishment, smiled into a pair of mesmerising grey-blue eyes.

'You are new in town, yes?' he asked.

'Just arrived,' I confirmed. 'Couldn't hitch a lift, so I rode the cog railway up from the valley. Bit freaky, didn't know if the rickety thing was going to make it, with all that clunking and straining.'

'That rack is over a hundred years old. You took a journey on a classic piece of Chablais transport history. What brings you here?'

'A bit of an unscheduled stop, really. I'm backpacking through Europe and read about this village in a student travel guide. Plus a college friend once told me about this bar.'

I hesitated. In reality I was looking for a few days' work. I had heard this resort, easily accessible on my Eurorail pass, was a good place to try. Amsterdam and Paris had sucked the money out of my wallet faster than any pickpocket. This guy didn't need to know I was flat broke.

'I was originally on my way to Greece for the summer. I know that's a long way from here, but I'm getting a bit short of cash.'

'Mm. The Med. Sounds romantic. Unfortunately you have arrived at the end of the season. There won't be many jobs avail-

6

able. People will be heading off soon, travelling south, perhaps to the same beach you are dreaming about. Some of us will stay here though; we have to work.'

The barman slid a bottle of Cardinal across the bar, a slight frown on his face. My new companion took a sip from the beer.

'You're lucky to live in such a beautiful place. What do you do outside the ski season?' I asked as I glanced at the barman, now moving away to serve another customer.

'I teach French at the international college. Pays the bills.'

He sidled in to sit on a recently vacated barstool in one smooth move, his body filling the space at my side, and he reached into his jacket pocket. He took a ready-rolled cigarette from a pouch of Drum, and lit the tatty end with a loud click of his Zippo. He noted my surprise.

'One of the few bars that still allows smokers,' he said, studying me intently through a swirl of blue smoke. No one else in the bar was smoking. He waved at a spark rising from a burning curl of tobacco, and studied me through creased eyes.

My face flushed hot and my belly flipped. A magnetism kept my eyes locked on his, despite the commotion around us.

And then he coughed, the harshness of the smoke catching in his throat, making his eyes smart. We both burst out laughing, his slick seduction technique exposed. I saw the barman roll his eyes as he served another client at the end of the bar, and as he returned, he leaned over.

'Buddy, you know the rules. Quit being a dick.'

My companion put his hand on my arm, pulling my attention back to him.

'Should give up the stuff,' he said, curling his fist towards his chest, cigarette still clasped between two fingers.

'Absolutely,' I agreed. 'Tobacco should be outlawed anyway.'

He raised his eyebrows. I blushed, and mentally kicked myself for sounding so prudish. He continued to smoke his roll-up, and I wondered which rules the barman was referring to.

'So what's your name, Pretty Travel Girl Heading for Greece?'

He picked a sliver of tobacco from the tip of his tongue, and I couldn't help thinking the roll-up cigarette routine was going horribly wrong for him today.

'Lucie, actually Lucille, but everyone calls me Lucie.'

'And my name is Matt, actually Mathieu, but everyone calls me Matt. *Enchanté*,' he said, holding out his hand to shake.

I would have commented on his patronising tone, but a physical static tick connected our palms, and we both smiled. My heartbeat spiked. He brushed a lock of brown hair, a little flattened from a day under a ski hat, away from his face. His broad shoulders hunched on one side as he leaned his elbow on the bar. He stretched his ski-honed legs either side of my barstool, and my vision of a golden beach and carefree days with suntanned beach bums slipped away.

'Do you ski?' he asked.

With my glass to my lips, I took a sip, and shook my head.

'You can always engage my services. Ask for Matt at the ski school.'

Now that sounded like a more practised marketing tag line.

'I can't afford to ski right now, though I'd love to learn.'

'Of course you don't ski! You are from the land of sailors. Do you sail, Lucie? Is that why you are heading to the waters of the *Mediterranée*? Perhaps you would like to sail with me, on my boat, on *Lac Léman. Mon premier lieutenant.*'

I shook my head, but not with disagreement. Did he really just say he had a boat? The concept seemed so contrary, up here on the mountain.

'I used to sail very small boats – Optimists – on a man-made lake near our home as a child. And although my dad was in the navy, we never sailed on the Med.'

I was still not entirely sure he was telling the truth about owning a boat. I might believe him more if he said he drove a Ferrari.

'Actually, my little sloop is also not much bigger than a bathtub. It was bought with a small inheritance from a childless aunt. Sounds good as a chat-up line though, doesn't it? Can I get you another?'

I buried my smile in my glass as I emptied the warm dregs and placed it on the bar near him. My cheeks flushed in acknowledgement of the heat in the pit of my stomach.

As we talked, other customers chatted around us, but I blocked them out, not allowing their gossip to interfere. I didn't want this to end. I felt myself sucked into the vortex of a schoolgirl crush. Finishing his second beer, Matt reached hastily for his jacket, stood up and leaned in to me, as though he'd lost his balance.

'Perhaps I will see you around, *ma Lucille*. It's time to change out of my office gear,' he said, indicating his ski uniform.

I'd always hated my full name, thought it made me sound like a faded Sixties' TV star, but the way he spoke made it sound like honey slipping off his tongue.

Mathieu cast me a last curious smile as he shrugged into his jacket and wove his way through the clientele towards the exit. I frowned as I watched him leave. A wedge of disappointment remained, the warm feeling he had invoked in me already a heady memory. An air of mystery floated in his wake. Our conversation remained half-finished, as though he intended to return to it later. I wondered if he felt the same physical and emotional pull. Or was this just another day at the office?

'He's a Casanova, that one. Watch out,' said the barman, absently drying a glass with a tea towel. I wasn't sure whether his tone was one of wistful jealousy or a warning.

'Does he really have a boat on Lake Geneva?' I asked, ignoring the alarm bells.

'Apparently.' He shrugged. 'Though I don't know anyone who has ever seen it. Could be a bullshit line. Watch yourself there, young lady.'

He moved away to stack glasses.

The bar emptied at the end of Happy Hour, and the barman, much friendlier in Mathieu's absence, introduced me to the manageress of the hostel.

'We close next week for a month or so, but we will need extra staff for the few days it takes to spring-clean,' she said. 'I can hire you for the week. It will be tough work, moving furniture, lots of cleaning.'

'I'm fine with that – I'd be delighted to help,' I said, relieved to the point of making it sound like we were doing each other a favour. If I had any hope of reaching my Greek beach, I needed more than a few days of work, but this would be a start.

'You can move into the staff accommodation and take your meals with the others. I know that look. I can tell you're desperate for cash. We'll deduct the rent from your earnings and you can set up a tab at the bar. You can take Sandra's bed. She had to leave early. Some family emergency back in Australia. Normally we wouldn't hire extra staff at the end of the season. You're lucky.'

* * *

As I entered the bar the following evening, after a day that had magically transformed the landscape with a spring snow, my gaze was drawn to a raucous group at the bar. They were playing the inanely stupid but enticingly addictive game of spoof. It was a game I had often played in the student lounge at college. Clutched fists thrust repeatedly into a circle at each other, hands then turned to reveal the number of coins in their palms. No prizes for the eliminated victors, but shots of the Swiss schnapps Pomme for the losers, the grimaces on their faces at the harshness and raw strength of the alcohol a prize in itself for the onlookers.

'Ah, here is our pretty Greek seaside girl. A little diversion on her way to the summer sun.'

Matt threw his arm casually across my shoulder, the weight of it implying possessiveness. Despite acknowledging the possible effects of alcohol, a flush crept up my throat at his familiarity.

'*Bonsoir*, Mathieu,' I said.

'What have you been doing with yourself today?' he asked. 'How did you like nature's last gift of winter to us? There were a few happy powder hounds on the mountain today.'

'It would have been great to be able to ski. Perhaps next season,' I said cautiously, not wishing to imply that I might rashly have made my mind up to stay a little longer. 'I had a pleasant walk around town. I'm not really prepared for wintry conditions. Today was a test for the soaking capacity of my socks.'

I pointed down to my sodden sneakers.

'Inappropriate footwear, huh?' Matt patted me on my shoulder. 'The slush will probably be gone by tomorrow. This little cold front was unexpected.'

The barman greeted me warmly with a tip of his head. His eyes moved away and cast Matt a steely look as he ordered us beers. Clutching our bottles in one hand, Matt returned the barman's stare and then turned away, putting his body between me and the bar. He placed his other hand firmly on my elbow, and guided me with a little more force than necessary towards the corner.

He pointed to a bench where we could sit and talk. I glanced back to the barman before allowing myself to be led away. I could only think that his reaction was due to jealousy. I had to stop myself grinning broadly. Matt had forsaken his colleagues and their entertainment for me. As far as I was concerned, it was game on.

* * *

When I moved into the hostel's staff accommodation, I enjoyed the camaraderie of my room-mates. But while they were all

11

winding up for the end of the season, for me it felt like a beginning.

On the first evening after work, I was lying on my bed reading a novel borrowed from the hostel library. Anne, the receptionist, burst through the door with a bag of items she had purchased from the local épicerie.

'I see you have thrilling plans for this evening,' she said not unkindly, pointing her chin at my book. 'Well I'm going to change them. I don't feel like going to the bar tonight before dinner, but I need some wine and I don't want to drink alone.'

She pulled a bottle from the bag with a packet of pretzels and a tub of olives.

'My boyfriend and his mother are disagreeing over one of my pieces, and I've left them to it.'

I fetched two glasses from the shelf in the bathroom and brought them back to the dorm. As Anne emptied the rest of her bag, I studied the posters tacked to the wall above her bed. A Hodler print hung next to a photo of a Giacometti sculpture; one of his classic tall thin bronze men. Beyond them she had pinned up her own photos of the surrounding mountains, glowing with sunsets or sunrises, and one spectacular shot of a sea of cloud filling the valley against a striking purple sky.

'You're an artist?' I asked over the noise of the pretzel packet being opened and the lid screeching off the plastic olive container.

'If you consider photography an art.'

She handed me the bottle of wine and a corkscrew.

'Of course,' I said.

'I love contemporary Swiss artists, as you can see. A salute to my fellow countrymen. Photography is more my own passion, a hobby inspired by our environment. My boyfriend François' father owns the Grand Hotel in the village where he works, and they recently agreed to hang some of my photos in one of their conference rooms. But they don't seem to want my advice as to which ones. It was as though I wasn't even there,' she said crossly. 'Are you also interested in art?'

She nodded towards the posters on the wall, curiosity quashing her irritation.

'I was halfway through a fine arts degree when I dropped out of university and decided to travel. It's backfired really. My parents obviously weren't happy, and I wouldn't have dreamed of asking them to fund a trip, but I can't believe how quickly the money I earned from Saturday and holiday jobs seems to have slipped like water through my fingers.'

I opened the bottle, poured some wine into our two glasses, and took a handful of pretzels Anne offered me as we sat on our beds facing the windows. The setting sun cast a pinkish glow on the toothy ridge of the Dents du Midi. She reached for her camera on the shelf by the bed and tucked it beside her, waiting for the perfect alpenglow.

'Then it's good they hired you at the hostel. But it's poor pay for cleaning work. Your funds won't last long in this country. I'm a bit better off on a receptionist's salary, especially after the peanuts I earned when I travelled in the States. *Bon appétit*,' she said as she offered me the pot of olives and popped one in her mouth.

'You speak excellent English.'

'The multilingual skills of the Swiss, I guess. What made you give up studying art?'

'I don't know really. I love my art, but I had the feeling I'd never be able to find a job I would enjoy. Plus I've always had this secret dream to travel abroad, and wanted to do it before getting bogged down with a career.'

'I can't wait to get out of this room,' said Anne, looking around at the three rumpled beds and a jumble of mismatched furniture. 'They want me to stay on for the next couple of seasons. But there's only so long you can spend living in a dorm. I've saved up enough money to rent my own flat. It'll be so much easier

13

for François and me. Will you look for another job in the village, or move on from here?'

'I'm not sure. It depends.' I turned to a poster. 'Your photos are beautiful.'

It depends on Matt, I had wanted to say, but now found it hard to admit that an impulsive decision might be based on the outcome of meeting one person. Anne's mention of her boyfriend made the heat rise to my face.

When we had finished the bottle of wine, she showed me some more of her photographs. I swirled the last of the Valaisan gamay in the glass tumbler.

'Do you know Mathieu, the ski instructor? The local guy?' The wine had loosened my tongue, and I blushed as I said his name.

Anne's smile didn't touch her eyes. 'Has he been flirting with you? He's a looker. I don't know him very well. Only that he often comes to the bar. He had … He and François don't get on, something to do with a group of students François' dad had to ban from the hotel after a rowdy night out in their college years. They don't mix in the same social circles.' Anne hesitated. 'And I find his attitude a little arrogant for my liking. Plus, I've heard he's … I would be careful.' Anne bit her lip.

I wasn't sure whether my heart beat a little faster at the mention of his name or hearing the edge to Anne's comments. Before I could dig further, she took her camera and opened the dorm window to click a few shots of the view, and I felt too awkward to ask her to elaborate.

'Come on, I'm starving,' she said, snapping the cover onto her lens. 'Let's see what chef has for the workers tonight.'

* * *

My life revolved around the hostel and the bar for the remainder of the week until I received my pay packet. The whole time I was stripping beds, scrubbing floors and cleaning windows, I couldn't stop thinking about Matt. The grudge work I was doing was worth every cobweb and dust ball if it meant I could see him at the end of each day. The anticipation of our budding romance was delicious. I relished the apprehensive thrill of not knowing whether he would be there when I walked into the bar. Or the expectation every time the door opened to admit new customers, and the powerful heated rush when he finally appeared on the threshold. I was behaving like a besotted teenager.

But he always came. Each night he captivated me with stories of his adventures, and at the point where his descriptions verged on bragging, he would reel me in with promises to show me his world. The lure of sailing in his sloop, the desire to mirror his tracks down the ski slope, all whispered in my ear, sending shivers down my spine, with the security of his arms around me. Fuelled with a blind hormonal passion, I knew I wanted this man beyond anything else I had ever desired.

How could I let myself fall so quickly? I knew I was throwing caution to the wind. I had only met Matt days ago; I knew nothing about him, and Anne wasn't able to provide much information, although the things she said, or didn't say, made me think she might be hiding something. But my yearning for him eclipsed the warning bells of losing control in my head. Despite being a relatively inexperienced 19-year-old, I knew the danger of succumbing to these emotions, but could do nothing to control the fire.

* * *

I am shaken from my reverie by a gentle fluttering at the window. It sounds like a moth batting the pane, and thinking I should let it out, I look up to see the first splats of today's rain blowing against the glass through the bars. The forested ridge to the east has disappeared in a smudge of weather released from the grey belly of the sky.

Fatima starts a keening wail. This is the one she usually saves for the middle of the night. It doesn't seem so unsettling during the day, lends itself to comical lunacy rather than ghostly guilt without the cover of darkness. But before I can feel sorry for her, I hear a loud '*Fertig, jetzt!*' from Müller in the corridor. Enough now!

Müller is one of the guards, or carers, as they like to call them here. Makes us sound like we're in an old people's home, or a mental institution, which is probably closer to the truth. She is assigned to our block and spends most of her duty time on our floor.

Fatima's tone reduces to a series of self-pitying sobs. I barely tolerate her ranting. But when I hear Adnan crying I go to pieces. By some administrative quirk, I ended up next to Fatima when I came in. She was already pregnant, and gave birth not long afterwards. She won't be on our floor for long though. There are only six units on the mother–child level, and one of them will become free in a couple of days when another inmate's toddler goes to a foster home. However sad it is for the mother, at least she had some time with her baby. Fatima might face the same fate if she is still here in three years' time. I've never asked how long she's in for.

It's a cruel coincidence that they are next to me, given that I would love to have my son at my side. There is already some confusion as to why I am here and not at La Tuilière prison in Vaud, the canton where the crime took place and where I was sentenced. My incarceration here is unprecedented in a country where the legal process is decentralised. It must be the ambiguity of my origin. Although I have lived in Vaud for several years, in the French-speaking part of the country, I never went through the procedures to become a naturalised Swiss citizen. But I have begun to suspect that's not the only reason I am so far away from JP.

My sketchpad is open on the desk. I pick up a pencil and try to draw, but can't concentrate with Fatima going on, so I take two paces to my window. I have to lean past the narrow shelf of the desk bolted to the wall to peer outside through drops of water on the glass. Blue curtains frame the window, a lame attempt at helping us to forget where we are, absurdly contrasting the lattice of the bars.

The sky lies like a wet blanket over the flat landscape. The prison sits on a slight mound above the village of Hindelbank. A forested ridge blocks our view of the sunrise, which isn't visible anyway behind today's miserable weather. Beyond the community to the north stretches the vast unexciting plateau where the River Emme meanders out of a broad valley. We are a long way from the romantic alpine meadows at the source of its waters in the Bernese Oberland, home to the cows producing the milk synonymous with the famous Emmental cheese. In the distance to the west lie the ancient mountains of the Jura, marching their sheer cliffs along the boundary of France. An almost static curtain of cloud spills slowly like Niagara down their gullies.

If only I could see the mountains on the other side, to the east. If only I could touch in my mind the familiarity of altitude, forever inciting a melancholic longing for home.

Or a place I used to call home.

Chapter 2

Yasmine is sitting on my bed. Today is Sunday, our day off. I was enjoying my solitude until she walked in. I'm a little irked by her attitude, thinking she can barge into my cell whenever she wants. I don't say anything, as it's better to avoid provocation in this place. Everyone is unpredictable, and I just want to get by without attracting attention. I'm not completely comfortable in her company. I busy myself watering my plants – a dragon palm, a small ficus and a fern. They will soon suffer from the brittleness of the dry winter air. I can pick and choose my house-plants. That privilege comes from having access to the greenhouse.

Yasmine sifts through a few photos of JP lying on my pillow, and stares at one of him as a baby. I want to tell her to take her hands off my child.

'You know they used to lock up young girls in this place who became *enceinte* when they were not being married. And they hadn't done anything wrong. No stealing. No kill—'

'It was called the "re-education" of unmarried mothers then,' I interrupt. 'The system was tailored for the likes of Fatima. Usually put here by their own parents who didn't know how to deal with their daughter's pregnancies.'

'The worst is they were still doing this thing until the 1980s,' she says. 'Imagine, in our lifetime! They will not take Adnan away from Fatima permanently. They cannot do this. To provoke such publicity again would be, how do you say, *une atrocité*.'

'Fatima must have the ghost of one of those girls in her room,' I say. 'She often screams as though she might never see Adnan again. Maybe tomorrow she won't. It's hard to imagine the destinies of the babies. Who knows where Adnan will end up if he is farmed out to a foster family? I don't know if it's any less barbaric than back then.'

Yasmine looks at me and raises one eyebrow. I'm not sure she understands everything I say, but she doesn't ask for clarification.

She has shuffled the photos out of order and my breath quickens to see the images carelessly handled. They are so valuable to me, and I'm worried she's smearing them with hand cream or grease from the kitchens. I doubt I'll be able to get fresh copies. The family didn't give these to me. That would never happen. These are photos Anne has sent me, copies from her collection. Her son Valentin is JP's best friend. I wonder what JP will look like the next time I see him. Kids change quickly in six months. I'm surprised every time.

'Don't …' I start to say, and am silenced by a look that either tells me I'm being too precious, or that I shouldn't mess with her.

Yasmine often talks about Hindelbank's history, repeating its horrors as if trying to make the events of the recent past more believable. To make her own imprisonment more of a fantasy. Or perhaps to kid herself that she is here even though she has done nothing wrong. She came to Hindelbank after me in May, from Basel. She was part of a gang crossing the French border in a transit van, periodically relieving pre-alpine villages of their bicycles. They indiscriminately loaded up bikes, using bolt cutters on even the strongest of locks. It was on their fourth or fifth foray into the country that they were finally caught.

Yasmine is Algerian, but chooses to converse with me in

19

English, despite knowing I can speak French fairly fluently. She pronounces all her th's as a soft zz.

I am quite the novelty. There was another English woman here until just before I arrived. She was rumoured to have murdered a man who had been stalking her family. But she was released before I arrived, and no one wants to talk about those who get out. So I am the only one here right now. Everyone wants to practise my mother tongue, except the guards who bark their orders in Swiss German. They are aware that most of the Swiss citizens, who don't even constitute half of the inmates here, can barely understand their guttural Bern dialect. Most of the guards speak only one of the four languages of Switzerland: the most discordant of them all.

Yasmine reaches for a pack of cigarettes in her pocket and taps it on her thigh, a pointless resettling of tobacco in those poisonous cylinders. I make a tutting sound and shake my head. First the photos, now she wants to smoke.

'No, Yasmine,' I say firmly.

She sighs and rolls her eyes, but silently places the soft packet of Gauloises on the table, and continues to look at the images of JP. I think back to when she first arrived, how she boasted about the bikes they used to steal.

'You would not believe how many people leave their VTT on the street without locking them, expensive ones too,' she'd said, using the French Vélo Tout-Terrain acronym for mountain bikes. 'I've heard that all the serious road-racing bikers prefer to sleep with their bikes rather than girlfriends or wives. In any case, there is not much business in France for second-hand road bikes. People are too suspicious. Road bikers are *puristes*, want to know the origins of such things.'

I'd marvelled at her expertise on the bicycle black market back then.

That was in spring this year, exactly seven years since I came to Switzerland. The season of beginnings and arrivals. I can't believe I have been in this country for that long. And I have been in prison for six months. That's the hardest thing to understand, given my innocence. I'm 26 now. My life should be entering the next exciting phase. I once hoped I could raise my family within Switzerland's safe society, as long as I kept my bike locked up. Its clockwork systems, true democracy and magical geography offered a dramatic but somehow tamed beauty. But in contrast, it is the rigid rules, chauvinistic values and xenophobic attitudes that have me trapped in a nightmare from which I fear I might never awake.

'Does he look like his father? Those piercing grey eyes are not from you,' queries Yasmine, squinting at my hazel eyes, which are now a little hot with the strain of my memories. Her eyes flick back to another photo of JP as a toddler.

'Yes, he looks a lot like his father,' I say, inexplicably choking up, not because of JP, but because I remember how he made me feel. JP's father. In the resurfacing of old hatred, old blame, I'm horrified that my body still betrays me. After all that he did, after all that I have endured, he remains in control of my feelings. I recall that pooling hot sensation in my belly when Matt looked at me with his smoky eyes. He made me believe I was the only woman in his life.

I glance at Yasmine, worried she has a window to my thoughts. I swallow the tears that threaten.

I'm ashamed of my vulnerability.

* * *

Seven years ago

On the last Friday evening of the season, with the pub full of workers spending their weekly wage, the barman turned up the volume on the stereo and played a series of Latin American numbers. A few people began to move to the music.

It was then I discovered that along with his other seductive traits, Matt was a talented dancer. He gathered me into his arms, moulding me to his body with one strong hand splayed over the base of my back, applying enough pressure to claim complete control without force. With my hand on his shoulder, he pressed my other hand close to his chest, gently sweeping the backs of his fingers across my breast. His warm dry breath raised the fine hairs on my neck, and he turned his hips slightly, his leg pushing between my thighs.

Not a flutter of air passed between our bodies as we danced a grinding merengue in the crowded darkness of the bar. Our movement together was hypnotic, arousing a fervour of unreleased passion as I involuntary pressed myself to him and felt his desire against my thigh. My cheeks burned as he swung me around to the desperate fiery strumming of 'Bomboléo' and I could hardly breathe with the anticipation of what might follow.

We drew apart when the song had finished. He took my hand to lead me out of the door of the bar. The night air chilled my cheeks, but my body was on fire. At the side of the woodshed, he leaned in to me, the pungent smell of creosote eclipsed by the sweet, beery scent of his breath. He kissed me deeply with his hot mouth, pulling my shirt and bra up to expose my breasts to the night. The tightening of my nipples in the sudden cold craved his touch and his lips.

Clothes crumpled, zips sawed, underwear pushed to the side and I welcomed the exquisite, almost violent force of him thrusting into me. Throwing my head back, my hair caught in the splinters on the woodshed wall. We wedged our feet into a drift of packed snow under the roof overhang, jeans pooled at our feet in a tangle. I gasped from the long-awaited satisfaction and release, oblivious to the discomfort of shoving against the rough wall.

Afterwards, the sounds of the night filtered back in. The bar door screeched open; a waft of voices strained over the music. As the closing door clapped the raucous voices suddenly mute,

I became aware of our stark surroundings. A weak moonlight reflected off patches of snow on the slope between a few chalets clustered in this area of the upper village. I was grateful for a copse of pines shielding a clear vision of the woodshed from the nearest house.

Two thoughts briefly crossed my mind: the sordidness of this quick bang outside the pub, and the fact that neither of us had used protection. Those thoughts were soon replaced by a blindly misguided feeling of smug possessiveness. Seduction complete, my bruised lips stretched into a satisfied smile. As the passion subsided, distinctly quicker than it had risen, the seeping cold and the worry that someone might have seen us made me hastily pull my clothes back into place. Matt gently stroked the hair off my face, drawing my worried gaze back to him.

'You surprise me, my beautiful beach-seeker. Such passion. You have been wanting me since we met, no? I love how you give yourself, this spontaneity. I think I need to explore you more.'

He kissed me again, holding my chin. His comments, initially making me feel slightly sluttish, warmed me with the thought that he wanted me again.

This was the one.

A handful of flings through the few months I'd spent at art school, and a disappointing initiation into physical love had never aroused such savage passion as this in me. I'd given myself to him so readily, and couldn't control myself. Thinking I had succeeded in making him mine, in reality it was Matt who had made me his. What would he be thinking? I was so easy, a conquest complete.

I hoped we would leave the bar together. Perhaps I would wake in his arms at his apartment, follow through with a sweet aftermath of that initial passion. But he led the way back inside. Music rang in my ears. Beer and sweat soured the air. Matt looked distractedly at his watch, a frown on his face, his focus no longer on me. And then suddenly: 'I have to go.'

Abandoned, pleasure still stinging between my legs. Just like that, with a fleeting brush of his lips on mine, he was gone.

* * *

I was the first girl back to the dorm room that night, and glad for a moment alone. Anne was on a date with François. It was possible she wouldn't even come back. She often stayed at his studio in the attic of his father's hotel.

I lay on my bed staring at the ceiling, forcing myself to stay awake and remember every rushed sensation of the lovemaking. I focused only on our time together, ignoring the abruptness of our parting, and hoped desperately it had not been a one-night stand.

The door opened and my other room-mate, Terri, one of the cleaning staff, came in. She threw her jacket on her bed.

'Hit it lucky with Mathieu, did we?' she said jovially.

My blush gave me away, and I was embarrassed to think anybody knew what we'd done. Terri couldn't taint my brief moment of euphoria, and if she hadn't seen me, I was strangely elated that Matt might have been boasting about his conquest.

'It was pretty obvious when you came back into the bar what you'd been up to. You were like the cat who got the cream. No hiding that look.'

I narrowed my eyes. Wary of Terri's perpetual chatter, I wondered whether she saw right through me.

'Look, I know Matt is a catch,' she continued. 'He's a good-looking, charismatic guy. But the truth is, he's getting his rocks off with you, Lucie. He just wants sex.'

Despite the crudeness, I detected a grain of sympathy. And a small part of me ignored the possibility that she was telling the truth. I squeezed my eyes shut, trying to quell the uneasy feeling in my gut. I was still riding high. *Let me have this moment.*

24

Since taking the place of the girl who returned to Australia, I felt comfortable in the company of my room-mates, despite the restrictions of sharing the small sleeping space. We all worked for the hostel in various capacities, and the others had reached the end of a busy season. Although I had taken a cherished colleague's place, I was never made to feel the imposter. I refused to let my feelings be hurt, despite the fact that I was currently back in the dorm and not going home with Matt.

The door opened and Anne came in.

'Not staying at lover boy's place tonight then?' Terri asked Anne.

I wondered if Terri was like this with everyone.

'No, not tonight. It's going to be a busy week. I have to help with closing the accounts and I cannot be late to work tomorrow. Was it a good night at the bar, *les filles?*'

'Ha!' said Terri, and looked at me, grinning. Anne raised her eyebrows, and I blushed furiously.

'Mathieu?' Anne asked. I nodded with a sheepish smile, which dropped as soon as Terri continued.

'What happened to that girlfriend of his? You know, that Somali girl he used to hang out with at the bar. Leila, wasn't it?' Terri asked.

I was sure she hadn't meant to wreck my mood, but her words were like a blow to the gut.

'She disappeared halfway through the season,' she continued. 'I heard things might have been a bit rough for her. Matt has a wild streak. I know he punched some guy's lights out in the Grand. Don't know what happened to Leila though. Do you?' Terri turned to Anne.

Anne cleared her throat. She knew how I felt about Matt. I needed to know more about this Leila she mentioned. My stomach churned.

'What do you mean? He hasn't said anything about a girl-friend,' I said, feeling witless that I hadn't actually asked him.

This was information I naively assumed would be shared long before things went too far. And tonight, things had definitely gone too far.

'I did know Leila. We were friends for a while.' Anne looked awkward, put on the spot. I knew she wouldn't want to hurt me, but she also wouldn't want to lie. Even in the short time I'd known her, I already felt we had too much in common to ruin a good friendship.

'She was a student at the international college for a few semesters, studying liberal arts.'

Now I really was beginning to feel like a slut. Or at least an intruder. I recalled the barman warning me that Matt was a Casanova. Jealousy instantly rose like the bow of a sinking ship, but Anne felt compelled to continue.

'She and Matt were together for a while. It was a highly forbidden relationship, not only because of the faculty-student rule, but also in the eyes of her family. When her younger brother Kafia enrolled at the college the following year and saw what was going on, he reported Leila to their parents, and they took her away immediately. She had to return to Mogadishu and plans are underway to get her married off as soon as possible to avoid scandal. She wasn't even allowed to write to me when she left. Kafia is still at the college, though I think he will graduate this spring, and he sometimes tells me about his sister.

'I think he feels guilty having ratted on her, but the family doesn't care, and to make things even worse, he has a beautiful blonde American girlfriend. The inequality of that makes me sick. Lucie, I don't think there is anything … but Matt, he's …'

'Did Matt and Leila have, you know, an intimate relationship?' I asked, knowing that prejudices around prearranged marriages meant people wouldn't look favourably on one of their princesses minus her virtue.

'Of course they were, Lucie; what century are you living in?' Terri said as she changed into her pyjamas. 'I heard she was

26

hoping to find a way to stay, or at least to come back later, but I don't know what's going on now that she's gone. I guess the link to her family was too strong. Too bad for her. Good for you, though, eh Lucie? He's quite a catch, despite his reputation. Guys like that usually get what they want and hightail it outta there. Know what I mean?'

Terri howled with laughter as she made her way to the bathroom across the hallway, and I smiled uneasily. I wanted to ask about Matt's rough streak, but I couldn't believe that someone who had laid his fingers on my cheek so gently could be violent. Her flippant comments validated the barman's assessment of Matt, but I was sure her judgement was false. People surely couldn't believe that Matt would remain faithful to a girl he might never see again.

I turned back to Anne, and saw the apology written on her face.

'Anne, thanks for telling me. You know, I've really fallen for him.' I leaned back on my pillow and closed my eyes.

'It's not too late to shut it down, Lucie,' said Anne quietly. 'That way no one gets hurt. And I mean you. You could be getting yourself into more hot water than you imagine. There's some weird stuff going on with his family. Anyway, it's not for me to judge. I knew Leila, but I don't know Mathieu very well, only rumours from François. I'm sorry to have ruined your magical night.'

'Oh, let the girl enjoy the thrill of the chase,' said Terri as she came back into the room. 'As long as she knows the consequences. They all think with their dicks around here.'

I pretended to laugh it off, but felt a fragment of sorrow as I turned on my side and tried in vain to sleep, thinking how naive I might have been to believe in a fairy tale.

* * *

'*Dis-donc*, Lucie, are you okay?' Yasmine asks.

I realise my eyes are hot with unshed tears. I rarely show my emotions. To protect myself in this place, and to protect my own sanity, I try to remain aloof. My supposed crime alone elicits a bizarre respect from the others, a morbid fascination. If the authorities thought I posed a danger to the other inmates or the guards, I would have been placed in the high-security block. But they know I am not an evil person. I didn't commit first-degree murder. I am even housed in the same block as the mothers.

'I'm getting a cold. I have a headache,' I say pathetically, blowing my nose loudly.

I screw up the paper and throw it into the toilet, flush it angrily to try to banish the memories. I'm still cross with myself for revealing vulnerability. I sit back on my stool and sigh, steadying the ragged breath in my throat.

'Do you have a partner, Yasmine? Someone in France? In Algeria? I've never asked you.'

Good to change the subject, but I regret sounding so chummy.

'Not really,' she says. 'There was a man I was seeing in Lyon. Jean-Claude. He was a sous-chef in a high-class restaurant. But it is not easy, dating a chef. His hours were so irregular. We could never see each other on the weekends.'

Yasmine's eyes glaze for a moment, then she laughs and shakes her head.

'I can't go back to Algiers. There is nothing there for me. My parents are … they no longer exist. They are dead,' she says with a hesitation that makes me think they haven't actually gone from this world.

She's a pretty girl, unusual yellow-green eyes and long dark hair. I think about her chef boyfriend. If he knew about Yasmine's activities, he might have thought it wasn't easy dating a bike thief. Irregular hours, erratic wages. In truth I think her timetable would have suited Jean-Claude, her work typically carried out during the hours of darkness, when the odd cyclist might be enjoying a meal at a Michelin-starred restaurant.

The irony is that Yasmine works in the bakery now. I don't think I could stand the job, too much of a challenge to resist all that warm, yeasty bread. I'd balloon up within days, constantly cramming in irresistible comfort food. I've seen others let their bodies go all too easily. But Yasmine has resisted. She's proud of her achievements in the kitchen. I wonder if she thinks of Jean-Claude from time to time when she's working.

I haven't asked her before about a partner. I often see her in the cafeteria holding another inmate's arm, Dolores. Yasmine hangs off her like a lover. I wonder whether she is merely a tactile Mediterranean type, someone who thrives equally on non-verbal communication, or if it's something more.

I keep my distance, especially in the confines of my cell. Perched on my stool, I watch her sitting on my bed. I'm itching to take my photos away from her.

I've become scrupulously neat, colour-coding my clothes, grey and grey and grey. We don't wear a prison uniform, and it's ironic that with the freedom of the dress code I have chosen to wear monochrome. As if my need for colour has been wiped from my palette. I keep my T-shirts and trousers neatly on my shelves like the new season's fashion in a department store, each folded to centimetre precision. I resist the urge to put the photos back in order. I'll wait until she's left the cell.

'You should hang more of your pictures on the wall,' says Yasmine. 'I hate all this white everywhere, so impersonal. If we cannot paint, then wallpaper is necessary, and yours will be … picturesque.'

'It's a prison, Yasmine; what do you expect, Ritz drapes and shag-pile carpets?' I laugh. At least I have a few plants to bring a little green into the room.

'Oh, you know what I am meaning, all that stuff,' she says pointing to the sketchbook on my shelf. She gets up from my bed, the pile of photos slipping back onto my blanket.

'Lock-up time soon, I'll see you later,' she says, raising a hand as she leaves the cell, the door still ajar.

'Yeah, let's do dinner sometime,' I shout sarcastically after her.

She laughs as she sashays down the corridor back to her cell. Could it be that she actually enjoys being in this place? Her air of purpose is unsettling.

Chapter 3

'What the ...?' I raise my voice, but as I see Müller jump guiltily back from my desk, I clamp my mouth closed. She's a guard after all. But I still wonder what the hell she's doing in my cell.

I'm clean. I have nothing to hide, have been the model prisoner. There's always a worry someone might plant something to get another inmate in trouble, usually to remove suspicion from themselves. We all have single cells, and they're locked when we're not there, so Müller has let herself in with her key. But this is one of those tiny borderline infringements, unless she's been instructed to search for something specific.

I've come back early from work because of the bad weather. I take my rain cape off and fling it over the radiator. Running water into the sink, I pick up the nailbrush to clean the loamy soil of the garden from under my fingernails, and wait for her to tell me why she's here.

'Be careful, it might melt,' she says, pointing at the cape, and I shrug.

I don't care. The head gardener can give me another one. The smell of the steadily warming synthetic material evokes an unidentifiable comfort memory from childhood.

I dry my hands on my towel, walk towards the desk, and see

she's been studying a coloured pencil sketch of an alpine scene I drew from memory.

'They told me you are an artist. You have talent.' She nods towards the picture.

Müller is one of the more amenable guards, one of the few who speaks passable English. She even takes part in a Wednesday conversation group, the only time I openly speak to the others. She's a tough-looking middle-aged woman with broad shoulders, but she has a gentle demeanour. She wears her greying hair in a messy bun, a schoolmarm-gone-wrong look.

'You like working there?' she asks, looking through the window.

The rain against the pane has eased. I take a step towards her, still drying my hands, but keep my distance as much as one can in this confined space. We both look down at the garden. It has been flattened by the chill dampness. Half the beds contain over-grown vegetable tops, extended seed-heads and the random mess of items ignored during harvest. They have faded from green to dark grey under this heavy humidity, collapsed with the putrid-ness of gradually rotting foliage.

The other flowerbeds have now been cleared and freshly turned. The evidence of our hard work is strewn across the field on the far side of the courtyard like a freshly knitted quilt. Straight dark rows of rich earth shaped into corduroy furrows are ready for planting. A corrugated canvas prepared for some colour, after the slumbering weight of the winter has passed.

'Your days of labour outdoors are not so many now. When the clearing is finished, we find you new work,' she says.

I don't need to be reminded I will soon be without the distrac-tion of cultivation. Most of us who work in the garden will be assigned alternative jobs for the winter months. Only a few will be kept on to work in the greenhouses. It saddens me to think I will have to work indoors.

'Do you know yet what your job will be? Or do you let them put you in the laundry?' she asks as I shrug again. 'You can choose, you know. You do not need to keep silent. You cannot close yourself off, cannot forever be so angry with everyone. It is not our fault that you are here. You can make your life easier.'

'You sound like the shrink,' I say not unkindly, and she's surprised to hear me speak, always expects silence, unless I have a teacher's book in front of me. 'Are you looking for something?'

'I want to find out whether you will think about working in one of the more creative work stations.'

'Jobs? I'm not bothered. We all get the same wage. I guess I'll let you lot decide.'

Müller turns back to my drawings. 'But you could use your skills, perhaps even enjoy what you do,' she says, and I snort.

'May I?' she asks, and waits for a tilt of my head before sifting through my sketches, devoting time to a few that interest her, while I think about what she has said about the job assignment.

Most of the women here used to fight for work that paid the best rates. Now everyone gets paid the same. It's not much, but at least there's less of a dispute.

Fatima and Dolores work in the pottery studio in the west wing. They have turned some beautiful pots. It's hard to believe that these angry, volatile women create pieces decorated with such delicately fashioned and carefully glazed porcelain petals and leaves. When I first came here, I visited the studio, admiring the rows of pots waiting to be fired in the kiln. But I snapped up the job I was offered in the garden to be outside in the fresh air. The regimental attention to detail of planting seeds, row upon row, helped to settle my mind. Nurturing a new generation of plant life, watching things grow. I forgot that by autumn everything would be dead.

We grow things for the community. Our goods are either used in the prison kitchen, or taken to local markets. And there's a shop inside the prison gates where locals come from the surrounding villages to buy our organically grown produce.

By Müller's reckoning I may automatically be assigned a job in the laundry for the winter, but I can see something ticking away in her mind, and I begin to think this is not the first time she has looked at my art. The more creative jobs of weaving and mandala design nevertheless incite a feeling of monotony in my mind. Don't get me wrong, I think it's great that everyone has a job, but I'll let them decide where to put me.

I look at JP's picture on the wall. My personal little icon. Something to worship. God, I miss him so much. I wonder if JP has inherited some of my artistic leanings. At this stage in his stick-man art, it's hard to tell. By his age I was drawing ponies at the kitchen table from morning until night.

Müller puts her hand on top of the pile of sketches.

'These are really good, Frau Smithers. It is pleasing to see you use your creativity.'

There she is again, going on about my creativity. But I nevertheless lap up her compliment, knowing it's a rarity between guards and inmates, and I award her the slip of a smile. She turns to leave.

'Take raincoat off heater. *Es schmilzt*,' she says gruffly, and I listen to her footsteps retreat down the corridor.

I glance at the pile of drawings and consider that they are hardly my best work. When I run out of reading material, it's the drawing that keeps me occupied. I have to fill my free time with something. To stop the chimera of bitter revenge raising its ugly head. The demons of injustice are still present, and it will be a while before I manage to exorcise them all. Probably not until the day I leave this place.

I sit at the desk and tear another sheet of A4 from my pad. It's not great quality paper, but at least I have something to draw on. I put in an order for some paper a while ago from an art shop in Lausanne, but it hasn't arrived yet. Pencil poised, I breathe deeply, relishing the smell of melting plastic on the radiator behind me, and prepare to create another illusion.

* * *

34

Seven years ago

My beach in Greece could wait. The wistfulness of saying farewell to those leaving for the summer, and the uncomfortable feeling that I was getting myself into something I couldn't handle, lessened each day. Anne's wise advice ignored, I was a bona fide love-struck teenager.

I didn't confront Matt with the story Anne and Terri had told me about Leila, not then, but kept it to myself. Instead I turned his unspoken confession into my own goal of healing his supposedly broken heart, without pressuring him into any kind of a relationship. I had no intention of tainting our courtship with questions about past girlfriends, painting myself as the jealous successor. If he considered his association with Leila unfinished, then I would wait for him to divulge it to me in his own time, would expect him to offer his honourable confession. But if he remained silent about her, then in my mind his liaison with her was over, finished. I was his new horizon. Ignore a smug cat for long enough and it will eventually crawl into your lap.

And the other rumour? I put it down to jealousy. Others will often find fault with someone they wish they could be like.

One day when the snow had melted, Matt and I hiked through the forest to a viewpoint known as the Eagles' Nest, high above the Rhône Valley. Perched on a boulder, we admired the view across to the French ski resorts. The cliff dropped a thousand metres vertically, a stone's throw from where we sat. Through the haze, Matt pointed out a village below us in the distance on the grey smudge of Lac Léman, and told me it would soon be time to put his boat back in the water.

'You fascinate me, Lucille. Most girls I meet want something more. They're always working a game to get a part of me, but you're so free and easy. You weren't looking for anything when you turned up on my mountain, and you haven't expected anything of me. I appreciate that.'

'I've enjoyed our time together so far,' I offered timidly.

I knew by not defining our relationship, he was under no pressure to categorise it himself. 'And maybe I'm happy to stick around. I have no plans, no obligations.'

'That's it, I think. The no obligation bit. It makes me want you to stick around.'

Matt put his arm tightly around my waist. I was impressed with his honesty. He surely wasn't hiding anything.

'Anne is letting me stay on her sofa while I look for work. She's now renting a place of her own.'

I winced inside with the memory of my conversation with Terri and Anne.

Matt and I leaned in to each other, enjoying the view. He took off his shirt in the unexpected warmth, the sun shining on the niche where we sat on the rocks, our bodies protected from the wind by the granite at our backs.

'You must let me draw you one day. You have perfect muscle form for the artist's eye. I could do you in pastel, charcoal, even acrylic.'

I ran my hands lightly over his broad shoulders. He leaned forward slightly, a small shrug away from my fingers.

'No, you will not draw me, Lucille. No drawings of me.'

I frowned. His sudden mood change confused me.

'Okay,' I said slowly. 'No sketching. But it's what I love to do, to express my appreciation of perfect form.'

I laughed playfully and trailed a finger down his bicep, but he didn't smile. Face still turned away, a muscle ticked at his jaw.

'Stick to drawing that,' he said, pointing at the view. 'Landscapes, mountain scenes. Let's not talk about painting any more,' he said abruptly.

Anger flared briefly, eclipsing the hurt at his initial shunning of my touch. I realised he'd never really asked me about my art.

'But it's what I love to do. You think cleaning toilets in a shitty hostel is enough to satisfy me?'

He turned to me, and in a flash, his dark demeanour changed

36

to playfulness, with that hungry look in his eyes I recognised. My irritation softened, and I moulded my hands around the shoulders I had, moments before, imagined drawing. As he began removing articles of my clothing, I panicked. Ignoring any negative signals, I put my niggling angst down to worrying whether our situation on the footpath was too exposed.

* * *

A few days later a flyer appeared in Anne's mailbox announcing a local art exhibition organised by a group of students at the international college. A series of personal interpretations of the modern masters would be on display. Intrigued, the two of us went along.

'I'm not really a fan of modern art,' she said as we walked past colourful renditions of Picasso, Kandinsky, Braque and Matisse. 'But these are pretty good.'

'Who's in charge? Who's their teacher?' I asked, studying a bold still life, in acrylic greens and blues. 'This is the kind of stuff I was doing at university. Hard to believe a little college in the Alps has students turning out this kind of work.'

'That's the professor over there.'

Anne pointed to a portly-looking gentleman at one end of the hall, his sparse white hair in disarray. He seemed a little awkward, seeking solace in a glass of wine the students were offering for their vernissage. He reminded me of an Oxford don, a tweedy mussed look. But nevertheless approachable. On the spur of the moment I introduced myself.

'Patterson, Iain. How do you do?'

His boisterous handshake rattled the bones in my arm. I introduced myself, likened the work his students had exhibited to a project my class had participated in during my first year at university. It turned out we had a connection. One of my mentors at Leeds was an old colleague of his.

'Haven't heard from old Hibbert for a while. Multi-talented chap. Great artist, but also wrote some excellent plays in his time.'

The professor waffled on, his tone wavering somewhere between didactic and aristocratic. The plum in his mouth, rather than marking him as pompous, suited his eccentric demeanour. I didn't want him to think I was another college dropout, but the association with my old professor made me wonder if I hadn't done something unwise by giving up my studies in a subject where my skills truly lay.

'So it must be half-term. You'll be going back for the end of the semester soon, won't you? Spring ball next month. Always a hoot.'

'Actually, no ... I'm not going back.' Then thinking this sounded like I was a failure: 'I've taken a break from my studies. I'm on a cultural tour of Europe.'

Patterson cocked an eyebrow, and changed the subject. He'd heard that one before.

'What do your people do?'

It amused me to hear him refer to my parents in such an old-fashioned way, especially as my relationship with them was somewhat strained with my unexpected voyage to the continent.

'My father is an ex-naval officer. My mother's a nurse. She used to be an expat locum, Middle East mainly. I suspect I have a genetic predisposition for travel. Which is why I've ... delayed my studies for a year,' I said, twisting the truth.

'Nothing wrong with a journey of self-discovery, throwing a few wild oats.'

I smiled, the misquoted idiom making him appear suddenly naive.

'You should come and visit the studio sometime. Pop by next week – we won't be too busy when this exhibition is out of the way.'

* * *

I wasted no time taking the professor up on his invitation. By the following week I hardly had two centimes to rub together. The few francs I had earned were long spent. I'd sold my Eurorail ticket to a departing backpacker when the hostel closed. But that money was rapidly running out, and Anne, although a generous hostess, must have been getting tired of my presence in her home. Her relationship with François was getting serious, and I could tell she wanted her space to herself.

'I was Professor Hibbert's assistant for a term in my first year,' I told Iain Patterson when I visited his studio.

I was trying my best to both charm and maybe impress the old fellow.

'A Hibbert protégé! I could do with an assistant in the studio. Are you looking for work?'

Yes, yes! I wanted to shout. Everything was falling conveniently into place.

Iain Patterson, self-professed artist and wine connoisseur, flaunted an ample belly upon which he would amusingly rest his brushes as he painted, tucked between the buttons of his brown smock. I had never seen anyone paint with so many brushes at once. He balanced the smaller ones over his ears. They even protruded from his mouth, a substitute for the tortoiseshell pipe his long-suffering wife insisted he smoke outside the studio, to avoid bringing home the cloying scent of Latakia smoke on his hair and clothes.

Patterson, as he preferred to be called, had enough seniority to secure me a job as his assistant, and although he was past retirement age, it was evident his teaching was highly valued.

I was unable to obtain official working papers, but the college secured me a study permit, to fool the authorities into thinking I was a full-time student. I was even able to earn one credit a term in Patterson's classes, which marginally satisfied my parents' concerns about taking up the reins of an education I had left behind in England. Although it was unlikely I would ever fulfil enough credit requirements for an undergraduate degree.

I soon blended into the village and local life, and after a slow start, learned to speak French. Not that it mattered in a resort where so many foreign tourists passed through, and given that non-language courses at the college were all taught in English.

Being seen at Matt's side, a local boy, should have made me feel secure, knowing the authorities were always on the search for illegal workers without permits. The news about my semi-legal permit status quashed his hesitancy about me finding a job at the same college where he worked. And my love for him eclipsed the feeling of unease everyone else seemed to have when I was in his company.

* * *

We are sitting at a table in the cafeteria when Fatima comes in with Adnan bound to her in a perplexingly fashioned wrap, resembling a haphazardly knotted sari. She moves along the canteen counter, collects random items of food for her tray. As she comes to sit near us I wonder how she can place so many opposing food groups together on one plate. Perhaps she still has the disturbing gastronomic leanings of an expectant mother in her third trimester, and yearns for unidentified chemicals her body is missing. I vaguely remember a craving for horseradish and caramel fudge.

She starts plucking morsels off her tray and pops them into her mouth before she has even reached the table. She looks slightly manic. Adnan whimpers and squawks quietly in his sleep at her chest.

The cafeteria, or eating area, is bare and orthodox. It's relatively quiet, compared to the school dining rooms of my youth, but it fills fast and voices crowd the fuggy air, thick with the smell of institutional food. Meals are brought in large warmers from the

40

main kitchen in the castle and distributed to each living block. Occasionally I take my plate of food to my cell and eat alone. But most of the time I eat in the dining area so the food doesn't stink up my living space.

Sporadic snippets of conversation in a multitude of tongues stab the atmosphere. Depending on who is sitting together, the room sometimes feels like a clinic for the deaf, communication reduced to sign language accompanied by 'mm's and 'aah's when an idea becomes too challenging to convey. Today it sounds like a telephone exchange where all the operators have been designated different languages. The Tower of Babel prior to the scattering of the people.

Dolores is sitting with me, and now that Fatima and Yasmine have joined us, I know she will want to use her limited skills to talk English. Dolores has been teaching me a few words of Spanish in return; it's useful to know the basics in any language here – Russian and Greek would be the next priorities on my list. I am fascinated by the anthropological implication of European linguistics, how languages developed from prehistoric tribes have blossomed like ink blots to fill the borders of the countries we see on a map. Pockets of humanity have been allocated their spaces, coloured within the designated lines like shapes in a painting book. Hindelbank has an extensive selection, jumbled within its cramped borders.

'Why you don't sit with your people?' Dolores asks as Fatima sits awkwardly at the table, almost tipping her tray. No one leans over to help. It's every woman for herself in this place, even if she's carrying a baby.

'They not my people,' Fatima says darkly, glancing briefly at a group of Balkans sitting by the door.

Fatima shoves her tray back onto the table. One side rises and bangs back down, rattling the cutlery. Adnan's fluffy head twitches at the noise.

'Why you not sit with yours?' She nods towards a small group

41

of Latinas sitting in silence not far from us. Colombian, Ecuadorian, Venezuelan.

I think I know why Dolores doesn't sit with them. For some reason she is considered an outsider. It might be because she helps teach a Zumba class in the activities room on Tuesdays. Perhaps like me with the English classes, she's seen as someone who sucks up to the establishment. But a more likely reason is her comrades and neighbours avoid her because she screeches down the phone in Spanish at her kids every time she gets permission to call home. She upsets everyone with her animated mourning of the distance between them. The Latinas must be sick of listening. At least the rest of us don't understand her emotional diatribe.

'Not today. Today I a citizen of the world.' She pronounces the w of world like the Spanish j in Juan. 'And I with my new friends.'

Dolores pats Yasmine on her thigh, and Yasmine passes her a handful of cigarettes. Nothing changes hands in return.

We sit back and chew on our food in silence. Yasmine looks thoughtfully at Dolores, but glances away when Dolores catches her.

The conversation among the group of Balkans in the corner rises in volume, taking the attention away from us. Whether from Serbia or Macedonia, the group is able to communicate in their various Slavic dialects. They are forever in conflict, even though the Balkan wars finished over a decade ago. Fatima bristles. She is Albanian, a non-practising Muslim, but she stares at them as though a terrible battle is still raging in her mind, ever aware of the nations who destroyed each other to the north and the east of her country in the name of ethnic cleansing.

'They are most definitely not my people,' Fatima says, a little louder than before.

The Slavic argument abates briefly, and they all lean in, one of them gesticulating in our direction. A Serbian woman stands and scrapes her chair back noisily from the table with the backs of her legs.

The guard in charge of distributing the food raises her spatula like a fly swatter. She is pre-empting intervention from a distance, and I can tell she's silently willing them to calm down.

The woman who has risen from the table stomps to the trolley and shoves her tray into a spare slot. The plate and cutlery crash against the edge of the tray, and a fork clatters over the side to the floor. Instead of walking out of the room, the Serbian girl marches over to our table. I can see her over Fatima's head. I gulp. Fatima hasn't seen her yet.

'You think you so high and mighty, sitting here with the bourgeoisie,' she says to Fatima. 'You think baby gonna protect you?'

She pokes Fatima's shoulder with a finger, and Fatima suddenly rises with a nimbleness I didn't think possible with Adnan strapped to her chest.

'No, no, no … the baby!' I try to shout after swallowing a hunk of unchewed bread.

Fatima doesn't hear me, and a stream of incomprehensible words fly like ammunition from her mouth. A bubble of spit lands on Adnan's head, and I reach up to grab her arm. Before I get there, her hand lashes out and she pushes the Serbian girl with her palm in the middle of her chest. The Serbian staggers backwards, but doesn't fall.

'Fucking bitches,' the Serbian says as she regains her balance.

Adnan begins to cry, and the Serbian turns abruptly, making a sucking sound through her teeth, and leaves. The exchange has ended with a phrase everybody understands. I don't take it personally. It causes me to smile involuntarily, feeling vaguely fortunate the universal language in this place is my mother tongue.

'What you smile about, husband killer?'

Fatima's question wipes the smile off my face.

She's gone from ally to adversary in a matter of seconds. I don't even try to explain. It's true that Fatima is wearing Adnan like a shield. Thinks she can say anything. Things would have been a lot messier if she didn't have the baby at her chest.

The low pressure of the autumn weather is getting to all of us. In the mugginess of the canteen, I am beginning to yearn for snow.

44

Chapter 4

Müller walks right up to my desk without checking my tidy cell, and I expect her to click her heels together like a sergeant major as she stops beside me. I look up from the letter I am writing to JP, annoyed that my train of thought has been interrupted. I clack the pen on the desk, and press my lips together.

'Come. We have not much time,' she says, turning to walk straight back out of the cell, and a retort of refusal sits unspoken on my tongue. I know I'm in prison and at the mercy of my captors, but I don't want to appear so easily compliant.

I follow her nonetheless, curiosity getting the better of my belligerence.

'Where are we going?'

'You will see,' she says, without breaking her stride.

We head down two flights of stairs to the door by the garden and she uses her key card to open it. A stiff breeze lifts the wisps of grey hair like wings at her temple and I shiver in the sudden freshness. It feels like a clandestine trip to a forbidden world. The cold blue-grey dimness of the autumn dusk plunges the bare plots into shadow.

Across from the allotment sits the main Hindelbank castle, its faux-Versailles annexes enveloping a courtyard at its centre, surrounded by a high brick and plaster wall. As we walk down the track to the main entrance, I peer through a gate to the courtyard, gravel raked to Zen precision. Red and white striped shutters flank the thick beige limestone frames of the arched windows, normally jolly in the daytime, but appearing menacingly violet in the fading light. Cupolas and round dormer windows adorn the shingle roof, sweeping down in an almost Dutch-style gable, darkened after the recent rain. The roof ridges are decorated with large urn-like finials, topping off an architecture that speaks of once opulent aristocracy. I told JP at the beginning that I was imprisoned in a castle. He drew me as Rapunzel for several weeks afterwards.

'The Schloss, is it not magnificent?' asks Müller proudly, as if it's part of her own ancestry.

'I guess, under different circumstances ...'

'It was being built in 1720, by a man named Friedrich von Erlach. When he died, the building was made a poor house for women. It is how this place developed into a prison. But there is something I want to show you. We go into the Schloss. Come.'

We walk along the wall into a cobbled courtyard and Müller leads the way up the steps into the castle. The door is unlocked. I wonder whether she always has access, or whether she arranged this for us.

Along the hallways and up the stairway of the castle, there are numerous portraits on the walls, but the paintings on the ceilings in the reception rooms are the ones that catch my eye. Müller throws the light switch and I stare up at the scenes painted between the plaster mouldings of what must once have been a great dining hall. There are exquisite scenes of angels and kings. I crane my neck, reminding me of a bygone class excursion to the Sistine chapel.

'Yes, yes, beautiful, but this ...' Müller opens the doors of what looks like a formal salon, free of furniture. The antique parquet floor creaks under our feet. It is a space designated for parties and gatherings. By trickery of the brush, the room has been made to look larger with rococo trompe l'oeil scenes of Tuscan pillars encircled with vines and Romanesque garden archways, through which there is a hint of dreamy Italian summer skies. The effect is striking, and a complete juxtaposition to the renaissance paintings in the other rooms.

But the final pièce de résistance, and different again, is a relatively small panelled room crammed from floor to ceiling with mountain and country landscapes reminiscent of the Swiss painter Calame or the German artist Bierstadt. The dozens of painted panels take my breath away. It is so hard to believe that this is located in the middle of a prison compound.

'There was a time …' Müller leaves her sentence unfinished and bites her lip.

'You paint too?' I ask. She shakes her head once.

'You think you can do?' asks Müller, my question unanswered.

I stare at her, blowing air through my lips. 'You are kidding.'

'I think you can do. Copies. You can copy these. I have been having the idea. You know that every year we have a market here. The Schlossmärit. Everybody makes something to sell. I think you can do painting. You can make your own paintings, but copies of some of these works would get good money.'

I narrow my eyes. Her enthusiasm makes me think she's not merely considering the lucrativeness of the prison market.

'I can't paint like this. I could never match this skill.'

'I think you should try. Come, let me show you where.'

Curious, I follow Müller out of the castle and back across to the prison outbuildings. We approach the block where many of the handcraft departments are housed and Müller uses her key to enter. The place is empty now at the end of the workday. We walk the length of the building, past the cardboard packing room, a room with computers, and a library where some classes take place for those wanting to study specially offered apprenticeship courses. A stairway leads to the weaving and sewing rooms on the first floor. Beyond the stairs is the pottery where Dolores and Fatima work. On the other side of the corridor there's a room called the Werkatelier.

'I'm not working in here!' I protest.

This is the place where those who can't concentrate or sit still for long periods of time are employed. Mostly because they're zoned out on drugs. Müller shakes her head and keeps walking. We pass tables of half-finished pre-printed mandalas. Simple, mind-numbing work.

It's quiet, except for the humming white noise of the kiln on the other side of the wall. A faint smell of porcelain dust permeates through from the pottery. We go through a door at the end of the block. A little light seeps in through the windows on the north end of the room, through which I can see part of the main greenhouse. The dark blue luminosity reveals easels folded against the back wall, jars filled with brushes and charcoal, trays of half-used tubes of oil and acrylic paints. Different-sized canvases, some blank, some half painted, lean against a cupboard next to rolls of butcher paper. The floor is splattered with the masterpiece of years of spilled and dripping paint.

The airless room smells faintly of turpentine. It feels like no one has been in here for a while, confirmed by a thick layer of dust that lies on the bench. It is almost the artist's Zion, if it were not situated within the walls of a penitentiary.

'I had no idea this was here,' I exclaim.

If I had known of its existence, I would definitely have been more proactive in seeking work in here.

'That's what you get for your solitude and *Indifferenz*. I have suggested to the administration that you should work in the atelier over the winter. I don't think you will do the asking, so I do it.'

'Why would you do that for me?'

'I have seen many criminals in this place over the years. Some have done terrible things without remorse. I would not normally speak like this. We are to be unattached, unemotional, and I don't know if you killed your husband. Maybe, but I'm sure not on purpose.' I narrow my eyes at Müller's grammatical errors. 'But it is our *Ziel*, our goal, to integrate all prisoners back into society and some have skills that can be used after you are free. You need to continue to build your skill. And more important, I am somebody who appreciates good art. These things mean that you have a little of my *sympathie*, Lucie.'

It is the first time any guard has used my first name. We are all referred to as 'Frau' and our last names, to avoid the very sociability in which we now find ourselves.

'Well, I think I should like that. Thank you. To work in the atelier ... What is your first name, Frau Müller?' I think she realises the line she has crossed, and ignores my question.

'I'm glad you have decided. It is time to eat. We must get back,' Müller says gruffly as though she has read my mind, and she herds me out of the door and down the stairs.

* * *

Seven years ago
'My father, Didier, is Swiss, and my mother, Natasha, who we all call Mimi, is Russian by birth,' explained Matt.

We were tucked into the corner of a rustic restaurant eating fondue. Matt showed me how to stir the cheese vigorously, to avoid separation or burning on the bottom of the caquelon.

'That makes my English roots sound so mundane in comparison,' I said. 'How come you speak such good English? You should be fluent in Russian.'

'I don't speak much Russian. The language at home while I was growing up was English. I think Mimi thought there was some sophistication in that – can't think why.' He smiled cheekily as I brandished a cheese-laden morsel of bread at him on the end of my fork.

49

'If your mum's Russian, how did she end up here?'

'Via London actually, hence the association with English, *ma belle Anglaise*.'

He held up his shot-sized Vaudois wine glass and we clinked, kissed and sipped before stabbing and dipping our next pieces of bread.

'Mimi's parents, my grandparents, escaped Petrograd which is now St Petersburg, and fled to England before the February Revolution of 1917. They could see that the Duma was gradually becoming unstable over the years since its formation, and had prepared for a possible uprising.'

'But the language of the aristocracy in Russia was French for many years, if I'm not mistaken,' I said.

Matt nodded. 'Even at the beginning of the twentieth century, French was the language of *la noblesse*. Mimi was bilingual until she was about 5, and then trilingual, as English became her third language. She and my aunt went to a private school in London for a few years until my grandfather was offered work as an *interprète* at the newly founded League of Nations, and they moved to Geneva. They lived in a big house on the shores of Lac Léman, near Versoix.'

'Could an interpreter's salary at the League of Nations support those costs – an expensive private school in London and a mansion on the lake?'

'My grandparents managed to, how would you say, smuggle, some accumulated tsarist funds out of pre-Communist Russia, probably in the form of gold and precious stones.'

'How did your parents meet?'

'Mimi met my father at an art conference in Genève. He dabbled with art in his youth, worked in acquisitions at a gallery for a few years until he realised his dream of becoming a writer. After they married, he persuaded Mimi to move to this more rural pre-alpine region so he could concentrate on his writing. He published a few books, but none became bestsellers.'

For all the romanticism a carefree seasonal fling with a ski bum conjures, Matt had an equally impressive background born almost of the stuff of Ian Fleming tales. I was happy he was opening up his past to me, but I wondered how Matt's parents could survive on the earnings of a writer of second-rate commercial fiction without the publication of a successful novel.

The fondue pot was now empty. Matt placed the cap over the burner to put out the flame. I folded my napkin and laid it on my plate.

'Not finished yet, *ma belle.*' Matt smiled, grabbing the caquelon.

He began scraping at the large coin of cheese burned onto the base of the pot with his fork, deftly lifting the golden disc and taking it between his fingers when it had cooled. Tearing it down the middle, he handed half to me. 'The best part – *la religieuse.*'

I was doubtful – a piece of burned cheese – but the salty offering tasted like the best crusty bits round the welsh rarebit my mother used to serve me as a child. It silenced my thoughts about heritage and financial means.

* * *

The first time I properly encountered Natasha and Didier Favre, we chose to meet at a busy Italian restaurant in the lower village. I figured the distractions of the animated chefs in the open kitchen and the bustle of the waiters around the customers would reduce the scrutiny I might be subjected to by Matt's rather exotic parents. I was flattered that for one who was keen to maintain our relationship on a casual level, he had wanted me to meet them.

Matt's mother, Natasha, was a beautiful, poised woman. She raised her chin and looked down her nose at me as we shook hands. There was to be no traditional Swiss embrace one would expect for the girlfriend of a son, and I was sure she didn't approve of me. Her supercilious attitude gave the impression that she didn't appear to approve of anyone, including Matt and his sister

Marie-Claire. His sister was barely out of her teens when she married and moved to California with the American husband she had met at the very same college where Matt also studied, and where we both now worked. Exchanging one surreal family situation for another.

'You never speak of Marie-Claire,' I said, and Matt shifted in his chair a little awkwardly.

'MC rarely returns to her alpine roots,' he said.

'*Mon Dieu*, I wish you wouldn't call her that,' said Natasha. 'Such a beautiful name, Marie-Claire, and she reduces it to some sobriquet of a delinquent musician.'

'Do you have any grandchildren?' I asked.

Natasha hesitated. 'Unfortunately not. Marie-Claire is unable to conceive.'

'But she's still so young, surely there is time.'

'No, she will not have children,' she said firmly, as though it was a family decree.

I raised my napkin to my mouth so she wouldn't see the shock on my face. Natasha cleared her throat before continuing.

'They think the world is far too populated and she is concentrating on her career as a designer. She cannot have children, something wrong, down there.' She waved vaguely at her lower body. 'She and that American husband of hers have decided not to adopt. I am grateful that Mathieu stayed on the mountain when Marie-Claire left for California. He may eventually provide us with the future generation when he finds the right girl.'

She stopped abruptly. Heat rose to my face. Not because she must be aware our relationship had progressed beyond simple courtship, but with indignation that she thought Matt had not yet met the 'right girl'. I looked down and sliced into a wild-mushroom raviolo on my plate. This was turning out to be harder than I had thought. The stereotype of a boyfriend's acerbic mother. I already felt sorry for Marie-Claire's husband, having to put up with all this family snobbery.

52

'When did Matt first become interested in sailing?' I asked to change the subject, continuing Mimi's habit of talking about him as though he wasn't there.

Having used the yacht as his trump card when trying to impress the girls, I wanted to find out whether Matt had been telling the truth in the bar on the night we met.

'Natasha's sister, Matt's Aunt Alesha, moved to London when she finished her schooling in Geneva to study economics at LSE,' said Didier. 'Unfortunately she died of cancer a few years ago, but she left Mathieu a handsome sum of money in her will on the one condition that he buy himself a sailing boat, to continue her legacy.'

'Alexandra ...' Natasha glared pointedly at Didier. She definitely had a thing against the use of diminutives. Ironic that everyone called her Mimi and she didn't seem to mind. '... was one of the first female students of her generation at the school. She married a London financier who was a great yachtsman, and they used to take Mathieu sailing with them on the Solent during the summer months. They had no children of their own, and became very fond of young Mathieu.'

I guessed we were skirting back to the subject of succession.

No matter the tack of our discussions, every conversation returned to Matt during the evening. It was as if he wasn't actually there, although he appeared to be basking in their passive attention. It was a relief to keep my own history to a minimum. After the initial questions about where I came from, what my parents did, and the awkward quandary about my forsaken studies – taking a gap year out seemed to be the most comfortable explanation, giving Natasha the satisfaction of thinking I might one day leave and return to my academics – they remained entirely incurious as to my feelings or ambitions.

'You've never mentioned your sister before,' I said as Matt took me home that evening.

'You never asked.'

'I thought it would be natural ...'

'I'm sorry, Lucie, I don't want to talk about her, okay?'

It was hard to believe he had been so open and forthcoming about his family a couple of weeks before in the fondue restaurant. The encounter with his parents left us both feeling uncomfortable.

We kissed briefly outside the door to Anne's apartment before Matt turned to leave, and I watched his back for a few seconds before letting myself in.

* * *

Matt's mother Natasha never warmed to me, even after I had been initiated into one of her traditional Russian evenings several weeks later.

It was Didier's birthday, and the first time I had been invited to the chalet. A heavy tablecloth adorned with richly embroidered silk tassels was flung onto the massive round table in the middle of the dining room. There were eight of us in total, including two other couples, friends of Didier and Natasha. A variety of Russian delicacies covered the table – blinis, rollmops, pirozhki with different vegetable and meat fillings, salty fish and caviar dishes.

'A stunning spread, Natasha.'

Matt's mother tipped her head to one side, acknowledging my compliment. I expected 'Please, call me Mrs Favre' to slide from her tongue, such was her supercilious look. I could see it was going to take some diplomacy to worm my way into this woman's icy heart. Although at that stage I already wondered if I'd ever want to. It was possible she thought only a superwoman would be the perfect match for her son.

'Thank you, my dear. There are some bourgeois Russian traditions we don't want to see disappear. I usually prepare food like this to celebrate Maslenitsa before Lent, but any special occasion deserves some flair, and Didier's birthday is a good excuse.' She smiled at her husband as he appeared from the kitchen, a bottle of Moskovskaya in his hand, vapour flowing off the frosting glass.

'Prepare your plates, help yourselves to food,' Natasha urged as Didier carefully poured the viscous vodka into eight pewter shot glasses sitting on a wooden tray. Conversation lulled as everyone watched Didier's steady hand.

'I couldn't help noticing those icons on your wall,' I said, as Natasha ceremoniously passed the tray around the table to the guests. Her hand shook slightly as I spoke, vodka shivering in the tiny frosted goblets. I looked at her.

'Those old things. They are merely copies. A sentimental reminder of my parents' plight. Like the Russian dolls.' Her eyes indicated a set of cheap yellow painted dolls regimented over the wide lintel of the kitchen door.

My gaze was drawn back to the icons hanging in the corridor leading to the entrance hall, directly in my line of vision.

'They're very handsome copies. A great example of Orthodox art. Wonderful to have a few of your cultural roots displayed in the home,' I said to Matt.

Natasha cleared her throat, taking the last glass of vodka from the tray.

'Quick, before it warms! Here's to my wonderful husband, Didier, many happy returns. *Vashe zdorovie!*'

She threw her head back, emptied her glass. Warm lips seared the cold pewter as the oily vodka slipped down our throats.

'Eat, eat!' urged Natasha, and we followed the drink with a mouthful of food to soak up the wickedness of the alcohol.

She claimed we could drink all night like this and never wake up with a hangover, but even in my youthful resilience, I never quite believed her. Once the first bottle of vodka had gone, a second appeared from the freezer, and Natasha brought out a heavy tureen of borscht, tender beef strips in a well-seasoned beetroot and cabbage broth.

Towards the end of the evening, Didier told the story of the first time he set eyes on Natasha at an art exhibition in Geneva. The vodka caused his tongue to sweeten and eyes to moisten. He turned to me and began to talk about the latest book he was writing. Natasha's eyes flashed at him as he was halfway through describing an adventure in her youth, and his sentence petered out. He changed the subject, passing the tray to collect our glasses for another round, leaving me to ponder what secrets Natasha had in her steely past.

On the way home afterwards, I asked Matt about his mother's Russian background.

'Mimi's got a bit of a thing about the old country. I don't know why really. She's more Swiss than most Swiss people. But there's a pride in her that doesn't come from the Alps. Something deeper. She has a fiery character. Since the dissolution of communist Russia, they've wanted to travel back ... But anyway, why the interest in her background?' Matt asked, a little irritated.

I thought of the icons on the wall, the traditional fare at the table. I shrugged. 'Curious, I guess. Have you ever been there?'

Matt shook his head. 'Papa's only started researching for his latest book recently, but they're planning to travel there soon.'

'Sounds like a great plot location for a historic romance.'

'He says he wants to write about the experiences of Mimi's family before the revolution. Mimi's not keen, keeps telling him to let sleeping dogs lie.' I looked at him curiously. 'I don't really know what she means, the revolution happened more than a generation ago. She's proud, but I think she's scared of something. She continues to look for links to her roots though. Maybe she feels like she never quite belonged in this Western society.' Matt stopped, as though he thought he was maligning his mother.

'I thought she fitted in well here, considering the cosmopolitan nature of Switzerland's population,' I said when he didn't continue.

'Mm. Maybe. You should hear my sister talk about her.'

I was surprised to hear him offer the opinions of the sister I hadn't known he had until recently.

'She calls Mimi such a hypocrite,' he continued. 'All this faff and ceremony about maintaining Russian tradition. MC always hated these Russian parties. Thought they were so fake, when Mimi never actually lived there, and my grandparents escaped when they were barely adults. They became more devoted Londoners than most Cockneys. I don't know where she'd be more happy – she can't seem to sink her roots deep enough here. But it's important the family try and stay together. Not that MC would ever come back here. It was a bit of a blow to Mimi when she left, despite our ... despite their differences. But Mimi's happy I stayed around after college. I think she likes having me close.'

'Marie-Claire doesn't get on with the family?' I asked cautiously, remembering his reluctance to speak about her the last time.

'No ... I ... no not really. She's a bit of a nonconformist. She's ... unusual. Pissed off with the world. Isn't willing to believe that fate can sometimes deliver some tough times with the good.'

'Do you miss her?'

'Not really,' Matt said hesitantly. 'We didn't get on. Anyway, she's made a life for herself in California now. Ron's a good bloke. Bit too American for my liking, but I think he looks after her.'

'Do you really think they'll never have kids?'

'No, of course not! I mean, no. MC's not really the family type. How come you're so fascinated with my sister? Let's drop her, okay?'

'Don't get short with me, Matt. I'm just curious. If I had a sister or a brother, I'd probably want to hang out with them all the time. I guess it's because I don't have one that the whole dynamic of having a sibling fascinates me. Surely it's natural to want to know about you and your family.'

I had obviously hit a chord with Marie-Claire. We weren't in a sober state for in-depth family discussions. I was trying to find reasons to like Matt's mother, but despite her fascinating background, it wasn't happening. I wondered how MC felt about her.

We arrived at Anne's place. I fiddled with my key in the dark, swaying a little from too much vodka. Tonight I actually looked forward to Anne's pull-out sofa bed, I was that tired, and was unable to analyse Matt's irritability. I figured he'd come right in the morning. We kissed and he held me tight, as though delivering a silent apology for his reaction.

* * *

'Why do you not draw your son?' asks Yasmine between mouthfuls of her food. 'She made a lot of great pictures,' she says to the others at the table, pointing a fork speared with a morsel of grey meat in my direction.

My eyes flash. I don't like talking about my art, but mostly I don't like being the centre of attention.

'I don't know. I sometimes think I've forgotten what he really looks like,' I reply. 'I need to see him to be able to draw the essence of him. It's harder than you think to draw my own son.'

I keep my voice neutral. Though I think it would break me to try and draw him, unable to wrest the detailed memories from my mind. The curve of his rosy cheek or the sweep of his fine hair. Those grey eyes that only started to turn green when I had to say goodbye, their colour enhanced by his tears.

'She has drawn me, you know. She's a real artist,' Yasmine says to Fatima who nods with eyebrows raised and mouth turned down at the corners.

She's vaguely impressed, or disinterested in my skills, I'm not sure which. A minuscule piece of bread crust sticks to Fatima's lip, then falls onto Adnan's head. She blows the crumbs from his crown as he sleeps. His fine fluffy hair puffs like gossamer. My throat tightens.

'Perhaps you could start a business. Lulu's Portraits,' Yasmine continues, thinking out loud. 'Yes, we could make a bit of money. Earn a few sous.'

'We?' I ask, amused. Lulu?

'Yes, I will be your agent,' she replies, presenting herself, flamenco fashion with a wave of her arm from head to chest, fingers splayed. 'Of course you will give me a cut if I am to do your marketing and *publicité*.'

'*Caramba*, Yasmine! You are to be my agent, remember? We have a business in cigarillos to organise,' says Dolores huskily, eyes flashing.

I have no desire to fight over Yasmine's attention, though I can see where this is going. Yasmine, with that look on her face that says she is the centre of our universe, demanding deference.

'I am not going to sell my paintings, okay?' I say, not wanting to darken any moods, but knowing that things like this can escalate alarmingly quickly into dissension in this place. Tiny issues can turn rapidly into thermo-nuclear reactions.

Chapter 5

'So, Madame Favre, here we are,' says Dr Schutz, as if we're on a bus that has pulled up to our stop.

I look around the sparse office, eyebrows raised with fake curiosity. I turn back to stare at the psychologist.

'I'm really sorry, I thought I'd already told you. My name is not Madame Favre. I prefer to be called Mrs, or better still Ms Smithers. I don't answer to Madame Favre any more. Sounds like a sordid joke in an opera. It was a sordid joke, Dr Schutz, the missus bit, if that's what we're here to talk about. I'm guessing you're going to get me to talk about my relationship,' I say, crossing my arms.

I fix my gaze on the name shield on the psychologist's desk. Frau Doktor Dagmar Schutz.

The guards have already learned to use my maiden name, their various pronunciations amusing me each time.

I'm wary of shrinks, especially after all the interrogation I've been through. Each party tearing themselves apart to prove either I am or I am not mentally stable. And nobody able to make their minds up about anything.

'Okay, Mz Smizzers,' says Dr Schutz over-patiently. 'You have requested that our interviews be conducted in English from now on, though I am not sure why. I thought you were Swiss?'

I'm surprised her English is so precise, except for the mispronounced 'th's. She speaks fluently, with an American accent, but I don't ask her how long she lived in the States.

'My French might be better than yours, Dr Schutz. But my mother tongue is English. I prefer not to be misunderstood in a language that is not my own. There has been plenty of misinterpretation over the past few years. And unfortunately, I never sought Swiss citizenship.'

Dr Schutz tilts her head to one side. I imagine she'd like nothing better than for me to break down in tears and spill all my thoughts and secrets. I've done enough crying for now. But I know she's a shrewd one, and she'd be used to belligerence in this place.

'I've heard that you are doing good things among the women on the block,' she says, trying a different tack. 'You have volunteered to teach them a little English. Do you think this might help to keep the peace among all these women who speak different languages?'

She looks up from her file at me, and I feel the flicker of a smile on my own lips. My pride has not been completely broken.

'And the guards are talking about your paintings. Frau Müller is interested to have your copies of Erlach's art sold at the next Schlossmärit. You must realise that all this is helping your case to show that you are ready to integrate into society when you are free. However, it doesn't help your case that you are so sullen with me every time we meet. You may be forgetting that it is possible my reports have an influence on your requests to be able to see your son.'

I check myself. I sometimes forget that Dr Schutz is not an emissary sent from Natasha to confirm that I am crazy and report back to the evil mistress. I have always assumed that her evaluations are of a negative nature, to persuade those in power that it would be better for JP to be raised by his grandparents. But I now realise she is working for my benefit. I must prove myself worthy.

'Maybe it would help if you can tell me exactly who you are angry with? Is it your husband?'

'I was, yes. I was angry with him for deceiving me, for betraying my trust. But he's no longer here to defend himself, and all I have is his wicked mother trying to keep me here.'

I feel the blackness of resentment smothering me again. It clouds my judgement, makes me bitter.

'But it was obvious from the circumstances that there was anger on both sides. Mrs Smithers – Lucille – I really think you need to talk about it. To help you. I want to help you.'

I uncross my arms, push the chair back, and look at Dr Schutz with renewed curiosity. Leaning on my knee with one elbow, I tear at a tag on my thumbnail with my teeth. That will hurt later. I'm displaying guilty body language, so I sit up quickly. I hear the judge's voice in my head. *Coupable*. Guilty.

'This is a country of rules – right, Dr Schutz? I don't know how easy it is to disobey those rules, but Madame Favre seems to be doing just that. She is keeping my son away from me and nearly always has an excuse to stop me from speaking to him on the phone. There are others in here, Dolores for example, who gets to speak to her children twice a day if she wants, and those are long-distance calls to Central America. My weekly phone call pales in comparison.'

I stop, and take a breath. A trapped bee buzzes against the pane behind Dr Schutz's desk. She rises to let it out. The bee hums out into the sunshine and she leaves the window open, as if the chill autumn air might persuade the bee to reconsider the warmth of her office.

'I think she would have found a way to keep him from me even if he was still a breastfeeding infant. If I make my call on Friday and she says "JP can't talk to you now, he's out playing" or "he went shopping with Poppa and they're not back yet" or, worst of all "he doesn't want to talk to you" that's it, that's my one chance. She doesn't answer if I call again. But the thing is, I'm holding up my end of the deal, and she's not. And nobody seems to be controlling that, in this land where you love your rules and red tape. In this bullshit country where I've been locked up for something I promise you I didn't do, she has the last word. Because she's Swiss. But that's a joke. She tells you she's Swiss, until it's convenient and exotic to tell you she's Russian. That's bullshit too. She hasn't even set foot inside the boundaries of her motherland, or her mother's motherland. It's bullshit. And yes, if you were wondering, I am still really, very angry about that. Can you tell?'

My eyes narrow at the open window. Dr Schutz sits patiently while my breathing calms.

'Do you think it is Mrs Favre's fault that your husband died?'

'Of course not. I'm angry about the situation now, about not being able to see my son. I don't need to analyse the reasons why my husband behaved as he did for all those years. Maybe that's her fault. I don't know.'

* * *

Seven years ago

On a bright Sunday in June we drove down to the marina and took Matt's boat out for a sail. It wasn't all talk at the bar. He really did have that yacht. Certainly not the equivalent of a Ferrari on water, but a handsome little sloop nonetheless.

While I was on an art excursion the previous weekend, he had spent the time sanding and painting the hull before putting it back in the water at its regular mooring after a winter on the trailer. We were ceremoniously affording the little yacht its first baptism of spring.

Lac Léman, like any other large body of water, is home to varied and unpredictable winds. The lake, shaped like a giant upside-down croissant, is separated into three regions. Geneva sits at the west end in the narrow area called the Petit-Lac. Matt's boat was moored in a pretty port at the southeast end in the Haut-Lac. The lie of the mountains to the north and south determined the temperamental direction of the winds, but most of the time, Matt was able to consult the forecast and know what to expect for the day.

We sailed across the Rhône Delta and far into the Grand-Lac, the widest and greatest body of the lake. Matt showed me the tricks of sailing a boat larger than the little Optimists of my youth. He was a patient and encouraging teacher. My captain. Once the sails were hoisted, we sat together on the cushions in the cockpit and he put his arm across my shoulders.

'One day we'll take a big boat out on the ocean. I started studying for my Yacht Master's certificate last year. I've done all the theory and navigation, but I'll need to spend time on the open water soon. And I can see you have great sea legs.'

Grinning like a kid, he smoothed his hand along the inside of my thigh. A belligerent gust caused the sail to flap, and our attentions returned promptly to the task of navigation, as we laughed into the wind. He had confidence in me, watching me judge the wind, deciding when to tack, folding the sails, and tidying the sheets, rolling them neatly from fist to elbow. I was elated, and felt our relationship had reached a different level. Not only one of respect and potentially lasting love, but cementing my position as that significant first mate.

As we distanced ourselves from port, we lazily scoured the water for some speed. A pleasant *Séchard* wind blew down from the north and we stayed with it into the Grand-Lac, knowing its strength would not fill our sails back on the Haut-Lac. Wisps of clouds floated high in the summery sky and I lay back on a cushion in the cockpit, enjoying the increase in speed over the flat water.

Matt stood up to potter with a few things in the cockpit and on deck, then busied himself fixing the brass rim of the compass next to the hatch of the cabin that had come a little loose. I had one hand on the tiller, keeping watch for other boat traffic.

As though somebody had closed a door, the breeze dropped dead, and we began to rock gently in the doldrums. The sail flapped and I sat up, paying more attention to our position. We were almost midway into the Grand-Lac, abreast with the lakeside suburbs of Lausanne. I checked my watch. It was mid-afternoon. I assumed we had plenty of time to get back to port. But as I looked around, I noticed the sky darkening towards the south over the imposing square-topped Grammont Mountain and its neighbouring peaks. It wasn't so much a cloud, as a dark-grey haze threatening the horizon. Looking directly above us at the clear blue sky, I noticed a group of birds very high up on a thermal. They were mere specks to the naked eye, and could have been kites or seagulls. My gaze was drawn back to the shore.

'Hey, Matt, the storm lights are on full.'

Matt stopped polishing the brass rim of the compass he had now fixed and stood to look around the lake. The storm light in Lutry harbour was the closest to us.

'It's flashing at sixty. I think we should head back. There must be a change of weather coming. It wasn't predicted until tomorrow. Let me check the barometer.' He peered at the instrument on the inside of the cabin. '*De Dieu*. Something big is about to hit.'

As soon as he had spoken, the storm light at Lutry increased its rate to the maximum ninety flashes per minute. I noted all the storm lights in the ports around the lake were now winking brightly at the same rate. We had to get back to port.

'I think it's best we start the engine. When the next wind picks up, it might not be very helpful for us. It will be a southerly, which means a lot of work to get back up the lake. I'll keep the mainsail up and take the jib down for the moment until we know how strong this will be.'

Matt started the outboard motor.

'Here, take the tiller,' he said as I shuffled along the seat to the rear of the cockpit. 'Just head directly back to port. I'll get the sail down.'

I was puzzled by his urgency. The sky above us was still a calm summery blue, the lake still flat, and the sun was still shining. We floundered in the doldrums with no wind, and I found it hard to believe that anything would change in the next few hours.

But it wasn't hours. It was minutes. The wispy clouds were soon masked by a muddy haze, through which the sun still shone, but cast a foreboding brassy light on the water. Matt came back to the cockpit and took the tiller.

'Allez, ma belle, plus vite,' he said quietly to the boat, urging the motor to make headway. And as I was about to open my mouth to question this absurd urgency, a gust of wind hit us in our faces like the slap of a cardboard box. I felt the boat shudder in the water, and even without a headsail we heeled over.

'Chier. C'est le Bornan,' said Matt. 'We have to head directly into it, then maybe we will be protected by the French coast and we can use a little sail to tack back to port. Lucie, can you close the hatches on the cabin here? I will keep the tiller. I think we'll have some waves.'

As soon as he said this, the surface of the lake whipped up in front of us. I could see it travelling towards us: a battalion of ripples followed by the frothing heads of horses. The boat seesawed, hull banging into the irregular waves, and spray flew at us over the deck into the cockpit. I scrambled to batten the hatches. My experience sailing Optimists in my youth had not prepared me for this. Matt only had one set of wet-weather gear on board. He made me put it on over my already sodden clothes.

The water felt freezing in the wind. It soaked Matt's cotton T-shirt, his muscular arms glistening. He ripped it off and put on a fleece I had retrieved from below before closing the hatch. It wouldn't keep him dry, but the synthetic material would keep him marginally warmer than the cotton of his shirt.

We made pathetic headway into the gale, the wind whipping my hair from my face. An angry purple sky loomed over the mountains ahead. We were experiencing the full force of the unpredictable weather patterns on an alpine lake. The enormity of its power was to be respected at all costs.

And then the motor died.

'*Merde, merde, merde*,' muttered Matt. I looked at him questioningly, wondering why he wasn't attempting to restart it.

'We're out of fuel. I had meant to refill the canister before we set out today. I completely forgot. I didn't think we would get this far down the lake. We'll have to sail home.'

I was prepared to go up on deck and hoist the jib back out of the forward hatch, but Matt shook his head.

'We'll stay with the main. I need to reef it. When we come round, you'd better hold on tight.'

I took the tiller as Matt hauled up the outboard motor, and pulled the kicking strap tight on the boom. I stowed the loose items in the cockpit under our seats, including the cushions on which we had been soaking up the early summer sun only minutes beforehand, and which were now soaking up gallons of the spuming lake.

The process of tacking up the lake back to port proved laborious. Matt didn't want to leave the protection of the hills near the coast as we could see the water rising in the centre of the lake, giant waves running into each other from all directions as the lie of the land caused the wind to swirl. The boat heeled, even with such a small sail area. Water banged against the hull, halyards screeched, and I swallowed my fear. Matt yelled his instructions at each tack, his face set in determined concentration, but not losing his cool. I had confidence in him, and tried to suppress the panic that lay squirming in my belly.

When we eventually limped back into port, it was with some embarrassment we were forced to use the emergency oars to bring the sloop back to its berth. With rain now lashing down, there were few witnesses to our homecoming, and relief shone from both our faces. The three of us were intact. Matt, me, and the boat.

'In any other wind I can usually sail right into her berth,' he boasted.

As I tied up to the ring on the jetty and Matt hooked the buoy to the stern, a satisfying exhaustion infused our limbs. We stood in the cockpit, the boat still rocking on the rough water lapping into the port. He wrapped his arms around me, and we shivered together. Despite my discomfort, I felt elated.

'I couldn't have done that without you.'

He looked lovingly into my eyes that were smarting with the wind. He stroked my cheek, gently pushed the tangle of hair from my face, and kissed the top of my head.

'What a team! Working hard together to survive. That was quite an adventure.'

'Were you ever really worried?' I asked, knowing my fear had lurked constantly.

'It's not knowing what's coming next that's the scary part. But we made it in the end. Together,' he said, still holding me.

The urge to get into dry clothes soon had us rushing to the Land Rover to drive home, the heater on full blast, fogging the windows as though it were mid-winter.

'Have you ever had another sailing partner to share experiences like that? I imagine that's not easy if you're on your own,' I asked in the mugginess of the car.

'No ... I'm nearly always on my own. I'm glad you were there.' He smiled at me.

'Did Leila ever come sailing with you?' I asked.

Matt continued to look forward, hands on the wheel as he negotiated a turn onto the main road. But his jaw clenched, and I felt stupid for having mentioned her name. How witless of me to ruin the camaraderie.

'Leila was scared of water. She never set foot on the boat.'

I don't know why, but this felt like a little victory. It could also have been time to let sleeping dogs lie. I pushed the niggling unanswered questions to the back of my mind.

But I did feel like we had endured a rite of passage together that day. No matter what I had felt before, the reality of the danger we had been in had somehow sealed our allegiance. We weren't merely a team, we were an invincible army. Nothing could break us.

* * *

A few days later I was in the art studio putting order to Patterson's chaos of painting equipment when I found an unnamed portfolio on a high shelf. I untied the ribbons and opened the heavy board cover. I gasped, and the paper I held between my fingers trembled. Without seeing the face of the figure in the drawing in front of me, I knew it was Matt.

I had inadvertently come across Leila's sketches. And it was as though I had caught them naked in the room together.

Heart pounding, I laid the portfolio on the table, and spread the pictures apart to reveal a series of still life and model sketches. There were several of a bowl of fruit and a vase of plastic cherry blossoms. I recognised the flowers as those still steadily fading near the window behind where I stood. I turned the pictures carefully; several works of a skilfully drawn middle-aged woman in chalks and charcoal, and then a whole collection of Matt's beautifully sculpted body. I felt instantly guilty, and shuffled the drawings together and slammed the portfolio closed.

I felt sick to think of them making love. She must surely have given herself to him as his reward for sitting for her. I could almost see the scenario playing out before me. The torturous mind of a jealous lover. Flustered, I looked around to make sure no one was in the studio and I slowly opened the portfolio again. I studied a sketch of him on top of the pile, my hands in the prayer position, fingers touching my lips. This body, so familiar to me, had been perhaps more familiar to her. Matt and I had only been together for a few weeks. They had been together for much longer. I now understood why he wouldn't let me draw him.

We were like a threesome, then, in that studio. I carefully pulled all the sketches out of the portfolio, and spread them on the table. I studied them more closely: beautiful simple lined sketches in charcoal, and a more detailed drawing in graphite. The familiar torso, the corded neck, drawn up to that distinctive jawline. I wanted to cry. I could feel the passion in these pieces. Matt remained so closed about his relationship with Leila, had never wanted to discuss her, but I now craved to know what was in his heart.

I should have taken the sketches home. If I couldn't return them to the artist, at least I should return them to the model, as if part of his soul was embedded in the charcoal dust. But I eventually shuffled them back into the portfolio cover, re-tied the black ribbon and laid it carefully back on top of the shelf where I'd found it.

Later I went to the college library and looked through the yearbooks for the terms when Leila had been a student. I found one photo with her name, her official class portrait. Her burnished skin glowed from the picture, her dark penetrating eyes gazing with innocence and passion simultaneously. Perfect white teeth showed through a blossom of lips in a playful half-smile, half-pout. A loose scarf surrounded her head in a swathe of mysteriousness, plaited hair like black snakes rising from the top of her head. An alluring medusa. Her gaze at me out of the yearbook page turned me to stone. I felt like a stalker hiding a secret. This exotic beauty had captured Mathieu's heart, and I was trying my hardest to wrench it from her grasp.

* * *

70

One afternoon I caught Patterson puffing his pipe contemplatively on the wide balcony outside the art studio.

I stepped through the glass doors to join him. He had set up an easel to one side, a half-finished canvas splashed with summer trees. He leaned against a pillar, gazing at the grounds in front of the college. I interrupted his puffing.

'These wide balconies are perfect for an art class in summer,' I said.

'When the building was a sanatorium, they would wheel the patients out in their beds to soak up the benefits of the healing sun,' he said. 'There are some photos in the lobby downstairs of rows of tanned bodies enjoying their TB remedy. Probably all cured of consumption, but died of cancerous melanomas later on.'

We laughed companionably and I sipped my tea while Patterson puffed away.

We watched a string of cars pull into the college car park, parents greeting their offspring as they arrived like guests to a wedding. Preparations were in full swing for the final year students' graduation ceremony.

'I've seen hundreds come and go, you know,' he said absently as I leaned on the wooden balustrade to watch the festive atmosphere below. 'It's a bit like saying goodbye to one's own children year after year. Never seems to get any easier. Poor buggers. You have to hope that they choose the right road in life.'

I had rarely heard Patterson speak of anything other than his beloved artists and paintings with any emotion.

'Patterson,' I said, always with the feeling that I should be addressing him as 'Sir' like a schoolmaster. 'Do you remember a student of yours, a Somalian girl called Leila?' I paused to give him a chance to pick an image from the yearbooks of student faces in his mind. 'She would have been in your classes about two or three years ago, I guess.'

Patterson puffed, a cloud of smoke hanging cloyingly around us on the windless summer air.

'Of course I remember Leila. Gifted artist, that one, though I'm not sure she will get an opportunity to use her talent.'

My heart skipped and I swallowed as he continued. 'Family came and whisked her away before she became too wound up in European society. Your young man had something to do with that.'

My heart spiked before he continued.

'They turned a bit of a blind eye in the college administration, actually. Seeing as young Mister Favre was an alumnus and all. And that draconian mother of his made a little donation to enable him to keep his job. If it had been up to me, I'd have fired the bugger, sorry to say. He wasn't always faithful to the girl, had a reputation for playing the field. There were rumours, but thank God she never heard them. She didn't deserve it. And he didn't deserve her.'

Patterson noted my open mouth and raised eyebrows, but didn't stop.

'Got a terrible temper on him, that one. I recall he caused a bit of damage in the registrar's office when he found out Leila had gone. Had his sister Marie-Claire in one of my classes for a semester. She also had artistic talent. Bad blood between them though. You want to watch that, his short fuse.' He looked at me pointedly.

We watched more vehicles arriving, students greeting relatives out of their rental cars or taxis after long journeys from the airport. They were temporarily reduced to displaying toddler-like behaviour, clinging to parents they hadn't seen for half a year.

It wasn't the first time I'd been warned off Matt by people I knew. But I had fallen so hard for him, I figured they were surprised at the speed our relationship had developed. They were telling me to take it easy. Take things slowly. Patterson seemed to treat me in a paternal manner. Matt's history at the college was just that. History. Now he had regular employment at the institution, things had surely changed. We'd all acted impulsively in our teenage years. People change when they mature.

And although I was convinced I'd found the love of my life, I figured it was time to exorcise my demons, to stop the doubt eating away at my self-destruct button.

* * *

We discussed the advantages of sharing a rent on our two salaries, and were about to move into a house together. We found a rambling early twentieth century faux-château complete with turret and chaotic gothic decorations reminiscent of stage props in a horror movie. Originally constructed for one of the pioneering physicians of the TB sanitaria in the village during the boom of the 1920s, it had been remodelled in the early Sixties into two duplex apartments. The house looked tired by Swiss standards, and Matt managed to negotiate a good deal on the rent. But before I could sign on the dotted line as a *co-locateur*, there was something I needed to know. With the papers in front of us, and my pen hovering, I looked across the table.

'Matt, I kind of need to know something. It's about Leila.'

If a split second could be stretched into a feature-length film and recorded, I would have pressed the replay button for hours to try and fathom the look he gave me then. Something between fire and steel. After the brief mention of her fear of water after our sailing adventure, he must have thought her name wouldn't be raised again. And I knew I shouldn't make her a regular topic. But I wondered if his heart suddenly beat faster. Mine certainly did.

For a moment I didn't think he was going to answer. My comment wasn't a question. Was he waiting for more? He slid a look sideways at me, his eyelids creasing imperceptibly.

'What do you need to know about Leila, Lucille?' He used my full name, leaving me with the uncomfortable feeling I had done something wrong. As though I had trespassed onto forbidden ground. I wanted to take my words back. Suddenly didn't want to hear what he had to say. Too late now. He had never once mentioned her name. I felt exposed, admitting that I knew about her all along. I'm sure he had questions of his own pitching through his mind.

'Do you ever hear from her? I mean, how are things between the two of you? Is there anything more I need to know?'

I felt these questions tumbling out, trying to justify my concerns before each one was answered. I knew he was uneasy about the fact that I was employed at the same institution where he worked, but now I wondered whether his uneasiness was more to do with the fact that I was employed in the art studio. Surely I shouldn't be so nervous about asking this kind of question?

'Lucie, it's okay. There is no future with Leila. I wouldn't be moving in with you if there were.'

I couldn't work out whether he sounded exasperated or simply sad.

'I know, I guess ...' I hesitated. 'It's just that, you've never really talked about her. From what I've heard, there was an element of ... something not quite finished in the relationship. I wanted to make sure that some ghost wouldn't be sharing our bed.'

'Of course not. Why the sudden interest in Leila? I've never asked you about your old boyfriends.' His voice rose in anger. He had a point.

'I'm sorry, Matt. I shouldn't have asked. It's such a big step with us moving in together,' I said, although I knew it was what I wanted.

His eyes narrowed as he rose from the table and moved towards me. He pulled me from my seat and laid his hand on my chest. For a moment I didn't know what to expect. Then he wrapped me in a hug, hiding his eyes by putting his chin on my shoulder. I found it difficult to read this man I didn't completely know.

'Come on, Lucie,' he said to the wall, voice now saccharin and slightly patronising. 'Our relationship is nothing to do with what's happened in the past. Don't go getting paranoid about some old girlfriend of mine. I'm with you now. You.'

He kissed me, long and deep. After I'd signed the rental agreement, he took my hand, led me past half-packed boxes to his room at the back of the apartment. Making love might make us both feel better. But there was an air of unease about the way he said her name, and in my love-struck state I needed more than a physical assurance.

* * *

I gaze out of the window of my cell, remembering the cool spray of lake water on my face and then another season, the freshness of snow. I wish I could feel cold crystals now on my face. I recall the thrill of seeing JP ski down his first gentle slope unaided. His little mittened hands were held in front of him, encircling a hug of air, ready to be caught by his proud mother at the base of the slope, while his excited father cheered him on from behind. I smile briefly. We were both quick learners. Matt was proud of us then.

I suppress a sob, and the pen trembles in my hand. These letters are probably pointless. I'm pretty sure Natasha doesn't read them to him. She likely drops them in the bin, leaving him clueless that his mother writes to him almost daily. I should be more inventive with my requests. Even if I ask JP to draw a picture, I am sure it would never reach the post office. I must remind him again the next time we are able to talk on the phone. I haven't received a picture from him since the summer, but I'm sure it's not through his lack of wanting to do one for me.

I draw a sketch of the castle at the top of the paper, colouring the shutters with their rusty red design, remembering the hues of my seasons on the mountain, their vividness a delicious agony for the eyes. This afternoon we will go out into our sombre grey world, dig over the garden, fork the weeds and dead foliage into the composting cages.

It stopped raining during the night, but feels no less damp, the cloying humidity trapped in the air. Waiting for the air to chill, ever hopeful that snow might fall at this low altitude. A dirty mist now surrounds us in our bland valley village, wiping away memories of the mountains. My vision is blurry with unshed tears, and I occupy myself by giving the plants in my cell some water, before returning to my desk and picking up my pen.

The aching sadness is like a hot poultice, but I must not let the bitter poison of vindictiveness infect my letters to my son.

My darling JP,

We picked the last of the carrots today and I thought of our window boxes last summer where we grew peas, carrots and broccoli. The weather is very grey, and the only colour in my world is now the red of the castle shutters – do you still remember them from your last visit? I hope you are above the clouds.

I haven't had a drawing from you for a while. I have included one of mine. I hope you like it. Can you draw me another picture? Please get Mimi to send it to me. Perhaps she will let you post the letter yourself, like a big boy.

I hope you are remembering your pleases and thank yous, and helping Mimi around the house.

I love you with all my heart, and hope that Mimi and Poppa will bring you to visit me very soon.

Lots of love and hugs, Mama

Chapter 6

The rain slants in thick needles again past the window. It's as though Hindelbank is situated in some depressing underworld where the weather is perpetually grey. A prison under the sea of clouded purgatory that separates us a thousand metres from paradise. We won't be forced to work outside today. Instead Müller has sent me along to the west wing. I am waiting for another guard to let me into the cleaning cupboard. Today my job is to help wax the floors, a random assignment. Supported by Müller, my petition to work as a painter in the atelier is still being considered by the chief warden, or Direktor as she's called here. But the garden first has to be completely cleared and hoed, hence the delay.

There is a row of chairs near the cleaning cupboard, close to the window where I sit and wait. I wonder why the floors need cleaning when I study their shine under the fluorescent strip lights down the hallway. One of the strip tubes above me needs replacing, and I sit in shadow.

So when Dolores shuffles along the corridor, she doesn't see me. I'm surprised to see her so far from her cell and am about to call out to her, a friendly '*Hola!*' when I notice she is agitated, behaving a little strangely. We all know Dolores can be unpredictable with her fiery temper. Something tells me to remain silent.

On the other side of the cleaning cupboard, a little way down the corridor, is a large metal box attached to the wall. Dolores clutches an object in her hand, heading straight for the box. She shakily opens her fingers and feeds the object into the side of the metal container. As she turns a handle, something clatters to the hole in the bottom of the machine. She reaches in and grabs a small plastic packet and without checking what is in her hand, shuffles back down the corridor from where she came, all the time ignorant of my presence.

A few minutes later a young guard shows up, and silently unlocks the cleaning cupboard. Together we wheel out the waxing machine, its bright blue buffer the only colour in the pale grey of the hallway.

'What's that thing for?' I ask in broken German, pointing to the metal box on the wall.

'*Spritzenumtausch*,' she says. I am nonplussed. '*Drogen. Heroin.*' She crudely mimes injecting something into the crook of her elbow. Jesus, they're giving away drugs? I am astounded. I know there are plenty of drug addicts within these walls, but I must have misunderstood the guard.

At the end of the afternoon, forearms aching from swinging my mechanical partner in great arcs on the lino dance floor of the hallways, Müller accompanies me back to the cleaning cupboard to lock away the machine. I point to the metal box as we pass.

'Did I understand correctly that the inmates can get drugs here?' I ask.

'Not drugs,' she says, hesitating. 'Drugs will always find a way into the prison. This is where the prisoners can get clean *Spritze*, syringes. It is part of our needle exchange programme.'

'But I don't understand. Isn't that encouraging them to take drugs in the first place? Shouldn't you be trying to get them off the stuff? Find a way to stop them getting in?'

I'm not shocked at the number of inmates here who take drugs. They're all pretty discreet about it. And it was how most of the foreigners ended up in Hindelbank in the first place. But with the strictness of censorship for the incoming mail, I wonder how drugs can possibly make it inside the prison walls. I wonder how they smuggle them in, and how easily the guards can be bribed.

'In the early Nineties, we started a project at Hindelbank,' says Müller. 'The Direktor wanted the prison to be a pioneer model for preventing the spread of infectious diseases. We provide distribution points for clean syringe needles. All users are registered with the counsellor. They can only get a clean needle by exchanging a used one with the new.'

'Do many women use this … this system?'

'Not as many as there used to be – we have a good, how do you say, rehab programme. Almost a third of the prisoners here take drugs of some kind.'

I'm not naive, but that seems like such a large proportion. It's the first time I've noticed the presence of these needle distributors. They are well hidden; this one is on a corridor close to the cleaning cupboard, an area seldom frequented. And Müller's explanation makes a lot of sense. The first priority is for the well-being of the inmates, and a clean-needle programme avoids the spread of diseases such as HIV.

I am incredibly saddened, though, to think of women like Dolores who have been forced onto a regime of hard drugs by the bosses who persuaded them to traffic for them in the first place. She has children back home in the Dominican Republic who rely on her money to survive. And now she's tied to the one thing that used to provide her income.

It's a far cry from dabbling in a few soft drugs that played a part of our teenage lives in the reckless social scene of a ski resort full of hedonistic travellers. I think of JP, and of Dolores's three kids. It might be so easy to succumb to that temptation if you have nothing to offer for your children's survival.

I don't know whether I should share the fact that Dolores is a user with the others. Our little group on our cell level has become ... not close, but I get the feeling we'd look out for each other. I had no idea Dolores was still an addict, although now I realise it would take months for a rehab programme to be effective. But I also don't know whether Yasmine or Fatima or Monika, a Swiss inmate in a cell down the hall from me, are users. We all still have our secrets, but I feel ashamed at my ignorance.

I guess there's a reason for discretion. Who knows whether it would help Dolores to know she has support. Sometimes it's easier to ignore the signs and all that crap, to kid ourselves we can maintain a semblance of normality.

* * *

Seven years ago
The sudden ringing made my hand jerk mid-stroke, and a fleck of green paint appeared on my pristine cream background on the canvas. It was a mid-week evening when Matt had papers to mark and a student to tutor at the college. I was working on a still life in the office space at home, tubes of acrylic paints spread on a cloth over the desk and a towel on the floor to catch any stray drops. I swore under my breath, wiped my hand on a rag, and went to silence the annoying jangle of the phone.

Dad sounded slightly strained, something he needed to say but didn't know how, and Mum was overly emotional to hear my voice. Something was up. The hair on the back of my neck prickled with anticipation. We began the conversation with news of weather, the newest Patterson anecdotes and my plans for the summer.

'Matt's planning a sailing trip to the Med this summer. I might finally get to that Greek beach I kept telling you about.' I laughed, then more soberly: 'I know you've never really approved of us living together, but I think things are getting pretty serious between us … I thought you should know.'

'Are you alone, Lucille?' my father asked with unaccustomed coolness.

'Yes … why?'

'Your father and I want to share our concerns,' said Mum. Your father and I. I could picture them on the phone, Dad at his desk and Mum in the hallway on the extension. I suddenly felt like a pre-pubescent.

'We called last week on Wednesday evening when you were preparing the set design elements for the senior theatre,' continued Mum. She called? Matt didn't say anything. 'The thing is, I mean, did you know that Matt wasn't alone that night?' My head went cold. 'Only … we heard laughter in the background. A woman's voice.'

My world tilted.

'Oh, Mum, come on, it was probably the telly. Are you trying to get Matt into trouble?' I joked, but felt unsure. Whose laughter?

'Oh look, darling, it's probably nothing; we thought we should tell you because, well, the whole thing sounded a bit odd, and you weren't there. Don't want to go putting a cat among the pigeons, but you know …' Mum's voice drifted as a sudden anger boiled in my chest at their attempt to make Matt seem not worthy.

To gloss over the implication I talked excitedly about an upcoming trip to Florence that Patterson wanted me to join. I told them he managed to get a budget for an extra supervisor on the trip as a dozen students had now signed up. I distracted them with my excitement about visiting the Accademia, finally getting to see 'David' after half a semester of studying Michelangelo and dropping out of the fine arts class two years previously. Not quite full circle, but a satisfying alternative.

'Lucille, no matter what we thought of your … abandonment of your studies, we are very proud of what you have managed to achieve. We're so glad you haven't ended up waiting tables from one season to another … We think we might come and see you this summer.'

'Oh, that would be great,' I said, excited. 'Once I know when we'll be away sailing, I'll let you know. We'll have such fun. You can stay in the office, the pull-out couch is very comfortable, and you'd have a great view over the village all the way to the Rhône Valley. I'll clear away my easel and paints. I think it's the best room in the apartment. And you'll finally get to meet Matt.'

'That's very kind, Lucille, but I think we'll look into staying in a bed and breakfast in the village, not far from you.'

I understood their awkwardness and concern. They thought I was too young to be getting into a serious relationship. They had yet to meet Matt, so I appreciated their caution, but couldn't understand why they would try and plant the seed of doubt about him. I knew he was 'the one'. I had my eyes open and was convinced fate had dealt me the opportunity to spend my life with the ideal partner.

My father had always steered reasoning away from my dreams that didn't match his. He'd never been enthusiastic about my art studies, and I figured he was using this cruel tool to convince me to hold off making a commitment. To think Matt had another lover while I was working on a project was inconceivable. For one thing the village was too small to allow such a thing to happen, and me not know about it.

After the phone call, a part of me accepted that my parents were protecting my interests as their only daughter. They simply didn't want me making rash decisions.

It would never have occurred to me that my father might have been right.

* * *

For the remainder of spring and on into early summer, I felt my life could hardly be more perfect. At the college I received credit in Patterson's classes, yet no one ever treated me like a student. As his assistant, I had cemented my place within the faculty, despite not having completed any undergraduate degree, and felt welcomed among them.

My favourite classes were spent lugging canvases and easels onto the wide balcony outside the studio, or across the road from the college into a field full of flowers on a sunny day. Although I spent much of the time helping the students to set up their equipment to paint, I enjoyed watching Patterson produce his works too, while working on some of my own. Rather than being a learning process, it was more a process of absorption, with the chance of earning credit for the classes a bonus for my future. Patterson took on a different persona when he stood at his easel. He was no longer the bumbling professor, but a delicate master balancing his tools cleverly and producing magic for the eye. I thought maybe I had found my mentor.

The vast alpine landscape, never the same from one day to the next, provided me with endless inspiration for works of my own, which in turn mustered enthusiasm to feed to the students. I felt settled in my vivid new home. I had it all – a satisfying job, a resident's permit, a beautiful home and a handsome lover. There was a kind of desperate shining to the edge of my desire to stay in this moment, to preserve time and emotions. I didn't want this to change, wanted these months to freeze-frame. I had found a niche where I could live forever.

Matt initially felt uncomfortable with me working on campus. He thought we might run into each other too often, a concern I understood to mean he wanted to keep work and play separate. But enjoying my work so much, it was hard for me to separate the two.

'That's the excitement about being with someone you love,' he said. 'It's all the more special to see each other again after a little time apart.'

I would remember that statement later on in the summer, but

for now his concerns were somewhat allayed by the fact that we never seemed to cross paths on campus. As the art assistant, I was often away with students, either on a class project or an excursion to a museum. We kept our professional lives separate from each other. Part of me wondered if he wanted to keep the phase of his life he had spent with Leila separate too.

* * *

'But we talked about it, Matt.' I couldn't prevent the whine in my voice. 'I thought we were going to go sailing together. And now you're saying you'll be gone for the whole two months?'

As the college wound up its courses for the summer holidays and the students headed home, I had been looking forward to the promised sailing time together on the Med with my captain.

Matt had finished his Yacht Master's studies in spring and provisionally received his captain's ticket. It was a long-term project that he had started long before we met. But to secure his qualification, he needed to log hours at the helm of an ocean-going sailboat. Time on an inland lake would not be valid.

'How exciting. I can be your first mate, official role,' I had laughed as he told me of his summer plans, holding me in his arms after we had made love one night. Matt cleared his throat.

'Lucie, I … I think it will be too distracting if you are there with me. It's not only about sailing the boat, I also have to complete my offshore navigation module. It's … I've been planning this for years. I think I must do this on my own. The guy I'm sailing with, he's not expecting me to bring anyone with me. Sweetheart, it's only eight weeks. It will go by so quickly, and then we can enjoy the rest of the summer together.'

I was hurt. When he had spoken about sailing on the Med back in spring, I had assumed he'd included me in his plans, especially as we were now living together. But at the time I guess he had never expected our relationship to last longer than the end of the spring.

'Even if you don't want me on the boat while you're logging your hours, surely I could hole up with some canvases and paints in some seaside town until you drop anchor. The old adage of a girl in every port ... I could be the same girl in every port,' I tried to joke, but he wasn't smiling.

'I'm sorry, Lucie ...'

'Me too, Matt. I'm so disappointed.'

I bit my lip, remembering that I didn't want to ever sound like the dissatisfied lover. Matt sighed.

'The skipper's name is Dave. I got his contact details some time ago, before we moved in together, through one of the students in my class. An uncle I think. He's in the yacht business and he's agreed to satisfy my logging requirements if I give him a hand to deliver a couple of vessels.'

I was gutted, but remained realistic. Yacht deliveries meant days, maybe a couple of weeks at sea. There would be little point me waiting forlornly in some port for my lover.

I looked at the positives. There were other reasons to be pragmatic. At least Matt was sticking to his guns. If this was something he had been planning for a long time, years even, then surely he could be relied on to see things through. Like moving in with his girlfriend. But at barely 20 years old, eight weeks to me felt like a lifetime.

I briefly wondered whether he questioned my loyalty. Whether he thought a young woman, suddenly single for a summer in the mountains, would still be there for him on his return.

'You'll be here when I get back,' he said.

So sure. A statement rather than a question. He knew he wouldn't lose me, and that was enough to know that this was a test I could endure.

Since our adventure on the lake that spring, I assumed I was the first mate, the premier lieutenant he couldn't live without.

Despite my determination to encourage him and not make him feel guilty with my over-reactive emotions, when he talked of his plans for the summer, he spoke with an added excitement that made me involuntarily sulky at his imminent break in our relationship. I couldn't control myself, it was childish and irrational, and eventually Matt stopped talking about it altogether.

The truth was, I realised the sailing trip Matt was planning for the Med had never meant to include me. The time apart would approach us silently, like an unavoidable medical procedure, and it brought to mind the very first night of passion together when his sudden change of heart led him to inexplicably drop me like a hot coal. Reading his moods and the signs, I realised I was still on a learning curve.

* * *

In the end, he was only away for six weeks. He said he had come back early because he missed me. But part of me didn't believe him. I wondered if there were simply no more deliveries on the schedule. Matt spent most of those six weeks transporting yachts between Italy's Adriatic coast and Turkey. He tried to make these deliveries sound like a hardship, but I could hear excitement in his voice that thrived on ocean adventure. We didn't speak often. With no mobile coverage at sea, he restricted communication to once or twice a week when he was in port.

I came to dread the calls. The part when they had to end, perpetually leaving me feeling like I had said something wrong. I could have forsaken them altogether in the hope that he might actually regret the length of his truancy, but missed his voice too much to act that proud. I tried not to doubt that he would come back to me after the summer, but still felt confused that he didn't want me to be part of it. I tried not to think of his muscular bronzed body at the helm of a yacht, surrounded by volunteer sea nymphs, first mates, premier lieutenants.

My parents came to visit as planned, and they agreed to stay with me in our apartment, confirming my suspicions that they were uncomfortable about meeting Matt. That saddened me. However much their indifference to my college, career and relationship had developed, they were still my parents, and their approval was a subconscious pursuit. The visit helped to fill a couple of weeks of emptiness, counting the days until Matt's return, wishing time would fly.

After my parents left, I spent more time with Anne. I began to enjoy a life with new friends, without the pressure of worrying whether I should check with my partner first before I went to a concert, a festival, a ride in the mountains or a picnic on the lake in the lazy heat of the summer. And gradually I began to enjoy my space on my own terms, and realised how pathetically reliant I had become on Matt, losing my independence.

And before I knew it, he was back, tanned golden, hair sunbleached. I couldn't help it, but like an abandoned pet, I remained aloof, perhaps hoping to make him think I hadn't been pining for him. The games people play. But he sensed a change in me, self-confidence I hadn't before displayed, not relying on his affection or querying his commitment, and I think it renewed his sense for the chase. His courting started afresh.

I felt something might have happened during the summer, an unknown incident or encounter that made him appreciate the effortlessness of our relationship. I believed in his integrity, trusted his fidelity and refused to let the doubts that someone had had an influence on him to the extent that he displayed an uncharacteristic neediness for a few weeks after his return. I had kept my side of the deal, never forgetting the old adage: if you love something, let it go.

I once found a message from a 'Selina' on his mobile. With heart pounding, thinking it might be a declaration of love-lust, I picked up his phone. But the message was innocuous, a query whether he had returned to Switzerland safely. No kisses, no hidden cutesy riddles. No indication that his ocean adventures had been anything other than nautical. I never asked who Selina was.

* * *

'Hi, sweetheart, what did you enjoy about school today?'

I've already learned from previous telephone conversations not to ask ambiguous questions like 'How are you?' or 'Are you well?' I try not to ask anything that requires a 'yes' or 'no' or 'okay' answer. I've even written a list, in case my emotions run away with me, which they inevitably do at some point. I have about ten minutes. It's my one phone call a week, if I can get through. I envision Natasha each time, furious that the court has forced it upon her. I am JP's mother, and nothing can change that. She knows I have my rights. If she manages to squirm out of the duty too often, some authority will make sure I am awarded this one prerogative. How distasteful for her to have to answer to a prison official.

'We played pirates in the big school gym today. Valentin and I climbed all the way to the top of the wall bars. Muriel Oguey didn't want to chase us, so we won. Mama, when are you coming home?'

His small sweet voice lifts me with joy. He still needs me. Even six months on. I want to dance a little jig, pump my fist. I imagine Natasha lurking in the background, monitoring the exchange. I ask more questions requiring specific answers, to stop me babbling. It's a joyous day when I get to speak to my baby.

'I'll be home soon, sweetie. Soon. Who did you play with at break time today?'

'You ask that every time. You know I always play with Valentin. *Tu sais ça …*'

'Well you're allowed to play with the others sometimes too, you know. What did you guys have for lunch?'

88

'Oh, Mama, I don't remember …'

I look further down my list, looking for something I didn't ask last time. I don't want to be the awkward hospital visitor talking to a patient, running out of things to ask. The unspoken elephant in our conversation is what am I doing in prison. He might as well ask what kind of cancer do I have. I don't want to give JP the chance to ask about me. I just want to hear his voice.

It disturbs me that I can hear a strong French accent. I hope desperately he doesn't forget his English. Natasha and Didier will both be perfecting his French, his schooling is all in French, his best friend, Valentin, speaks French, and I would not expect Anne to digress from her mother tongue to satisfy my desire to maintain a good level of English.

'Has it snowed again? What kind of games are you playing?' I ask.

An excited diatribe ensues about the building of an igloo in the park near Valentin's house with a group of friends, including Anne and François. I file away this information in the pending tray of my brain so I can ask Anne about this later. To get her to describe the scene in more detail. Anne is good at recounting these events so I can replay them in my mind, vicariously participating in the action. She even takes notes, a kind of diary, which she brings with photographs with her when she visits. She's like my own personal investigative journalist.

I let JP ramble on, don't interrupt. I'm grateful that Natasha doesn't know how close Anne and I are. She might forbid JP the chance to play with Valentin outside school hours.

'Do you have any special plans for the weekend?'

'Mimi and Poppa are taking me to the zoo!'

He's excited again as he remembers, and begins to tell me all the animals he hopes to see. I look at the clock on the wall. Our time is drawing to a close. I know that any moment now, Natasha will tell him that's enough. His voice starts to sound a little mechanical and I'm sure she is hovering. JP has no concept of the fact that it might be days before he will speak to me again. I want to cherish every word.

'JP, I want you to do something very special for Mama this week.'

Like many mothers I refer to myself in the third person, and can only imagine I do this because instructions sound less like militant commands and he is more likely to react.

'I want you to promise you will draw Mama another picture.'

'Of course I promise, Mama. I draw you a picture every week. My day for doing that is …' I can hear him thinking. 'Vendreday!' he says, pleased with himself. I don't correct him. He has mixed the two languages, and it's probably the wrong day anyway. It's likely he draws for me on Wednesday when he has the afternoon off kindergarten. But my head is singing. He's drawn me a picture every week! My heart is ready to burst. I wish I had those images, things I could stick on the wall, to feel like I am still part of his tangible life. My voice shakes as I continue, a combination of anger at Natasha for never sending the pictures, and overwhelming love for my son who has never forgotten his promised task.

'JP, I want you to send the next picture to me like a big boy.' I dispense with the third person. 'You must ask Mimi to write my address on the envelope and make sure she sticks on a stamp. Ask her if you can post the letter yourself. She can take you to the post office. Can you promise me you will do that? You must ask Mimi. Can you remember everything?'

'Okaaay,' he says, uncertain of the urgency in my tone. 'Do you want to speak to Mimi? I don't know if I can remember all that. She's …'

'It's okay, JP, I don't need to talk to Mimi. I know you can do this.'

The last thing I want to do is talk to Natasha. I'm not sure JP can manage all these instructions at 6 years old, but the request has to come from him. I wonder if Natasha is listening in, perhaps

90

on the extension, or if she's standing next to him, arms crossed, tapping her feet with impatience to get her criminal daughter-in-law off the line.

'I have to go, JP. I love you very much.'

'I love you too, Mama.'

'I love you more,' I say, wondering if he will remember our little bedtime ritual when I sat on his bed and kissed him every night before he slept.

'No, I love you more, Mama.' I smile, tears spilling silently down my cheeks.

It's a heart-wrenching game of chess, with JP the unsuspecting pawn. Natasha is a mother too, and I know every mother would want to apportion blame in her situation, but I'm still unsure why she is fighting so hard to win the game. We are all walking on eggshells with JP, each of us trying desperately to gain his favour.

Chapter 7

It's official. Yasmine and Dolores are a couple. It doesn't take long for both of them to advertise the fact, seeing as they're the two most vocal inmates in our block. There's nothing secretive or subtle about their liaison.

A part of me is jealous. I'm envious of the closeness, and the ability to lose themselves in each other. Sometimes I just crave to be held. I don't really care who would hold me any more, aside from constantly wishing I had JP's little arms around me.

Yasmine no longer comes into my room. I guess she spends all the free time she can with Dolores, with emotional responsibilities now. I'm unsure whether she knows about her partner's little habit. If I hadn't seen Dolores with my own eyes, I might never have suspected.

I still feel ashamed that I was ignorant enough to need the clarification from Müller, could slap my forehead with naivety. Since then, I see signs of drug use everywhere. Personality disorders manifest themselves daily at our workstations. There's always someone flipping out, and I realise now that it's not only the frustration at being incarcerated. They're chemically influenced.

Dolores has always insisted she was clean when she came in. I remember a conversation around the table in the cafeteria when

I first arrived, and before Yasmine turned up on the block.

'Carlos, he my man in Santo Domingo. *Que mierda!* He start me using. I was 14. Then I had to move stuff for him so I could afford to buy more gear for myself. We run shit out of Haina. Sometimes on boats. This happen for years. He violent too. Should have walked away, *Baboso*. But I needed him for my gear.'

She had moaned, and slapped herself on the side of her face, in a way that told us something was still not quite right with her.

'I stay in rehab clinic in Bellinzona before coming here,' Dolores continued.

Unlike most of the others in here for trafficking, she was caught in Ticino, the Italian part of Switzerland, crossing the border at Chiasso. Most of the others were arrested at the airports in Geneva or Zürich.

'I clean, honestly.' Dolores rubbed the cheek she had slapped, dragging the sallow skin upwards and then down, pulling the red lower lids of her heavily mascaraed eyes and leaving a streak of lipstick on her chin.

It seems so obvious now, that after so many years selling for an abusive pimp in the Dominican Republic, she could hardly expect the vicious shackles of addiction to be broken by one short stay in rehab. It's the insistent denial that saddens me more than anything else. After seeing her exchange her needle, and Müller's subsequent revelation, I'm not sure about anybody any more.

* * *

I have finally started working in the atelier, although my first task is unexpected, and I'm mildly disappointed not to be wielding some paintbrushes. I've been asked to pick up some flour and salt from the bakery. We are going to prepare salt dough decorations for the Christmas market, which takes place in a few weeks' time.

When the guard lets me in to the bakery, Yasmine is pulling

trays of *Semmeli*, crusty white rolls, out of the oven. The yeasty aroma is comforting, conjuring a vision of family and festive occasions. Soon the bakery will have the added ingredients of spices for the Christmas *Guetzli* they will make for Advent and the market.

'Lucie, *ma belle*!' After Yasmine pulls out the last tray and places it above the others in the cooling trolley, we walk together to the pantry.

'I know this might seem like an indiscreet question, Yasmine, but are you using?' She raises an eyebrow. 'Drugs,' I specify.

Yasmine's expression saddens. 'No, I am not, Lucie, not after the things I have seen. I would never sink to that level. It's a dark place to be, and I know I'll be getting out of here someday soon. Ça m'agace that you need to ask.'

'It's just … it's just I don't recognise the obvious signs. I don't doubt you, Yasmine, I simply needed to know.'

I want to tell her about Dolores, but her vehement self-denial keeps me silent. The things she has seen? I don't want to make her annoyed with me, ratting on her girlfriend.

I take a kilo of flour and a box of salt. We remain silent while the guard signs the supply chit and locks the pantry behind us, before walking slowly back towards the entrance.

'One day I will tell you how I watched my brother die in Algiers,' she says. I draw in my breath. 'Bad drugs. Bad shit. For his sake I could not take drugs. Never. My father … well, depressing stories like that are not for the warmth of the bakery.'

Yasmine opens the door for me. It's a short walk across the yard to the block that houses the atelier. My breath clouds around me in jagged vapour. Despite my recent scepticism, I believe her, and now feel sorry I even asked.

'Make me a pendant to hang from my tree,' shouts Yasmine merrily, any chagrin forgotten. 'À bientôt!'

The door slams shut and I'm on my own. Usually the guard in the opposing block would hold the next door open to let me in, but she has it firmly closed against the bitter cold, and waits for me behind the reinforced glass. I stop for a moment to enjoy the solitude, raise my face to the sky and let the chill air clear my nostrils and cool my throat. The cold burns my ears, and I take a deep searing breath before continuing on my way. Behind the square window of the door, the guard shifts and stands straighter, before she flings it open and tells me to hurry.

It's the first time I've spoken to Yasmine for a while. No wonder the girl wants to leave the memories of Algeria behind her. She hasn't only had to deal with a raucous bunch of bike thieves. I wonder what she was going to say about her father. There's so much we don't know about folk.

Some people can surprise the hell out of you.

* * *

Seven years ago

The closest Matt ever came to a genuine marriage proposal, was when we were intoxicated on ouzo, dancing the Zorbas under the buzzing fluorescent strip-light of a café in the tiny Eastern Peloponnese port of Plaka. I had finally made it to my Greek beach.

It was his idea to go away during the autumn break, just the two of us. He wanted to sail again, and I wanted to be a part of this thing that had taken him away from me for a summer, wanted to feel the fascination. We booked a two-week stint on a bareboat yacht rental out of the Greek island of Poros during the autumn college break. I was a decent sailor, could read the currents and the winds, plotted charts for our adventure, tied knots, hauled sails, kept the vessel shipshape above and below deck and loved waking each morning in a different port, limbs entangled with Matt's.

In Plaka I was transported back to the very thing that had first sent me down the blind road of passion. His dancing.

95

The youngest clientele by a good forty years, we were made to feel special among regular patrons comprising mostly farmers and a few fishermen. They were celebrating the arrival of rain after their long week of hard labour under a scorched sky. We had stayed in port, choosing to take a day off sailing as the deluge had deadened the wind. We spent the morning restocking our provisions in the tiny store in town, and the afternoon swimming off the stony beach behind the harbour wall, stair-rods of rain hissing on the grey water around us.

Following a dinner at the café from the only item on the menu – tender goat stew swimming in thick herb gravy – a farmer with brown weathered skin approached us. He introduced himself as Cristos. Tufts of grey hair sprung from under a flat beret and he smiled, revealing a missing front tooth. With sparkling eyes, he indicated we should dance. He delighted in holding my hand. I was flanked on one side by Cristos and on the other side by Matt in the traditional regimented dance line. He insisted joining us at our wobbly steel table afterwards, exchanging Greek vocabulary to learn a little English, and he toasted our youth and beauty from glasses stained with dishwater.

When Matt held me in his arms, slow dancing to a Greek love song playing on the tinny cassette player on the top of the fridge in the corner, he had eyes only for me, the intense blue-greyness of them sucking me in. He made me his all over again, taking me back to the excitement of our first dance in spring several months before. Emotion always heightened the blue in his eyes. He asked me if I could envision living like this all our lives, as a team, together. He surely meant marriage? His loving look didn't waver from my eyes for one second until I answered 'Yes! Yes!' thinking I had never been happier, never been on more of a high.

We walked back to our boat in the rain, shoes in hand, bare feet sliding through the puddles pooling on the smooth hewn limestone rock of the harbour wall. After a blitz of passion in the stuffy, humid fore-cabin, we slept deeply until the sun beating down on the deck the next morning had us gasping for the rain-washed air. Opening the hatch, Matt called to me.

'Luce, you've got to see this.'

I held my pounding head, the cloying smell of aniseed wafting about me. I pushed my way up through the hatch beside him, scraping my shoulder on the rim. About to give a retort, I was silenced by the sight in front of me. The deck of our thirty-foot sloop was covered in oranges, most still attached in clumps to their branches, the waxy orange fruit and green of the foliage a jolly festival bunting against the bright white of the decking.

They signified a Greek blessing from the locals for having revived the sweet wild memory of their youth, revelling in the power and pureness of a young love.

As I sat on deck sipping a mug of tea, the tangy perfume of the oranges clearing the last of the aniseed fumes from my head, it occurred to me that we hadn't seen any other young adults during our short stopover, just the merry old group in the bar and the children now playing on the harbour wall.

Matt had no distractions, with nothing to prove to anyone other than me.

And although in that moment I was convinced that he truly loved me, away from the frenzy of the real world, I was not too naive to realise we had created a kind of illusory bubble of isolation. I wondered whether this moment would have been different if we had been among our peers.

We left the fruit on deck until we sailed out that day. I had wanted to motor out of the harbour with them still covering the boat, but there were too many oranges for us alone. Before casting off we gave away armfuls of them to the happy sun-bronzed children fishing from the harbour wall. We were sailing on to new horizons, but an apprehension that I had too willingly consigned myself to something in the heat of the moment wormed its way into my conscience. I wondered if I was truly ready for such a commitment.

But the seeds of unease didn't have a chance to germinate yet. I would devote my energies over the next months to learning French and mastering the ski slopes, all with an underlying goal to impress Matt and ensure our compatibility.

As we sailed away from paradise, convincing myself of love's perfection, I ignored the signs of a storm gathering on the horizon.

Instead, the seed of something else was growing inside me.

* * *

Dolores can be heard all the way up here on our floor, through three fire doors and a flight of stairs. She is screaming down the phone in Spanish, her incomprehensible chatter rattling off her tongue like a jackhammer. The Colombian girl down the corridor is shaking her head.

'I thought there a fight. I don't know what she say. Just a phone call! How her kids understand her? *Loca!*' She throws her hands up, and goes back into her cell, but leaves the door propped open in case something escalates.

The fire door to our level flies open. Dolores marches down the corridor towards her cell, puffing with indignation. Her mascara has run and her lipstick is smudged in a gash across her mouth. It amuses me that she puts fresh make-up on before her regular phone call to her family, especially as it's inevitable she will cry. Maybe she thinks if she looks presentable, she will act presentable.

And I'm pretty sure her family doesn't care. They're only worried about where the next meal will come from. The money they receive each month from Dolores in her Swiss jail is more than she could ever hope to earn in Santo Domingo. They're the ones who should be feeling a double-edged guilt. The fact that she attempted to traffic drugs for them, and their consequent gratefulness for her incarceration in a place that pays her to work.

It's the risk some of these drug traffickers take. For them it's a win-win situation. If they get away with their crime, they'll be several thousand dollars richer. If they get caught, their incarceration ensures them a roof, a bed, warmth and regular meals, with the opportunity to send money home to their families.

Dolores has told us her kids are being cared for by their maternal grandmother. But the story is confusing. It sounds like up to twenty people might be living in the house at any one time. Uncles, cousins, lovers. I can only imagine the chaos. She told me the shoddy brick and plaster building with a corrugated iron roof only has two rooms. She once showed me a photo of the kids sitting on a dusty red-painted porch, banana and mango trees framing the colourful but crumbling plasterwork. She takes it with her to the phone cabin whenever she calls. In her state of madness, I now wonder if it is so she can remember to whom she has spoken. If she's stoned, she might need a reminder to make sure she connects with all three of her kids.

Dolores passes Yasmine, touches her shoulder briefly in a surprisingly lucid gesture, before heading into her cell and trying unsuccessfully to slam the door. All the doors are on pneumatic hinges, and her action is comical. The corridor sings with tense silence, and for a moment no one moves. Then we hear crashing from inside Dolores's cell. The Polish girl puts her hands to her mouth, but none of us move.

It feels like several minutes before two guards hurry through the door to our floor. One of them is Müller and she barges at Dolores's cell door. As it opens, we hear the hollow sound of cheap plywood smashing against something, a slight pause and then a repeated thumping of a metal object against glass. I imagine Dolores wielding her desk chair against the thick safety glass of her window. It's pure anger. She has no intention of escaping. Not only would the bars on the window impede her exit, we are three floors up as well.

'*Hure Spinner!*' yells Müller. 'Crazy bitch!'

Yasmine is standing in her doorway, but doesn't approach

Dolores's cell. She knows at least this much, to keep out of her way, to avoid that fiery Latin disposition.

Instead, she chews on a nail, arms crossed over her chest, head lowered. I know this will lead to a few days' solitary for Dolores. I try to catch Yasmine's eye, but she blatantly avoids my look, a slight frown knitting her brows.

Chapter 8

'Hello, Dagmar. How are you today?'

The psychologist looks up sharply. She wasn't expecting me to be amenable, especially using her first name. In a pretence at respect, everyone is Frau this or Frau that. But today I'm in a good mood.

I can see her looking at my file as I come through the door, a frown on her face. I wonder whether she feels she's getting through to me, or whether I am an enigma for her. Last time we spoke, she might have departed thinking I considered her the enemy. But not even the Serbian girl in here for grievous bodily harm treats her as the enemy. Sometimes Dr Schutz's methods might be questionable, but most of the women regard her as friend rather than foe. I'm not yet sure if she's capable of getting something I need, but I now realise I should keep her on my side.

'I am fine, thank you, Frau Smithers. It is nice to see you have settled in,' she says.

I guess I might have been shocked three months ago if she had come out with such a statement. I imagine she has a big red biro mark next to my name that says: *Don't forget to call her Smithers.* I smile disarmingly. Natasha and Didier are finally bringing JP for a visit on Friday. They've waited until the very

101

last moment in the once-a-month court requirement to bring him. But they're bringing him nonetheless, and it feels like Christmas. The prospect of seeing him has lifted my mood.

'The bed is a little hard, and I'm none too impressed with the shower accessories, oh and the sommelier could do with stocking some new vintages in the cellar, but in general, yes, I've settled in.'

I sit back in my chair, but don't cross my arms this time, instead putting my hands on the table in a semblance of supplication. Dr Schutz clears her throat and smiles briefly before consulting my file. She didn't get my joke.

'I see they have taken you off horticultural work. You are now in the art atelier. How do you feel about that?'

'It's okay. They only keep a skeleton staff in the greenhouse now. I was the last one to arrive, so I'm the first one off. But I like it in the atelier. I never thought to ask about painting. It makes sense with my skills. I don't really consider it a job. It's more like part of my life. I might actually call myself an artist at some point.'

'Do you draw or paint outside work hours? Do you do any art in your cell?'

I think of the sketch I finally tried to draw of JP. How I started from one of his photos. I know his little face will have changed during the months that I haven't seen him. It broke me knowing he's probably changed even in the last few weeks. I had to stop. I can't wait to see him again.

'Sometimes. The others often ask me to draw them. I practise sketching. They want to trade them with me. Cigarettes mostly. I don't smoke. But they're the second currency here. I take them to swap for the occasional bottle of shampoo or a jar of Abuela's chilli salsa.'

Dr Schutz is holding a pen between her first and middle finger, balancing it back and forth slowly. I keep thinking she's going to take a drag and reckon she must be a smoker.

I haven't spoken this much to anyone in weeks, apart from encouraging JP to deliver more than one-word answers every

102

time I ask him a question. And all those repetitive queries Anne has to deal with every time I talk to her. It must be annoying. If it's my mother or, God forbid, Natasha, I clam up like a barnacle.

'Your mood is different today. Has something happened?' she asks.

'It's because I get to see the light of my life on Friday. My son is coming to see me.'

'I can see that this makes you very excited. Frau Fav – Smithers, can I ask you more about the boy's father. Your husband?'

She asks this carefully, but I still draw in my breath. There used to be two lights in my life. I tilt my head on one side.

'We did not get a chance to talk about him the last two times I have seen you. I am curious to know how you feel about him. What kind of emotions still exist.'

Dr Schutz touches her chest, fingers splayed wide, except for the first and second where her pen is still wedged. Her hand covers her heart.

My emotions? How do I feel? She talks about him as though he is still alive.

'I want you to think about your husband carefully before you answer. Not to think about what happened, but to think about him as the boy's – what is his name? Jean-Philippe? Jean-Philippe's father.'

'JP,' I whisper. 'We named him JP.'

I'm so quickly deflated, knowing I won't ever see Matt again. Each time it comes back to me at the most unexpected moments. Perhaps that's why I used the upbeat tack at the beginning of our session, enhanced by the excitement of JP's visit. But why did I ever think Dr Schutz would gloss over the stuff that's hidden deep inside? It's inevitable she'll try and dig at things I didn't want to acknowledge.

I close my eyes, my throat aching. Jesus, don't cry now.

* * *

Six years ago

Matt's Land Rover was parked outside the house when I came back from work. I had hoped he wouldn't be home yet. Unusual that he was back before me. I'd had all day to work out what I was going to say, but it still didn't seem like enough time. Loving someone that much, I thought I would know how he'd react. But this … I wasn't so sure. This was a life-changer.

'Hey, Luce, glad you're home,' he said as I came in the door. 'You've got to hurry. Yves wants to try out some new Arapahos, these cool bike-scooter hybrids he might stock in the shop for next summer. But we have to get the last lift up the mountain. Quick, go get changed – he's waiting at the cable car station.'

Matt stood in his bike gear, helmet in his hand. He had been waiting for me, assumed I would drop everything and follow him on an adventure, as excited as a little kid. It could only go down-hill from here, so to speak.

'We won't be going with Yves, Matt. You have to tell him we can't make it this time.' Matt's face hardened, his plans under threat.

'Oh come on, Luce, you're always game for something like this. Don't wimp out on me now.' Matt started to put on his helmet.

'I'm not wimping out. We need to talk.' I took a breath. 'I'm pregnant.'

'You're … what? How the fuck did that happen?' Darkness swept across his face, excitement shifting to fury in a matter of seconds. My heart skipped a beat.

'How do you think it happened? I guess we've been a bit care-less.'

Matt clicked his helmet closed, stepped towards me, and before I knew what was happening, slapped me across the face, enough to make my cheek sting. I stared at him in horror. He'd just hit me! I was silenced, catatonic, my cheekbone aching dully to the beat of my heart. More than anything I was confused, seeing this stranger before me for the first time.

He stepped back, and for a moment I thought he was going to storm out of the house, go and try out Yves' new toy without wanting to deal with this news. But he lifted his hands to his face, looked almost comical with his bike gloves covering his mouth and his helmet slightly askew.

'Jesus, Lucie, I'm sorry. I'm so sorry. It's such a shock.'

He didn't move towards me though. Like I had some sickness, and I might be contagious. I raised my hand to my hot cheek. I wished I could stop my eyes smarting.

'Matt, call Yves. You have to tell him you won't be there. We need to talk about this,' I said, rubbing my cheek.

And with the realisation of what he had done, Matt stepped towards me and wrapped me in his arms, pressing my face to his chest. My cheek still stung.

But I hurt more on the inside. I imagined his face looking over my shoulder into unidentified space, thinking: 'What the hell are we going to do now?'

* * *

My first thought as I took the pregnancy test that afternoon had been that we couldn't possibly keep the baby. Neither of us were ready to start a family yet. Even in my dreams this was something that would happen years ahead. But as the double blue lines on the test stick darkened on the edge of the sink in the bathroom, I was overwhelmed with a fierce emotion to protect the tiny being that was growing inside me.

'Matt, we need to think about it before deciding what to do. Please think carefully before you say anything,' I said after we had pulled apart.

He nodded silently, his mouth tightening into a thin line, revealing a simmering annoyance.

'You may as well get dinner on the go. I'll call Yves. He'll be dead disappointed.'

I was sure Yves wasn't the only one. And not just about the bike ride.

I prepared a salad with some cold chicken left over from the previous night. The clinking of Matt's fork around the plate as he stabbed pieces of his food rang louder than usual at the table. I barely ate a morsel. My hunger had long ago been extinguished.

Every now and then Matt glanced at me and then looked away, and the air between us was thick with tension. At one point he frowned and I recognised the spark of anger in his eyes as he was about to voice his thoughts.

'Let's sleep on it, Matt,' I said, to stop him speaking. 'There's nothing we can do about it tonight. Tomorrow we'll discuss this like adults.'

The fire lit his eyes again.

'Lucie, I just … don't …'

'Tomorrow, Matt.'

As his cutlery clattered to his plate, he stood up from the table and walked to the window to stare out with his back to me. The trees across the street silhouetted the orange sky of an autumn dusk. I wished I knew what he was thinking, but was afraid to ask, which was why I wanted to wait for the calm of morning. He ran his fingers through his hair, shook his head, and walked from the room without lifting so much as a finger to help me clear the table.

But as I brushed my teeth before bed, Matt surprised me by hugging me from behind. I looked at him in the mirror, his lips nuzzling my neck. At first confused by this sudden change of mood, I felt a warm glow growing inside me. He was happy, accepting at last. I bent over, spit as elegantly as I could into the sink and turned to face him as he lifted my T-shirt and pressed himself to me. His playfulness ignited synapses in me as his fingers trailed enticingly down my body. I was glad not to feel the wretchedness of morning sickness at that moment. He pressed his hand to my stomach, still flat and muscled. My skin flushed a radiance not even the harsh lights of the bathroom could dull.

'You're sexier than ever, Luce. I want you now,' he whispered in my ear, and led me towards our bed.

Lowering me gently to the mattress, his warm lips traced my abdomen and thighs. I raised my hips to his as he entered me, and we moved together in slow luxury, rocking on an ocean of passion. It had been some time since we had made love, my mental calculation guessing somewhere down the Peloponnesian Coast. The power of this loving sealed the pact. We savoured the moment, making it last, the intensity of our pleasure bringing tears to my eyes. So different to the frantic snatches of sex at the beginning of our relationship. This was a nurturing love. I felt my whole belly opening up like a flower, pulsing with the little life inside.

Afterwards, I lay in the crook of Matt's arm, drawing invisible swirls with one finger on his chest. He stared at the ceiling.

'You know I'll support you completely through all of this,' he said.

I pushed myself up onto one elbow, and smiled at him. So grateful that his shock and anger had subsided. How could I have doubted him?

'I mean, I'll take you to the clinic and everything. See you through this,' he continued. My smile flickered. The naivety of a new father. The clinic would be a long way off. About seven months. There was a lot to go through until then.

'It makes sense, doesn't it, Luce? A kid now … We're so young. There's so much to do and see before we get tied down with a family. There's plenty of time later for you to have a nest full of babies. There won't be a problem with the finances for a proce-dure. I think my parents have some cash stashed away that we could borrow …'

I suddenly realised what he was saying.

'Matt! Are you saying you want to take me to an abortion

clinic?' I sat up in the bed, pulled the duvet across my naked body.

'How do you think we're going to keep it? It's the only answer, Lucie, for both our sakes. You'll have to get rid of it.' Any passion now forgotten, he spoke with such distaste, I put my hand to my abdomen as though to protect my invisible child.

'I think you've got me wrong here, Matt. I'm not getting rid of this baby. It's not like I corralled you into this. It takes two, and I thought you were agreeing that we could do this thing together. I wanted to talk about this tomorrow, but you should know now I don't want to terminate this pregnancy.'

'But, Lucie, we have no money saved. We have years of adventure ahead of us. Pistes to ski and oceans to sail. Come on, think about it.'

I could almost see the reflection of the shackles of responsibility shaking in his eyes. He had a point. But I knew we could make this work. And if he still didn't agree, well I knew I could make this work somehow.

'Look, even if you don't want to have anything to do with this baby, I'm not going to get an abortion. I'll find a way to look after it myself. But think about it; we can make the baby another adventure. Imagine passing on all your skills to a little image of yourself. How cool will that be?'

Never having experienced parenthood, it was difficult to know how to lighten the potential load.

'A kid ...' he said uneasily, then gulped. 'Shit, we have to tell my mother. She's going to flip.'

'I don't care what your parents think, Matt. We are grown adults. We can deal with this. Together.'

'I don't know, Luce. I need to think about it.'

'What exactly is there to think about? I'm not sure what you think your choices are, but I can tell you now, I'm going to keep this baby.'

I didn't say with or without you, but it was implied, and he knew it. After my initial insistence I wasn't entirely sure how I would be able to deal with this alone. Realistically, I couldn't afford to raise a child by myself, but I was determined not to terminate my pregnancy.

'We're currently sharing this massive house. Maybe we can get in a lodger to help with the rent, at least until the baby's born,' I said, watching Matt swallow. My statement didn't hold much conviction. 'There are plenty of solutions. Let's not complicate things now. Please.'

I leaned over, kissed him on the mouth, his lips barely moving in an automated pout. I was exhausted, needed sleep, but when I turned gently on my side and closed my eyes, a wave of nausea caused my head to spin. Morning sickness, or fear of losing Matt, I wasn't sure.

* * *

'You will naturally check into a clinic and deal with this as soon as possible,' said Natasha, hardly pausing in her work as she pressed a heather plant into the soft earth of the pot from which she had removed a geranium moments before.

I wondered about the wisdom of telling her while she was holding a trowel, but I was glad we didn't have eye contact. Matt was sitting on the garden wall, legs dangling, watching his mother. Didier was repairing a trellis that had come away from the side of the chalet. He smiled briefly when Matt told them I was pregnant, then packed away his look with Natasha's last comment. I was disgusted at his weakness. I covered my eyes with the palm of my hand and dragged it to the side, tears of frustrating pricking.

'I can't believe I'm hearing this!' My voice was dangerously raised. 'Don't I get a say at all? I'm sorry, but I am not getting rid of the baby. I already told Matt. He's okay with it. He understands.' I hesitated. 'It's not your choice, Natasha.'

At that moment I hated Natasha. She rocked back on her heels and looked pointedly at her son.

'I hope you will be able to talk some sense into the girl, Mathieu.' She addressed him as if I wasn't there. 'Of course she cannot keep the baby. What are you even thinking, considering this?'

'Natasha, did you hear me? What is wrong with you people?' I stamped my foot.

Matt jumped down from the wall, the muscles of his jaw working in frustration.

'Mimi, listen, Lucie has made up her mind. She wants to keep the baby. We can do nothing about it.'

I tried to read Matt's tone. I couldn't work out if it was accepting or exasperated. Certainly patronising. I wished we'd never come to tell them.

'What will you do then, my dear? I assume you will be better off going back to England, where you will have family support.'

Mimi looked at me for the first time. The crow's feet around her eyes developed a rosy hue and her nose took on a pinched look. I stared at her, mute with anger. I turned to Matt, who wore a neutral expression.

'I think I am going to leave you all alone now to deal with this information.' My voice strained to control my anger.

I stood in front of Matt, hands on my hips.

'I hope you'll take what we've discussed at home to heart, and will decide to do the humane thing here. I can't listen to this bullshit any more. I'll come back and get you in a little while.'

And with that I walked back through the French windows, across the living room and left through the front door, slamming it behind me. I didn't want to give them the satisfaction of seeing me cry.

Natasha and Didier's chalet backed on to a swathe of beech and pine woodlands. I smelled balsam on the autumn air. Taking a farm track through the woods to the other side, my feet swished through scrunching leaves, before I sat on a bench next to the footpath to think. Through a gap in the trees, the view stretched across the wide Rhône Valley to the jagged peaks of the Dents du Midi, the upper north-facing gullies pale grey with a recent early snowfall.

I loved Matt with all my heart, but knew I couldn't get rid of the baby, no matter how sensible that solution would have been. Something had clicked inside me the moment I saw the result of the test. I put my hand absently on my belly, unconsciously demonstrating my loyalty. I clenched my jaw. Of course a baby would change our world, jeopardise our youth, change the way we dealt with the adventures we still had before us. But I knew one thing for sure – I could not face an abortion. I couldn't live with the guilt, knowing I wanted kids at some time in my life. I couldn't turn down the chance now.

And exactly what kind of hold did Natasha have over Matt? Despicable woman. Exercising some kind of Oedipal right over him. I shivered.

Looking up, I saw a veil of high cirrus cloud had pulled across the sky, washing out the intensity of the late afternoon sun. The lilac haze of an early evening mist began to chill the air. Jacketless, I walked briskly back to the chalet. If Natasha had convinced her son that life with a partner and child was out of the question, I was prepared to let him go. It was as though I loved him too much to tie him to something he might end up resenting. And I didn't need their damn approval.

I walked slowly down the stone steps of the chalet and went in without knocking. The three of them had come inside from the garden and were sitting in the living room, watching Didier set kindling in the fireplace. Matt stood up as I came in. I was about to tell them all to go to hell.

'So it is decided, Lucie,' Natasha began, and I looked at Matt, who seemed a little pale.

'You must marry. Mathieu has spoken your case. If you are

to keep the child, we cannot possibly have our grandson and eventual heir disappearing off to some hole in the corner of England to be brought up. Mathieu will do the honourable thing.'

My jaw dropped and I stared at each of them. I could hardly believe what I had just heard. Natasha sounded more like a crass pompous aristocrat than a sophisticated multilingual European. I thought it was a joke. I almost laughed, wanted to spit in her face, turn around and stomp all the way back to England. Then I registered what she had said.

'Matt? Is that what you want? Truly?'

My wide eyes gazed at him. A crooked smile touched his mouth, but I couldn't tell whether he was displaying happiness or looking down the barrel of a gun. I felt sorry for him. What I thought was resentment must have been resignation in those beautiful eyes. My stomach rippled with a bubble of hope, or something else. I looked down, touched my belly again, the miracle of life no bigger than my fist, or a small bird, fluttering.

'I guess,' he answered faintly.

'There's no guessing about it,' said Natasha standing up and smoothing the front of her woollen skirt. 'Arrangements shall be made as soon as possible so decorum and creation can be presented in the correct order.'

Matt chewed on his lip, and I felt unsure. This suddenly seemed like coercion. From banishing me, to making me sound like a surrogate carrier of their grandson and heir. I didn't care that Matt's mother was a control freak, but I did want Matt to love me enough to hope that marrying me was the right decision. I went to him, held both his hands, gave them a little shake, and put my arms around him. A minuscule hesitation, and he hugged me back, kissing the top of my head.

I thought back to the port in Plaka where I would have been ready to marry Matt right there and then.

This was hardly the fairy-tale betrothal.

112

As I'm wandering back to the living block, I see Fatima in the distance walking jerkily down the path leading to the Schloss. She has a scarf wrapped around her head, although I know this is not for her beliefs, but against the cold *bise* that has picked up since the sun descended behind the ridge to the west.

I call to her as I approach. She's rocking Adnan from side to side. He is swaddled in a blanket against the cold, crying the desperate rasping screech of an infant in pain.

'Colic?' I ask as I approach them.

'I don't think so. He only seems to suffer from colic at night. I think he is constipated. He has not soiled his nappy for over a day, and he is always straining. Now again. Look at his little face.' She shows me, and Adnan momentarily stops his squawking to screw up his nose and eyes into a purple crease.

'Orange juice,' I say. 'Feed a little to him on a spoon or with a straw if you can find one. That'll clear him out, and pretty quickly.'

'It's so hard sometimes. There is no one to ask these things. A baby cannot tell you what he is feeling, what he needs. My mother ...' Fatima's eyes cloud a little. Adnan resumes his tight-throated crying.

'Plenty of us are mothers in here, Fatima – you only need to ask us. It's just that ...' I don't know whether it's wise to point out the obvious. 'You won't make any friends who want to help you if you keep pinching people's stuff, the cigarettes.'

I feel a little bold having said it outright, especially when Adnan's behaviour is causing her stress, but Fatima looks abashed.

'You have to set an example for this little guy. Give him a chance.'

I can tell by the look on her face that she knows what's right and wrong. Maybe she doesn't realise how much damage she can do to herself in prison. Here, even the thieves are sick of thievery.

'There will be someone in the kitchen now,' I say. 'Go and ask for some juice. It will work, Fatima, I promise you.' I put my hand on her arm. 'Wait. I'll come with you.'

The kitchen is situated in one wing of the Schloss, and we manage to get a small cup of orange juice. We walk together to the living block, and in the warmth of the day room I help to spoon a little of it into Adnan's tiny mouth. His eyes widen briefly with the sweet new taste sensation, and he smacks his little button lips together.

'Not too much, little man,' I murmur as I manage to get a bit more of the juice into his mouth. I wipe the rest away from his face with his cloth.

Later, after I return from eating downstairs, I find a note taped to my door. It reads: '*Will not see you for dinner. Adnan will bath, then cell will need clean!!!*' and I know the trick with the orange juice has worked.

Then in my cell, there is another note from the admin office that's been pushed under the door. I have to read it three times and get my dictionary out to translate, but I kind of guessed from the outset that the family have found an excuse not to bring JP for a visit this week. Again.

Chapter 9

Everyone is very wary of Fatima since the *Zigi* incident. Many of the inmates are ignoring her without really making it obvious. It's easy to do that when she has Adnan with her. The baby gives her purpose, something to occupy her outside her work, so the others mostly avoid her. I hope my advice to her sinks in before she makes too many enemies.

But some of us are constantly thinking of ways we can get a glimpse of Adnan's little face without getting too close to his mother. He's like a little ray of sunshine in our grey world, especially now he's smiling all the time.

She's lucky to have him, or she might be completely ostracised. Once a thief, always a thief. I guess for some it's a compulsion that the confines of a prison will never cure. I know the Polish girl is new and open for testing, but as Dolores might say, 'you don't shit in your own backyard'.

It brings to mind my father-in-law. To Didier's credit, I remember him saying the same thing once to Matt, when he thought I wasn't listening in the hallway.

* * *

Six years ago

Before I first found out I was pregnant late that summer, I'd contracted what I thought was a violent case of stomach flu. After several days of cramping sickness, I experienced an exhaustion I had never before encountered. Of course, at the time I had no idea I was pregnant, and this was certainly no ordinary morning sickness, but the doctor who came to the house didn't even think to check. I had a high fever and all the symptoms of a typical gastroenteritis. He administered some rehydration salts, plenty of water and bed rest for at least a week while I recovered. At this stage, JP was the tiny grain of a miracle, clinging doggedly onto the walls of my womb through a series of wild end-of-season parties, evenings where Matt and my passion was consummated with little regard for contraception after too much alcohol.

Matt, not wanting to contract the 'sickness', slept in a pull-out bed in the office, bringing me the occasional fresh bottle of water, ready-made soup and toast, staying briefly by my bedside to ask how I was doing. These visits up to our room became less and less frequent, until I only saw him when he came to pick his clothes out of the wardrobe in the morning.

One evening, I thought I felt well enough to go downstairs to get a fresh bottle of sparkling water from the fridge. Still very tired, my progress was slow, so I tiptoed barefoot down the stairs. All the doors were closed off the hallway, and I was about to head into the kitchen, when I heard laughter coming from the living room. It didn't sound like the tinny output of a television speaker.

As I opened the door to the living room, Matt and a girl I had never seen before leapt apart like drops of soapy water on an oily slick. A couple of books lay open on the coffee table. A student. My mind was fuggy. What the hell were the two of them doing on the floor?

I looked again at the books. French verbs. A study session. But I felt too wretched to engage, couldn't even muster the energy for conversation. I said hi and bye in quick succession and left the room. Matt must have been giving the student a private tutorial. I took a bottle of water out of the fridge, and crawled back up to bed, thought nothing of it, my physical wretchedness muffling the sound of alarm bells.

* * *

A few weeks later, after we found out I was pregnant, that student – Marlena her name was – turned up one afternoon on our doorstep with a boyfriend. She spoke with a Scandinavian accent, her dark-blonde hair softening a ferret-like smile exposing slightly yellow pointy teeth.

'Matt said we could stay in your spare room for a few days.'

She was sulky, a little belligerent. I couldn't work out what her problem was.

'I'm sorry, but he didn't say anything to me. You'd better come back later when he gets home. If you made a deal with Matt, I don't know anything about it, so you'll have to talk directly to him.'

We hadn't yet made a final decision on getting a lodger. It irked me that Matt hadn't discussed it with me. I vaguely recognised the girl, but had no idea who she was at the time. I wasn't about to let some stranger move into our home.

By the time I had come back from an evening session at the college that night, Marlena and her boyfriend, Damien, had already moved into the spare room. I hadn't been consulted, didn't have a say in the decision.

I figured it would be good to save a little of the income we earned for the room rental to compensate for my lack of work for the first weeks after the baby's arrival.

It was only after a few days, with her hanging around our living space, that I realised it was the same girl I'd seen in our home when I'd been ill the month before.

* * *

117

I couldn't work out whether it was the effects of my pregnancy, but it felt like a whole string of events was unfolding with information kept from me. I was the one who had suggested getting a lodger to help with our rent, and I assumed Marlena and Damien would pay Matt directly.

'How long will this be for?' I asked Matt when we were on our own in the kitchen one evening. 'I wish you could have talked about this with me first. I've got an uncomfortable feeling around Marlena. I didn't even get a chance to vet her as a potential candidate.'

Something about the girl annoyed me, but I couldn't put a finger on it.

'Is she one of your French students?' I asked.

'No ...' he said, and I frowned, remembering her in our living room. 'Not any more. Look, Lucie, we need all the help we can get with the rent, now that you're, you know ...' he said, pointing at my stomach with the knife he was using to slice an apple.

I placed my hand protectively over my abdomen.

'You think the college is going to keep you on after this thing's born?' he continued.

I was surprised at his vitriol. This thing? It was our baby.

'Jesus, Matt, you sound like I'm going to give birth to an alien. I didn't get pregnant all by myself. What's got into you? I thought you were okay with this.'

His face changed, and the knife clattered onto the counter as he put it down. My breath caught in my throat as he crossed the kitchen. I braced myself, not knowing what to expect.

And he gave me a hug.

'I'm sorry, Luce, it's going to take a while to get used to the idea.'

I breathed out. 'Matt, you've got six more months. Get used to it.'

I went through to the living room where Marlena and Damien

118

were sucking on bowls of spaghetti, flicking tiny spots of tomato sauce around the room.

'It would be great if you guys could restrict food to the kitchen and dining room,' I said crossly.

I was fired up by Matt's attitude, and glared at my rug, my favourite cushions and the beige sofa. My sparking eyes finally settled on the couple. These two people had somehow wormed their way into our household without me really understanding why.

'Oh, sorry, of course,' said Marlena politely, but not making a move.

I left the room and let the door close heavily. I knew I was coming across as a grumpy girlfriend, but I was unable to work out why Matt thought he owed this particular girl a favour. I would have preferred to take on a lodger who wasn't a student.

I guessed they were looking for a room off-campus because she was living with her boyfriend, but one afternoon a few days later my curiosity led me to the computer with the intention of looking up Marlena's records in the college database. I accidentally typed her name in the Google search engine open in an adjacent window instead of the college intranet, and as I was about to correct the error, her name highlighted in a Swedish tabloid news article caught my eye.

Using a translate facility, I flew through the article about the case of Marlena's baby brother Frederik who went missing from his school when he was 9 years old. The mystery of his disappearance was never solved, and the article described the family's plea to keep the case open with the *Kriminalpolisen* in Stockholm. I felt vaguely sorry for Marlena, but the feeling was brief.

There was a picture of Frederik, a handsome little dark-haired boy, standing next to his older sister. The photo split Marlena right down the middle from head to foot, but both her hands were in view, placed on the boy's shoulders. There was a propri-etary look in her one eye, and I could almost sense her hand squeezing the delicate hollow above Frederik's collarbones.

I shivered, and logged off the computer without checking her college file.

* * *

My pregnancy continued to make me irritable through the first semester, and I had the added stress of having to organise my own wedding, without much help from my mother who was a thousand miles away. My parents' disapproval meant it would be even less likely that they would visit more than their annual weary obligation, although I wondered whether this would change when a grandchild came on the scene.

Although Natasha insisted that Matt 'did the right thing', she still found it difficult to welcome me into the family with open arms. With her lack of offering to prepare for her grandchild's arrival, the atmosphere at both the Favres' chalet and in our home became progressively more strained.

My patience broke one evening when I came home and all the ingredients for a goulash soup I had been planning to cook were missing from the fridge. Marlena lounged on the couch in the living room. Dirty bowls and cutlery were strewn across the coffee table. I asked her if she knew where the food in the fridge had gone, the stewing beef and vegetables.

'Oh, I thought Damien had bought that for us. I'm sorry,' she said, drawing the apology out in a tone that said she wasn't sorry at all.

I exploded. 'Marlena, this arrangement isn't working. I'm sorry, but you guys are going to have to find somewhere else to live,' I shouted.

'Well you need to talk to Matt about that. He was the one who made the agreement with us.' Marlena remained annoyingly calm.

'This is my home too. Matt and I are equally responsible for how our household is run. This agreement you have should have been approved by me as well. And I'm telling you, it's not working. It's time for you to leave!'

She frowned, and something told me she had finally got the message.

I was surprised to face little resistance from Matt. He mumbled something about losing the useful rent, but didn't contradict my decision. He must have seen how this couple were walking all over us.

It was with great relief that I came home one afternoon to find them gone. The spare-room door hung open, motes of dust floating on shafts of light. My joy was short-lived. The room was empty. Completely empty, except for the bed. They had taken everything with them, sheets, towels, small furnishings, even a poster of Turner's 'Snowstorm' I had hung in a cheap frame on the wall. I was furious.

But that wasn't all. As I was waiting for Matt to come back from work, I began preparing a few things for our meal that evening, and discovered mugs, glasses and cutlery missing from our kitchen cupboards and drawers. Even food from the fridge. Most of the objects were second-hand cast-offs, but they were still ours.

When Matt came home, I couldn't face eating – there was nothing to cook – until I had addressed the issue of our missing chattels.

'Can you believe what's happened? Those assholes have taken half our stuff! What right do they think they have?' I was shaking, feeling violated.

Matt didn't say anything.

'Come on, Matt, doesn't this piss you off? These are your things too!'

I stood in front of him, arms out straight, palms up. Angry as hell.

Matt shrugged, and I snapped, stamping my foot. Something weird was going on here. Why was he reacting like this? Or more to the point, why wasn't he reacting?

'Did you tell them they could take our stuff? What's going on?' I shouted.

'No, Lucie, of course not.'

I was silenced by his apparent nonchalance. He had a sheepish expression, looked bizarrely awkward.

'Well, we're going to get it back! They have no right to do this. Do you know where their new place is? We need to go together. Show a united front. Matt, what the hell's wrong with you?'

I was exasperated. I couldn't work out what I was missing.

* * *

I stood in front of Marlena and Damien's front door, heart pounding as I waited an eternity for someone to answer. It was the evening following their departure from our house and I'd persuaded a reluctant Matt to come with me for the confrontation. The day between had not lessened my anger, and as I stood there shaking with indignation, a cool sweat broke out on the back of my neck.

Damien answered the door, his strawberry blond hair in disarray. A shirttail hung out of his jeans. They'd either been fighting or having sex. I didn't wait for pleasantries.

'You guys need to return the stuff you took from our place. Our stuff. Everything,' I said, shaking even more, beyond being able to communicate properly.

'Okay, okay,' said Damien. 'Marlena thought we could borrow a few things while we set up here. Thought it would be okay with Matt, you know …'

'No, I don't know, Damien. What right does she think you have to take someone else's things?'

I clenched my fists at my sides. Why wasn't Matt saying anything? Why wasn't he ready to pop this guy one on the nose?

'Ask Matt. I thought it would be okay. The stuff is pretty much junk anyway,' said Marlena, coming to the door. 'Here. Here's a few of them.'

She held out a supermarket carrier bag.

'We'll bring the rest back in the next couple of days,' she said, mouth in a hard pout.

She must have heard me from the hallway, and had hastily tipped a few things into the bag.

'The next couple of days? You'll bring the rest back tomorrow!' I shouted. 'All of it! This is theft!'

I couldn't believe Matt had remained quiet throughout this exchange, but when I turned to look at him, he had a desperate glint in his eye. He was looking straight at Marlena, communicating something … I wasn't sure what. Marlena stared back at him. Jaw squared, she began closing the door, and had to pause while Damien stepped back from the threshold. She looked at me, open resentment on her face. I couldn't understand why she would be so hostile towards me.

'I'd appreciate no more shouting in our hallway,' she said. 'You'll get your junk back, Lucie, don't panic.'

The closing door finally blocked our view. I wanted to scream at her, tear her hair, but remained silent, tongue-tied, staring at the closed door.

'Come on, Luce, let's go home,' said Matt, taking my arm below the elbow and steering me away from the apartment.

I shrugged out of his clutch. 'Matt, I'm going to the police. This isn't right.'

I looked at him. He brooded silently, something troubling him, but left it unsaid.

It was only much later that I understood what had been at stake. There were plenty more Marlenas vying for the attention of the handsome French tutor at the college, and I had inadvertently thrown a minuscule spanner in the works.

JP.

* * *

I finally get to paint. My brushes flow frantically across the canvas. It's like lancing a boil. There's something sensual in the escape from ugliness, the release from affliction.

I've been back to the Schloss several times. One of the tutors in the apprenticeship programme brings a digital camera with her. Studying the panels I feel would be easiest for me to paint, she takes a photo, and produces it A4 size for me on the printer in the office. This way I can stay in the studio while I work, to be supervised by the guards who also oversee those in the *Werkatelier*.

It's not always easy. Tempers are volatile in the workroom next door, and I'm obliged to keep the door open. I can't always concentrate when someone is losing the plot, shouting or crying, or simply complaining. But I get used to it, and eventually block out their voices.

At the beginning, I brought in my little CD player and listened to Verdi or Mozart, a habit left over from painting next to Patterson in the college studio. The women next door could hear my music and thought this was a great idea. They requested to have music of their own, until the inevitable argument ensued about whose choice of music should be playing. With more than a dozen different requests, it became impossible to monitor, so we've gone back to silence.

* * *

After lunch, everyone works from one until four o'clock. This afternoon is clear and sunny. Following a frosty start this morning, the window frames in the atelier click loudly with the change in temperature, sun beating directly against them. One end of the courtyard between the work blocks sits in a square of light. The few round wrought-iron tables have all been dragged to the warmth, resembling a setting outside a Parisian café. The scene is enhanced by the handful of women designing their mandalas. Swirls of blue surround the smokers, and the occasional murmur of conversation relaxes the mood.

I'm not allowed to take my easel outside, but I can take my sketchpad and some drawing materials to enjoy the clement weather. I sit alone, away from the tables, and lean my sketchpad against a crossed knee. I hold my face briefly to the sun, a copper light fizzing on the inside of my closed eyelids. Then I survey the scene, unusually quiet as everyone enjoys a rare moment of warmth at this time of year.

I don't know anybody particularly well here. A young girl is sitting at the next table in profile to me, filling in her pre-printed mandala with precise purple lines. Her long hair hangs in front of her face and she brushes it back behind one ear. There is a tattoo on her upper arm, a bracelet of black swirls, faded to a dull greenish-blue, and I note white spidery scars around her wrists. I begin to sketch her with a stick of charcoal.

'Smeethers!' shouts a young guard through the door to the *Werkatelier*, making me jump. A black smudge appears on my paper where I had been about to complete a brow and the bridge of the girl's nose.

'*Der Anwalt ist da!*'

My lawyer! What was I thinking? It's already three. Leaving the sketch on my chair, I hurry to the office. Two hours is all I have, and if there's something we need to restructure or repeat for my appeal, we may need all the time I can get. Stupid to have forgotten, but it's pretty easy to slip into a life of forgetfulness in here. For some it's the only way to survive. I have to pinch myself sometimes to remember that the other women probably deserve their incarceration. I treat mine like an unknown sentence on death row.

* * *

'*Bonjour*, Madame Smithers.' My lawyer is an athletic, swarthy type. He looks more Mediterranean than Swiss. I'm trying to work out if he's gay or whether he is an extremely snappy dresser with a creative barber. He could be about my age, but I suspect he's younger. That's probably because I feel so much older all the time. In any case, I don't imagine he's had much legal experience. I'm pretty sure he's been assigned to my defence as a kind of apprenticeship. See what you can do with this foreign woman's case.

'Monsieur Pittet.' I acknowledge him as I sit down.

'A little bad news, I'm afraid. You will not be moved back to La Tuilière.'

My shoulders slump, but I had already suspected this. He's afraid because it takes him over an hour longer to get here. But it won't hurt too much. He'll be billing the extra time anyway. His sympathetic eyes scan me briefly before continuing.

'The Tuilière prison is full. And although a cell may free up over the next couple of months, they want to keep them for women of Vaudoise origin. There are still several cells free here, so ...' More space for foreigners, I think, to finish for him, but I don't say anything.

'But anyway, you should know that compared to La Tuilière, this place is like a resort.'

I snort. 'Did you manage to fix a date for my appeal?' I ask eagerly.

I'm pretty sure Pittet believes my story. He was equally baffled about the outcome at my trial. He argued my case well, considering his inexperience – not that I have any experience of a Swiss court of law – but the prosecution had other ideas. To them my guilt was clear-cut, and the police themselves seemed to have decided without a second glance at any evidence to the contrary. Pittet's case was swept aside like a schoolboy's.

I felt so helpless at the time, but have become very suspicious since. This is a country boasting a perfect democracy. You'd think their judges would be totally unbiased. Thankfully Pittet's enthusiasm and the curiosity of youth are on my side. Due to our proximity in age, I think his sympathy for a peer who doesn't belong in prison has driven him to delve a little deeper, despite the fact that I'm a foreigner.

His expression is forlorn.

'I'm so sorry, Madame Smithers – Lucie. Our request for an appeal has been denied.'

'What?' I shout, as my hands slap down on the table.

He glances at the guard.

'How can that be?' I practically wail.

I stand up and the chair bounces back on the lino floor. The guard takes a step towards us from the door and I hold out my hand, eyes closed, jaw clenched, and sit back down.

'It's complicated,' Pittet continues. 'There were not sufficient documents to support the evidence. The judge does not want to use the reports from the prison psychologist. First he asked for an independent assessment, and then he looked at the police report again, and said it was solid. The report is clear. There will be no appeal.'

'But that's so unfair. Can't anyone see that the information has been ... manipulated?'

I bite my lip. I am no expert. I'm only just getting used to criminal procedures and criminal terms. But it seems like so much was suppressed.

'Lucie, you must not forget that the civil judicial system here is different to yours in England.'

I reach up and push my hair back from my forehead with both hands. I remember the courtroom. No jury, a small panel

127

of judges, but fewer people to convince. And all in a language that was not my own.

But I do appreciate the need to have as many allies as possible, and don't want to let Pittet go. I look at him with determination.

'I cannot believe my fight is over. There must be something else you can do.'

'I ...' He's lost for words. A most unlawyerly trait.

I flare my nostrils, force air out of my nose, trying to control my shaking anger, but tears of despair are not far away.

'Can we keep a line of communication open ... if I have any more questions?'

'Of course,' he agrees, I think with some reluctance.

'My parents will pay for your time,' I assure him, although I haven't consulted them yet about available funds.

I always bid farewell to Pittet thinking both of us had more belief at the beginning of our meetings than at the end. Today, this is more true than ever.

It's beyond the end of the workday, but I have to go back and rescue my sketchpad from where I've left it on the chair in the courtyard. When I reach the work block, a guard lets me in, and although the door is locked to the courtyard, I can see the sketchpad is no longer on the chair. It's not in the studio either. You can't leave anything lying around in this place. I squeeze my lips together and take a deep breath, to stop myself from crying.

* * *

'Lucie, you want to hold Adnan? Can you take him for a moment? I have to go pee.'

Fatima turns to me as I finish eating. We're in the cafeteria, and she unwinds Adnan like a turbaned Christmas present. I want to say yes. Then I hesitate. There's an inner protective shield telling me to remain emotionless. But she's already handing him to me, and my arms reach automatically, one hand ready to cup

128

his head, the other arm folding him to me. It's as though my limbs have a mind of their own, disobeying my mental orders. And she trusts me, since my help with his sore tummy. She knows I care.

He still sleeps. I lay him against my lower belly, pushing my tray away with my elbow. His little fluff of hair is so fine, it's almost transparent. He wears an expression of slight irritation that he has been disturbed, a crease at the top of his nose, eyes squeezed slightly, but he doesn't wake.

'You must miss your boy,' Dolores says, sliding along to sit beside me.

The tubular legs of her chair scrape the floor, making Adnan's little hands suddenly fly up in brief fright, but he sleeps on. I lift him to me, breathing in the smell of his baby hair. I can't speak.

'When do you think they will bring him to visit you? Do you think they ever will again?' she asks.

I shrug. A single tear runs down my nose and drops onto Adnan's forehead. Suddenly his eyes open. They are the dark myopic blue of infancy, and for a moment he studies my face with a curious look well beyond his age of several weeks. He's trying to work out who this is, this woman who is not his mother. I expect him to cry out, a stranger is holding me! But he closes his eyes again, pokes his tongue out from between his little button lips and makes smacking sounds with his mouth. He lifts his fist to his chin, and settles back into slumber.

'My mother brought JP last time, but she's not sure when she will be able to come again,' I finally feel strong enough to say. 'I know England is not as far away as the Dominican Republic, but it's still hard for her. My dad hates to travel.'

I don't explain the irony about a man who travelled more of the world during the war than most of us could ever hope to.

'And the father's family? Could they bring him? JP?'

Dolores obviously hasn't thought through what she is asking.

'Are you kidding, Dolores? I've had no contact with the family for over five months now. I can't imagine what poison they're putting into JP's mind. That's the worst thing.'

I remember the last time my mother came with JP. It was a strain for all three of us. JP doesn't know his other grandmother very well, and I could see she felt awkward in his company, not sure how to deal with a little boy. He's so different to how I was as a child. He hugged me, unsure whether he thought he was allowed to. I could feel him letting go before his arms had even clasped me. It broke my heart to see him apprehensive about how to behave in the company of his own mother as well.

I rock Adnan in my lap, eyes glazed, staring at the scabs of food on my plate. I wonder again what the family has been telling JP. The appropriate words describing the reasons I am here have never come from my mouth.

Chapter 10

I'm alone in the shower room when Yasmine enters with her towel hanging round her neck, and I think this is the perfect time to mention Dolores. She passes by me, smelling faintly of spice, humming to herself, some Arabic tune wavering in her throat. As she stands in front of the mirror, she pulls her long dark hair out of a tightly banded ponytail. I watch the curve of her neck as she turns her shoulder, and she catches me looking at her reflection. I furiously wish I wouldn't blush, and turn to start the shower.

'Hey, how's it going?' I ask casually over the sound of the water.

She immediately looks at me with a downturned mouth and a creased brow. No one ever asks how it's going. Stepping into the cubicle, I leave a little gap in the curtain. I busy myself adjusting the hot water, surrounding myself with steamy comfort, and squirt some shampoo into my hand. Through the opening in the curtain, I can see her turn and begin to undress. I'm not sure she's going to answer, then she speaks as she shakes her hair free from the dent of the rubber band.

'Ça va, ma biche. Just cleaning up. Got a date.'

Her eye catches mine in the mirror. She winks, and I swallow.

After months of being totally unaware of each other's bodies in the shower block, I suddenly feel modest. I think of the time she told me about the boyfriend, the chef – Jean-Claude was it? I wonder how serious this thing with Dolores will really be.

'Did you know that Dolores is still using?'

I simply come out with it, keeping my eye on Yasmine to judge her reaction and begin to smooth the shampoo onto the crown of my head. She's bending over to take off her socks, and pauses.

'Dolores is clean. What do you mean?' she asks, looking at the gap in my shower curtain in the rapidly fogging mirror.

But her voice is a little uncertain. The mirror has steamed up now, and I can't fathom her expression. I wish I hadn't said anything. The foggy screen I created for my own embarrassment has backfired.

'It's just that I'm concerned for you. I saw Dolores swap a syringe.'

I massage my hair into a foamy hood, raising my voice over the sound of the water. 'I don't know where she's getting her gear. I wanted to be sure that you knew. With her temper, and all, I thought it might help you in your . . . your relationship with her. And I know you are clean. I hope you won't be tempted, or can avoid an accident.'

'Lucie, *ma chère*, Dolores is clean, I tell you. You must be mistaken. She would have told me. It's just that family of hers that drives her crazy. We have no secrets. Like a couple should be.' Our eyes meet in the mirror. She looks at me poignantly and I blush even further, this time with indignation. 'Stop trying to, how do you say, *foutre le bordel*, stir the trouble,' she says with a kind of patronising patience.

She enters the cubicle next to mine and turns on the water, doubling the level of white noise. I raise my face to the shower, rinsing the suds out of my hair. I will have to shout, and I don't want anyone to hear me talking about Dolores, least of all Dolores.

'Look, I'm not trying to stir trouble. I want you know that Dolores can be unpredictable. She has always had these black rages, even before you came here. You've seen that now and … I did see her take a syringe, and when I realised … I don't know. I don't want to see you get hurt, Yasmine.'

My shower curtain rips open, making me jump, and an icy wad of air slaps my body. Yasmine stands there, naked and shiny, dripping onto the ceramic tiles. Her hair lies in black snakes over her shoulder, goose bumps rising on her arms and thighs. One of my eyes smarts from the shampoo.

'*Habibi!* Are you jealous?' she asks. 'You could have had me, you know. I was yours for the taking.' Hand on one hip, she does a little sideways thrust of her pelvis. 'But I could tell you wouldn't be into that kind of thing. That man of yours hit you with somethin' hard, girl.' She lets the shower curtain drop and returns to her cubicle to finish her ablutions. My heart beats faster.

The twisted irony of her words shocks me. For some reason I want to cry. I've been so intent on keeping my emotions and opinions hidden over the past months. And now I feel like I've been exposed as a fake. For some reason I think of the first time JP managed to master the pivotal movement of a swing at the park on his own. This monumental point in his development more significant to him than his first word. Never questioning the faith of my guidance that would lead to the thrill and his sense of satisfaction.

I shouldn't try and mother anybody else. More than wanting to take back the words that Yasmine does not believe, I am afraid that I will recognise guilt finally knocking on the door of my regret.

* * *

Six years ago

It was the end of my impromptu hen night. Matt's sister Marie-Claire had arrived that afternoon from California and was shocked to discover that nothing had been planned in the way of a pre-wedding tradition for the bride. Anne had wanted to take me out for a meal and find a place to dance, but had been struck down by a stomach bug two days before. To ensure she would be fit enough to act as my maid of honour the following day, and for the sake of the little life blossoming in my belly, she decided against going out. Matt and a group of his mates were spending the evening at the Casino in Evian.

'Everyone in California calls me MC,' she said when we shook hands for the first time that afternoon. 'Those traditional double-barrelled names are so cumbersome. It pisses off my mother, but I'd love you to call me MC too. Gives me fuel to fight the Russkies.'

I was bemused to hear her speak with such disdain against her mother; we had only just met. Now after a bottle of *chasselas*, I must have felt like her only ally. She had mustered a handful of girls together to meet at the Italian restaurant.

'I've become such a cheap drunk,' I said, waving the waiter over to order another bottle of water.

MC and I sat at a large table in the Italian restaurant, surrounded by empty glasses, bottles and little shiny dessert bowls bearing the remnants of an excellent Tiramisù.

My head began to spin, and I berated myself for the second glass of white wine. I shouldn't have been drinking at all, but this was a special occasion.

'But you're still here,' slurred Marie-Claire, placing a hand on my arm across the table. 'The others are all a bunch of wimps.'

'When was the last time you were in Switzerland?' I ask, curious why Matt never talked about his sister.

As an only child I often wondered how I would have treated a sibling, but was sure I would have remained in close contact, no matter how big our differences.

'God, years ago. I wouldn't come back to live even if they forced me. But I was kind of summonsed to the wedding by the powers that be. I bet Ron is pulling his hair out right now at the blackjack table with Mathieu. I hope my brother doesn't say anything to make my husband punch his lights out. Their relationship is on pretty thin ice, given our history.'

My curiosity piqued. History? MC might have declared herself my ally, but concern crept into my relative sobriety. Why would there be such animosity?

'I can see you love him, though,' she continued. 'And he obviously thinks you're pretty hot. Well, honey, you are hot. Wouldn'na asked you to marry him otherwise, eh?'

I blushed. Was my adoration so obvious? Then I squirmed, remembering Natasha's desire to keep the pregnancy quiet until it was too obvious to avoid.

I looked at MC, sitting opposite me, her body scrunched in her chair in a tight black dress and dagger heels, a clatter of silver bangles filling her arm from wrist to elbow planted on the table. I swallowed.

'MC, do you know I'm pregnant?'

This revelation might have me teetering in dangerous territory. Everyone would know soon enough anyway – they were all capable of doing the maths. MC's heavily kohl-rimmed eyes widened.

'No shit! Well that changes the stakes. I bet Natasha's pissing her pants.'

Her face dramatically developed the over-concern of someone who's had too much to drink. She tapped the table with her other hand.

'Honey, promise me you'll be mindful of my brother's wicked temper,' she said.

I laughed, poured her another glass, and pushed the bottle away. I took a sip of my water.

'Oh, I assure you I've already experienced that.'

'Jesus, has he hit you?' she asked, suddenly serious.

'No!' I was shocked, faltered.

I wouldn't have called it a hit ... Why did I lie? I wanted to give him the benefit of the doubt. I was sure that slap was a one-off that wouldn't be repeated.

'But I'm sure with a bit of provocation ... He's pretty hot-tempered.'

MC looked down into her drink, her spiky dark hair flapping forward over her eyes. Goth without the threat. She swilled the wine in her glass and studied the eddies, a frown on her face.

'I should tell you something about our tarnished past.'

Warning bells went off in my head. Whatever she was about to say, I didn't want to know. But I did want to know. What was I getting myself into? This man I had fallen so deeply in love with had a tainted history.

'Something happened when we were kids. Something ...' MC shook her head.

I leaned towards her across the table, eyebrows raised, my look saying: Go on ... My hand held her arm in silence. She finished the rest of her wine in one gulp and reached for the bottle.

'My parents and brother never talk about it. They probably hope I've forgotten. My idiot little brother, the prodigal son,' she said without the sardonic humour one might expect.

'I must have been 10 or 11. Mathieu would have been 9. We were mucking about on the wall next to the chalet – the one surrounding the patio on the west side. I was walking along the top of the wall, something neither of us were ever supposed to do.'

MC poured more wine into her glass. I put my hand across the top of my own.

'Didier had taken the fence down in preparation for winter, and Natasha thought we were old enough to know better. Anyway, I'd picked some mushrooms, some *bolets* growing near the trees on the edge of the paddock, and Mathieu began taunting me, telling me to give them to him. He had this big stick, one of the fence posts. I knew he wanted to destroy the mushrooms. I wanted to take them in to Didier, maybe get him to cook them for lunch, I don't remember.

'Anyway, Mathieu became angrier, wanted me to give him the mushrooms. He hit me with the stick, and I dropped them. As I bent to gather them up, he went ballistic, started hitting the ground, smashing their soft brown caps. Then the stick came down on my back and my arms. And just like that, maybe he whacked me a bit too hard, but I lost my balance and fell off the top of the wall.'

I put my hand to my mouth. The retelling of the incident was so matter-of-fact. A memory too long-established to incite any more anger.

'I would have fallen flat on the patio and probably only sustained a few bad bruises. But on the way down, I hit an old milk churn used as a flower box hanging from the rock wall. I fell strangely. Broke my pelvis.'

'Oh my God, that's terrible.' I finally spoke, feeling ever more stupefied as she talked.

'Not finished.' MC hiccupped, holding her hand up, either to stop me interrupting, or excusing her wine consumption.

'I was in hospital for a while, not because my pelvis took time to heal, but because I developed an infection that went undetected for a couple of weeks. It spread, and well, rendered me infertile. I can't have children. *Terminé. C'est comme ça.*'

To hear her suddenly speak French reminded me that this was Matt's sister. His sister. And his action, albeit indirect, had led to her infertility. Matt had done this thing.

'Natasha would piss her pants if she knew I was telling you this. "You won't bring up all the sordidness of your incident, will you, Marie-Claire."' MC mimicked a surprisingly accurate rendition of Natasha's accent.

She looked at me, noting the wide-eyed concern on my face.

137

'I'm sorry. Jesus, you probably don't need to be hearing this at this stage. I'm sure you're clever enough to work him out. I was always sure he would get his comeuppance one day. I'd like to think someone like you has made him a better person. All I'm saying is … be careful, honey.'

She patted my arm, took two big swills of her wine. I winced. She wouldn't feel good in the morning. She sat up suddenly, slapped her hand on the table.

'Fuck me, I've just realised. You know your kid's going to be the first successor to their twisted little dynasty? No wonder they want to keep you under wraps.' She spoke with bitter sarcasm.

In my sobriety, I still found it hard to hide my shock. I was flooded with conflicting emotions. I wanted to hug MC, comfort her, but at the same time wanted to defend the man I loved.

Accidents happen.

* * *

'I tried to reason with Natasha, but she wouldn't budge. She's quite the domineering type. I can see those Russian characteristics coming out in her. Some kind of misplaced pride.'

My mother is sitting with me in the visitors' room, and for the first time in many days, I feel tears prick at my eyes. She has flown over from England for the weekend, and in agreement with the prison is allowed two consecutive visiting days, each for two hours. Every prisoner is allowed three visits per calendar month. She tried to persuade Natasha to let her bring JP, although I am not sure she would have been able to deal with the logistics of fetching JP and bringing him by train all the way here. It would have involved three changes and a taxi ride in two languages unfamiliar to her. My heart had wrenched when I saw her walk through the gate alone. I'm reserving the third visiting privilege in case someone else brings JP.

'It's okay, Mum, you did your best. Thanks for trying.'

I unclench the fist lying in my lap.

'She's a despicable woman. I'm surprised the warning bells didn't ring loud and clear when you first met her,' my mother continues. 'Like mother, like son.'

'Oh come on, Mum. Were you ever that in love with someone, that you were willing to overlook the faults of their family? Didn't you ever feel like that about Dad?'

As I say this, I wonder how much Mum loves Dad, or whether it's the security he brings her. Her eyebrows crease and she briefly looks away, biting her lip.

'Don't you ever stop and wonder whether Matt had the same reservations about you, my parents?'

My last comment is spiteful. I'm getting sick of my parents saying everything in a 'we told you so' tone. But I remember Matt mocking the traditions of my family, and I flush with the memory of irritation. There were many things I overlooked in our relationship. But there are also many things I have overlooked in my parents' relationship.

'I … You do realise that your father and I also had to get married?'

'Of course you did, Mum. People didn't live together in your generation.'

'No, Lucie, I mean, we had to get married, because of you.'

My mother looks sheepish, and takes a deep breath as though a load has been lifted.

'Holy shit!' My eyes widen.

How naive could I have been?

'Lucie!' she automatically retorts at my bad language, and we both laugh at the irony. A mild swearword shocks her world more than unexpected pregnancies.

'I didn't know. I never made the calculations. Has it bothered you all these years? Like mother, like daughter?' I say without rancour.

'No it hasn't bothered me, but honestly, Lucie, I'm not sure

139

I would have married your father in such haste if you hadn't made such an early appearance.'

I've always wondered how my gentle, mousy mother ended up marrying the handsome but militant workhorse who is my father, so many years her senior. I assumed their match was one of complete opposites meeting in the middle for the perfect relationship. They displayed only discreet affection towards each other while I still lived at home.

'I would still have married Matt if he had asked me. I even kind of told him that when we were sailing in Greece that first summer. He seemed so in love with me, I thought it would last forever. I never imagined he wouldn't deal well with it ... And now I have a fatherless son.' My eyes water.

'You don't need to tell JP everything about his father. He needs an image to help him become the person he wants to be. But he needs to know how quickly a brash decision can change lives. I thought by telling you, it might help when you come to explain things to JP later.'

I get up and hug her, and glance at the clock on the wall. Visiting hour is almost up, but I now feel warmed by the fact that she will return tomorrow. I have time to mull on the information she has shared with me, to process it and try to work out why my parents have seemed so distant. I immediately feel renewed warmth for my mother.

'Did you eventually decide to stay in Bern?' I ask, changing the subject, lightening the mood. I don't want her to walk away from today's meeting remembering the sadness floating over her daughter.

'Yes, in the end. The hotel is delightful. Right in the middle of town. I love the cobbled streets and the arched arcades. It's a beautiful city. Everyone is friendly and most people speak English. On Monday it's the famous *Zibelemärit*, the Onion Market. I'd never heard of it, but there are plenty of tourists who are here only for the event. The hotel is full tonight.'

'I'm glad you've found things to do around the visits. Mum, you know I really appreciate you making the effort. It's a shame Dad didn't come with you. I'm sure he would have enjoyed the market too.'

'Yes, well, he doesn't like to travel much any more. He likes to stick close to his roots now.'

No longer curious to see his wayward daughter, I think. I wonder if he is at all curious about his grandson.

'I brought you some things.' She reaches down to a satchel-style bag she brought with her.

Things I have missed from home appear in a line on the table: extra strong tea bags, digestive biscuits, coarse-cut marmalade and my favourite shampoo. Another seed of gratefulness tips the scale and my eyes brim. It is no longer awkwardness that grips me with the thought we may not have enough to talk about tomorrow. I now look forward to the opportunity as much as I dreaded it two hours ago. The 'nice Indian taxi driver' who is waiting for Mum outside the gates will bring her back for a reunion that has been waiting years to happen.

Chapter 11

'*Te quiero*,' Dolores says to Yasmine, and I roll my eyes.

'*Me gusta*,' Yasmine replies, breaking off a piece of her cake and placing it melodramatically into Dolores's mouth with two fingers.

I smile as everyone around me laughs. I have no desire to participate, but know that if I don't at least watch what's going on, my reluctance might be seen as sulky jealousy, especially after the awkward shower scene.

Dolores has organised a little ceremony for her union with Yasmine. I'm unsure who she thinks will benefit from the open display. I can see she needs to assert her proprietary personality. And everyone else is enjoying the excuse to have fun and eat some cake, although the mixture for the latter was obtained none too honestly from the bakery.

I agreed to sketch the happy couple. But a session where they sit in front of me for hours is neither possible nor desirable. One of the guards took a photo last week and had it printed out for me in the admin office. I worked from that in my cell each evening and I'm quite pleased with the result. The work is a sketch in soft graphite, and I believe I managed to capture a look on both their faces of freedom and complete contentedness.

Dolores has her head slightly thrown back in a characteristic burst of laughter, although her eyes are still open, not screwed up, and Yasmine displays a closed-lipped smile with shining eyes. The ubiquitous look of captivity that we all carry with us is not present in the work.

I am pleased with the piece, which is now propped up in a tastefully decorated cardboard frame covered in bright woven cloth, made by two inmates in the weavers' studio. I wonder which of the happy couple will display the work in their cell, or whether they will take turns. They will still be separated at night. The illusion of togetherness can only go so far.

The Polish girl has lent Dolores a flowing pink kaftan she usually wears as a nightshirt. It looks a bit theatrical on Dolores. Pink is not particularly becoming on her. I study her carefully, wondering how much drugs have been required to maintain composure throughout the short ceremony. Yasmine has made the cake herself. She borrowed a tin from the kitchen and used the cupcake mix that was supposed to be for an order for the village bakery.

After declaring their union and respect in Spanish and French, they finish feeding morsels of cake to each other. I sigh, and sip a beaker of cold fruit tea.

They are probably happy to have a distraction, however bizarre. If any alcohol could be thrown into this mix, I imagine there would merely be tension and tears. In the end, it's much like any other wedding.

* * *

Six years ago
We were married on the last balmy day before the arrival of the snows. A group of friends and family gathered at the *maison de commune* in the vine-shrouded town of Aigle in the valley. Golden autumn colours stretched to the slopes of the iconic toothy peaks

of the Dents du Midi and Dent de Morcles above us to the south. Cirrus clouds capped the deep blue sky above the mountains in strands. The perfect day for a wedding.

I didn't have much time to get excited about the event. It all seemed so hasty. Although the promptness of the nuptials was at the insistence of Natasha and Didier, I think my parents were also relieved that tradition was taking place in the correct sequence. They seemed to be enjoying themselves, despite their reserved feelings about Matt. A kind of bubbling thrill floated between my stomach and my throat. My heart felt ten times bigger. Like being on the upward turn of a playground swing.

After the official signing of our marriage certificate, we walked from the registry office along the narrow walled streets to the thirteenth-century château on a small knoll overlooking the town. The area around the castle bustled with the flurry and traffic of the *vendanges*, the vintners hurrying to gather the grape harvest before the first destructive frosts of winter.

I was five months pregnant with JP, but you could barely see the bump beneath my cleverly tailored oyster-coloured silk gown.

My jaws hurt with the smiling, despite the occasional queasy feeling in my stomach, more through nervousness than any residue of morning sickness.

'You look stunning, my darling.' Matt leaned in to me, reassuring me this really wasn't only an obligation for the baby. I beamed.

'I don't recognise half the guests. I feel like I'm at someone else's wedding. It's like a dream. It's only when I look down I see the dress and – oh look, I'm carrying a bouquet! It's our wedding day!' I laughed.

'Most of these people are friends of Mimi and Papa. Your parents seem to be having a good time. I don't think they really approve of me, you know. But I'm glad to see they're happy for you,' he said.

'Oh that's not true, Matt. They're just getting used to your

144

rakish ways.' I pushed against him playfully. 'Any partner of mine, is a partner they'll love,' I lied.

I blew my mother a kiss and surveyed the crowd. MC wore a pair of dark glasses, nursing her predictable hangover. She clung to Ron's arm on the periphery, not really wanting to be there. I regretted not asking her to be a bridesmaid, though I doubt she would have agreed to step out of her traditional black into lilac for the day. Anne was my maid of honour; there to adjust my veil, hold the bouquet and make sure my champagne was laced with plenty of mineral water. 'Sacrilège,' wailed Didier.

Our other witness, the best man, was a colleague of Matt's who managed the local sports store. Yves and Matt often met for a drink at the bar and sometimes played a game of poker or backgammon by the fire through the winter. Standing within this gathering of our supposed nearest and dearest, I realised that Matt had as few close friends as I did, at least those he and his parents thought important enough to invite to our wedding. This struck me as odd, considering Matt had lived in the region all his life. Being so new on his social scene, I left it up to him and his parents to send out invitations. I thought there might be old pals he had associated with before he met me, but any friends from his history were sadly lacking. Where were the work colleagues, the barmen, the ski teachers, and what did this say about him?

* * *

In the courtyard at the château, people gathered around us for an informal receiving. I felt a soft thud against my leg. I looked down to see a piece of fruit slipping from the rough silk of my skirt, the juicy remnant of a peach or an apricot. An orange stain bloomed, seeping into the threads of the material. I drew in my breath. No, my dress!

'Oh! Where did that come from?' I looked up into a blue sky

strafed with vapour trails, and studied the sea of faces mingled in the courtyard. My gaze rested briefly on my father, smiling only with his mouth. I saw my mother chatting to a member of the college faculty. Nobody seemed to have noticed the mess on my skirt. My throat tightened.

'What a shame. My dress,' I said to Anne who quickly bent to minister a tissue to the stain.

She dabbed ineffectually at the smudge, already a permanent bruise on the raw silk. It wasn't until I looked across to Matt that I felt unease. I followed the direction of his frown to a figure walking away through the château gate, pale blonde hair flying behind her like a frayed banner. I didn't know this person, but I was sure Matt did, judging by the twitch of his body language, and a slight flush at his throat.

I glanced at MC, who also followed Matt's gaze. She removed her glasses to examine the retreating figure, rolled her eyes, caught me looking, and dressed her exasperation with a wry smile. My eyes prickled, and I had to swallow repeatedly so my make-up wouldn't smudge. MC's warning rang in my mind.

Be careful, honey.

* * *

The informal reception was a modest affair. Drinks continued to be served for a couple of hours, accompanied by some exquisite canapés and snacks served on large silver platters. When the sun dipped below the edge of the western turret of the château, I felt exhausted, another bout of pregnancy hormones taking their toll.

But the celebrations weren't over yet. We drove back up to the mountain village in convoy, leaning on car horns to traditionally announce our nuptials. Natasha organised a meal at the village's most exclusive restaurant, and although I was exhausted, I sat happily at the head of the wide table with Matt on my left.

Seating tradition ceased at that point. On the long side of the table to my right sat Didier and Natasha, opposite my mother and father, like proud adversaries. I placed the crisp white linen napkin across my lap, covering the stain on my skirt, dearly wishing Anne, who sat on Matt's left with her boyfriend François, could have been seated at my side. My head had begun to ache dully.

'I don't know whether you realise this, my girl, but there are thirteen of us at this table,' my father said.

I was unsure whether his comment was patronising or an attempt at his own special humour.

'But of course! Thirteen is a Russian lucky number,' chirped Natasha, whose hawk ears had overheard my father's comment. Her slanted eyes widened with champagne-infused enthusiasm.

'Why is that then? Lucky?' my father asked, his need to know every last detail.

I could feel trouble brewing. He had made it to the wedding, but had not made peace with the reasons for our marriage. I feared his political view of our relationship might cause him to pick a fight with anyone.

'Thirteen has little significance to us in itself. It would not be lucky to have an even number around the table. Like never having an even number of flowers in a bouquet.'

I suppressed the compulsion to check the number of flowers in mine, now lying in the middle of the table.

'Well, in our books, thirteen is unlucky. The Last Supper,' said my father.

'Oh, don't be so morbid!' Natasha laughed. 'We didn't see any black cats today, and the girl sitting at the corner of the table is already married. Superstition is for the whim of the cynical.'

She waved her hand, giving away her tipsiness. She leaned in to Didier, who had driven us back to the village and now made up for lost drinking time with a bottle of Bordeaux.

'Who do you think is the Judas here, Dad?' I asked, but

regretted the question as soon as I had spoken, fearing I didn't want to hear his answer.

My eyes surveyed the table. To my right sat Yves, the best man. He had brought a girlfriend I didn't know well. I suspected her presence was a carefully planned motive on Yves' part, aside from someone he could talk to. With fine food and champagne on offer, a seduction strategy must have played a big part. I glanced down the table past Matt's parents and son-in-law Ron, to Didier's brother Serge, who I had never met until today. Seated opposite me at the foot of the table, he had come from Geneva alone. His wife had fallen ill the previous week and didn't feel well enough to make the journey. I felt a pang for the absence of Patterson. He and his wife had made a brief appearance at the reception at the château. But in many ways I would have preferred his paternal presence at the wedding breakfast table to my own father's.

I smiled briefly at MC sitting on the corner to his right. She gave me a wink and I looked back at my father with a questioning look. Judas?

His eyes rested coldly on Matt before he tucked into his smoked trout and caviar.

* * *

At the end of dinner, in a reversal of bridal tradition, we were the last to leave. Uncle Serge left first, followed by my parents. Then the younger crew departed. Yves, Anne, MC and their partners intended to continue the celebrations at the tavern. Matt looked longingly after them as they left, a wild alcoholic celebration of his nuptials almost too tempting. I felt like telling him to go with them. I was dog-tired and longing for my bed.

But Natasha and Didier remained seated for one last task of the evening. The waiter cleared away the last of the espresso cups and dessert plates, upon which lay the remains and smears of a traditional French éclair cake covered in spun caramel. Didier placed a package on the table.

'We have a small gift for the two of you,' announced Natasha proudly.

The present lay on the table between us, the size of a large book, and I pushed it over to Matt to open.

'No, I think Lucie should open it,' declared Natasha. 'I know it is something she admires.'

Matt raised his eyebrows uncomprehendingly and passed it to me.

My curiosity piqued, I carefully tore open the package to reveal a box into which was placed a small Russian icon. I recognised it as one of the fakes that hung on the Favres' living-room wall. A cynical snort stuck in my throat as I looked up into Natasha's blandly smiling face, and cleared my throat.

'Wow, thanks so much, Natasha, Didier. You remembered I commented on your collection.' I smiled neutrally.

'Our grandchild will need to learn all about his or her traditions and Russian roots that go back generations. I'd like assurance that the baby will have access to both sides of his or her family history. This is a good start,' said Natasha.

Was this some kind of a joke? I looked at Matt, who seemed equally nonplussed. Roots? What about Didier? Wasn't he proud of his Swiss traditions too? I couldn't help thinking this was some kind of an insult. That they thought I needed to prove myself to join their cosy little Russo-Swiss club, that I was somehow forsaking my own identity so they could have control of it.

'Thank you, Mimi, Poppa,' Matt said as he got up from his chair and kissed his mother on her forehead, before shaking Didier's hand. The scraping of his chair brought my thoughts back to the icon I still held in my hands.

'Take good care of it, won't you?' said Natasha as I looked at her. Did she mean the baby?

'Yes, thank you. I'm so glad to have your blessing.'

* * *

'I almost got away with it,' volunteers a Swiss inmate one afternoon.

Her name is Monika. She says she likes to paint, but I haven't seen anything she's done. She's wandering through the atelier looking at the acrylics and charcoals on my bench, turning containers to examine their contents. Right away I know she's talking about her crime, but I don't want to voice the question 'Murder?' It's taboo, like never saying Macbeth in the theatre.

'I used toxins gathered from some old paints my father had in his garage. Put a little into his food every day.'

I'm shocked, look at the tubes of paint, but keep a neutral face.

Deep down a little part of me thinks that was a clever idea. To think I had my own multiple tools and plenty of opportunity at the time Matt was playing me for a fool.

'How long did it take?' I ask.

'Too short. A couple of months. I thought the process would be much longer.' She makes it sound like she's weaving one of the rugs on the loom where she works. 'Slow suffering. That's what I intended. I don't even think I wanted him to die. I wanted him to feel *desolat*.'

She moves away from the acrylic colours and starts looking through some of my paintings.

'I read about these people in Japan who had a disease they called itai-itai – that literally means "it hurts-it hurts". *Armi Schweine*, poor sods. They contracted it because they ate rice grown in cadmium-contaminated water. Some mining company in the mountains was releasing poison into the rivers. They were eventually sued for it, but many people died in the meantime. You'd think they'd have suspected something when all the fish turned belly up in the paddies and the rice didn't grow very well. They thought it was some kind of bacterial infection. My father

150

developed the same pains in his limbs and joints – flu-like symptoms. But he died quickly at the very end. Simultaneous kidney and liver failure. That's why the doctors were suspicious. He ingested too much, too quickly. I should have been more careful. Should have watched him suffer more.'

Monika's complete lack of emotion makes me shiver. I bite my tongue to avoid an involuntary expletive.

The other forty murderers – I can't believe there are so many – are in the high-security block, and I often think Monika should be there too. Of those convicted of murder, we're the only two with zero danger status on our files. We're considered harmless for the other inmates and guards, I guess through the circumstance of our crime and psychological assessment. It makes me think that someone out there knows I would never be capable of intentionally hurting my husband.

Despite her broad shoulders and big hands, Monika produces incredibly intricate designs. She's never asked to change stations. She's been a weaver for several years. Most of the others like to change from time to time. There are nine jobs on offer. Everyone has to stick with their assigned stations for a minimum of eight weeks. The women doing the cardboard packing must be bored out of their minds with the monotony, but there has to be a job that doesn't involve skill, for the ones who can't concentrate for more than a few minutes at a time, for the ones who are stoned.

Monika is tall and imposing. She always wears lipstick, a shiny gloss that doesn't match her hard eyes. Her hair is dyed black with a few bright red streaks in the front. She wears bulky sweaters that hang off one shoulder, the strap of her bra greyed from years of mixing colours in the laundry. Being Swiss, she is able to communicate effortlessly with the guards, giving the impression of congeniality with them. But who knows what manipulation she's playing.

It's given me back some of my pride, painting in the atelier, and I know I'm lucky, especially when I detect wistfulness in

Monika's examination of my bench. It's not one of the officially assigned jobs, but they still pay me the twenty-six francs wage. Most of this goes into an obligatory savings account. Everyone has one for their eventual release. All the inmates work, no exceptions, even the old biddy in here for life, who's way beyond retirement age. She needs the money for her chocolate and cigarettes.

Monika's indifference to her crime borders on supressed pride. She wouldn't be interested in my thoughts about unfair imprisonment. No one seems to want to believe me. No one wants to listen. Everyone's entitled to say they're innocent, but when so many women say it, it loses its impact.

But of course everyone's curiosity is piqued. We'd all like to know each other's misdemeanours. There's always an unspoken tension.

No matter what Matt did to me, whether or not I suspected him of adultery, I could never have seen him suffer, despite my fleeting thought about the possibility of poison. I still loved him at the end. I still love the idea of him now. Monika's cold recounting of her sins makes me feel sad. I would still be loving Matt today, even if he had thrown me into jail himself.

Chapter 12

I'm walking out through the gates, although I'm not free. But this is real, not a dream. It's the first time, and of course I hope it will not be the last, but I feel reckless with the uninhibited view at ground level. The fences are not high, but from my cell the bars are always a reminder, even if I put my head right near them through the open window and concentrate my gaze into the distance.

As soon as the gate closes behind us, a pair of invisible hands releases its grip on my throat. I suck in the air as though I have been holding my breath under water. A tiny voice screams 'run, run' inside my head, but there is nowhere to go. Nowhere to hide. The cropless fields stretch for miles around, with a clear view to the village in the distance.

This is an unusual sanction. Müller is taking me to the Hindelbank church in the centre of the village. Something she wants to show me. I'm almost in shock to be outside the prison's fenced perimeter. I'm not sure what to think of my grain of almost-freedom. We drive in the prison van along the narrow road around the fields to the village. We can see the spire of the church from the grounds of the penitentiary, and I would love to have been able to go on foot to the village. But the distance is considered too far for the other guard accompanying us, whose dodgy hip causes her to walk with a swaying waddle.

I feel like the teacher's pet, the privileged one, although I know that Yasmine has been to the local bakery a couple of times to help deliver bread when one of their ovens broke down. Rarely are the inmates given the opportunity to leave the grounds. This is unprecedented. It's Müller's idea. She thinks I could sell my sketches, wants me to check out some sculpture in the church crypt.

'The man who built Schloss Hindelbank also built this church. His son commissioned Nahl to sculpt a memorial for his father in the church,' she tells me.

'Johann Nahl, the German artist? I've heard of him,' I say.

'It is a miracle the sculpture was not damaged in the fire of 1911,' Müller explains as we walk up the path to the arched doorway of the church, our feet crunching on the gravel.

The heavy wooden door is protected from the drizzle by a simple square wooden portico. I tuck my sketchpad under my arm to protect it from the damp and hike the bag containing charcoals and pencils over my shoulder.

I feel vaguely uncomfortable about going into the church. The last time I entered a sectarian establishment was on the college field trip to Florence when we stopped off in Milan to visit the 'Last Supper'. I'm not religious, but feel slightly rueful that Matt and I weren't married in a church. But that's not because of my holy sense of duty. I guess it's more a sense of tradition.

I'm not prepared for the sheer beauty of two sculptures that Müller has brought me to see in this simple rural church. She first points to a vertical carving, and the awkwardness I felt entering a place of worship is replaced by an emotion I can't put my finger on.

'Hieronymus von Erlach's resting place,' she exclaims, as though she is announcing his entrance to a ballroom. On the wall is a pale rose marble carving of a sarcophagus. A Greek mythological character is draping a cover over the stone slab. The folds of cloth, hewn out of rock, are so delicately velveteen I want to touch them, but a railing spans the alcove. An angel cries at the side of the coffin, holding a handkerchief to her face, while two more cherubs fly overhead, one blowing a trumpet and the other holding a golden shield.

As I grab the swirled cast-iron handrail, which keeps observers from stepping into the niche, I look down and draw in my breath, my eyes stinging with the poignancy of a second sculpture, set horizontally on the floor. It is not something you would expect to see in the austerity of a village church, and the divine work brings a tightness to my chest and a lump to my throat.

'She is Maria Magdalena Langhans,' explains Müller. 'She was the wife of the pastor here at the church. Nahl was working on the tomb for von Erlach when they became acquainted. Langhans' wife died tragically in childbirth and Nahl took it upon himself to create this piece in recognition of the pastor's hospitality and generosity. The sculpture was not originally here. They were not initially together. After the big fire, this piece was found in the crypt, covered with beams and wood, forgotten for almost two centuries.'

Maria Magdalena appears through the pieces of a broken tombstone split three ways, escaping some unseen Hades. One of her hands is trying to push away the broken slab adorned with snakes and skulls. The other holds the arm of her baby. One of the baby's chubby little hands presses against his mother's breast; the other perpetually reaches out to some unseen wonder. I want to touch the little fingers of the baby.

'There is an inscription – "*Herr, hier bin ich und das Kind so du mir gegeben hast*",' I quote.

'Here I am Lord, and thou hast given me the child so,' translates Müller, the irony that I spoke the words in German and she in English not lost on either of us. 'Or something like that. The baby died shortly after his mother. She did not survive the birth.'

I don't know if it is a boy or a girl, but it occurs to me that neither did Maria Magdalena, having died during delivery. She would never have known the love of her firstborn, the visceral love a mother and child have for each other, and that in itself deepens my melancholy. It's the perfect resurrection. My eyes prickle with tears.

'It was a boy, a son,' says Müller, as though she has read my mind.

This is a piece of such beauty and sorrow and passion, I can only imagine that Johann Nahl was himself in love with the pastor's wife.

And I know what it is to love a newborn son.

* * *

Six years ago

JP was born on a stormy night in the busiest part of the ski season, his pale skinny body slithering into the world on Valentine's day. I was thankful for Matt's Land Rover forging through the drifts formed by the blizzard on our early morning descent to the hospital. I nervously counted the decreasing minutes between contractions. The hard, unforgiving suspension of the car made me want to scream.

Through the window of the labour room, the mountains we had driven from were shrouded in deep blue clouds, and sleet spattered the windows. I was grateful to have made it to the hospital. I felt a certain safety there, a vast contrast between the storm outside and the harsh lights of the labour room. Once we had settled, the room's lights were dimmed, but with the pressing weather, it was still brighter inside than out.

Matt's fascination and eagerness to welcome a little clone of himself into the world was clouded by his new image of me in the throes of labour. Clammy and sweating, my animal-like growling shredded any of my remaining dignity, enhanced by my choice to use the birthing stool resembling a makeshift toilet in the middle of the labour room. At one stage I thought Matt might faint, and in a brief moment between contractions I sent him into the hallway to call his mother, to report on their grandchild's progress.

Afterwards, in my room, he perched on the edge of my bed. He seemed afraid that I had changed, perhaps having witnessed a savage part of me he was fighting to deal with in his mind. He tentatively pulled the covering away from our son's velvety little face.

'Jean-Philippe, *mon fils*,' he said lovingly, proudly. Through my exhaustion, an exhilaration rose in my chest. This little human being could reconnect us in so many ways. I looked at Matt studying our baby, and my heart filled with a desperate love for them both. I gently handed him the swaddled bundle, showed him how to hold his vulnerable little head.

'I'm going to teach you such things, JP. You're Papa's little boy,' he said.

This moment was worth every effort it had taken to make the right decision, and I was prepared to allow Matt the thought that this little miracle was all his own work. His life's biggest achievement.

Jean-Philippe – JP. The acronym stuck, despite Natasha's protest.

'Of course you're not going to call him JP. Such an American vulgarity, using his initials. Jean-Philippe is such a fine name.' She must have been thinking of MC.

Matt had brought Natasha with him in the Land Rover, and she was still complaining about the poor heating and uncomfortable seats when she marched into the ward, perpetually fussing with her neatly pleated hair and necklace at her throat. Didier chose to stay at home. I would bring the baby to the chalet to visit Poppa as soon as I came back to the mountain.

I asked the doctors every day when I could go home, not

wanting to leave Matt on his own for too long. But I had to stay for a few more days. JP developed jaundice, and although the golden colour looked healthy on his skinny little limbs and chest, I stayed in hospital to avoid the lengthy trips up and down the mountain for monitoring and blood tests.

Matt visited once a day, but stayed a little less each time. We found there wasn't much to say to each other, hospital wards being the great silencer of dialogue. The smell of cleaning products and antibacterial wash sanitised our warm cosy thoughts. JP mostly slept, so we didn't even break the monotony by walking to the hospital cafeteria. Natasha had insisted on paying the extra fee for me to have a private room. I would secretly have preferred the company of another mother in the room, if only to share the anxieties of young parenthood. But I knew if Natasha came to visit, she would be horrified to have to share her time with a stranger.

Matt's cooing and staring gradually lessened. 'Doesn't do much, does he?' he said.

But if JP squawked one single protest of hunger or thirst, he handed him back to me.

Matt talked woodenly of his current ski class, a group of giggly Belgian schoolgirls on an academic sport week. He described a raucous evening spent with the lads to celebrate JP's birth. He wasn't sure if it was the cigars or the whisky that had made him ill at the end of the evening. I wanted desperately to be home, to nurture our family, to make Matt climb back in that cosy cocoon with us.

Postnatal hormones spread their seeds of instability. I felt a strange distance between my new life as a mother and the freedom I had left behind. The two eras pulled apart like a piece of stretchy putty, the strands becoming ever weaker. Matt on one end, JP and I on the other. I hoped we could find a way to mould ourselves back into the same ball.

By day four, Matt was genuinely perturbed that I couldn't come home. Aside from the daily journey from the village to the valley, I think he missed my company. He sat on my hospital bed, holding me and stroking my arm while we watched JP sleeping noisily in his bassinette.

'We've certainly come through a lot in the last year,' he said reflectively the night before we were due to be discharged. 'I'm looking forward to our next adventure. We'll be a great family. I'm very proud of you, Luce. You've given me a beautiful son.'

I was surprised at his genuine warmth, and doubted my irrational worries over the past days. I was always aware that our union and a child had not been in his plans, but when he gave me that melting look of his, the one that made my lower abdomen now ache with discomfort rather than passion, my faith returned. He stroked the hair off my face, whispered my name, and I knew it was going to be all right. Our hands would shape themselves back around that putty. We would make it.

* * *

'You're not going back to work for them, after snubbing you like this,' Matt said furiously when I was told the college had managed to wangle their way out of paying maternity benefits for the six months I had taken off.

We assumed we would still receive two salaries, but I was officially a student. Matt wouldn't dream of fighting for me from his seat on the faculty. It was my battle. The one-sidedness of our parenting responsibilities had already been determined by the fact that Swiss paternity leave was restricted to one day's paid absence from work.

'The college has already done me a favour by slipping me through the system for Patterson's benefit,' I insisted. 'I'm not going to kick up too much of a fuss or they might see fit to let me go,' I told him.

'Well I think you should find somewhere else to work anyway.'

'I can't believe you just said that! Why are you so determined not to have me work at the same place as you? It's not like we ever run into each other on campus. And what about your employment there? They hardly pay you a top-notch salary either. Perhaps we could benefit more from you seeking out a higher paid job.' My voice was rising dangerously.

'It's different, Lucie. There's more than my job at stake. There's my loyalty to the institution. I've been with them through my studies. And I love my job.'

'I love my job too! It's not as though I have some mediocre alternative to waitressing or cleaning hotel rooms. I've finally found something I care about, and now you're trying to take it away from me.'

I forced my raised voice to calm, afraid I might wake JP.

'If I feel okay after a few months, I'll approach them about working part-time. Patterson says he can manage on his own for a while, but he's not getting any younger.'

I was so determined to make the transition of JP into our lives as seamless as possible, to carry on as though nothing had changed. But with one less salary we would have to tighten the purse strings.

This issue would have been irrelevant had we been able to secure Swiss citizenship for me, after which I would not require a working permit as a foreigner. But a new law meant that I could only apply for naturalisation after three years' marriage, and at that time I would have to be resident in Switzerland for at least five years. And the plan to take in another lodger was now on hold with the spare room transformed into JP's nursery.

'I hope we can make ends meet in the meantime,' Matt grumbled.

* * *

'*Merde alors*, Lucie. Matt's family has enough money to support you both. Don't let anybody make you feel guilty.'

Anne had come round to visit a few weeks later and I admitted I was feeling more than a simple post-partum anxiety.

'I don't know, Anne. I feel so guilty all the time. Guilty that I insisted on keeping the baby. Guilty that I somehow forced Matt into a situation he couldn't have foreseen. Guilty that I am standing in the way of something in his life.'

Guilty that I might love him more than he loves me. But I didn't say that.

'You think it's your fault? It takes two to get pregnant, so quit blaming yourself. I think you should remind Matt of his responsibilities. It is time for him to grow up a bit.'

'We had another blazing row the other night. It's always about money. But at least he conceded he would have to give up teaching skiing for a season and work at the college full-time.'

'Well that's a start, Lucie. Don't keep beating yourself up about it.'

In a way I was relieved he would receive a regular salary, and not rely on the occasional profits of a good ski season, where he was paid on supply and demand, suffering if a warm front brought an abrupt and early close to the winter season.

And the last thing I wanted was for him to go begging his family for funds. I was determined to make up for his sacrifice by being the model partner and mother. The good wife.

But after his initial paternal enthusiasm, Matt didn't engage with JP the way I had hoped. He developed an indifference to his own child. In my grumpier moments, I saw it as a kind of wariness that his offspring might prove a greater competition for his vanity. My beautiful baby versus my handsome husband. Eventually, even Matt's indifference turned to impatient annoyance. He complained that the baby wouldn't do anything other than 'cry and piss and shit'.

He said he couldn't wait to get JP on skis, or at the tiller of his boat. I laughed uneasily, and wondered how many years I would be left nurturing this future skier or sailor on my own. At this stage, JP hadn't even smiled for the first time.

I tried delegating some of the soothing night duty, when all I desperately craved was an extra half-hour's slumber.

'Can't you shut the thing up?' Matt asked during one particularly colicky night. The thing. Was this what it had come down to? An unfortunate visitor in Matt's ideal hedonistic life of parties and pleasure?

One night I caught him shaking JP. Matt's biceps were tense, hands under JP's armpits, thumbs pressed into the little hollows on the baby's chest while he administered a controlled series of little jerks. JP's delicate head teetered back and forth.

'Jesus, no ... No!' I said as I entered the nursery on my way back from the bathroom. 'Give him to me. I'll take care of him. I know his crying is frustrating, but the little guy is in pain. You could really hurt him doing that. He could ... Look, why don't you go and sleep in the office. I'll get you some earplugs tomorrow. Matt, he has no idea. His little tummy is feeling bad. I don't know why, but he can't deal with my milk. It will pass. This happens to many babies. Please!'

I gently took JP. He still cried, but I calmed him with my breast. I turned away from Matt, not knowing whether to feel outrage or sorrow for him, but mostly grateful I had passed the nursery at that moment.

This phase would pass, but exhaustion was making the days stretch agonisingly. Matt ran his hand through his hair, and walked out of the room.

'I didn't realise it would be this hard. It's like our lives have been put on hold. We shouldn't have to change so much for him,' he mumbled as he headed for the office.

As I heard the door downstairs slam, tears pricked at my eyes. Such resentment. I wondered if he resented me too. For putting JP in the way of his plans. Perhaps I was in the way too. I couldn't rid myself of the vision of him shaking my baby.

'Shhh, little guy. Let's not go making Daddy all angry. He needs his sleep, little one, so do you.'

So did I. The team wasn't working out quite as I'd hoped. I sat on the bed and rocked JP until he finally fell asleep. I leaned upright against the headboard, JP lying against my chest. This position seemed to ease his little tummy. I desperately hoped the colic would soon subside. Because now I knew I couldn't leave him for a moment alone with his father.

* * *

Those first stressful months of JP's life felt like they might never end. Each new infant crisis exhausted me more, but I was determined to hold our family together. But the more JP and I tightened our apron strings, the more Matt loosened his hold on a bond that I had started to think was never really there. I no longer conferred with Anne about my disappointment. She had never warmed to Matt, and I could tell she was careful about her opinions of him in my company.

On JP's first birthday, I prepared a little party, not quite sure whether Matt would remember this small commitment. If he had, I hoped he would come home straight after class at the end of his workday. I cracked a bottle of beer, waiting for Anne and 4-month-old Valentin, plus another woman from the local crèche with her 1-year-old, and Matt's parents.

Watching JP flailing with his paper plate and scrunching at the plastic tablecloth, enjoying the sensation of his nails on the shiny surface, I raised my bottle.

'Well, it's you and me, kid. Better get used to it.'

As members of the party showed up, Matt's absence was practically forgotten in the celebration.

I could no longer rely on him. He played no part in the string of shopping trips, doctors' appointments and disturbed nights. I hadn't expected him to take a practical role, but I had hoped he would involve himself more emotionally.

Hassling him about small commitments brought an exasperated string of excuses about his heavy workload, insipidly emphasising the fact that he was now the sole breadwinner. He spent increasingly more time 'in his office' at college after class. I wasn't even sure where his office was.

But I stupidly allowed myself to fall into this unsatisfactory routine. That part was my fault. When I saw how involved François was with Anne and Valentin, I felt a pang of jealousy, but kept silent. I preferred to keep the peace than raise another issue for argument. My domesticity provided him with clean clothes and hot meals, when he chose to come home for them. He seemed to be hanging on, tolerating his wife and son.

All I could think about was keeping the family together for JP's sake. But it was breaking my heart.

* * *

From the time JP was 2 years old, Matt's impatience led him to use smacking as a punishment. JP might not even have done anything particularly naughty. But I could see that Matt himself was frustrated with something, and took his anger out on his son. Instead of a single flat slap across his buttock, he would repeat the punishment several times in succession, each time allowing the force of his hand to rock JP's body a little more, until he lost balance or stumbled forward with the momentum of Matt's arm.

I shouted at Matt to stop, not to punish an innocent child because he was the one in a bad mood. On more than one occasion, he turned to me as I approached and raised his hand as though to slap my face, his blue eyes glazed in a state of obscure fury. As I flinched, he withdrew in a huff and inevitably left the house to cool his temper elsewhere, while I calmed JP. At least my comments had turned the focus from JP to me. But I began to worry about his simmering temper. I felt like we were a split second away from an explosion.

Anne and I saw a lot of each other during this time, particularly as JP and her son Valentin had become such good friends. I tried not to lay too many of my worries on her table. I thought maybe everyone's marriage faced the challenges I was experiencing, but I noticed she no longer complained about her own partner's annoying quirks at home.

I never called my parents, avoiding the inevitable questions and scepticism. I doubted myself too often, and I didn't want to be reminded of the time my father had tried to plant the seed of uncertainty in my mind.

Through this deterioration, Matt and I still managed to make love from time to time, although it became something I felt obliged to mark on my mental calendar. Our passion became mechanical. The enjoyment we gleaned from our bodies was a physical formality. But it was necessary to touch base, so to speak. There was no question of a second child. I was paranoid about forgetting my contraceptive pills. I couldn't imagine loving another baby as much as I loved JP. Matt and I told each other we still needed my part-time salary. But in truth, I couldn't imagine being left to do the difficult baby stuff all on my own again. I knew another child would break us.

Another summer rolled around, and Matt sailed off for six weeks on a new yacht delivery. I kept hoping each approaching summer was the year we could meet him at the end of one his jobs. We could take JP on a sunny holiday to the Greek beaches of our romantic days. But somehow it never happened, and I couldn't help feeling that having JP around was only hindering Matt's lifestyle. I was forever reminding myself it had been my decision. No regrets.

I lived in some kind of illusion that eventually everything would come right. As if the love I knew I felt deep inside would bathe him in an adoring light, one day to be reciprocated and rekindled in the intoxicating manner of our courtship.

There was a certain truth to the saying hope springs eternal, but it wasn't until later that I realised how much of a walkover I had been all those years, purposely ignoring the things I should have had more self-respect to address.

* * *

After Matt came back, and before college was due to start again, I ran into our old lodger Marlena one day at the supermarket. She was on her own, hadn't seen me, so I skipped into a neighbouring aisle to avoid her. JP giggled in his seat in the front of the trolley as my sudden change of direction caused his head to sway.

But alas Marlena and I ran into each other at the checkout, our trollies bouncing off each other, almost toppling the sunglasses carousel. I said nothing, and gave a false half-smile, fury at her audacity still firing in my chest after two years. JP reached out towards Marlena, and I gently nudged his arm away from her.

Marlena's smile didn't reach her eyes.

'I wasn't aware, you know,' she said defensively, pointing towards JP. She wore an almost desperate expression. She couldn't possibly imagine that I was going to forgive her now for all the trouble she'd caused us as our lodger back then. What warped sense of justice did this person have? She was lucky I hadn't been to the police. I remember finding the things she'd taken from us – stolen from us – in front of the door when I'd come back from work the following day.

'You weren't aware of what?' I asked, exasperated at even having to communicate with her.

'I didn't know you were pregnant. Together. You and Matt,' she said uncertainly.

I had no idea what she was talking about. It all felt like so long ago.

'I didn't know either at the time,' I said, slightly confused. 'Why would you have needed to know? Biology 101?'

Marlena gave me a long look, smiled again without smiling, a forlorn brassiness touching her eyes, then turned to push her trolley towards another checkout. I recalled the grainy picture of her in the news article I had found in the Swedish tabloid. I placed my hand protectively around JP's shoulders and kissed the top of his head, relieved I had never let her stay in my home, and hoping I wouldn't run into her again.

It wasn't until later that I understood my own naivety had stopped her flow of words. She realised I still didn't know the whole story.

* * *

I shift the sketchpad on my knee and begin to draw the outline of the tomb, but can't take in the enormity of the sculpture as a whole. Instead I concentrate on the infant's head, and his hand reaching up, not for the reassurance of his mother, but to some unknown angel or light above to their right. Maria Magdalena's face is also turned towards this unknown source. I'm intrigued. My pencil hovers. I can't stop staring. Hot tears pool in my eyes. But I know I must come away with something on my sketchpad, to justify any future visits to the church.

I am convinced the sculptor was blinded with love for Maria Magdalena. He depicted this beautiful woman, a desperate mother, looking to him, reaching for him, the child … reaching for Nahl. This creation, this work of art out of stone, was surely no ordinary favour to the woman's husband. The baby is sculptured with such intense love and longing, not simply the face of the cherubs he has created around the tomb. I've convinced myself that this child could even be his own. He might have been a father who loved his child enough to immortalise him in stone with such love. Forever reaching for him.

I've been here for two hours this time, sketching until my fingers are numb with the cold. But those two hours have flown by. My melancholy has faded to a serene peacefulness in the ecclesiastical surroundings. I feel a little like Maria Magdalena, helpless to save her son. I can relate to her. It's as though I have fallen into a bizarre state of prayer. Not that I have found God or anything.

Perhaps this is the temple I didn't realise I needed.

Chapter 13

'I'm not sure, Lucie. I know she doesn't read all your letters to him. It's becoming harder to get information out of him. I hate to say it, but I think JP is getting used to you not being around.'

I can tell it pains Anne to say this. She knows this news will hurt me, but that's what I like about her. She's honest. But her comment doesn't stop my silent tears. She puts her hand on my arm.

Anne looks tired, wrought almost. Her curly dark-blonde hair is showing streaks of grey, and she's not even 30. Have I done this to her, my best friend? I feel terrible putting her into the position of go-between, interpreting the life and random thoughts of my 6-year-old for me.

'I'm so sorry to make you do this. It's so manipulating. But I can't believe how hard Natasha is working to cut JP's strings to me. Pittet, the lawyer, is working on getting me more visitation rights, but he doesn't see how he can make them enforceable. There are so many ways to slip through the net. Because I'm not Swiss, I have little input. I feel useless.'

'I'm sorry I couldn't persuade Madame Favre to let me bring JP. That woman is as hard as granite.'

Anne rubs a hand across her forehead. It has taken her more

169

than two hours in heavy traffic to get here, and a string of road-works around Bern had her complaining about that busy section of motorway the moment she walked into the visitation room. I know she values our friendship, but these visits are putting a strain on her. She has a son to look after as well.

'I'm so tired right now. We have other news.' She paused. 'I'm pregnant again.'

'Oh my God, Anne, why didn't you say something? That's fantastic. I'm so happy for you!'

I feel genuinely uplifted to hear something positive. Anne smiles weakly.

'We're really thrilled too, Lucie. I can't believe I feel so awful at the moment. So tired. I'm sorry to be a grumpy visitor. I know you don't get many. Visitors I mean. I'm sure you see your fair share of grumpy people.'

'Don't worry about me. You don't know how much I appreciate the effort.' I lean across the table and hold her arm. 'But listen, you can still help without coming here. Your letters are like a bible to me. You don't have to drive all the way up here. I'm so grateful that you can pose the odd delicate question while Valentin and JP still get some playtime together. I can't see the Favres moving out of the village just so JP can go to another school.'

'I don't know, Lucie. I'm not sure of the extent of that woman's influence,' Anne says.

'I'm pretty sure Natasha doesn't read my letters to JP. If I send them to you, perhaps you could read them to him, so I know he's getting my news.'

'I can do that, I guess, as long as she doesn't find out. Imagine how crazy she would be with me if …'

'I can't think of another way. It will be good while it lasts. I hope it doesn't jeopardise their friendship.' Meaning JP and Valentin.

It's my turn to feel weary. It's also getting harder for me to think up things to tell JP. The garden and the atelier can only swing a few seconds of interest with a child that age. I wonder whether I should talk about some of the people I've met. Make it some kind of kid's fantasy for him.

'I guess Mimi has already told him that I'm a wicked woman and I've been sent away because I did something terrible to Papa. I don't want him to grow up hating me, Anne. It's the thing that scares me most.'

'I always tell him not to forget that his Mama loves him,' Anne says. 'Lucie, are you okay? I mean, are you doing okay in here?' She looks around, as though the visitors' room is my cell.

'When I think of all the things I could have done, the things that could have happened, in retrospect ...'

'They happened, Lucie. You can't change that. You've got to work on your lawyer more. I've revised my character reference with him, asked the college to provide a report too. It's not over yet. We've got to get you out of here.'

'The memories are killing me,' I say softly.

She's about to speak, looks around redundantly for someone to support her, to help me in my despair. I'm so grateful to Anne for all she's doing. She's my lifeline. I realise it's only been seven years, but Anne has turned out to be the best friend I ever had.

'There's this bird ...' Anne looks at me uncomprehendingly, but lets me speak. I can see she's unsure whether I'm losing the plot. 'It's always been a mystery to me where the native birds go in autumn,' I continue. 'My ears were filled with the sound of them when I arrived here in spring.' I smile as I remember the birds. They smothered our garden, pulled worms from our freshly turned soil, and stole seeds from our tailored rows.

'Luce, what's with the birds?' Anne patiently humours me, although our time together is running out.

'Now that summer has long gone, there's barely a peep in the garden. But, Anne, there's this one bird who even now often sits on the limestone ledge outside my window, always singing his

171

heart out. What kills me is that it's the same birdsong that stirred me the first morning I woke alone in the bed I shared with Matt ...'

* * *

Four years ago

The bird woke me first, its monotonous peeping piercing my unconscious through the gap in the window. We often left it ajar at night in the sapping dryness of high altitude, even in winter. I moved my arm into a shaft of sun shining on the mattress, motes of dust winking in the strip of light. Matt's side of the bed was empty.

The moment his absence registered alarm with me, JP called 'Mama! Mama!' from his cot down the hallway. There was wonder in his voice, likely at the fascination of waking in daylight. I went to him, ruffled his hair, and picked him up.

'Good boy,' I said, kissing his cheek. He had slept through dawn. It was now past 8:00 a.m.

It was the beginning of spring break. I had agreed to help Patterson tidy the studio until late the previous evening, and was exhausted after a busy week at work. Matt said he had a 'thing' at the campus lounge. A few of the students were sticking around during the break because their homes were too far away, and had met up for an impromptu evening together.

JP spent the evening at Anne's, playing with Valentin. I picked him up when I had finished work, and he was already asleep in my arms when we walked through the door a couple of hours past his bedtime.

'Papa?' JP asked. I assumed Matt had come back late, and had fallen asleep on the couch in the living room, something he was prone to doing recently.

'I don't know, sweetie, he's already up I think. He's probably downstairs planning something exciting for our day. Is it time for breakfast? Go and choose some clothes.'

JP shuffled off the bed and ran to his room, an infant still spellbound to wake each morning to a new day.

I gathered my bathrobe around me, went downstairs and knew immediately Matt was not at home. I looked first in the living room, at the empty couch. Pointlessly inspecting each room of the house, knowing with certainty he wasn't there, but checking anyway. Each new door opened onto growing dread, or disappointment, I wasn't sure which.

I tried his mobile phone. It went straight to voicemail. I left a brief message.

'Hi, Matt. Would be great to know where you are. Don't forget we have lunch at your mum and dad's today.' And then as an afterthought, to remind him of his paternal duties. 'JP thought you might have something special planned for him this morning. He's asking after you.'

I am asking: Where the hell are you?

* * *

Snow lay in patches around the plants in the garden, crocuses pushing their way up between clusters of melting crystals. I stood on the step outside the chalet with JP at my side, unsure whether to knock. Usually Matt was with us, and he would walk straight in. I hesitated, my stomach aching, and my whole body trembling from the chagrin I felt about Matt's absence. This would teach him a lesson, telling his draconian mother that I don't know where he slept last night.

'Papa must be meeting us at Mimi and Poppa's,' I told JP as we began walking through the upper village to their chalet. 'He was up early this morning, must have been held up running an errand.'

I tapped the knocker against the hard oak door. Waited. When no one answered, I rapped again louder. Didier answered.

'*Les gosses sont là!* The kids are here!' he yelled back into the house. 'Why did you knock; why didn't you come in? Natasha and I were wondering who this could be.' Didier looked around as we entered. '*Il est où*, Mathieu?'

'Mimi, Mimi, Mimi!' chirped JP, running through the hallway to the living room where the mouth-watering smell of a Sunday roast contrasted my uneasy constitution.

'Matt's not here?' I asked Didier mechanically, knowing the answer.

I briefly considered it unfair to say anything without Matt being able to defend himself. I was always making excuses for him, but he might have a valid reason why he fell asleep in his office at college, or perhaps he had to deal with an emergency. There could be any number of reasons. But logic was banging on my mind like a stray brick.

The domesticity of the aroma of comfort food, a neatly laid table, the stereo quietly playing Verdi in the background, and the distant clattering of pans in the kitchen tightened my chest.

'Matt didn't come home last night,' I said quietly.

Shocked – was that guilt I recognised in my emotions? There was my loyalty, fighting the compulsion to snitch on Matt.

In the distance I heard Natasha welcome JP, her voice raised over the white noise of the extractor fan above her hob.

'*Voilà, Jean-Philippe, mon petit bijou!*'

Didier looked at me, mouth turned down at the corners. My comment needed no clarification. He understood. I wondered if either he or Natasha had ever been unfaithful to each other. If so, which one of them would have been the guilty party? I suspected it would not have been Didier. He knew which side his bread was buttered. Matt was turning into the archetype of his mother.

Natasha entered the living-dining area, looking around.

'Where is Mathieu?'

'Papa gone run error.'

Didier and I made eye contact. While I was absorbing the fact that this was JP's first sentence, I knew the trace of a smile on Didier's lips was for the irony of his grandson's comment.

* * *

Three years ago
'I suspect Matt is having an affair. And I don't think it's the first.'

Anne and I sat on a grassy bank above a narrow road in the upper village, a gentle *föhn* wind blowing from the south. It was the second week in June, time for the farmers to move their milking herds to the high alpine slopes. We could hear the pounding rumble of a dozen heavy cowbells far away.

'Mama! Mama! They coming,' shouted JP, pulling on Valentin's arm.

'*N'allez pas sur la route!*' called Anne, afraid the boys might be trampled if they climbed down to the road. 'Are you sure? What are the signs?' She turned to ask me.

'He didn't come home again last Saturday morning. He says he fell asleep in the student lounge after a film night, but I don't know. It's not the first time he's stayed out all night. He always has the same excuse.' I picked a marguerite and began twisting the stalk between my fingers. Every time I thought of Matt's absences, I felt a little sick. Anne searched my face to place my emotions.

'He's always been a womaniser,' she said. 'If he wasn't hanging off Leila at the bar, it was someone else.'

I turn to stare at her. To hear her talk about Matt's indiscretions before me made me feel strange, excluded, especially after all this time. Part of me believed that my real life only started the day I met Matt.

'Don't be naive, Lucie, he had a life before he met you, you know.'

'No, it's not that … Was he with other women while he was with Leila too? I thought she was the love of his life.'

We could hear the first of the farmer's calls in the distance, a faint 'Heyup, heyup, heyup', encouraging his herd to keep moving.

'So what if he was with other women? Weren't you the love of his life?' she asked.

'I thought so, but maybe he's not capable of remaining faithful to one person. A kind of serial philanderer. It's just that … I'm afraid to confront him. I'm not really sure I want to know the answer.'

'Lucie, there is such a thing as a pathological liar, you know. I don't know him very well, and he and François have never seen eye to eye, but it's possible he has convinced even himself that he is faithful to you. He's not thinking with the right part of his body, that's all.'

My relationship with Matt on the outside had cooled to a mutual tolerance of each other over the past couple of years. But all that time, inside, my emotions still simmered. For months I longed for the fireworks again, longed for his hands on my body to trigger those switches I knew were still present, deep down. Where had the magic gone?

Just when I was about to accept dark despair for our marriage, knowing, but choosing to ignore he no longer thought I was the centre of his world, he would surprise me with a family weekend away, suddenly finding a gap in his marking of papers. He might suggest a romantic night at home, cook us a meal and offer enough pampering to keep me on that line, keep the fires smouldering. To stop me asking the questions.

'Do you think François is capable of adultery?' I asked Anne.

'*Chérie*, every man is capable of cheating on his wife. François wouldn't dare make that mistake. He knows I could take him and his family's hotel business to the cleaners if that ever happened. But no, I know he loves me. And I'm sure Matt loves you too, in his own way. I'm sorry I didn't see this coming, Luce. Sometimes you can be so involved, you can't step back and notice the little things.'

'I guess it helps that you're Swiss. You have a grasp on the legal aspects of society and the system should you require it. I still don't want to rock the boat, for JP's sake.'

As I said his name, JP knocked into my shoulder with his legs. 'Look, Mama, moo cows!'

A collie ran up the road, barking excitedly. It was followed by a young farmer dressed in a traditional short black jacket embroidered with edelweiss. He strode up the road with a long stick in his hand, a felt hat sitting jauntily on his head. He opened the gate to the mountain track a little past where we sat.

The first of the cows lumbered into view, her massive bell clanging so loudly, conversation became impossible. JP put his hands over his ears, a tentative smile on his face. The lead cow wore a tall headdress of spring flowers, signifying her place in the herd, determined by her milk yield. Her bovine followers wore decorations on their heads and leather collars, bells swinging in a deafening clamour.

The cortège passed by, followed by the farmer's family and a flatbed truck transporting the churns to the makeshift barn on the alp where the herd would be milked during the summer. We gathered our belongings and made our way back to the village between islands of fresh patties on the road. Anne touched my shoulder.

'You should think about yourself for once, Lucie. You can't go on ignoring crap because you think JP will have a better upbringing. It will rub off on him in the end.'

* * *

I confused Anne yesterday, all that stuff I told her, dwelling on my past. Some sadistic part of me must be fabricating my guilt. She left tired and perplexed, but promised to keep in touch. She probably thinks I'm losing the plot.

Today I have other things to occupy me. It's my second visit to the church. Any enlightenment I might have felt on my first visit has dissipated. My awe is purely directed at the beauty of the art I see before me. With my rotting disdain for the shackles of religion itself, it disturbs me that churches are museums for so many pieces of beautiful art. I shun the very ideals for which the building was constructed. But there must be something in the divine that has inspired these works. These artists and sculptors have been influenced by the very thing I consider a hypocrisy.

I spend most of my allotted time staring at the marble figure of Maria Magdalena reaching for something unseen. I wonder if it's a kind of hell this woman is also breaking out from. The symmetry is somehow comforting. I know her pain. The difference is I survived, and I must find a way out of here.

Chapter 14

'But, Mama, only bad people get sent to prison. You're not bad. Why can't you come home?'

JP is sitting on my lap in the visitors' room. The joy of finally seeing him.

'I'm very sad about what happened, but not everyone believes me, and I have to stay in this place until we can sort everything out.'

I hug JP tight to me and breathe in the juvenile mustiness of his hair. I glance at Didier through the window, sitting outside smoking a cigarillo. He makes me sick. He is so weak, happy to be Natasha's puppet. I know Natasha doesn't want to bring JP to visit, but neither does she want to entrust him to Anne, so today Didier has done his duty. When he brought JP into the room, he merely nodded in my direction and then went straight to the door. Sometimes I think it's almost like Matt wasn't really his son.

'I want to go home,' JP says.

I panic. He's only just got here and he already wants to leave?

'Can you visit Mama a little longer? I don't know when I'll get to see you again.'

He is sitting on my lap while we draw a picture together at the table.

'No, Mama, I mean I want us to go home. You and me. To our home.'

My heart warms, and I hug him a little tighter.

'Don't you like staying with Mimi and Poppa?'

Perversely I want to hear that he doesn't like living with his grandparents. But I also don't want him to be unhappy. He looks towards Didier with an expression wise beyond his years.

'I want to live with you, Mama. Do you think I could stay here with you?'

I think of Fatima and Adnan. If this had happened five years ago, even though I should have been permitted to keep JP with me, I'm sure Natasha would have used her influence to prevent that from happening. Depending on the length of the sentence, the authorities prefer children to be looked after by family members rather than in the confines of Hindelbank. Natasha would have had her bony veined hands on him even then.

'But what happened to Papa – that was a addicent, right?'

'Yes, my love, it was an accident.'

My throat constricts as I control the tremor in my voice.

* * *

Three years ago

A heavy atmosphere wedged between us like a wad of cotton wool whenever we were in the same room together. Our big beautiful Victorian-style house had become a labyrinth for us to lose each other in. One evening when Matt didn't claim to have a class, we silently prepared dinner in the kitchen. The air between us was static, water bubbling on the stove and the soft slicing of mushrooms the only noise. I put the paring knife down next to the chopping board, and stared at the velvety gills on the wooden surface.

'Matt, there's something I have to ask you,' I said, certain I had to ask now, while I had the courage.

'What is it, Lucie? What's up?'

'I ...' *Ask! Ask now!* I couldn't look at him. His eyes would stop my words.

'Are you ... are you seeing someone else?' My voice caught. 'It's just that I'm not sure what's been going on over the last couple of months or so. I never see you. You seem to be avoiding me, and, well, I don't know, but I get this feeling I'm missing something.'

This last disjointed diatribe slipped rapidly from my tongue like cod liver oil, knowing its goodness, but tasting foul. I waited with dread, the seconds until he answered ticking as slowly as minutes in my head. I expected to see him break down, admit his wrong, ask for forgiveness, or beg me to understand.

But none of these happened. He stopped mid-pace across the kitchen, a baguette still in the baker's bag in his hands. He turned slowly towards me, his face at first neutral, then reddening, eyes sparking. I didn't now know what to expect, but suddenly I was frightened. Sometimes it was hard to believe I had been married to this man for four years. I could still remember the sting of his hand on my cheek.

'Luce, how can you ask me such a thing? Our relationship has always been based on a deep trust of each other. How can you doubt that? What are you thinking?'

At first I couldn't answer. I shrugged, my emotions unclear to me. Should I simply deny all the signs? I didn't know whether I should believe him, whether I should be relieved.

'I need to know, that's all, Matt.' I paused. He hadn't directly answered my question. 'So, are you? Seeing someone else?' I looked at the bread in his hands, strangely resembling a weapon.

He took it and smacked it like a stick against the kitchen counter. The baguette broke in half inside the bag, and the paper around it finally split, showering crumbs all over the kitchen. He threw it to the floor and the two halves spiralled against the wall near the fridge.

He turned to me and placed his hands heavily on my shoulders. I flinched and turned my head, waiting for the hit, then jumped as he shouted.

'Of course not, you silly woman. Didn't I just talk about a breach of trust? I would never do that to you! I am shocked you feel you have to ask that question. It makes me think something is going on with you here, how can you abuse my – no – our confidence?'

He pushed me backwards with both hands, and I stumbled. Spittle flew, and just like that, I was the bad guy.

I felt wretched, wanted the floor to open up, wished I had never asked the question, and could take it back. Matt was angry, furious even, both his fists clenching, his knuckles white. Tears sprang to my eyes.

'Mama?' JP called from his room upstairs. Matt's hands loosened and he stretched out his fingers on both hands.

'I'm so sorry, my love,' I said. 'I'm so sorry I doubted you. I guess it's because of all the evenings you've been away, all those times I didn't really understand why you had to be at the school. The individual student tutorials. I'm so sorry.' Tears streamed down my face.

Matt turned around and kicked at the bag that had held the baguette on the floor. I could hear JP stirring in his bed upstairs. Soon he would come down unless one of us went to him. Matt took two paces across the kitchen to me. I braced myself, hesitated, eyes wide with apprehension.

And then he hugged me. I held my breath, wanting to look deep into his eyes, drink in his sincerity, but he pulled me to him, buried my face into the space below his shoulder and I gave in, leaned against him. Thinking of my beautiful son upstairs in his bed, the innate faith he had in us as his parents. I wondered how much I could ignore or endure to ensure his stable and happy upbringing.

* * *

I lay in bed later, begging for the relief of sleep, to stop the turmoil going on in my mind. I felt like I was learning a side to my husband I didn't know before.

As I heard his foot creak on the warped wood transition in the doorway, I closed my eyes and feigned sleep. My heart was beating so hard I felt my body moving rhythmically on the mattress, like a boat lapping in the brewing storm waters of a port. Any attempt to resurrect the conversation of the evening would make us both angry, so I remained on my side, facing away from him.

I could hear every article of clothing unbuttoned, unzipped and discarded on the floor. He padded to the bathroom, left the door open as he let a noisy stream of urine echo loudly into the toilet bowl. The bathroom cabinet opened. He flossed, brushed, and I could see him in my mind spending a moment too long vainly examining his chiselled features in the mirror. I imagined his every move, his every breath.

The mattress sank as he sat on the bed, and he gently peeled back the duvet. A moment later I felt his lips and tongue on my shoulder, a playful bite. How could he even think about sex when we had set each other at such unease a short time ago?

I blinked, mouth opening in dismay. He looked over my shoulder at my face and interpreted this as a sigh of pleasure. In moments his mouth was all over my body. I wanted to resist. My head said stop, but my body, as usual, fell completely at his mercy. He whispered how sexy and beautiful he found me, assured me I was the only woman for him, and touched me in all the places that set me on fire. And I once again doubted my unease.

This was the father of my child. We were a family, and we should do everything possible to keep it together.

'It's okay, Luce. It's okay, sweetheart,' Matt said as he stroked my back afterwards.

But do you still love me?

I couldn't ask the question – I had already caused so much angst.

'Everything will be okay,' he continued. 'You're my baby, you know that. We're here for each other. I forgive you.'

My heart froze.

'Mama?' I heard JP calling again from his fitful sleep in the room across the hall. Matt's arms fell away as he felt me automatically turn to go to JP before he was fully awake, to soothe him back to sleep. I sat on the edge of the bed without looking at Matt, couldn't bear to deal with what I might see in his eyes.

I forgive you?

* * *

All hell has broken loose. I hear several women shouting. I recognise Müller's voice yelling something down the corridor, accompanying the sound of rubber soles slapping on linoleum in desperate applause.

Throwing on some clothes, I open my door, and look down the hallway. The Kosovan woman, Adelina, holds both hands to her mouth, eyes wide. The Polish girl comes to the door and glances cautiously at me. A guard is looking into Dolores's cell. There is commotion, confusion, and then a piercing scream. I don't recognise the shrill cry, but I can guess. My thought is confirmed as I see Yasmine being led out of Dolores's cell by another one of the young guards, and Monika follows, shaking her head. Yasmine is sobbing, and wipes her eyes as she steps into the hallway. A couple of girls who have approached Dolores's cell step away from Yasmine, as though she has some contagious disease. They don't want to catch her despondency.

Work has been postponed for the inmates on our floor. Seven of us sit in a room next to the office downstairs. Yasmine is still in her pyjamas. She's silent now. Disbelief has moulded her into a catatonic state. Monika is next to her, an arm across her shoulders. They both sit bent in on themselves.

'I knew she was using, but I didn't think she would be so irresponsible,' Adelina says in broken English.

Yasmine darts her a look. We are all thinking the same thing. Is that where Dolores got the crack?

Monika remains next to Yasmine, a little hunched, chewing a nail. Of all the women I thought would try her hardest to save a life, Monika was the last one on my list. One of the guards described her attempted heroics to us. With Swiss efficiency, Monika tried in vain to use her CPR skills, pumping Dolores's sternum and administering mouth-to-mouth. But no one can blame her for failing. It's hard to revive someone who's taken an overdose.

There is such a pointless sadness to all this. I lean back, realising why we have all been sequestered here. The guards suspect that one of us traded or sold Dolores the drugs. There will be harsh consequences to pay, especially if it's true and Dolores was clean when she came here.

I've learned a lot over the past weeks about the drug scene. The counsellor who sees the addicts would have had Dolores on her list – she pays special attention to those who might be vulnerable. She's a good egg, really cares for her patients, for want of a better word. They are like her sisters. She's proud of the fact that in her reign only one person has ever been known to start taking drugs after their internment. She will be so disappointed that she couldn't prevent Dolores from using.

Yasmine's eyes are still red-rimmed and her cheeks blotchy. It shocks me that this sassy, confident woman has been reduced to a wreck. I get up from my seat and approach her, feeling a sympathy I haven't felt for anyone else since I've been here, not even Fatima. Monika shifts out of her seat as I sit down. I wrap both arms around Yasmine and pull her to me in a tight hug. It's a brief display of comradeship that defies the edicts of etiquette in this place, but I want to make a statement. As I have been one

185

of those inmates who rarely socialises with the others, they all stare at me now, as if I've changed into a different person. But I know that Yasmine is not only grieving for Dolores.

'*Ton frère?*' I ask quietly in Yasmine's ear, knowing she's comparing Dolores's plight to her brother's.

She nods, trembles with renewed dejection, and puts her arms around me.

So much physical contact after months of sensory isolation feels a little strange.

'*Merci, Lucille,*' she whispers.

* * *

Two years ago

The college administration called mid-week towards the end of the semester.

'We need your key, Lucie, for the supply cupboards in the art studio.'

I looked at my watch. I'd just put JP down for a rare nap. He had been up late the night before with a stomach ache, then woke this morning full of energy, only to crash and burn after playgroup at lunchtime. Patterson would be finishing an art history lecture now in the projection room.

'Can't you wait for Patterson outside his class? My son is sleeping now.'

There was a momentary silence on the end of the line.

'Oh, Lucie, I don't think anyone has told you. Patterson died of a heart attack last night. His wife called this morning.'

I suddenly felt very alone.

* * *

The cemetery occupied a slope on the outskirts of the lower village, headstones rising like lichen-covered steps towards a beech forest. Between each grave lay a carpet of well-mown grass, a challenge for the gardener on the steepness of the slope. I looked towards the south. Patterson had a spectacular resting place.

It was late autumn, and the snow hadn't yet arrived in the village. The rusty crispness of the beech leaves lay like fallen cloaks under the trees surrounding the cemetery. The turf was still soft enough to dig, the frosts of winter yet to harden the ground. A black hearse was parked on the road below, ahead of a string of vehicles belonging to the mourners. I chose to walk from the village church to the cemetery with two of the college professors.

Matt said he was too busy to attend, but he was sure everyone would appreciate that I represented the family. He never had much to do with Patterson, but I think the real reason was that they never saw eye to eye. I had the feeling the professor's loyalty lay with Leila back then. Like my parents, he had always been wary of Matt's integrity. Now I wish I had opened up more to him, and had shared my anxieties. Anne was a great sympathiser, but it would have been reassuring to have his paternal support.

As we stood around the grave listening to the priest blessing the coffin, the wind whipped up a tumble of leaves from under the trembling trees, and they blew around us like golden shards on a canvas. They reminded me of Patterson's seasons of colours. I felt a deep sadness, knowing I had lost more than a father figure. It was as though I had lost my own father.

Patterson's wife, Jennifer, stood near me, tucked onto a woman's arm who appeared a little older than me. Probably a daughter. The conversations between Patterson and me in the studio had rarely wavered from the subject of art. Tears chilled on my cheeks in the breeze. I had missed so many opportunities, had ignored so many signs. I approached Mrs Patterson to offer my condolences.

'He spoke fondly of you, my dear. I know we never had the chance to see each other socially. Spoke of you like he might his own Phoebe here.'

I smiled at the woman standing next to Jennifer Patterson whose arm she held. The real daughter.

Between waves of sadness, I felt a panicky loss of stability. My position as Patterson's assistant, a sporadic part-time duty since JP's birth, was now in jeopardy. I suspected the administration office had wanted to recuperate my key on a permanent basis when they called to ask for it. They would have to hire a new art professor, someone with more youth and energy. Someone who wouldn't need an assistant to manage the number of students who chose the minor elective.

I hadn't thought to ask who might be teaching Patterson's classes, but with no official qualifications and no official work permit, I knew they couldn't ask me to take over his teaching schedule.

'He loved the change of seasons for all the colours, did Iain,' mused Jennifer Patterson. 'But most of all he loved autumn. Said it had a special light in the Alps that cannot be found anywhere else in the world. Appropriate that he should go before his canvas is wiped clean with the snow.'

Staring down at a wreath of flowers at the head of his grave, I remembered him describing the flora as though the blooms themselves were on his palette. Spring brought a brightly coloured carpet of wildflowers to the meadows, beginning with the buttery yellow of cowslips, dandelions and ragworts. As the days lengthened, nature mixed in the altitudinous blues of campanula, cornflower and gentian, finally warming into summer with the pink glow of wild geraniums, marsh orchids and thyme. All sprinkled throughout the seasons with the snowy smatterings of butterwort and marguerites. He loved to emphasise the names of the flowers, as he mixed his colours, almost too vivid to paint, nature's kitsch.

Jennifer said her husband's favourite season was autumn. The ochre, oranges and reds of the leafy autumn foliage competed with the bright golden needles of the larches, sweeping in wild strokes down the mountains from stony peaks, dusted on some mornings with an anaemic sprinkling of snow. This was Patterson's favourite canvas.

We lived within these changing masterpieces, like the constant changing virtues of a lover's heart. But my world seemed to turn to shades of grey that day. Ghosts hovered in the trees. Ghosts of innocence, Patterson, Leila, even Matt. As we stood gazing over the vast Rhône Valley, I knew then that something in me had perished too.

Chapter 15

My door is ajar and I'm working on a pencil sketch when Yasmine comes into my cell. It is still a while until lock-up. I didn't notice her in the canteen at dinner, but I was a little preoccupied with Adnan, rocking him for most of the mealtime, in the corridor, while Fatima ate. Getting my baby fix.

I am pleased to see Yasmine looking relaxed, her face no longer one of sadness and confusion. I smile. She smiles back. She stands there in silence, hands hanging at her sides, looking at me. I sit up, wondering what she wants. I put the pencil down beside the sketch. It's a male torso from my imagination. Partly from the memory of the bare chests of Nahl's angels, and partly with a sad longing for the perfect muscular body of my husband. My emotions are confusing. I had another one of those dreams last night about Matt, and today's perplexing feelings of both loss and remorse have put me in a strange mood. I put my hands on my knees and turn to Yasmine in my chair, throwing a quizzical look.

She gently closes the door behind her, turns to me and slowly takes off her shirt. She's not wearing a bra. At first I laugh. What is she doing?

'Yasmine!' I say jokingly, then see the smouldering look on her face.

My cheeks are burning with embarrassment, or shame, I am not quite sure which. She truly has a beautiful figure. She stands proud, unabashed. I recall the dream I had about Matt, our passion. Yasmine's olive skin is glowing. I remember the water dripping from her lithe body in the shower, and my belly is suddenly, uncontrollably, on fire.

She walks towards me and I lean back in the chair. She takes my shirt, lifts it above my head, throws it to the floor, and deftly undoes my bra at the same time. I am rooted to the chair, knowing I should slap away her hands, slide away from her. But nervous curiosity overcomes my embarrassment.

'You are truly beautiful, Lucie. So slim, so fit, so …' and she touches my breast.

I gasp. An intense flash sears my lower abdomen, my nipples harden and I am astounded at the sensations racking my lower body. I'm in a state of shock. I don't know how to react. Like a stranger drawing a nail across the sole of your foot.

'Yasmine, I … I don't …'

'Oh but, Lucie, you do, you need this. We all need the release. Come …'

She takes my hand. No one ever comes into my cell, but I look with concern past Yasmine to the door, expecting it might suddenly open. We sit on the bed and I turn to face her, looking at her body, avoiding her eyes. I don't want to. But I want to. Inviting touch, sensation. I tentatively reach my hand to her breast, my thumb moving against her hardening nipple. She lifts her chin, leans towards me, a laugh bubbling in her throat. To see her physical reaction to my touch sends streaks of unexpected pleasure through my body.

She leans towards me, shiny dark hair masking her face. Her tongue is on my breasts as she pushes me back on the bed and my back arches in forgotten need. Her hands move down my body, pulling my underpants down to my knees. She lies on me, our pubic hair crushed together. I am hot, so hot. She places her

191

hand between our moistness and somehow, she is moving her body and her fingers so we are both gasping with the intensity of orgasm within minutes. Tears squeeze from my eyes and I am pulsing against her touch. The sweetness of a physical memory unlocked.

When I close my eyes, it is not Yasmine's face I see, but Matt, devouring me with his look, his body. I swear I do not wish him dead. I have never wished it. I miss him too. And in this minute of ecstasy I can believe that he is still here with me. A brief, but yawning escape.

'I know you wanted this,' whispers Yasmine in my ear, and the cold fingers of something indefinable creep up the back of my neck. I turn my head away from the smoky scent of her breath.

'Yasmine, this felt good. You made me feel good, but I'm not, you know. I don't want to start anything.'

'Too late now, girl. If that ain't starting something, I don't know what is.'

'What I'm saying is, it's not like you and Dolores. I can't replace her. I don't want to replace her.'

I never questioned the motives behind Yasmine and Dolores's relationship, the sub-cultural role it represented in this place, but I wonder now if there was a more sinister incentive than physical comfort. Perhaps economic manipulation. Racial or gang protection. I have been stupid to let my guard down without considering the consequences.

Yasmine has pulled on her clothes, and I am wrapped in the blanket from my bed, knickers still round my ankles.

'I know you still belong to that man of yours, *ma belle*,' she says, speaking as though Matt will visit me next week and we'll get privileges in the honeymoon suite. She opens the door to leave, then turns. 'Live that fantasy for as long as you can, *mon amour*.'

I guess that's what we are all doing. Dolores had her drugs;

192

Yasmine has her physical escape. What do I have? I look down at my sketches. I feel weird. I would not have thought in a thousand years that I would let a scenario like that unravel. My inner shame now clouds the residue of physical pleasure.

As if I didn't have enough to worry about.

* * *

'Do you believe you've made any friends since you've been here?' I shrug, and Dagmar continues. 'Frau Müller tells me you're a bit of a loner, but you've become very involved in your art. Do you feel that is enough for you?'

Her office is on the ground floor, facing the outside of the compound. Through the window and past the chain-link fence, the spire of the village church pokes up through the leafless trees in the distance. I have a strange yearning to go there. I turn back to Dagmar.

'I don't know if anyone really makes friends in here, Doctor.' I address her as doctor to emphasise that we are not about to 'make friends' in her office, despite already having been on first-name terms. 'I have a few colleagues, acquaintances if you like. Mostly through circumstance. I like to help Fatima with Adnan. They let me do that, Müller and the others. There are a couple of women on my floor – we sit together sometimes at mealtimes. Now I'm working in the atelier, I'm pretty much on my own during the day, and don't talk much to people. I used to visit Dolores in the pottery, but well, since she's gone … and there's Yasmine …'

'I've been told you and Yasmine have a special relationship.'

I study her face as she says this, looking for a sign of disgust, empathy or ridicule. But her expression remains passive.

'Yasmine has been doing a lot of talking. It's got a bit out of hand. I was stupid to let my vulnerability take over. It's not … I'm not …' I squirm in my chair, mortified that we are talking about something I'm pretty sure I wish never happened.

'Lucie. It's normal that things like this will happen. Don't beat yourself up about it. You might be surprised to know that more than half the women in here have had sexual relations with other inmates at one time or another. It's considered normal for so many of the same sex in such close situations.'

She talks about it as though half of us have tried wholegrain bread.

'It's just ... I'm not like that.' I swallow. 'It was something I couldn't really control, the physical thing. I still feel ... not quite right about it. Now I'm here I feel like I've turned into a different person, and when I get out, everything will go back to normal. Except it won't go back to normal. Because Matt won't be there.' I pause, take a breath. 'I feel awkward about the Yasmine thing, a little ashamed.'

'Where's the shame in it? Nature's given you that body.'

I look at her sharply. Is she coming on to me?

But no, she's being neutrally clinical. 'You're only recognising the natural signals.'

Nothing fazes a prison psychologist. I'm sure they've heard it all, and seen a few things. What I don't say is that this character I am playing who has the occasional physical fling with Yasmine, is secretly excited to alleviate the boredom and loneliness, and that sometimes my character likes to have a pair of arms around me, to be held. I don't tell her I still dream of Matt at night, and sometimes wake in the dark hours with my heart beating and my body hot, to a plunging disappointment that he is not in the bed beside me. I haven't made sense of it all yet. It's taking its time, but you'd think I'd have got it by now.

'If you don't consider that you're having a relationship with Yasmine, do you think she does?'

'No, I don't think so, despite her publicity. I told her I didn't want this to be a thing, a relationship, if you prefer to call it that. I think of Yasmine as one of my colleagues. There are a few women in here I might consider colleagues, but relationships? Friendships?

You never know what you're going to get from one day to the next. Aside from the nutcases and the drug addicts, everyone is unpredictable. They probably think that about me too.'

'Do you feel that you're different from your ... colleagues?'

'You mean aside from the fact that I have been wrongly convicted? In that case, yes. Otherwise ... no, I guess we're all women who may have fallen off a path.'

'Do your ... colleagues make you happy?'

'Some days we have a few laughs, yes. And some days I wake up sad, and I can't tell you exactly why. Apart from the obvious, of course.'

'What are the obvious reasons?'

'I miss my son. I miss my home, my family. I miss my husband.'

I hadn't expected to feel anything as I said this, but my voice cracks, and all I can think of is: Don't cry! That ingrained dread.

'There's no need for you to hold back, Lucie, if you want to let go. Crying is a natural cleanser.'

Despite the fact that we are now on first-name terms, I try to keep something to myself. We all have other people hiding inside us in this place. Inside our actor bodies. We have to protect ourselves somehow. It's imperative that I learn to control the tears. I take a deep breath. Think 'calm'.

'Tears in here are like your death sentence,' I tell her, wondering how to steer the conversation away from my inner feelings to stop the flood. 'As soon as anyone sees them, you're either avoided like the plague or bullied, and there's always a fear that someone will use your emotions to manipulate you for something they need, and I'm not just talking material things. You can't put a value on pieces of your soul.' I take a deep breath, force strength into my voice. I guess she wants to hear about my regrets.

'We had such a good life, had so many experiences. It's hard to believe that in a split second that can all disappear, be forgotten.'

'Yes, over the past weeks it has been almost breathtaking to hear about your adventures. The sailing, the skiing, life on a mountain. It is a life most people would envy.'

'It was magical.' I pause, gazing again through the window, my eyes damp. 'He taught me all that, Matt. He was a good teacher, an expert in every field.'

Dagmar nods. 'His outdoor pursuits were almost as numerous as his indoor ones,' she says without thinking.

She's not supposed to offer an opinion on my dead husband, and knows this. She darts a look at me and I flush. But ultimately I think she has shown a little anger that I put up with his behaviour for so long. Perhaps she's disgusted that a human being could treat his partner with such disdain. I wonder if she ever met a convincing pathological liar like Matt. She clears her throat, as though to put her thoughts back on track.

'Do you think you are ready to tell me what happened? The day you were arrested?'

* * *

One year ago
JP and I returned from England where we had been for the best part of a week, visiting my parents and spending time with relatives. We arrived back on a Friday afternoon when Matt was at work, unwilling to wangle a few hours off to pick us up from the airport.

A small bag lay by the front door with a note taped to it. It was from MC. She was in town for some boring family business, and would pop by later to say hello. In the meantime, here was a packet of Oreo cookies JP might be allowed to share with me. I smiled. A treat from America. It was a while since we'd seen MC and I looked forward to her jovial banter.

With JP reminding me he was dying for a pee, I fumbled with the key, and practically fell through the door with the bags, the package and the buggy. I was glad to finally be home.

But as JP rushed to the bathroom, I stood looking around the apartment, smelling something unfamiliar. The flat was pristinely tidy, but the sour odour of exotically spiced food hung in the air. The kitchen bench sparkled and everything was put away in its place. I found this odd, expected chaos. At first pleased that Matt had deigned to keep our living space so tidy, a niggle pushed its way into my mind.

I carried our bags upstairs to unpack and sort laundry. The duvet on our bed was not quite pulled tight into the corners of an old set of linen I kept only for emergencies when we had visitors. My first thought was: How considerate, clean sheets for my homecoming. But riding instantly on the back of that was: Why would he change the sheets? He'd never done that before.

As JP's voice bubbled from his room, familiarising himself with toys he had not seen for a week, I unpacked my clothes and divided them between the wardrobe and a pile for the laundry. I carried my toilet bag to the bathroom and began filing items away.

JP stamped along the hallway, dragging a toy noisily along the radiator. He came into the bathroom brandishing a Lego Bionicle, the clunking of its mechanical feet still echoing among the tubes of the heater.

'I missed these guys, Mama!'

He had two of them by their waists, clutched round their various armour.

I smiled, ruffled his hair.

'Let's go and get you some tea, young man. Papa will be home soon. You can tell him all about our trip.'

JP skipped back down the hallway to his room.

As I closed the bathroom cabinet and caught my reflection in the mirror, alarm bells rang in my head. A split second of comprehension caught up with an image of something inside the cabinet. A loud humming in my head dampened another burst of boyish laughter from JP's room. I slowly reached for the mirrored door, my reflection swinging away from me like a slinking secret.

I held the edge of the basin, and stared unseeingly at the plughole. My focus zoomed in on every tiny piece of detritus in its drain, water pulsing menacingly in its depths. Stomach churning, my head felt hot, then cold. A slow realisation.

I went to the laundry room, rummaged in the basket looking for the bed sheets. But any sordid evidence had been washed. The sheets now lay clean and crumpled in the bottom of the tumble dryer. I went to the kitchen, pulled out the bin below the sink, but all I found in the bottom was an empty yoghurt carton and a stale heel of bread. Naturally, rubbish collection day was yesterday. I went to the living room, moved cushions, looked under furniture. I had to think what I would say to him, not sure I ultimately wanted to learn the truth. I finally began to feel like a fool.

'Change of plan!' I yelled with forced gaiety. 'Shall we see if Valentin is home? I'm sure he's missed you.'

'Yaaay!' JP yelled, running down the stairs after me, still full of energy and forgetting the offer of food.

Before he could remember he might be hungry, I grabbed his coat from the hook, opened the door and watched him skipping down the lane in front of me to his best friend's house.

* * *

Back home alone, the minutes until Matt returned slowed to hours in my mind. My heart pounded as I tried to predict the confrontation, preparing the territory, feeling a total mess. I sat on the couch, staring at the detail on a faux-Provençal vase on the coffee table, turning the lipstick over and over in one hand, hot and clammy. There remained the one speck of hope that I was wrong about the signs, but logic kept telling me that deceit lay in all their clues. I snapped off the gold cap of the lipstick, wound the half-used shaft fully out, studied the slope of caked colour, drew it absently across the top of my hand. I stared at the glistening, metallic bruise it left on my skin, before putting the cap back on.

I assumed Matt would be late home as usual. He generally used his free Tuesday afternoons to mark papers, and I had no idea whether he would stay at college to do that today. But as I heard the rattle of his Land Rover passing the kitchen window, I suddenly wished I had a little more time to coherently formulate my line of interrogation.

As the front door slammed, I heard the rustle of his jacket as he threw it over the hook in the hallway. My heart raced and I stared at the living-room door from my place on the edge of the sofa, rapidly clicking and unclicking the lipstick from its cover in my hand. As he came through the door, I felt a rush in my head and heat in the lobes of my ears. I wanted to run to him, have him hold me, kiss me, welcome me home. But determination kicked my conscience as I remembered why I was here. I wanted to hate him rather than feel this sad disappointment.

He stopped three paces in, shrugging the strap of his book bag off his shoulder. He bent over to put the bag down on an armchair, and I unhinged slightly, his broad shoulder moving under his plaid shirt, jeans creasing at the knee as the outline of his muscular thigh strained against faded denim. I could not control the physical reaction.

'Hey, Luce, how was the trip?' A pause. A tiny muscle ticked at his jaw. 'Where's the kid? What are you doing here?' he continued with a neutral expression before I could answer.

Was that a brief flash of panic? I frowned.

'No, what I meant was, why aren't you in the kitchen? Oh Jesus, that sounds really bad. I mean … Luce? What's wrong? Why are you sitting on the sofa, just … sitting there?'

His stuttering loss for words gave me a sliver of satisfaction.

I had caught him off-guard, having to back-pedal his unintended chauvinistic comment. That and the fact that he referred to our son as 'the kid'. It gave me the confidence to finally speak.

'Can you tell me who this belongs to?'

I hadn't intended on a sarcastic tone, but it satisfyingly covered my nervousness. Matt peered at the lipstick in my hand and shook his head, confused.

'What is it?' he asked.

'It's lipstick. Maybelline. Summer Plum.'

'And ...?'

'It's not my colour, but that's irrelevant. I don't even wear lipstick, Matt. I found it in the bathroom cabinet. Inside our bathroom cabinet. Just now.'

'I – I don't know. Maybe it's Mimi's. I don't know. Honestly, I've never seen it before. This feels like the Spanish Inquisition, Luce, get a grip.'

'And why would you change the sheets on the bed? I've only been away for a few days. And how come the house is so clean? You've never been so domesticated. What's been going on while we've been gone?'

I jabbed the lipstick in his direction like a tiny fencer's foil.

His jaw slackened. He suddenly looked defenceless, arms hanging at his sides, lost for words. I faltered, wanting desperately to hear another of his clever excuses, wanting the lipstick to belong to his mother, wanting to hear how much he loved me, wanting the make-up sex. But knowing a terrible truth lurked below the surface of his deceit.

'Lucie, I ...'

'Who is she, Matt? At least give me the satisfaction of knowing who I lost out to. This time.'

I waited, mouth flat, nostrils flaring to control the pooling of tears. The radiator ticked in the corner of the living room.

'Her name is Sylvie,' he said faintly.

His quiet voice was like a sharp knife to a poison cyst. I stood up abruptly, drew my arm back and threw the lipstick in his direction on the wave of a strangled roar.

'Hey!' he chirped, surprise masking the pain as the edge of the lipstick lid glanced off his brow.

And as though I had hit the button on one of JP's Transformer toys, he strode towards me. My anger now finally released, I was too full of adrenalin to yet feel fear, but I recognised the look in his eye.

'You cheating bastard!' I yelled, as we met in the middle of the room. I pummelled his chest with both my fists, the acknowledgement of his adultery a vitriolic catharsis.

'You bast …' My voice finally caught and I sucked in a ragged breath.

He grabbed my wrist, twisting my arm.

'Ow, ow, stop! You're hurting me!'

A drop of blood appeared on Matt's brow from the lipstick lid. 'You suffocating bitch,' he said, and twisted harder.

Fear flooded in on my anger, and I knew things were going to get a lot worse.

* * *

In that moment of silence after I fell, helplessly stuck in the frame of the table, I stared curiously at the antique coving around the light fixture and the edges of the high ceiling of our living room. I was still partially deaf in my right ear from Matt's brutal hit, but then sucked in my breath as a thumping crash vibrated across the floor. Something shoved against the table with an animalistic grunt, and the tinkle of a heavy object shifting onto the broken glass filtered to my limited hearing.

Then complete silence.

I blinked. The radiator ticked again in the corner.

As I tried to compute what had happened, a searing pain spread down from my hip. I pulled myself up, hand gripping the glassless table frame, and placed my feet carefully on the floor, shards crunching beneath my slippers.

I looked down where Matt lay. His body had turned during his fall.

No longer angry.

No longer anything.

His handsome grey-blue eyes stared at a point below my knees as if he had been looking past me to the offending radiator. I stepped around his body to allow him to focus. His eyes didn't move. The picture he had knocked off the wall was the Russian icon. It lay next to his ear as though he was listening to a hidden message. I registered the angle of his head, the corner of the iron table frame, darkened and shiny, and clasped my hand to my mouth.

Chapter 16

One year ago

Stooping briefly to look into Matt's soulless eyes, I picked up the icon that had fallen off the wall. It looked as though it was making him uncomfortable, nestled next to his temple. I backed away from him, still clutching the frame, fearful he would suddenly blink, shift his body, rise on an elbow, shake his head or curse. As I reversed all the way to the door, the significance of the scene spread like a bruise in my mind. The irony of him lying on my favourite rug where he had probably fucked that student Marlena all those months ago not lost on me. The tragedy of it, so quick.

Oh God, Matt, what happened?

My simmering anger was replaced by a raw sorrow, tinged with fear. Shock was the wedge holding the door open to loss.

My gaping mouth finally closed, jaw clenched, and tears coursed down my face. JP would be wondering when he would see Papa after a week's absence. He must not see him like this. And if Matt somehow regained consciousness, I would be in deep trouble. I'd felt his hand on me before. He would come after me. I had seen his intentions when he strode across the rug towards me.

That notion galvanised me. With barely a thought for the

consequences, I ran upstairs, threw the icon down on the bed and pulled some clean clothes out of my wardrobe and a few items from JP's drawers. I retrieved the passports and ID cards from the desk where I had flung them only hours before and added them to the pile on the bed. I could not stay here. I had to get JP out of here, out of the village.

I paused briefly, thinking I heard movement. I closed my eyes, recalled Matt's body lying on the floor, and sobbed. JP must not see his father ... like this. Hauling a backpack out of the cupboard, I stuffed everything in. I changed out of my torn jeans, grabbed a wad of tissues to shove against the deep cut on my hip and pulled on a clean pair.

I went back downstairs and crept past the living-room door, as though my footfalls would wake him from his sleep. My breathing quickened, and tears pricked at my eyes. Such passion gone sour. Such love torn. I began to shake as I reached the front door, and pressed my tears away with a thumb.

* * *

'Shay-Pee!' Anne shouted into her apartment, one hand on the door. 'Your mama's here! Time to go!'

Two pairs of feet clattered along the hallway, the friends chasing each other. Anne looked back at me, smiling. She turned away briefly to watch the two boys arrive. There was a delay as she registered my blotchy face, turned quickly back to me, smile gone.

'Are you okay? My God, Lucie, what's up?'

'Anne, something terrible has happened.' I sobbed. 'I – I can't tell you, you'll find out soon enough. I have to leave, I'm taking JP, but you mustn't know where.'

'But you only just got back! Luce, what do you mean something terrible? Has Matt been messing around while you've been gone?'

I checked myself. So she did know it too. I wondered how I

could have been so stupid. Any desire to dig for the truth was now masked by my fear. I didn't have time for twenty questions.

'Look, I can't explain, but I – please, I want you to know that what happened ... it wasn't my fault ... JP! Come on, sweetheart, we have to go!'

'Jesus, Lucie, what happened?' Anne asked again. 'You can't just go like this. Is there something I can do?'

My hip and leg had started to throb. I shook my head, and wiped the tears from my face with my sleeve. As JP appeared under Anne's arm, I grabbed his hand and turned to go. Anne stood there, mouth hanging open in shock, but I couldn't look back at her as we left.

I grabbed the pack from where I had left it leaning against the wall outside Anne's building, and glanced worriedly down the lane towards our house, before turning in the opposite direction.

'Mama! I want to go home, to the toys!'

Not to Papa. He hadn't asked yet. *Don't ask.*

'I know, but something has ... come up. We're actually still on holiday. And I know you've been such a good boy, but we have a little further to go.'

'Still on ... holiday? Okaay,' he said uncertainly, and short of dragging him, we hurried to the train station.

* * *

I looked across the table at JP, his face screwed into a vision of concentration. His lips moved slightly as his finger traced the giant letters across the speech bubbles of his comic book. Inventing his text. His eyes gritty, I knew he would be asleep by Lausanne. This had been a long day for him and we were back on the train.

'Mama, are we getting on the plane again?' Despite his fatigue, a hopeful excitement. 'Where's Papa? Will he meet us somewhere?'

I swallowed, mouth dry. No matter how indifferent Matt had become towards his son, he was still JP's father. JP wouldn't know how a father was supposed to react. His alpha male.

'No, honey, no planes, but this is a bit of an adventure. Papa … he has to work. We will be on trains and buses and this time even a boat. I'm not sure of the timetable just yet.'

The train rocked slightly and I looked away from his excited face, out of the window to the peaks of the receding Alps, biting my lips together to stop renewed tears. The geography of my undoing receded in the distance, jagged teeth of granite growing smaller with each passing kilometre. My stomach fluttered. I didn't really know where we were going, but could only think of putting as much distance between ourselves and Matt as possible.

'JP, sweetheart, can we change seats? I'd feel better facing forward. Would that be okay with you?'

I needed to be looking in the direction we were heading, to the welcoming levelled landscape of our future, to the direction of our freedom.

'Sure, Mama, here.' JP pushed the comic book and his Thomas the Tank Engine backpack over to my side of the table and we shuffled around each other to change seats.

'We're going to have such a fun holiday, sweetheart,' I said, gently squeezing his arm. He pulled his water bottle from his pack and took three loud sips, put it on the table and beamed at me.

'Love you, Mama,' he said, making my eyes sting.

'I love you more,' I replied in a wobbly sing-song voice.

'No, I love you more,' returned JP, and chirped a giggle before returning to his book, head bobbing with the movement of the train.

I concentrated on his reflection, a perfect twin image against the dark window as we passed a copse of trees. The train gathered speed as we left Lausanne, each minute bringing us closer to France, the rising hopefulness of our escape clouded sporadically with visions of the obstacles that might face us crossing the border. I felt the tight coil in my stomach unwinding as the scenery rushed past, and repetitively went over the plan again in my mind.

I had purchased round-trip tickets for rail and boat at the station, as yet unsure what my options were. When we boarded the train, I had no idea where we were heading, but as the movement gradually calmed my panic, I worked out a plan. We would get off the train at Geneva, head down to the water and catch the ferry heading back to Villeneuve on the eastern end of Lac Léman, back towards the Alps. But we would get off the boat at Yvoire, a stop on the French side of the lake. At this time of year, there would still be crowds of tourists clamouring to visit the walled medieval town. We would mingle with the people leaving the boat, our two faces easily forgotten. We could disappear inconspicuously into the Haute Savoie, travelling west into the depths of France, making our way across the country.

* * *

The train stopped at the town of Morges to let passengers alight. As predicted, JP had fallen asleep, and I finally let my tears flow unchecked, but the squealing of the brakes and stillness of the train woke him. As we sat in the station, the hiss and bump of doors closing and reopening to admit fresh travellers merely exacerbated my frustration of being on the stationary train. JP looked out of the window, and perked up.

'Look, Mama, there are two gendarmes. And they've got a doggie. He's so cute,' he said.

A cold chill clasped my throat. I turned to follow JP's curious gaze. Two policemen wearing bulletproof vests stood on the edge of the platform, backs to the train, one of them talking on his radio. A German shepherd sat patiently at their side.

'Doing a routine check, I guess,' I said unsteadily.

Panic threatened to engulf me. I looked at my watch. We'd only been gone a few hours. Surely the police wouldn't already have been alerted? But I was suddenly uncertain. Should we stay on the train? Would they get on the train to check? Maybe we should surreptitiously sneak off. But it didn't look like the policemen were going to get on. I had the feeling that my impulsive emotions might cause me to do something stupid.

As the train doors closed, the policemen walked slowly away down the platform. They nonchalantly checked people heading to the stairway. Were they looking for us? We'd be easy to spot, a mother and toddler. I withdrew from the window and leaned back in my seat, heart thumping. JP pressed his forehead against the glass, straining to follow their progress. I wanted to pull him back, but didn't want to alarm him, and the policemen were concentrating on the passengers, with their backs to us.

JP finally turned back in his seat, having lost sight of them, and reopened his comic. A high-pitched whistle announced the imminent departure of the train. The piercing noise caused the hairs on my arms to rise. Relief flooded through me. My heart continued to beat; I could see its movement fluttering the fabric of the T-shirt against my chest.

The train pulled slowly out of the station and I smiled at JP as we gathered speed westwards.

'What about Papa?' The inevitable question.

'I … Papa is … He has to work. A project. He still can't leave. I'm sorry.' I wanted to cry, and closed my eyes to prevent JP seeing them.

'Will I get to see Valentin tomorrow?'

'Perhaps the day after,' I lied.

The rocking of the train sent JP back into slumber. By the time we stopped at Nyon, I had controlled my tears, but panic set in as I looked at JP who had woken again, and took out a drawing book and his box of coloured pencils. I wanted to cram

208

everything back in his pack, thought there was too much para-phernalia to clear up and run if we needed to. But I didn't disturb him. He looked up briefly, his pencil raised to study the station platform, then went back to the puppy on his page. I tapped my foot with impatience. No police here. *Let's go!*

On our way again, no sooner had we reached top speed, the train began to decelerate once more. It was too soon for this to be the next and final stop of Geneva. We slowed, the squeal of brakes an intrusion into the normally clockwork timetable. We remained stationary for several minutes, the undercarriage ticking. Silence prevailed. My neck began to prickle with sweat as each minute passed. JP looked up.

'Mama, why have we stopped?' he asked, suddenly aware that no one was getting on or off the train, and that we weren't in a station.

'I'm not sure sweetheart, I ...' and the dong of the speaker preceded an announcement.

'*Mesdames et messieurs, nous vous prions de nous excuser ...*' The flurry of an apology followed by a message. In an unusual deviation from Swiss rail efficiency, an unscheduled freight train was hindering our journey. There would be a few minutes' delay. I breathed another sigh of relief, but as I reached for JP's water bottle to take a sip, my hand was shaking.

'I hope it won't take long,' I said quietly.

Why isn't the damn train moving? I looked at my watch, then out of the window, willing us to continue. The lake had come into view. There was France, lying temptingly across the water. *Come on, come on!* I didn't know how much time we had.

'It's okay, Mama. Remember you said we shouldn't worry about the tabletimer. This is part of the adventure, remember? Can I have one of those choccy biccies now, please?'

JP's cheesy grin made me smile and I took MC's Oreos from my pack. I tore off the outer wrapper, the paper trembling. I handed one to him, and put the torn wrapper in the bin under the table along with the bag and MC's note. A thought nagged me, before the door of the compartment slammed open, making us both jump.

Bile rose in my throat. But it was a middle-aged man in a trilby, his old-fashioned hat at odds with his Iron Maiden sweatshirt. Our eyes connected, and I slid my gaze back to the window as the train lurched forward. I smiled nervously across at JP.

'On our way again,' I said, with false jollity.

I stood up the moment I felt the train slow before Geneva station. I methodically helped JP pack his things, promising he could finish colouring in his puppy later. The delay meant we risked missing our boat. We would need to hurry.

It took me precious moments to focus on the signpost to the ferry outside the station. JP dropped his backpack and Thomas the Tank Engine's beaming face skittered away from us on the pavement. As I bent to retrieve it for him, the battering wings of a flock of pigeons made my heartbeat spike.

'Birdies!' JP shouted, and as I followed his pointing finger, my gaze fell on the CCTV camera at the entrance to the station.

'We need to hurry for the boat now, JP, we're a bit late,' I said abruptly.

'Mama!' JP protested as I pulled on his arm.

My own backpack suddenly weighed a ton, hindering a fast run. JP skipped along beside me, his pack clattering with pencils spilled from their box. The road sloped down to the lake. I could see water glinting between the buildings. We pushed past people and shoppers on the busy street, many of whom saw our plight and stepped out of the way. *Almost there!*

The boat came into sight as we reached the end of the street facing the lake.

'Mama! A fairy!' squealed JP with delight.

'Yes, honey, that's our boat, our ferry,' I said with relief.

A male body blocked our path onto the gangplank and my

first reaction was one of annoyance. *Get out of our way! We have to be on that boat!* My heart sank as I focused on a uniform that wasn't that of the ferry company.

'Madame Favre? Lucille Favre?'

My '*oui*' came out as a strained whisper.

'*Viens avec moi, jeune homme.* Come with me, young man.'

The cop looked at JP, then back at me. No! No! How could this be happening so quickly? He took him gently by the hand. Confusion and awe flashed across JP's face. 'You get to ride in a police car,' the cop told him.

I felt pressure on my arm, and turned to see another policeman, a disapproving look on his face. Patronising. I wanted to tell him it wasn't my fault. In the end I figured silence was the better option.

* * *

My emotions are in turmoil. I can't fathom exactly what I am feeling. The thing I can identify is that I feel kind of sick every time I think about what happened with Yasmine. I can't believe I showed so much vulnerability. I let myself become putty in her hands, and my guilt threatens to overwhelm me.

Guilt that I don't feel for Yasmine the same thing she feels for me.

Guilt that I have committed adultery to the memory of Matt.

Guilt that I jeopardised my life with JP by running from the scene of the crime.

Dagmar has listened carefully to my story, but our session already went over time. She's with someone else now. I think I need to see her again as soon as possible.

The one positive in my life at the moment is a renewed confidence that JP is still on my side, especially after talking to Anne on the phone today.

I've been imagining the horror stories that Mimi might be

telling JP about me. But I am still his mother, and he knows it. Hallelujah for today's proof.

'He drew a picture of you today, Lucie,' she told me. 'You and him, holding hands, each of you holding a suitcase in your other hand. I asked him to tell me about the picture, and he said: "Mama and I are planning a big adventure together. I'm waiting for her to come home." It was so cute, Lucie. He's like a faithful puppy, expecting you back any moment.'

Anne's voice broke as she said this, and my throat constricted. But I subsequently sighed with joyous relief. He hasn't forgotten me. That's always my biggest worry.

I had asked Anne to do some detective work for me, to casually ask JP one day what Mimi had told him about his father.

'Lucie, you cannot believe it, and I could not hide my shock. I even think Valentin was a little alarmed. He said: "Mimi says Mama did something terrible to Papa. He died." Just like that, "He died". But without emotion. He went on rolling play dough balls and said: "He was so shouty sometimes with Mama. It made her sad. I don't know why they've both gone." He picked up the drawing and then looked at me and said: "Is Mama dead too?" It was horrible. I was shocked. I told him: "Of course not, chérie. She's only gone away for a while." God, I had to leave the room to avoid JP thinking that all this wasn't absolutely normal. He doesn't seem to miss his father, but I know he misses you. I know he does.'

I'm horrified that Mimi came out with it. But JP, my shining light, at 6 years old, could not fathom the emotion. When Billy his hamster died, the stories I created for him about Billy's better life practically had JP wanting to experience heaven himself.

'Has Pittet been back to visit you?' Anne interrupts my thoughts. 'I went to see him, you know. I wanted to rewrite your character reference. I am not sure it was strong enough the first time. If he can get you an appeal, you will need all the help you can get.'

'I'm so grateful to you, Anne. But I'm afraid my appeal has been denied.'

'*Mon Dieu.* I didn't know. What will you do now? You know you can count on me to help you any way I can.'

'There's something odd about the trial, and I'm trying to get to the bottom of it. I may need you to be an intermediary for some correspondence.'

'Of course, Lucie, you know I'll help.'

'I don't know what I would do without you, Anne. I don't know what JP would do without you and Valentin. Thank you. Thank you for being a friend.'

My voice finally breaks and I let out a sob.

Chapter 17

A new girl has moved into the cell next to me, empty since Fatima was shifted to the mother–child floor. This new woman is about my age, and holds her head up proud. But she exhibits high manners and education rather than obstinate snobbery or hierarchal toughness. I wonder how long that will last in here.

I smile as she passes down the corridor, carrying a pile of towels as though she is about to offer a precious gift to a pharaoh.

We meet later in the day in the shower block. I feel sheepish striking up a conversation in the humiliation of the communal space where private ablutions take place. And to be able to do so, I have to make sure Yasmine is not here. I feel as though this person needs to be offered the deference of royalty, polite silence rather than prying curiosity.

'Hi,' I say. 'My name is Lucie.' I smile, don't ask her whether she speaks English, I am so sure she does, and it has been a long time since I've been able to hold a real conversation in my mother tongue.

'I am Zeinah. You are English? What on earth are you doing here?' she asks incredulously.

Her English is impeccable. I knew it. But now she's asking that one question that will probably trigger her mute button.

People don't tend to talk to me very much once they learn what on earth I am doing here.

'I am – was – married to a Swiss. Although I don't hold a passport, I'm a resident, but they don't know how to classify me. I have to serve my sentence here.'

'But you are a foreigner nonetheless. And you are serving a sentence for something that might involve extradition? You do not look like a terrorist,' she says.

I'm taken aback. A terrorist? How about a murderess? I'm relieved that this woman doesn't see me as a hardened criminal.

'Neither do you!' I laugh.

She has smooth olive skin, shoulder-length dark hair falling stylishly into wavy curls as if she has stepped from a salon, and her eyes tell me she is no ordinary criminal. They are a striking pale green, registering intelligence and pride, but not arrogance. They make me want to engage with her. She has something no one else has in here. It's sophistication.

'Well, that is a big shame,' she says, 'because that is precisely what I am trying to portray.'

A small frown creases her perfectly plucked brow. I wonder how long it will be before she lets herself go, forsaking the crispness of her presentation. Trying to portray?

'I cannot go home to Damascus,' she continues. 'I will be arrested and made to disappear instantly on arrival. Although I am a dedicated academic, I have been labelled a political usurper, a danger to the future of my country, like the rest of my family.' Her voice catches. 'I have to hope that I can remain in this place for as long as possible. Extradition is my death sentence.' As she says this she looks around at the blue-grey walls of the shower block and finally stares at her face in the warped fake glass of the mirror above the sink. 'Here, I am safe.'

I learn more about Zeinah in a few short days than I have about any other inmate over a period of months. It's not the first time I've heard someone embrace their residency in Hindelbank.

Dolores always said she could earn more money here than back in the Dominican Republic, and that's certainly the case for the Latina women who are in here for trafficking from the Colombian ghettos.

'Do you have any advice for new guests?' Zeinah asks, smiling.

I roll off a few tips. 'Avoid any meat in the cafeteria that you can't identify. Don't be alarmed if you hear Fatima wailing when they take away her baby. Don't trade with the Latinas, no matter how much they beg you. Try to get a job you think you will enjoy, if you're given a choice.'

We are standing next to each other at the sink, and I almost feel like we're discussing something in the cloakroom of a posh restaurant. I imagine Zeinah reaching into her handbag to extract mascara, pat some powder onto the perfect skin of her face, fix a diamond earring dripping from her ear.

'Well, there are certainly a few considerations for a start. It's nice to talk to someone in a language I understand. I don't speak German and the guards don't speak any French or Italian.'

Oh, so she speaks French and Italian too.

'Actually, I suspect the guards do speak French, but they choose not to,' I say. 'This country is a bit of an enigma in that respect. The north seems to despise the south, and vice versa, but they keep alarmingly quiet about it.'

'That sounds like Syria. North and South. Although there's nothing invisible about the hate and loathing that has manifested itself among my people,' Zeinah says sadly. 'It is far from a democracy.'

We've been in the shower room for too long. The Polish girl comes in, then a Colombian woman. I wonder where Yasmine is, and I break the conversation with Zeinah to avoid speculative gossip.

She sits next to me later that day in the cafeteria and I enjoy her attention until Yasmine arrives. Zeinah looks from me to Yasmine, a little confused at my sudden fickleness. But she's wise enough to remain silent. I save my questions until later, knowing that Zeinah is in the cell next to mine, and it will be fairly easy for me to engage with her. I feel like I need to say something about Yasmine, if only to warn about the potential danger of jealousy.

* * *

'You'll have to excuse Yasmine's attitude towards me,' I say later. 'I'm not sure how to distance myself without creating animosity. It's a delicate thread.'

Zeinah nods, and I'm sure she wants to ask something else, but I continue before she can speak. 'How come you're here? In Switzerland?' I ask.

'It is a long story. My father was one of the architects of socialist reforms that encouraged investment in our country at the beginning of the millennium. But his politics backfired when living costs began to rise alarmingly and the employment situation in my country was too slow to improve.'

We're in Zeinah's cell. It is still bare. She has no trinkets or photos. She's folding clothes she has brought back from the laundry. I find it ironic that she's wearing a scarf around her hair, when in the corridors of the prison she chooses to bare her head.

'The great drought that has lasted for years in the northeast of my country has not helped to improve the economic mood. And with Assad's government controlling all the media in Syria ...'

'I always wanted to visit Syria,' I mused. 'I hear Damascus is a beautiful city.'

'Was a beautiful city. Assad's regime has instilled such a state of fear into the people. My country no longer has beautiful cities. They are all made ugly by their personalities, and many of them have been destroyed.'

217

'How did you end up here?'

'Assad sent spies from his secret service, the *mukhabarat*, into every area of society. My family funded my travel to Switzerland, but his secret network extends far beyond the borders of my country. I had to get arrested to give myself more time, to avoid being sent back, where I would be made to disappear.'

'But how come you couldn't ask for political asylum? There are plenty of asylum seekers arriving every day. There's an integration centre in the village where I live – used to live.'

'It was a question of time. The asylum application was going to take too long. I'm talking hours. This was the quickest solution. Although I have to say, it's not that easy to get yourself arrested when your heart's not really in it,' she says, and I smile with the irony.

'What did you study? Does it play a big part of the witch hunt?'

'Most definitely. I am a lawyer.'

* * *

Ten months ago

'Why did you run? It doesn't look good from our perspective, you must understand. There was no attempt to resuscitate your husband.'

A police detective sat across the table from me in an interview room at the Aigle gendarmerie. They had brought me back here from Geneva, to the jurisdiction of the Vaudois cantonal police and closest administrative centre to the village. I had spent most of the journey in the back of the police car in a state of shock after one of the policemen confirmed Matt's death. At the station, I realised we were sitting within walking distance of the château where Matt and I married.

I had no idea where they had taken JP. I spent most of the night awake in a small holding cell, asking constantly where they

218

had taken my son, if he was okay, to please treat him gently. Nobody would speak to me, except a gravelly male voice in the cell next to me who at 1:00 a.m. yelled, 'Ça suffit! Silence, de Dieu!' I finally fell asleep at about 4:00 a.m., exhausted with tears and worry, and pondering the very question the policeman was now asking me.

'I don't know what I was thinking. Mathieu, my husband, was angry. I felt threatened. I wanted to protect JP from his ... his rage. I don't know where I was going, maybe to see my parents in England. I had to get away from the violence and anger. Look, it was an accident. I didn't know he was dead. I thought he would come after me again. He acted as though he was going to hurt me, and who knows what he could have done to JP. He never ...'

I suppressed a sob, and rubbed my arm absently, a barely visible red mark and a faint bruise the insubstantial proof of my statement.

After a night of reflection, my biggest worry was that everybody involved in an investigation would be guided, or I should say manipulated, by the so-called sage advice of my mother-in-law. I could think of nothing that would satisfy her more than finding me guilty of a heinous crime. She had, after all, just lost her beloved son.

Detective Genillard told me it was Natasha who came to the house and found Matt. I thought it might have been MC, as her note said she would see me later, but I didn't say anything to the police. Natasha dropped by to leave a couple of books for Matt only minutes after we had left, and had hoped to see JP after our week away. I was fully aware that finding Matt must have been horrible for her. Mothers need someone to blame in the event their children are hurt. In her anger, Natasha had probably not hesitated to plant the seed of menace into the minds of the detectives, perhaps even a judge.

She had immediately alerted the police, pointed the finger at me even in my absence. As I hadn't taken the car, the first place they checked was the funicular station, and the man at the counter instantly remembered me buying a ticket for the train and the boat. It was hardly rocket science to put officers on guard at the main stations. They hadn't managed to reach the Geneva terminal, but another team had already been sent to the ferry jetty on the lake. A suspected murder was sure to get things moving in this country.

'How is my son? Why am I not allowed to see him?'

'We need to ascertain a few things first, Madame Favre. We are not sure of your motives in taking him away.'

'My husband's violence was … unpredictable. Are you seriously suggesting I was abducting my own son with sinister intentions?'

He ignored my question. 'Can you explain the significance of this item in your backpack?'

I was genuinely confused. The icon I had thrown down on the bed had somehow made its way into the pack. I hadn't realised it was there. The detective noted the confusion on my face.

'I … I don't know. I hadn't intended to put it in there. It's a cheap copy of some Russian art. It's nothing. A wedding present to Matt and I.' My voice broke as I mentioned Matt's name. 'There was no malicious intention with my son, I can assure you. He is the most precious thing in my life. I merely wanted to protect him from the horrors that would ensue, after the … incident. That's why I … we ran.'

I was babbling to the French-speaking detective. I could be sure that half my conversation would be misinterpreted, especially if Natasha had anything to do with it. I could hardly carry on living in the same village as the woman who believed I had killed her son. I couldn't tell Genillard that deep down, I was sure that's why we were running away. It would make me look guilty.

'Who is looking after him – JP – Jean-Philippe? Who is looking

220

after my son? Is he okay? Has someone explained to him what happened? Because … Please be careful, don't be cruel, he didn't see Matt, his father, he doesn't know …' My throat closed.

I thought I didn't have any more tears, but I had to stop speaking to avoid a sob. I lowered my head.

'Madame Favre, there is an investigating team at your home right now. We need to let them verify the circumstances of your husband's death before I can consider giving you any kind of … *privilège*, like seeing your son. He is in good hands.'

'Whose hands? Surely I have a right to know who is looking after him? Where is he, Monsieur Genillard. Where is my son?'

'He is with people who know and love him. His grandparents are looking after him, as the next of kin.'

'I am his next of kin!' I shouted. 'I should choose who looks after him. His godmother—'

'I'm sorry,' he interrupted. 'You are currently not in a position to make that decision. And your son's grandparents are also your husband's next of kin.'

Detective Genillard looked awkward. He seemed momentarily confused. I suspected this was his first case dealing with a death other than sudden illness, suicide or a car accident.

'Monsieur Genillard, I want you to note the most important thing on your record. I did not kill my husband.'

A sharp knock, and the door opened. A smartly dressed young man entered. He looked at me, briefly flattened his tie against his chest with his hand, and nodded to the policeman. I shifted in my chair. A cold drop of perspiration ran down the groove next to my spine. He wasn't wearing uniform, and didn't exude much authority.

'Madame Favre, you will be allowed twenty minutes with Monsieur Pittet.'

I shrugged, shook my head. I had no idea who this person was.

'He is the gentleman who has been appointed your lawyer by

the court, as you have stated that you do not have a preference for legal representation.'

'Shouldn't I have spoken to you before I was interviewed by this detective?' I asked Monsieur Pittet, ignorant of the procedures involved. It was the protocol I remembered from the movies.

'I'm sorry, Madame Favre, I would have been here sooner, but I had some documents to drop off at the Parliamentary offices in Lausanne this morning. There was some confusion – I thought you were detained at the cantonal police headquarters in Lausanne, which would be normal procedure for a ... homicide.' Monsieur Pittet glared at the police detective.

I felt a moment of alarm. Procedure had taken an abnormal route? I hoped I hadn't said anything that would go against my case. There was no knowing the lengths someone might go to to jeopardise my innocence.

The detective left, and a young rookie who looked barely out of his teens slipped in to stand by the door. Monsieur Pittet pulled out the chair and sat opposite me.

'We do not have much time. Again, I am sorry. You should tell me as much as you can.'

He took out a notepad and clicked the voice notes app on his smartphone.

'This is all a terrible mistake,' I said. 'I know it looks bad, the running away. And they will find my fingerprints everywhere, on that vase. It's my home too.'

'Madame Favre, I need to know from you exactly what happened. I do not have the police report as it will only be filed once forensics and the investigation at your home has been completed. Please, you must tell me everything. Later we can talk about procedures.'

I sighed, looked at the clock on the wall, and recounted the details as best I could from the moment I entered the house with JP on our return from the airport. It felt like days ago, not hours. The memories still raw, my anger rose as I recalled the realisation of Matt's betrayal, and then genuine bewilderment that he could no longer defend himself. Emotions raging a war of attrition in my mind. As I hurriedly finished my account, I asked again about JP.

'I will enquire after your son, Madame Favre, but I must ask you a few things first ...'

'Please ... Please don't call me that. My name is Lucie.'

Monsieur Pittet raised his eyebrows and I immediately regretted the comment. It looked bad, as though I had always hated the name.

'I'm not my husband's mother,' I tried to qualify, not sure how it would be interpreted by the lawyer. I waved my hand dismissively, didn't have the energy to embellish.

'Madame – Lucie – do you think this is the first time that your husband was *infidèle*, unfaithful?'

I looked carefully at Pittet. His suit hung comfortably on his slim frame. His dark hair, a little longer than the Swiss norm, shone under the fluorescent lighting. His glasses, rather than giving him an air of legal wisdom, made him look like a rakish James Bond type.

'Monsieur Pittet, I have lived for many years blindly ignoring certain things my husband did. All for the sake of providing a stable family environment for my son. I realise now that was a stupid philosophy. There's only so much a woman can take. I know it wasn't the first time.' My voice caught at this point, remembering Matt wasn't here to defend himself. Suddenly alarmed that I may have sounded like a scorned wife seeking revenge, I added pathetically: 'I did not murder my husband.'

The door opened and Genillard entered and spoke directly to the lawyer. It hit me. I was now a murder suspect. Any respect I had ever been afforded by strangers had disintegrated. It felt like a cold flannel on my face.

'I think you will be detained here one more night,' said the lawyer, turning to face me again. 'I will interview you again

223

tomorrow. By then we should have a police report to – to quantify your story.'

'It's not a story,' I whispered. 'It's the truth … Please, Monsieur Pittet, I am worried about my son. I believe that his grandmother, Madame Favre – senior – will do anything in her power to prevent me regaining custody. He is all I have left, but I also think she believes he is all she has left too. Please.'

Pittet shook my hand as he left, a parting phrase stuck on his tongue as he wasn't sure what to call me.

The police officer accompanied me back to my cell and I sat on the edge of the thin mattress covering the concrete bed, my mind spinning. I assumed I would be able to make a phone call, but was unsure who to contact. It would be pointless to try my parents. They would be clueless what to do from the UK. I would have called Patterson, but he was dead. My only other ally was Anne, but really, what could she do? I purposely hadn't told her a thing to avoid her being implicated. The realisation began to sink in. The circumstances made me look terribly guilty. What had I done? Running away was a dreadful mistake. I put my head in my hands.

What irked me most is that Natasha knew I was a good mother. She could always see that JP was being raised correctly, always said his pleases and thank yous, ate with his mouth closed, greeted strangers with a polite '*Bonjour*'. She could not see, however, how her son had behaved so deceitfully, who he had become. Didier had a suspicion, but was too weak to stand up to his wife.

I wondered if Matt had inherited his pathological lying from his mother. Regardless, I was sure I was about to see how powerfully that tool could be wielded.

* * *

'Everyone will tell you they are innocent, so I'll leave it to you to decide.'

Zeinah and I are walking in the castle grounds. It's exercise time and I try to imagine we're strolling through some stately home grounds in a free world.

'From what I understand, and I am no criminal lawyer, I would say that even if it is deemed you killed your husband with an object, with this vase you mentioned, and that even if it cannot be proved that you acted in self-defence, you were surely committing a crime of passion after years of abuse.' Our feet crunch on the gravel path. 'How long is your sentence?'

'Ten years. First-degree murder would have been life.'

'Even so, I do not believe you will be in here for very long, but I think your priority is to get your lawyer to first find enough evidence to have a retrial, to make an appeal. It obviously wasn't enough the first time. You also need to examine all the levels of prosecution and take the one that offers you the quickest release, which may involve you resubmitting a plea of guilty to one or more of the charges. I'm sorry if it sounds brutal, but what is more important – clearing your name completely, or getting out of here as soon as possible?'

Zeinah wrings her hands as she says this. Her own plans must be fraught with challenges. Switzerland would surely not grant political asylum to someone with a criminal record.

* * *

Later, I am sitting at my desk when I sense someone's presence and look up with a frown to see Monika standing in my doorway. Her greasy hair is pulled back into a tight ponytail, making her eyes slant, almond-like. The smell of fresh tobacco smoke wafts in.

'*Was isch los?* What's up? Why the anger? Someone got out of bed on the wrong side today,' she says.

I've been making notes, and I am stumped by Natasha's vindictiveness while I'm working out how to reunite myself with JP. I'm suddenly aware that my exhalations have been accompanied by a soft growl in the back of my throat.

'It's that damn mother-in-law of mine.'

'Not the *Schwiegemutter*, but the *Schwierigemutter*. How do you say in English? That pain-in-the-arse?' She laughs.

'I have the recipe for a little potion you should be feeding that woman,' she continues. 'I saved some for my husband's lover, if I would have got away with it, of course. Maybe when I get out of here in all those years' time, I will still have enough anger to use it on her too.'

I wonder if she expects me to laugh. I'm not getting her dark humour.

'How will you find her then? Surely she will make sure you never know where she is.'

'Oh I don't think that will be too difficult. She is my sister.'

The cynical laugh dies on my lips, replaced by a look of disbelief. Monika's story is like nothing I've heard before – her husband cheated on her with her sister. I wonder vaguely if her story is true. Perhaps she has made it up to try and place herself on that hierarchal scale of people who should not be messed with.

Monika walks slowly into my cell and studies JP's pictures next to mine on the wall. I lean back in my chair, watching her with renewed curiosity and not a little wariness.

'Did you truly believe you would get away with murdering your husband?' I ask. 'It's very rare that murderers don't get caught in the end.'

Monika shrugs.

'I did a little research. Obviously not enough, but yes, I could have got away with it. If it had not been for his family's curiosity and surprise, the police would never have suspected me. The poison might have been something his body absorbed through his work, or something he ingested at the cafeteria, in a restaurant, on a train. But never the wife. Murder is not usual police business here. They are not familiar with it. They prefer prosecuting people who don't pay their taxes. Now that's something you can never get away with.'

Monika wanders back to the door, chirps a clipped '*Tchuess!*' and disappears down the hallway.

I turn back to my desk, and stare at the doodles on my sheet of paper, tapping my pencil thoughtfully.

Chapter 18

'You must open the package,' says the office administrator.

'It's just a letter. Look no drugs, no weapons,' I say, holding the envelope in front of her eyes and squeezing it. She wants to make sure there are no contraband items. I hope I haven't crushed any precious photos in my belligerent manipulation of the package.

I never get packages, but I have nothing to hide. It's the principle of it. They can't trust anyone. I sigh, and tear open the top of the envelope and pull out a letter and a folded newspaper. I spread everything out on her desk for inspection. She waves me away with my wad of papers.

I start reading Anne's letter before I reach my block, the crunch of my feet on the gravel path slowing with each step. My head begins to buzz. It's like I have opened a puzzle box, and I have to sit down, hoping to link the clues together before I reach my cell.

I may have a lot more to be thankful for than Patterson's paternal whims.

The letter explains that Anne ran into Patterson's wife Jennifer at the supermarket a few days ago. Mrs Patterson asked after me, and wondered whether I still managed to find the time to paint. Anne didn't tell her where I was. Mrs Patterson had not heard the village gossip, probably too consumed with her own grief. She told Anne she had almost finished clearing out her husband's studio office at home in preparation for her departure to England. She intended to return there to be closer to their two children, and to enjoy the years as a grandmother to their offspring.

She mentioned that while clearing Patterson's desk, she found a publication open to a page with 'Must show Lucie' written on it. Did Anne know my whereabouts? She would like to be able to let me have it, in case it meant anything to me. Anne casually told her that she would be seeing me over the next couple of weeks but that I wasn't currently in the village – she could pass it on to me if Mrs Patterson would like.

I carefully unfold the paper. It's a past issue of the *Antiques Trade Gazette*, almost eighteen months old. I guess Patterson was a regular subscriber. His red pen has arrowed an article with a photo of an icon held in white-gloved hands by some unseen custodian wearing a dress shirt and cufflinks. The title reads '16th-Century Orthodox icons on the auction block'.

The article announces the upcoming auction of a set of four icons at Sotheby's the following month. The date is now well in the past. I'm amazed that Sotheby's has a department devoted entirely to Russian art and artefacts. It doesn't give any details as to the origin of the icons, but their authenticity has been confirmed by 'experts' at the Hermitage Museum in St Petersburg. The event was an evening auction requiring entrance tickets, indicating the objects would fetch an extremely large price, in the millions. The seller is not named, discretion being essential in such transactions.

Initially unsure why Patterson wanted to show this to me, I continue my journey to the block and my cell. Possibilities are now creeping like spider fractures across my consciousness. I remember showing him the icon Natasha and Didier had given to us for our wedding present. We had joked how tacky it was, and that the gift was bordering on an insult.

I wonder if Patterson had intended to expand this joke, or whether he had changed his tune about the origins of the Favre icon. I sorely wish I could consult him now. I haven't a clue who to ask. I have so few allies and certainly none of them are art experts.

I go to the shelf where my clothes are stacked, and rummage through a pile of sweatshirts. At the bottom is the icon. It was returned to me with the items in the pack I had the day JP and I were stopped in Geneva. The backpack is next to my bed. JP's clothes are still in it, and from time to time I take them out and bury my face in his sweater and T-shirts. I imagine I can smell him, but in reality I can only smell the laundry detergent we use at home, and even that has now faded to the musty smell of cotton cloth stuffed inside a canvas bag.

I place the icon on my desk, next to Patterson's publication. Realisation is beginning to dawn. But locked up here with no access to art libraries, I'm missing the ease of picking up a telephone and making casual enquiries. Each task takes so long to administer by letter, and sometimes days are added to the end of the chain for incoming mail to be censored. And now that Patterson has gone, I have no idea who I should contact to ask the questions starting to form in my mind.

* * *

Yellow Post-it Notes cover the wall above my desk like roof shingles. I managed to get a half-used pad of them from the same lady who gives out the mail in the admin block. I swapped them for a sketch I did of her cat.

It's the start of my mind map. The top note reads: 'Russian icons'. At the bottom, above the desk is a picture of JP and a note with 'Freedom' written on it and a fat love heart. It's quite the cliché, but it keeps me positive. In between are a series of Post-its with names, some with question marks and some with contact addresses.

My first task is to write a letter to Jennifer Patterson. I know her husband had a colleague in the lakeside town of Vevey, whom he regularly visited to share the latest fine arts news over a glass of chilled chasselas and companionable sessions of pipe smoking. The ideas and information he brought back from this colleague were used to create field outings and excursions to museums for his classes. It's at times like this I wish I'd paid more attention to the small details. I don't know this gentleman's name, and my fifteen minutes' access on the computer downstairs renders no results. I only know he is an evaluator, specialising in antique art.

I'm unsure whether Jennifer Patterson will be kind enough to impart a contact from her husband's address book if she knows I'm currently sitting in jail. People react to that information with more disgust than an infectious disease. I finish my letter to her and start another to Anne, emphasising the urgency in sending Mrs Patterson's reply on. The return address I use is care of Anne. I hope Jennifer Patterson assumes I'm staying with her. This way, I should be assured of getting a reply.

When I've finished the letter, I tuck the icon back under my clothes on the shelf. Every time I look at it, I'm reminded of Natasha, so it's best to keep it out of sight.

The process will be agonisingly slow, but I guess I should be happy to focus on something other than my incarceration. I'm still straining to see any light at the end of the tunnel.

* * *

Ten months ago
It wasn't until we drove from the police station in Aigle to the East Vaudois courts of law in Vevey where I was to be detained

until trial, that I realised I was saying goodbye to my freedom. Pittet sat next to me in the back of the police car. There was so much I wanted to ask him, but I sat in silence, letting him attempt to justify the reasons for my detention.

'I'm sorry, Frau F – Smithers – Lucie. With a report of accidental death, you would not normally be detained until trial. I am not sure why the police investigation is so certain of your guilt. They have decided you must remain in custody until the trial. It is because you tried to leave the country. I'm sorry.'

His tone was more one of embarrassment than pity. I was to be detained for 'security'. They couldn't risk me disappearing again. I wasn't to be trusted. In their eyes I was already guilty, not innocent until proven so. My biggest mistake had been to run away with JP. This was the one thing I constantly mulled over, biting my lip until I tasted iron.

I was fortunate to be sitting on the left-hand side of the car, and attempted to calm my raging emotions by staring across the waters of the lake, focusing on a small sailing yacht heeling in a stiff breeze. My time on sailboats seemed so long ago. I couldn't believe this was happening to me.

* * *

My trial took place after six weeks' incarceration in the cold impersonal cells below the tribunal building in Vevey. They were the most depressing weeks of my life, my sadness compounded by the loneliness. Even the realisation that my husband had been constantly cheating on me didn't compare to those empty days. My mother came to visit once. Her helplessness through poor language skills and lack of knowledge of court procedures was distressing, and the unspoken disappointment of my father lay thickly between us in the stale air.

During that time, they brought JP to see me only once, despite being allowed more visits. Through Pittet, the court administrator finally intervened on my behalf and insisted I should see my son. I'm not even sure whether it was Natasha or Didier who brought him. A female police officer accompanied JP to the visitors' room from the unseen entrance of the tribunal building.

Until the moment my case was heard, my only knowledge of a court hearing was the stuff of Hollywood films and British TV series. I wasn't sure what to expect – a great high-ceilinged oak-panelled room with benches like church pews and a judge sitting high on a dais wielding a gavel perhaps. No, it was more like a conference facility you might find in any company, with panelled blinds covering the windows diffusing the room with a little natural illumination in addition to the harsh tube lighting. The room contained regular tables and chairs, a couple of computer screens and some recording equipment. Simple, sterile. And aside from a few murmurs from the back of the room, quiet. Suffocatingly quiet.

The first people I saw as I entered the courtroom were Natasha and Didier sitting behind the prosecutor, whose head was bent over a sheaf of papers. Natasha's eyes narrowed to razors as she saw me. So much hate. It felt like a bad dream. I still couldn't believe I was on trial for killing my husband. Five judges sat patiently waiting for me, backs to the window. They looked at me sternly as I slipped into my seat. I felt like they had already made a decision. So many negative vibes flew at me. It didn't look good.

Glancing at Natasha's face, I panicked, almost sure of my fate before the words were dealt. I sat next to Pittet on the other side of the courtroom, feeling more helpless than ever. At the back sat a few members of the press. It had been a while since the canton had seen a murder case. They whispered, coughed and shifted in their seats, breaking the silence as I sat down. I looked briefly for Anne among the small crowd, but couldn't find her, and chose to study the hands in my lap rather than look around, despite my curiosity.

The trial went by in a blur. The prosecutor droned on in a nasal, slightly *paysan* accent. As he spoke, although my knowledge of judiciary vocabulary was limited, it became apparent that the prosecuting team, which included the repugnant Genillard, had completely ignored any pleas on my part of abuse and insubordination during my marriage to Matt.

Our main hope, the medical report about the bruising on my arms, was dismissed as insubstantial. The witness report from Anne about my years of mental abuse and Matt's adulterous behaviour was also dismissed. She hardly knew Matt. I couldn't expect her to lie, so she was unable to give specific details in the police report. Of the foreign students Pittet was able to track down, they all refused to denounce Matt and would not make a statement in my favour. Beyond the grave, he still had his fan club. And although many of our colleagues must have been aware of his infidelity, when asked to testify, they didn't want to become involved in what might turn out to be a lengthy murder trial. It was all too messy.

And then an ambiguous note that had been found in the rubbish bin in our office, a half-finished message to Anne explaining I couldn't meet them at the park one afternoon because I needed to 'do something about Matt.'

I remembered it was one of the times I almost had the courage to ask him about his infidelity, but when he didn't come home when expected, I scrunched up the note and went to meet Anne at the park anyway. Genillard kept banging away about how this proved I had a premeditated plan.

Not once was my claim to have acted in self-defence recognised. Even the torn jeans with my blood on them from the coffee table were dismissed. They were happy to admit that my fall had been accidental, but not Matt's. Much was made of the fight scene. A flip chart was produced, with angles and trajectories drawn in different coloured pen. The pretty Provençal vase became a weapon of horror, transforming itself from a stage prop to a samurai sword. When Genillard was asked to describe Matt's body at the scene, I finally began to quietly sob, and could not stop. Léon Pittet handed me a tissue. I wanted to howl out loud but suppressed the urge. My eyes bulged hotly and my head pounded with the containment of grief.

The case was tainted with Matt's blood on the vase, the lack of signs of violence against me, the Favres' statement of our idyllic and blissful marriage, the misconstrued note they found in my bin, the precise time of death, and of course, my attempt to escape the country with my son.

Because we thought my case would be cleared, Pittet hadn't even investigated the possibility that someone else could have been on the scene after I left the house, emphasising his lack of experience in researching all avenues. Pittet became more and more flustered, pointing to documents in evidence, hardly believing that my story had transposed into such a dark tale before our very eyes. It sounded so weak to me, riding on the back of an already twisted prosecution. I felt myself walking to the gallows, and all the while Natasha sat there with an unreadable expression on her face. She had lost a son, had buried him weeks ago without allowing his wife to mourn. She could not accept that I was upset too. I had lost a husband I still desperately loved. I wanted to scream at her that I never wished him dead. I only wished him loyal.

* * *

I'm still puzzling over the Russian icon in my mind when a guard casually informs me I'll be receiving a visitor after work. They haven't told me who it will be. Normally I'd be told at least a week in advance, and Anne usually confirms it in a letter, even if it's a couple of days beforehand. But it must be her. Then I realise with sadness, even if it's Anne, she can't have brought JP. I mustn't get ahead of myself. I know Natasha will stick to her guns. I can't see her relenting.

It won't be Pittet again, because he always calls the administration first, to organise the best visitor room, given that he has more freedom to see me.

My excitement ebbs and flows on an emotional tide. I feel I haven't had much time to prepare myself for this next visit, whoever it may be. It's like Christmas has come a little early, but I'm missing the days of preceding excitement, something to look forward to. I usually set up a list of questions, monotonous snippets of information that Anne must be sick of dishing out to JP.

I can't concentrate on work. I'm not alone in the atelier today. A Russian inmate called Vasilisa has been using the studio for a couple of weeks. I don't know her very well. She's housed in one of the other blocks. She's painted some wooden cups she made in the workshop, to sell at the Schlossmärit next week.

Vasilisa huffs quietly as my paintbrush clatters to the counter and I begin to pace. I can feel her irritation. I know she'd like to yell at me to stop fidgeting. So I turn my attention to a series of painted cups drying on the bench, and nod appreciatively.

'They look impressive now they're all together,' I say as I turn two cups in each hand.

They're painted with cows, chalets, pine trees and mountains.

'They remind me of Russian dolls painted for the tourists,' I continue.

Vasilisa laughs.

'I wanted to make set of matryoshka dolls like that,' she says. 'But they said to create something more … Swiss. I tried to make set of pine trees that fit inside each other, but was too difficult. Swiss cups, for Swiss market. This market will not be Ploshchad Ostrovskogo.' She answers my frown. 'Ostrovskogo Square where St Petersburg Christmas market takes place every year.'

At the mention of St Petersburg, my lips press together.

'My mother-in-law has many sets of dolls all over her house, along with little egg-cups that are too small even for Swiss eggs, and a load of icons we thought were tacky art,' I say, and boldly continue. 'In reality they are probably worth a fortune. She hangs them next to the cheap tourist art.'

I can't believe I've blurted this, voicing my theory to an almost complete stranger. It must be the festive atmosphere loosening my tongue. I don't know what Vasilisa's in for. Maybe I'm half hoping she will send round the heavies to steal the icons off Natasha's walls.

'Mother-in-law has icons, eh? Of course they must be displayed. My family says bad luck to hide religious art. God cannot keep his eye on you from locked cupboard or bank vault. My mother very relieved after communism. She openly pray again. She take this routine from my grandmother, who had one icon, but keep it hidden. Icon small enough to hide from communists.'

'But the fact that they might be worth so much money, and are hanging with all her other worthless art. That I don't understand. I wonder if they're even insured,' I muse.

'Probably not. You cannot put a price on icons. She Russian? If anyone try to steal them, Russians have other ways to insure their things. We proud people. Stick to our own. We have ways of getting back stolen goods. Do not underestimate the pride of Russian people.'

Her tone is sinister and I clam up. I've already said too much. I'm blabbing because I can't concentrate, knowing visitors' hour is approaching.

What if ... what if I get to see JP? What if Anne has brought him? I put my hands together in silent prayer, and I recall an image of my son.

'Mama, you know Valentin is named for my birthday? We will be best friends forever!' He once told me about Anne's son. I would love to see JP's little face today. But I must stop. I don't allow the flame of excitement to take over.

I've made that mistake before.

* * *

237

When I walk into the visitors' room, MC is sitting there, and I cannot hide my surprise. I know there was little love lost between her and Matt, but I still figured she wouldn't want to have anything to do with me since his death. Blood runs thicker, and all that.

MC gives me a tentative smile as I approach the table, and I think it's going to be all right. But I still pull my chair back slowly, a curious look on my face.

'Hey, it's okay. I come as friend, not foe.'

'It's good to see you, MC. I …' My voice catches.

'You eating properly? You're looking a little thin,' she says to allow me to recover my emotions. 'You've got to take care of yourself. For that handsome little boy of yours.'

'I didn't murder your brother, MC,' I blurt, looking at her plaintively, not sure what to expect, and wondering why on earth she would be here.

'Don't you think I'd be the first person to know that? You might be a little naive, Lucie, but I can tell you're a good girl. I know you wouldn't have taken his life intentionally.'

MC sounds like a wise elder, not someone only a few years my senior, and I narrow my eyes at her. The last contact I had with her was the note she left outside the door on the day JP and I arrived back from England. With a shudder of unease I decide to limit the conversation to JP, my innocent angel in all of this.

'That's not what your mother believes,' I say. 'I know it's not my place to tell you, but I think Natasha is doing her best to wrench JP from me. I think she's trying to get sole custody.'

'Honey, I know that too, and that's why I'm here. I'm afraid it's not good news. She and Didier asked me to come over again from the US to sign some papers, sort out some family business. She's got some shit going down you wouldn't even dream of. That doesn't bother me. She can sink in her own ship for all I care. But what does bother me is this whole thing with JP …'

'Have you seen him? Does he seem okay to you? I miss him like crazy.'

'Of course you do. But there's something you should know. They've been working with the Russian consulate to get JP and Didier citizenship papers. For Russia.'

MC puts her hand on my arm as my eyes crease with incomprehension.

'My father has always talked about writing his magnum opus. A biographical study based on my maternal grandparents' escape from Russia before the revolution. They're planning a long-term sojourn in St Petersburg. That's great, good riddance and good luck I say. But, Lucie, the thing is, they're planning to take JP with them.'

My jaw drops.

'They can't do that! I'm his mother, and I may be in prison, but surely I have the right to decide where he lives!'

I stand up, the chair falls backwards, and a guard starts towards our table from near the door. MC puts her hand out, palm raised. The guard stops. I get the feeling MC could stop a riot. She gets up to put the chair back on its feet.

'It's okay. It's okay,' she says to the guard, who retreats back to the corner of the room. Tears are now coursing down my cheeks.

'Lucie, look, I know this isn't fair either. But my mother has influenced a lot of people in this whole process, if you know what I mean.'

She rubs her thumb and first two fingers together rapidly.

'How can she get away with it? More's the point, she's bribing people to make things happen. Where is she getting the money?'

Until my recent suspicions, I've never questioned their finances. Never questioned how they could afford to keep a fine chalet and live like royalty on the paltry earnings of a second-rate writer, despite Didier's insistence that he is the one who puts the family's bread on the table. But it has been niggling at the back of my mind since Matt first told me about the family history, and the photograph in the antiques gazette springs to mind.

'She's planning her own little Perestroika, Lucie. It's like she's on some kind of ancestral mission. But listen, your point is valid. How have they been able to afford to live this kind of life in the mountains? How have they been able to send Mathieu and I to private schools and colleges?'

MC swallows, suddenly doesn't seem so confident. She sits back, and a frisson goes through me.

'Lucie, I'm going to tell you something now that you may or may not be able to use to influence the return of your son. It's to do with those icons, the ones hanging in the chalet. Remember how Natasha always told you they were copies, fakes?' I nod, ears buzzing. 'Well they're not fakes. They're the real deal. Sixteenth century. Our grandfather, Natasha's father, was apparently a curator at the Winter Palace in Petrograd.

'When they knew the revolution was coming, they took a handful of icons from the museum collection and smuggled them out of the country through Finland and made their way to London. He said he was protecting them from the destruction being wrought by the Bolsheviks. But, Lucie, it's only since I've been an adult that I wonder why they never took them back, at least not all of them. Every few years there was one less icon hanging on our wall, and I don't think they've gone back to claim their rightful place in St Petersburg.'

'Jesus, and they were hanging on the wall all this time?'

My suspicion about the authenticity of the icons is confirmed.

'No one knew. All that crap around the house, the matryoshka, the pendants, the flags. It's all tacky stuff. People would think the icons were part of that vulgarity. It's Switzerland, after all. I guess they thought the icons were safer on their walls than in some bank vault. Certainly more accessible each time they wanted to do a discreet deal. I guess it's like hiding smuggled diamonds among the change in your pocket.'

I don't say anything. Apart from the information about JP, I'm confused about MC's motive for telling me all this. I don't know what she expects I can do about it while I'm in Hindelbank, and I wonder what she stands to gain from this.

MC doesn't know that Natasha and Didier gave us an icon for our wedding. Better to tell no one at this stage.

'I don't know how you can get the judge to change his decision, but I hope you have a good lawyer who can help you,' continues MC.

I think of Pittet, probably younger than me. His inexperience allowed the prosecution to walk all over him, likely with the influence of pressure from Natasha. But I could tell he was a quick learner. He was pissed off when the judge made his ruling. He truly believes me, believes it was an accident, and tells me from time to time he feels terrible to see me locked away for a crime I haven't committed. I'm hoping he hasn't lost the will to set things right.

'Why do you want to help me, MC? We don't really know each other very well, although I can't tell you how grateful I am that you've shared this with me.'

'Lucie, I know they're my parents, but I've been angry for too long about their total lack of support of everything I've ever done. I don't want to appear jealous, but they've only ever had eyes for my brother. I never really felt like he was my sibling.' I draw in my breath and swallow as she continues. 'I always wanted a sister ... I know that sounds like a cliché, but I like you. And I don't have kids. Can't have kids. But JP represents the goodness somewhere in our family. He's my nephew. We share some of the same blood. And I believe that child's place is with you, his parent. My mother is playing him like some pawn, thinking she can use him for retribution.

'You need to concentrate on getting out of here, and you must regain custody of your son. I'm telling you this because I think you'd better hurry, before my parents disappear into Russia and lose themselves somewhere on the floodplains of the Taiga. They probably know you're not stupid enough to let yourself kick back in here while they carry this out. There's no time to waste.'

Chapter 19

It's the middle of the night. I wake suddenly. I think someone must have shouted out on our floor, but when I strain to listen, there is silence. The window creaks quietly as a gust blows against the pane. The wind passes through the metal lattice bars with the hint of a moan. Something woke me. A thought. A dream. Something Monika said. Something about taxes.

'That's it! I have to call Pittet!'

My voice booms in the confined space of my cell. I know I cannot cause a fuss until daylight. My outburst might be misconstrued for belligerency. Or insanity. I can't risk solitary, removal of privileges or psychiatric restriction.

Now that MC has confirmed my suspicions about the Favres' wealth, I have to talk to Pittet, bounce my idea off him. After writing a few notes, I lie awake for a couple of hours and then fall back into a deep slumber, knowing I won't forget my theory because I've written it down, ready to revisit a plan in the cold light of day.

Waking a little later from a heavy sleep, my nose is dry from the radiator I cranked up with yesterday's cold weather. I forgot to turn it down before I went to bed. Aside from an annoying whistle as I breathe through one nostril, there is complete silence.

The silence of the deaf. Like my ears are stuffed with cotton wool. I feel my heart beating slowly, steadily. It's this silence that has woken me, for I am still emotionally exhausted. But it's not even 6:00 a.m. and it's still dark outside. Dark, but somehow not. A purple light infuses the cell. I get out of bed to turn down the radiator and look out of the window.

Snow!

I should have known yesterday when the temperature dropped drastically in the evening. There are at least twenty centimetres of fluffy powder on my window ledge, and I can barely make out the outlines of the other living blocks and the corner of the greenhouse. All the contours are softened in the slowly brightening dawn. I don't turn on my light, so I can watch the indigo night turn to a royal blue.

The lights eventually come on in the block opposite and the general noises of morning are mixed with the excited chatter of several women who have never seen snow before. The corridors soon sound like a primary school.

We all wear inappropriate shoes and shuffle along the slippery path to the work block. I'm reminded of my first days in Switzerland. Wet socks. I recall Matt's comment about my unsuitable footwear. Security has cleared a narrow channel through the snow. One of us will be assigned a more substantial shovelling or sweeping job later. In front of me there's a squeal, and a snowball flies past, narrowly missing my shoulder. And suddenly it's mayhem.

The snow deadens the screeching and giggling, as though we're at the beach and kids are frolicking in the surf hundreds of metres away. Like a kind of mournful echo swept on the wind with the cries of seagulls. A couple of guards come to the door of the work block and simply watch. They cross their arms and lean on the doorframes with smiles on their faces. The security guy who has been clearing the area around the main gate rests on his shovel but doesn't reach for his radio. There is no harm in this.

'I have never seen snow. It's so … cold!' laughs one of the Latinas.

I would stay for a snowball fight, or help to build a snowman, but we are severely punished if we're late to our jobs. We either get a hefty fine, or free-time privileges are curtailed. And I have an urgent call to make. I hurry to the phone cabin in the work block. I have to ask Pittet to research my nagging question about taxes before my workday begins.

* * *

The snow lasts several days on the ground, the shovelled piles growing smaller each day as a light drizzle reduces the novelty until it sadly disappears altogether, revealing the grey winter anew. I practically wear out the pathway between the housing and work blocks to the mail office.

You'd think I'd be happy to get any letters, but when I pick up an envelope with my mother's writing on it, I impatiently ask if anything else arrived in the post. Correspondence with my parents has been sporadic. I know they are sympathetic to my cause because they guaranteed my legal costs at the beginning of this whole messy affair, but I'm sure they feel I somehow brought all this on myself.

My mother's letter talks of nothing more than their village life. She doesn't ask one question or express hope about me. She doesn't even mention JP. I find her letter depressing, especially after we seemed to reconnect during her visit a couple of months back. However, I'm glad I no longer get 'We told you so'.

Turnaround time for the other eagerly awaited correspondence is about ten days.

I now have the address I need and I'm signing a letter to someone I have never met in Vevey. Normally my letter-writing time is filled with senseless notes to JP, offloading to Anne, or occasionally, perfunctory obligations to my parents.

I have to be careful about what I say to this man in Vevey. I know this old colleague of Patterson's can speak English because the art professor found the French language, beyond titles of fine works, quite a challenge. For once I can focus on something very specific. I'm so glad Jennifer Patterson came up trumps. Once I know I have him on board, I have to find a way of getting the icon to him for an evaluation, and Anne is my only possibility. I'm not ready to trust anyone else.

My door is open and I hear the shuffle of footsteps down the corridor. I press the flap of the envelope closed and look up to see Zeinah passing.

'Hey!' I call, but she doesn't turn, keeps her head facing forward, still shuffling. Her hair is uncombed, her shirt hangs creased from her sloping shoulders.

'Zeinah, hey!' I call a second time and I hear her stop, but she doesn't return to my door. She continues to her cell.

I have too much to do, must finish this letter. There are some things I still need to ask Zeinah, but I feel it's better to have my complete list prepared before I sit and bounce ideas off her. So I don't go out to the corridor.

But at dinner in the canteen, Zeinah doesn't appear. My list of questions is ready, and I'm almost irritated that she's not here. She's agreed to help me. She must help me, I silently plead. Her legal mind has been invaluable to the way I have been forming questions to the social services and my lawyer. She has reignited the fight in me to get out of here and get my son back. I wonder where she is.

Yasmine sits down beside me with her tray and pats me twice on the thigh. I smile thinly. I feel guilty about ignoring her recently, but tonight I don't feel inclined to deal with her flirting. I finish eating quickly, excuse myself from the table without a second glance and go in search of Zeinah to allow us maximum time before lock-down.

Zeinah is sitting on her bed, door open. She usually has her

246

nose in some book, so I'm surprised to see her gazing away from me out of the window.

'Is something wrong? Are you not feeling well?' I ask. She turns to face me and I gasp. Her left eye sports a massive aubergine swelling and her puffy lower lip displays the zip of a vertical split.

'Oh my God, did Yasmine do this to you?' I ask. She shakes her head, winces with pain.

'Then who? And why?'

'Go away, Lucie. You'll get into trouble yourself. Somebody doesn't like us being seen together. Either they don't like what I represent for you or they don't like what we discuss. Either way, I need to distance myself from you. I see now what you meant by watching my back.'

Zeinah speaks slowly, her swollen lip causing her speech to sound almost loutish. I walk towards her bed, but she holds up both her hands, pushing away the air between us.

'Oh Jesus, are you okay? Can I do anything?' I ask.

'One of the guards is bringing me some soup and a straw. I'm hungry, but I cannot eat today. I'm sure it will be better tomorrow. The doctor thinks my eye is okay, but they have to wait for the swelling to go down to do some tests. They are worried I may have a displaced retina.'

'Where did this happen? When?'

'This afternoon, after work. In the shower block. It's okay. Don't go getting revenge. It's none of your business.'

I'm not so sure. I still think that Yasmine might have something to do with this. She's been moody and withdrawn over the past couple of weeks, despite a stern clarification of my relationship with her.

'It is still not as bad as the things that could have been done to me in my own country,' says Zeinah. 'I'm okay, Lucie, just a little bruised.'

I go back to my cell, sit on my bed, and hold my head in my

hands. I've been so selfish. So careful not to allow myself to get close to anyone else, until I saw that this new girl could help me. My 'relationships' with the other women have been one long string of sisterly distance, one fickle chapter after another. Fatima, Yasmine, one step too far, and now this. I've been behaving irrationally, cheating myself more than anyone else. In the end, someone will always get hurt.

Remembering Anne's latest letter, I pick it up and read it again more thoroughly, having thrust it aside to deal with the other correspondence earlier.

She has dispensed with the trivialities of how life carries on in the resort without me, and tells me she has been hassling Natasha and Didier into bringing JP for a visit. They are reluctant to let her bring him herself, but she assures me she will use her powers of persuasion.

Until my last letter to her, she was unaware that it's been over a month since I last saw JP. She's been in touch with my lawyer, Pittet, to make sure my rights are being respected, and has been doggedly questioning the authenticity of the investigation following Matt's death. We all know that something doesn't ring true.

Her questions seem to have sparked new enthusiasm on the part of Pittet, and I am ever more grateful for Anne's friendship. She has never doubted me and has been a steadfast friend since I arrived in Switzerland.

I think back to the beginning of our relationship, when my time with Matt dominated my every waking moment. I'm so glad I still found time to nurture a friendship with her. That first summer, Anne started work as a receptionist at an upmarket hotel in the village, then fell in love with François. I thought our situation would be ideal, a social foursome. But with some history between François and Matt, they chose to avoid each other. When Valentin was born the summer after JP, I still hoped life would fall into a more domestic model with the six of us doing things together, but it was not to be.

Maybe Anne can work out a time with JP's grandparents to bring him next time, but I try not to get my hopes up. It can destroy you, wanting something so much, expecting it, and then having the opportunity snatched away from you at the last minute. It's happened before. A court of law will never convince Natasha that her son was a victim of his own temper.

* * *

My free hours in between waiting for the mail are spent researching sites I am allowed to access on the computer in the work block. That's if it is not occupied by anyone else. This afternoon I offer the Polish girl a handful of cigarettes that might have been hers in the first place to take her session when none was available.

I sit down at the computer and type key words into the 'news' section of the search engine bar.

I come up with an article in the *Guardian*, one of the few newspapers that displays free online articles. It's a feature, several years old, about the current curator of the Hermitage Museum in St Petersburg. His life mission has been to restore the museum's collection to its full original glory. I read the first paragraph, then stop with a jolt.

The photo of a small Russian icon that looks much like the one I have in my possession makes my eyes keep sliding away from the text. My eyes skip through the article and the words 'missing', 'en route from Moscow' and 'absconded' leap out at me.

The curator's name is Alexey Mikhailovich, and he is supposedly related to Tsar Nicholas II. In an interview with the journalist, he speaks of many missing imperialist treasures that were ransacked by the Bolsheviks. Many of these were either destroyed by anti-religious Communists or recovered and restored.

But there is one mystery surrounding a set of miniature icons from the fifteenth and sixteenth century. They are referred to as 'travelling icons'. They were en route from the Tretyakov Gallery in Moscow to St Petersburg when they mysteriously disappeared in early 1917. It was mid-winter, and it is unclear exactly how the icons were to be transported between the cities, but they never arrived at their destination, and in the chaos of the riots around imperial Russia's capital at the time, the icons were lost.

The curator expresses amazement that anyone ever intended to remove the icons from Moscow, where they were relatively safe. But there seemed to be a sense of urgency to protect them during socialist unrest. The curator suspects that before his abdication, Tsar Nicholas II may have been amassing smaller items of his own he thought might eventually be destroyed in Moscow by revolutionaries.

I sit back in my chair and put my hand to my forehead. Could Natasha's icons be a part of these missing pieces? In which case, Natasha lied to MC about their origins too. This is not merely a case of protecting ancient art, but outright theft.

I want to call Pittet straight away, and rush out of the building towards my cellblock, but in the corridor of both floors of the living block are lines of inmates waiting to make pre-Christmas phone calls. Once I've jumped the queue with the remainder of the cigarettes I've been keeping for such occasions, I offer two more inmates five francs each to get to the front. In the space of one day I have managed to spend a whole month's salary on simply bribing my way to communication.

'What did you manage to find out? Do you have a contact at the tax office?' I ask hurriedly when I get Pittet on the line.

He coughs and sniffs. He is stuffed up with cold.

'It's not so simple, Lucie. They are not willing to act in such haste. They have made their calculations, and it is true that their declared income' – from Didier's paltry writing royalties, I think – 'is not very much, but there is no discrepancy with the funds declared in their bank accounts. They must have another account abroad somewhere.'

'Of course. If they are getting paid by a fence in the art world, they would have an offshore account,' I muse. 'They're not that stupid.'

'Are they an influential family in your village?' asks Pittet.

'Not really. The chalet must be worth over a million, although I don't really know much about their social life.'

'Then that is probably why they have not been reported. They have no apparent enemies who would inform on them. That's the usual route. A jealous neighbour or a business partner … how do you say, *méprisé*.'

'Scorned,' I say.

'Yes, then the tax office would probably never find out.'

'How about a scorned daughter-in-law? Surely it's not too late to expose those offshore funds. But I don't know how. What will the tax office do now that you – we – have reported the art?'

'They will organise an inspector to visit their home spontaneously, to ascertain the presence of these … icons. If they find them, they then need to have them valued. But they are in no hurry. The process could take weeks, months.'

'And in the meantime, here I sit in prison, and the Favres might simply disappear.' I feel like wailing.

'And, Lucie, the tax office may not think the whole process is worth pursuing. What if they find out these icons are not worth so much? They will only charge tax retroactively to ten years ago. You say Madame Favre brought them with her to Switzerland, but this they cannot prove.'

My heart sinks. 'I know now for sure these icons could possibly amount to several million,' I say quietly.

I can almost hear Pittet raise his eyebrows. A bubble of hope rises in my chest, the urgency of a new idea causing my heartbeat to spike.

'Monsieur Pittet – Léon?' It's the first time I have called him by his first name, although he has long been calling me Lucie, unsure of which last name he should use with me. Time to dispense with Swiss etiquette.

'I need you to do something for me. I need you to contact the Russian embassy.'

Chapter 20

'*Schön*,' says a guard over my shoulder, making me jump. 'If you do not sell today, perhaps I make an offer.'

I laugh cynically as I prop a painting against the boxes placed for that purpose on the red-clothed table. It's the weekend before the first Sunday of Advent, and the second and final day of the Schlossmärit. We've all been preparing for this Christmas market for months, making objects, or in my case, painting pictures to sell. The inmates are asked if they would like to help set up the stalls or to serve hot punch or Christmas cookies, *Guetzli*, to the public. Only a few of us volunteer. The others will stay in the cellblocks the entire time the market is open. Although everyone gets a chance to visit the stalls before the public comes through the gates on Saturday, I'm amazed that more inmates have not jumped at this opportunity to feel normal for a day or two.

I'm at a stall with two guards, selling the paintings and a selection of hand-made candles. The stall next to us displays *Adventskränzli*, balsam-smelling cedar and pine branches woven into beautiful wreaths. Each one is topped with four candles to be lit on the four Sundays of Advent. Vasilisa is with me, stamping her feet in the cold, behind a display of her wooden cups.

The courtyard in front of the *Schloss* has taken on a festive atmosphere. Our canvas-roofed stalls are colourful, crammed full of our creations. The pretty red and white shutters of the castle building surrounding us are open, some wreathed in pine garlands. Twinkling lights shine out of every window, and with traces of snow remaining from last week's fall, it brings a melancholic longing for the Christmases of my youth.

I clap my hands together in an attempt to bring them warmth, and reach into my pocket to put my gloves back on until the next customer. Our breath puffs clouds of vapour in the cold.

Suddenly there is the frenzied patter of feet on the cobblestones.

'Mama! Mama!' JP is running towards me, and my heart about explodes. Anne must have persuaded them to let her bring him! This is the best Christmas present.

The few visitors to the market who have started to wander between the stalls look around as he pounds towards me. Faces are warm with memories of vicarious childhood joy as he throws himself into my arms. I want to cry. It's as though I am picking him up from school, or we've just met in the street.

Anne arrives on his tail, half-heartedly admonishing JP for running away from her. I hug Anne tightly and thank her for coming, especially for being able to bring JP. The guard I have been assigned to lets me show JP the other stalls within the courtyard. I'm not allowed to wander beyond the perimeter. It might be easy to get lost among the crowds, but I know I would not make it past the main gate of the prison. With barely more than a hundred inmates, I would be recognised instantly, and the public has been carefully chaperoned from the minibuses bringing them from the village train station to the gates.

JP looks through my paintings, most of them no bigger than a newspaper. He's not impressed with the copies of renaissance-style art, and would certainly have preferred a Pingu or a Tintin. I show him the Christmas trees some of the inmates have made out of recycled plastic drink bottles.

'Great idea,' says Anne. 'We'll try and make something like that at home, eh JP? On one of our crafting days?' JP smiles and nods, rushing on to the next stall.

'Mama, what are these little houses? Can I have one?' I've told him he can buy one thing from the market, as long as I have enough cash to pay for it. He crouches down near a tiny wood-framed narrow house with a shiny metal roof. Within the frame of the house are sawn-off pieces of bamboo, creating a honeycomb effect.

'They're called bee hotels,' I tell him. 'Not all bees are honeybees. Some of them just help to pollinate the flowers and the trees, and that's still a very important job. You see these little pieces of bamboo lying sideways? The bees crawl into the holes at either end and chew on the wood. They mix it with their saliva and make little nests for their babies in there. On a quiet summer's day you can actually hear the bees' little scratchy chewing noises. They stay in the hotel for the season, then fly away. Do you really think Mimi and Poppa want more bees in their garden?' I was sceptical.

'Mama, I really want one. I really want a bee hotel.'

'You realise that the bees won't come until spring? It's a long time to wait.'

I'm suddenly very sad. I'd love to be with him to see the first bee come and visit. Spring. That feels like a long way off.

We sit together at a long picnic table in one of the painted rooms of the *Schloss*, which has been converted into a seated dining area for the day. JP recognises a painting on the ceiling, similar to one on my stall, and exclaims a husky 'waw' as he looks up, appreciating the skill I have used to paint a copy.

We eat spicy pumpkin soup with thick wedges of farmer bread, fresh from the bakery. I wonder if Yasmine has made this batch. I buy JP a chocolate bar, which he concentrates on eating while Anne and I chat, trying to keep our attitudes nonchalant, as though we have met for an informal lunch somewhere at a local market on the mountain.

255

While JP plays with the bee hotel on his lap, already imagining a community under construction, I push my bowl aside and lean towards Anne across the table.

'I'm so glad you were able to come. The Christmas market is a great distraction for JP. For all of us. I know you're feeling a bit stressed with the pregnancy, but I'm hoping you'd be willing to help me one more time.'

Anne leans towards me, a curious frown on her face. Other visitors are bustling around us, eating soup and *Bratwurst*. I know her whole day has been inconvenienced for this brief visit, for which I feel guiltily grateful.

'*Mon Dieu*, Lucie, what is this? Are you going to ask me to help you escape?' She laughs a little nervously.

'No, but I think there is a possibility I can get out of here soon. I have some people who are doing some things. But I don't know how long that will take and I need you to do something else for me.'

A tray of cutlery drops on the floor in the next room, silencing the conversation around us. I wait until the festive murmurs build again.

'I have something that might be the key to my freedom.'

Anne looks at me like I've lost the plot.

As I lean forward, I surreptitiously slide the icon I have wrapped in plastic and tucked in my waistband from under my thick sweater. Anne stares at the package.

'It's a Russian icon that was gifted to us on our wedding day.'

'Jesus, Lucie, is it one of Natasha Favre's tacky Russian souvenirs? Everyone knows her house is covered in that worthless shit. What's so special about this one?'

'I want you to take it to a man at this address in Vevey. I'm not sure how delicate it is. Better to leave it wrapped and let an expert take off the plastic.'

I push an addressed envelope across the table with the icon. I glance at a guard who is standing at the door of the dining room, keeping an eye on the few inmates who have been allowed to mingle with the market visitors for the day. She shows no interest in these small objects crossing the table.

JP continues to play with the little wooden house, flying imaginary bees in and out of the holes.

'What's the deal with this icon?' Anne asks. 'It's so ugly. But ... an expert. Do you mean ...?'

She suddenly realises what I have said. I don't have the time for an Eastern European art history lesson.

'It's not a cheap copy, Anne. I'm pretty sure it's an original, and it could be extremely valuable. But there is also the possibility that the Favres' icons have been obtained illegally. This expert in Vevey will be able to determine the icon's origin and evaluate it for me. Here is a document I've prepared that you should get him to sign for receipt of the icon. He is expecting the object for appraisal.'

'Why on earth did you take it with you when you tried to escape with JP? Didn't Natasha know?'

'It was a total fluke. It fell off the wall during ... A complicated story. It got mixed up with my clothes while I was stuffing them in my backpack. But the police thought nothing of it, and gave everything back to me when I was sent to prison.'

'I wonder why she gave it to you?' mused Anne.

'I reckon Natasha gave us that icon for our wedding as some kind of financial insurance for Matt in case he fell on hard times, and in case she ever got caught with her own hot goods. He just didn't know about its value.'

'Hot goods? You mean these are stolen?' Anne asks, wide-eyed.

I wince. This must all sound like a farce to Anne.

'I know this sounds crazy, but can you help me? I know I've already asked you for so much ...'

'Of course I can, Lucie. I have a check-up with the doctor in Montreux on Tuesday. It's not far from there to Vevey. I will do it then. Valentin will be with François' mother for the afternoon.'

Anne tucks the icon and the letter carefully into her bag.

'Promise me you won't tell a soul about this. I don't know how far Natasha will go to make sure I don't discover her dirty little secrets. The less you know, the better. But please stay clear of the Favres. They could be dangerous. I mean it, Anne.'

I look at her with pleading eyes.

Anne is obviously tired, and I know she has almost two hours to drive back to the village. JP must be back with the Favres at 6:00 p.m. That's the rule. As the sun disappears behind the west wing of the castle and the shadows deepen, I hug first Anne and then JP, and I can't help the tears welling. I know I won't be seeing him before Christmas. And if something doesn't change, I might never see him again.

My heart aches as they say goodbye and turn to leave. JP sees I am upset and holds on to me a little bit longer.

'One day soon, we'll be together again, sweetie. Remember every day that I love you.'

He tightens his arms around my neck.

'I love you more, Mama,' he whispers.

'No, I love you more,' I say smiling. He hasn't forgotten our ritual.

After they've left, I start crying. They are barely out of the castle courtyard on their way to the main prison gate, and I move through the space JP occupied, hoping to feel an essence of him, hoping desperately that Anne can help me.

* * *

'I'm afraid, Lucie, the Russian consulate was rather … unhelpful.'

Léon Pittet is sweating slightly, although it's not warm in here. But he doesn't remove his jacket. He looks smart in his dark suit and white shirt, making me feel messy in my sweat pants and hoodie. I put my hand to my hair, and pat a stray lock behind my ear.

'I wonder what they have done with our information.' I remember Vasilisa's conversation in the studio. 'Although they told you they can't help, I'm now worried they might follow up with someone from within their own art foundation. Or their own policing methods ...'

I gasp as I realise what I might have set rolling. My hand covers my mouth.

Pittet can see I'm stressed. He puts a hand on my arm across the table, moves it down to my wrist.

'They spent all those communist years defying any belief in God. Why would they care about a few missing icons?'

He's trying to make me feel better. I stare at his hand, enjoying the warmth of the touch of another human being. I don't pull it away.

'It's to do with pride in their heritage, even pre-twentieth century,' I say, thinking again about Vasilisa.

I look up into his face. I try to fathom whether his dark eyes reflect a determination to help me, or compassion for a helpless situation.

'What about the Swiss police?' I continue. 'Could they help? Surely something can be done for suspected child abduction? JP is a Swiss citizen. Wouldn't they be interested in protecting one of their own?' I can't avoid a whine creeping into my voice.

'It's a little complicated. Because the Favres have been given temporary custody of the child.'

The child. As if JP is someone else's.

'I appreciate the case is unusual. But please could you ask someone about this? Can you ask the judge for advice? The one who awarded the custody? Surely someone can help?'

'Normally your son would be interviewed and examined by social services, but he is only 6 years old. His logic and sense of loyalty cannot be easily assessed. A case like this has not been challenged before. I will try to set up a meeting with the judge. Anyway, we need to determine the length of custody awarded. There are some open ends we might be able to work with.'

'Léon, it is imperative that you work on this as quickly as possible. That child is my son, JP. He could disappear within days. Please. You have to help me. You know I'm innocent. You know I don't deserve this.'

My eyes are glistening. Léon gives a slight smile and takes his hand from the top of mine. It's only when I feel the cool air against my knuckles that I realise it has been resting there for much of our conversation.

* * *

That was probably the last visit I will be allowed for a while. This morning one of the guards tells me I have a postcard in the office to pick up. I find this odd, as Müller has recently been bringing my mail when it doesn't require inspection, and a postcard is a small enough item to easily pass through the system. She's been doing this as a privilege for the past couple of weeks, and I've never been sure what she expects in return.

'Müller sick today?' I ask as I make my way to the office.

The guard shakes her head.

I get to the office. MC has dashed a scribbled message on the back of a postcard of the Golden Gate Bridge: 'Move set for soon, before the end of winter.'

There is also a letter from Anne confirming that she has delivered the icon to the art evaluator in Vevey. But along with that news comes a small bombshell, supporting MC's comment. François' brother runs the estate agent in the village and has been instructed to rent out the Favres' chalet for a long-term lease of two years, with a possibility to extend at the end of that period. The start of the rental period is undisclosed, to be negotiated by the interested party. This means they could be moving any day. Panic grips my throat.

On my way back to work, I see Müller in the yard and ask if she has heard anything from the administration about another visit from my lawyer. She shakes her head, doesn't look me in the eye, and walks on. She's been a little strange with me over the past week. I wonder what's bothering her. With a flutter of hope, I wonder if it's because she believes I will be leaving this place soon, and will no longer satisfy her little artistic project. She's disturbed about something. The guards should never be seen to fraternise with the inmates, although they do have their favourites, but I always thought Müller had a soft spot for me. Because of my art. Her cool distance is disconcerting.

* * *

The next day, when Müller previously promised me another visit to Hindelbank church to finish some shading on one of my pastel works of Maria Magdalena, Dr Schutz turns up unexpectedly in my cell before breakfast. My first thought is that something terrible has happened to JP. Why else would the shrink turn up unannounced? I'm tying the ribbons of my portfolio when she shakes her head.

'You will not be going to the church today, Lucie. Your privileges have been rescinded.'

'Why? What have I done?'

'The warden has reason to believe that you are planning a *flucht*, an escape from Hindelbank.'

Dr Schutz sounds awkward about delivering this news, as though she doesn't believe the information.

'You're kidding! How would I do that? If only!' I laugh sarcastically, but her face doesn't change. 'On what basis has the warden formed these suspicions?'

'I am not permitted to give specifics on the information they have received, but you will no longer have the privilege of going

261

to the church, and for the moment your visitors' rights have been revoked.'

'What?'

This means I won't get to see JP. A vice closes around my heart. I won't be able to see Anne, and I imagine the mail correspondence going both ways will now constantly be examined, lengthening the precious time it takes for me to receive and send information.

'Does that include my lawyer?'

Dr Schutz shrugs. 'I'm … not sure.'

'What has been said? And by whom? Someone in here is messing with me. I haven't done anything wrong!'

I think about Müller's attitude towards me the day before.

In spite of this setback, at least I'm not on solitary. I continue to work, so I'm still allowed to paint in the atelier, and as I work, I mull over the scenario that makes the most sense in my mind. I'm also still allowed half an hour a week on the computer to research, and have been able to make some notes.

It's likely that Natasha has been interrogating JP. Somewhere along the way I must have mentioned Müller to Anne, probably because she was the one who got me all fired up about my art.

I can imagine Natasha asking JP: 'Does Mama talk about any of the friends she's met in the castle where she's staying?'

Chapter 21

Something struck me as odd during my trial and at the juncture of my conviction. I was naturally shocked that the prosecution's evidence was so readily accepted by the judges. They didn't seem to want to hear my side of the story. It was as though they had decided at the very beginning that Léon Pittet, my court-appointed lawyer, was only in it for the learning experience, an observing apprentice.

But what floored me was the absolute certainty of the detective in charge of my case that I had committed murder.

A question was raised by Pittet that with so much philandering in Matt's life, someone else could have caused his death. I'd told him about Marlena, about the suspicions surrounding her brother's disappearance. A revengeful woman might be capable of something terrible if she already has a history of aggression and knows who her adversary is. She'd been dumped by Matt for another woman or women. But a dramatic revenge after a lover's rejection was thrown out by the investigation as ridiculous, so we never pursued it. Finding any of his other lovers had been impossible, including the ultimate Sylvie. No one wants to get involved in a legal case of adultery.

And there wasn't the slightest doubt in Genillard's mind that this could have been an accident, let alone it being a simple case of self-defence.

I can be thankful my case was deemed to contain elements of a crime of passion, and my punishment determined accordingly, or I might have been issued a life sentence. Despite having been denied an appeal, I have always hoped that something might turn up at a later stage.

But now, fighting for my innocence has been completely eclipsed by the desperate need to stop JP being abducted.

I'm allowed one last call to my lawyer before my privileges are rescinded. Then the prison authorities will discuss my case at a higher level to determine whether I will even be allowed to remain in contact with him. But they want to make sure it's the lawyer, so a guard is instructed to dial his number to verify that it is indeed Pittet's office. There is some confusion while a receptionist, who doesn't speak very good German or English on the other end, finally manages to put the call through to Léon.

My call is being monitored. The guard stands with her foot wedged against the door of the cabin. I feel exposed speaking in front of her, so I switch to French. I still find it ironic that there is a bigger risk of my conversation being understood in English than one of the nation's four official languages.

'*Salut*, Lucie,' Léon greets me in the familiar.

I realise I have looked forward to hearing his voice as much as I might Anne's, although it would prove to be an extravagant expense merely to hear an ally's input.

'Léon, Natasha Favre is bribing people to keep me in here.'

Now I've said it out loud, my accusation sounds petty, childish. Like I'm pointing the finger of blame in a kindergarten dispute.

'What are you talking about?' He sounds exasperated, any warmth gone from his voice. 'This is not America. You have been watching too many television crime dramas. It's not such a circus. What proof do you have of this?'

'Well … none. But I'm pretty sure it's one of the guards here.

Someone has caught wind of my research into the case. My privileges have been removed, which means I can no longer have visitors and this is my last phone call until ... I don't know when.'

I thought I was angry, but as I say this, my eyes suddenly well with tears and my voice catches, rising in a suppressed sob at the word 'when'.

'Why do you have your privileges taken away? What have you done?'

'I've done nothing. But they think I'm planning to escape.'

'*Mon Dieu*. This is absurd. What have you been doing to make them think that?'

It hurts to think he doesn't believe me.

'Nothing, Léon! Someone has created this suspicion from absolutely nothing. I know I have been more active in using the internet when I can, and I've had more correspondence in the last month than in all the time I've been here, but everything is so transparent. They already know everything about me. Know everything I do. I don't know why they think this!'

I try to keep it together. The guard frowns and looks at a colleague through the internal window who is waiting out in the corridor with his back to the door. I lower my voice to an urgent whisper.

'I'm convinced there have been other backhanders, Léon. How come your defence was so quickly ignored in court? Didn't you ever wonder?'

'We're talking about a regular court case in Switzerland, although homicide is not common. This ... This bribing cannot happen,' he continues. 'I could understand if more was at stake ...'

I make a strangled sound. The guard looks at me again sharply. JP is at stake.

'I'm sorry, I realise that for you a lot is at stake,' he corrects himself. 'But, Lucie, aren't you getting a bit carried away?'

'Listen, I now know many things that I haven't told you before.

I'm sure Natasha has bribed one of the prison guards to keep me in prison. I believe she bribed someone to keep me in Hindelbank rather than housing me in La Tuilière closer to home. I also think it is possible that she was able to influence the prosecuting counsel in my case.'

I look straight at the guard still holding the door of the cabin. She doesn't react to my conversation, so I'm pretty sure she doesn't understand.

'You once admitted to me that you never understood why the evidence was so clearly determined as unintentional homicide, right? If that didn't make sense, then don't you think it's possible someone could have been influenced?'

I'm repeating myself, but have to convince Léon Pittet of the possibility.

'That is a big accusation to make, Lucie. I'm not sure I can deal with such a thing. Rules here are so … concrete.'

I take a deep breath.

'Listen to me. During my last session on the internet, I decided to look up the names of the people who were involved in my prosecution. I simply wanted to find out where they all lived, whether it's possible that there is some local connection to the Favres. Some social link, maybe a favour to be returned. You know how easy it is to do that.'

'You mean to return favours?' He sounds affronted. Maybe he thinks I suspect him too.

'No! To look up personal information on the internet. Hardly anyone in this country is ex-directory.'

'Did you find anything relevant?'

'Not with the addresses, but when I googled the *Poste de Gendarmerie* in Aigle, a newspaper article was highlighted in the search engine. It was reported in the *24 Heures* last week that something bizarre has happened at the police station. Some pornography has been discovered on the office computers and there is some kind of investigation going on.'

266

Léon laughs sceptically.

'The police, Lucie? Think about it, do you think they would reveal information about an investigation in their own offices? I think not. There must be a mistake. We would have known this straight away. Even if this were true, and it sounds incredible, this has nothing to do with your case, and the corruption you are describing.'

'*Die Zeit ist um!*' shrills the guard, making me jump.

My time is up. I ignore her and continue speaking into the phone.

'No it doesn't, but an analysis might uncover something else, if the investigation team knows what they are looking for.'

There is silence on the other end. I can almost hear Léon's brain ticking.

'I have to go. They are going to end my call. Please, Léon. Please ...' The bossy guard leans into the cabin and cuts the line before I even have a chance to say goodbye. I squeal one short angry protest, smash the phone noisily back in its cradle and slam the door on my way out. Jeez, I want to say, feels like prison in this place!

And I laugh out loud at my own little madness.

* * *

'Do you truly believe that one woman could have so much influence on all these people? The policeman in charge of investigating the case, the prosecution, and now even a guard within our prison? I find it highly unlikely, Lucie. This is not Syria.'

Zeinah and I are sitting at the end of the corridor by the window, watching the sky trying to snow.

There are certain times when I can still mix with the other inmates, and it's a relief to talk to Zeinah again. Her left eye bears the scar that split her eyelid through to her eyebrow. I feel a shadow of guilt every time I look at her, knowing that the purple line on her skin might fade to a pale blemish, but will probably never completely disappear. She could have lost her eye.

'I don't know. She's always played the domineering mother-in-law but now I think she could be … evil. Dr Schutz won't listen to my ranting about her any more. I think she believes there's something more deeply rooted in my psyche about what has happened. Not to say that she doesn't believe I'm not guilty of murder …'

Monika steps into the corridor from her cell, a towel over her shoulder and her toilet bag in hand. She's on her way to the shower. As she walks away from us, Zeinah and I remain silent, so as not to draw attention to the fact that we are alone in the corridor. If I thought I was an innocent human being who has been the victim of betrayal when I came in here, my eyes have certainly been opened to the extent of the lies and games played within the walls of a prison that can leave cracks in the strongest of personalities.

Yasmine has a visitor today so she's not around. A cousin from Lyon. At least, she says it's a cousin. She never told me she had family there. I'm hoping that it's her old lover, but if she felt compelled to lie to me, she wrongly believes I might be jealous. I simply want her to stop feeling like she owns me. But at least I know it's safe for Zeinah and I to talk for a while.

'If Natasha has influenced all these people, she must have left a trail behind her. You need to find someone you can trust to investigate your theory.'

'I've asked my lawyer to do exactly that, but I'm not sure how easy it will be. It was already a pointless exercise blowing the whistle on them to the tax office. Can you imagine? Forty years' worth of back-tax, and a fine for misrepresented tax on millions of francs of assets? They didn't care. They told Léon they would only tax retroactively to ten years anyway.'

'If you can uncover even one of her bribery tracks, I'm sure the judges who decided your case would look at it in a different light.'

'Unless she has lined the judges' pockets too.'

* * *

'Someone got to you, didn't they? You're the reason I've had all my privileges revoked. Why, Müller, why?'

I know why, but I want to hear her say it. I still don't know her first name, but don't want to stoop to the usual etiquette of calling her Frau Müller. I'm angry. She's done the dirty on me. She's been turned. The result of which has me panicking even more about being able to get my son back.

We are standing in the hallway on the ground floor of our block. I haven't seen her on our floor for a while, so I suspect her area of responsibility has changed. Since the *Schlossmärit* we've seen very little of each other. She doesn't say anything, but glares at me with her jaw clenched.

'I thought we had a special connection. All that time we spent in the church together. I thought you were my ally in here. I respected you.'

Müller flinches, but still remains silent. Respect is the one commodity that is priceless in this place. I'm wondering what bounty it has taken to abuse it.

'I don't care about not being able to go to the church and paint your precious Maria Magdalena. I don't care about not participating in the group activities. I don't care about having my mail ripped apart and inspected for clues of dissension. But I do care about not being able to see my little boy. My 6-year-old son. Do you think he understands that? It's like you've ripped out a part of me. Here.'

I rap my fist against my chest, tears of anger pricking. Her eyes flicker down to the floor, and she turns to walk away.

'I don't know what you are talking about,' she says over her shoulder as she waves her key card at the box by the door and leaves the building. I'm tempted to run after her, but I'm not allowed outside.

* * *

A few days later, I'm busy tidying up the art atelier. I no longer paint copies of the masterpieces in the château. The ones that were unsold at the market will be packed away, and I wonder if I'll still be here next year when they go back on sale.

As I'm stacking the canvases, a drawing with a photo attached to it slips to the floor. It is a half-finished charcoal sketch of JP. I pick it up and stare at the photograph paper-clipped to the top. JP's face has started to take on some of Matt's handsome features.

I'm gripped with a sudden sadness, and a sob escapes. I cannot stop the onset of tears, and my eyes and nose feel hot and raw with physical emotion. There is no one in sight, so I let myself cry, perhaps expecting some form of cleansing from the tears. I hear a movement in the hall outside and slip across the room, hand over my mouth, to lean against the wall behind the door.

Müller walks in holding a large sports bag. She hasn't seen me, and as she approaches the bench at the back of the atelier, I don't know whether to run at her and beat my fists on her back, or make a quiet escape through the door. Instead I simply stand there.

She unzips the bag and spreads it wide on the bench, revealing that it is empty, then reaches for the smaller stack of my remaining paintings leaning against the wall. I stare, wide-eyed. When she turns and sees me watching, she jumps. Her gaze flickers to the bag she is about to haul over her shoulder. I narrow my eyes.

'Intending to make a little profit of your own?' I ask.

Her eyes flash with fear.

'I guess that's not your only form of income at Hindelbank,' I say. '*Die Rektorin* might be interested to know how you're profiting from the inmates' skills.' I nod towards the bag, now containing three canvases.

Her gaze drops to my hand where I'm still holding JP's photo and her look softens momentarily.

'I – I didn't know they would stop the visits,' Müller blurts, and then checks herself. 'I didn't know they would stop you seeing your son. Normally they still let children see their parents when privileges have been revoked, even fathers in the male prisons. I didn't know. It was supposed to stop you getting information …'

Müller bites her lip.

'Don't stop now. How did she get to you?'

'She? It was a man.'

My surprise shows.

For a moment I think I have made a terrible mistake. Perhaps I'm armed with the wrong artillery. Then I narrow my eyes. Natasha must have had an accomplice. Who else but her faithful partner?

'What did he look like? Was he French-speaking?'

Müller describes Didier to a tee. It figures. He must have some role to play in this sinister affair, to be able to profit from her misdemeanours. He leads the slovenly life he loves, no hard work, a few chapters of second-rate writing every few months. I've always thought he had no spine. A puppet. Well now she's got him doing her dirty work too. He was never worth trying to create a comrade anyway. He must have always known where his financial allegiances to secure his future lay.

'It was easy for me to accept a supplement to my imminent retirement fund. A few words in the chief warden's ear. They were already dubious about allowing you to go to the church so often. It made it simple for me to make a recommendation, to tell them I thought you might take the opportunity some time to abuse that freedom.'

'I thought you had more integrity.'

271

Müller's face briefly shows shame as I say this. I've finally touched a nerve. Then she shrugs and continues to dig into the grave of her justification.

'You think I'm going to get a handsome pension when I retire in a few years' time? This is a shit job. You must be naive, to think that nothing like this goes on all the time within the prison walls. The guards, the warden, everyone turns a blind eye. Usually only small amounts. And I won't get much for your paintings. But that other thing was not something to be turned down. I deserve a little extra reward for my time served here. It's like I have been in prison myself all these years.'

Müller narrows her eyes at me. She has calculated the risks. They must have offered her a tidy sum. I want to blurt that my lawyer is on the verge of obtaining more solid proof of the Favres' misdemeanours, that she will be implicated in all of this. But there is no advantage in spilling my guts to Müller. She is now the enemy. Any information could be used against me. I exercise my right to remain silent.

'I am a good citizen, Lucie Smithers. You think they will listen to you, the *Ausländerin*, the foreigner? I have obeyed the rules all my life, have been a model citizen. I have paid my taxes – that is the only thing the Swiss government really cares about, that we all pay our taxes.' *Except for Natasha Favre*, I think. 'There is no reward for this.' Müller throws her arm in an arc, fingers feathered like a dancer, strangely delicate at the end of her muscular arm.

And for a moment, fleeting though it is, I feel sorry for her.

* * *

It's Christmas Eve. Whatever each woman's creed or colour, we are all celebrating. It's not really about the Christianity of Christmas at all. It's about trying to make the best out of a bad situation, and just for today and tomorrow, everyone will be a little friendlier, chasing away the melancholy of not being with family. I think it's more like the way Christmas should be, taking the occasion back to the simple roots of goodwill, tolerance and compassion.

Müller has gone. The rumour is that she took early retirement. But I know better. I could embellish the scandal, but choose instead to concentrate my emotions on the procedures to get me out of here. Proof of prison backhanders is nowhere near proof of a tainted police investigation, and because of the Christmas and New Year holidays, I am not a free person yet. There is still my dead husband to be considered at the end of the day, and whatever chain of events led me to being locked away in this prison, his death can't be undone.

One thing is clear: Natasha Favre used her money and her influence to manipulate the proceedings. Somewhere in those chapters, a proclamation of self-defence leading to a verdict of accidental death has been twisted into a completely different story, one which I must rewrite before it's too late.

* * *

The telephone cabins are occupied every minute of the day. The handset is hot and sticky. The Polish girl gazes at me from across the hallway, waiting for her turn, arms crossed over her chest, knee bent with one foot flat against the wall as though she will hurl herself towards the cabin once I've finished. She has a softer look on her face than usual, the anticipation of talking to a loved one.

It's a minor miracle I manage to get through to JP on the first try. Natasha cannot refuse. It's Christmas.

'You must not take long, Lucille,' she says. 'We are going to a Christmas Eve event in the village.'

That's my son you're taking out, just remember that! I want to scream. She promptly passes the phone to JP and I defuse my anger.

'Mama, Mama! It's snowing! Big, fat juicy flakes!'

I automatically look out through the scratched Perspex wall of the telephone cabin towards the window at the end of the hallway. It looks grey and drizzly outside. Not the snowy landscapes of Christmas cards. It's sometimes hard to imagine we're in the same country. JP chatters excitedly. I wonder how many presents are waiting for him beneath the tree.

'Tomorrow Mimi and Poppa are taking me on a horse and sleigh ride.'

I can hear him beaming, bursting with seasonal exhilaration. My chest aches.

'I wish I could be there with you, sweetheart. I would love to spend Christmas with you.'

'I know, Mama, but you have to stay there. It's because of what you did to Papa. Made him disappear.'

I catch my breath. I can't imagine what is going on in JP's mind. Can't imagine what Natasha has been telling him.

'I'm sure we'll have dozens of Christmases together,' I say.

On the one hand I want him to be sad that I'm not there to celebrate with him. On the other, I am happy that he is still being given the magical Christmas memories a young child carries into adolescence. I have to believe that we will have many more together.

When the call is over, I hurry away. I spoke to my parents earlier. It was a stilted conversation this morning with nothing to ask, nothing to offer. I couldn't even begin to clarify the information we have uncovered. I feel too tired to explain it to them, to maintain the optimism. My mind swings from hope to darkness so often, both Anne and Léon must be sick of my invective.

I intend to avoid the area near the two cabins in our living block for the next two days. There are so many tears being shed for families who are whole continents away. I don't want to feel any sadder than I already am.

Léon has arrived for another impromptu meeting. I'm not allowed to receive calls, so he must have contacted the administrative office to get permission. They can't stop a visit from my lawyer, especially after the farce of Müller's so-called 'persuasion'.

There was a note stuck to my door when I came back from the atelier. I'm surprised he's arrived unannounced. I can't even begin to imagine how much this is all going to cost me, or my parents, when this is all over.

I don't bother entering the cell to change my paint-splattered smock, and run along the corridor to the stairs. The interview rooms in this block are on the ground floor. A guard yells '*Langsam!*' as I pass the office on the first floor. I have to wait for another guard to let me into the admin block, my mind racing as I tap my foot. I bite my lip, hoping Léon's presence doesn't mean bad news.

He's smiling as I enter the room. Not the smile of a greeting, but some smug look that tells me he is expecting approval for something that he's proud of. I recognise the expression from JP, of all people, when he's built a Lego tower or drawn me a special picture. My heart leaps with hope.

'We got him! The detective, Genillard. We found the link to Natasha Favre.'

Léon speaks quickly, words tumbling out in his enthusiasm to convey the news. I shake my head. It's taking a while to absorb what he has said. I walk over to where he stands, holding a sheaf of papers he's taken from his briefcase. He shakes them at me like a victory scythe at a Bolshevik uprising. I hold out my hands, palms pressing down.

'Whoa. Slow down,' I say, confused. 'What do you mean? Backtrack. Genillard?'

'You were right. They found a large sum of money in his bank account. Paid directly from an account in the UK. In the name of Natasha Anastasia Orlov.'

My hands finally fly to my mouth. That has to be our Natasha. Without thinking, I grab him by the shoulders, hug him and press the side of my face to the lapel of his expensive suit jacket. He pats my back gently, and uncertainly leaves his hand flat between my shoulder blades. A faint waft of musky cologne makes me close my eyes and breathe deeply. My heart skips a beat.

'Oh shit, I'm sorry.' I push away, brush at his jacket, hoping I haven't left a trace of paint anywhere on his suit. 'Just as well I work with acrylics. They dry quickly.'

I leave the palm of my hand resting briefly on his chest. He smiles down at me a little awkwardly. I am floating.

'So, tell me! How come they were able to search his financial records in the first place? Surely that's not easy?'

'They were not initially looking for the *pot-de-vin*, the bribe. But after you told me about the article you saw in the *24 Heures*, I talked to a colleague of mine who works in the IT department at the cantonal police headquarters. Genillard's laptop was confiscated for inspection after the porn allegation, and with a little encouragement my colleague managed to get himself on the investigating team. They found Genillard had been accessing some soft-porn websites. A further question was conveniently raised about some dubious sexual services he may have initiated from his laptop that were linked to these sites.'

'Conveniently? For us?' I am mystified.

'Yes, of course! My colleague insisted that they should investigate Genillard's bank account to ascertain the destination of these payments. *Et voilà!*'

'I always thought Genillard was a creepy guy. But how did they make the connection to Natasha? The bribe? How did they know that this was the same person? The name Natasha is not that unusual. They could have assumed she was some Russian hooker, and he was merely paying for a generous service. Someone must have been looking out for the abnormality. Something involving the case.'

I look at Léon. He's still smiling.

'I may have, how do you say, put a bug in someone's ear. Something to watch out for, unrelated to the porn. The amount paid to him by this Natasha Orlov was significant. Enough to set alarm bells ringing. Genillard had already been placed on forced leave until his files could be examined. I asked the same colleague to try to find out who Natasha Orlov might be. It was not difficult – the head office of the bank listed on Genillard's credited account is in London, and when a police investigation is under way from this country, banks are pretty open about the information they give now. They know that with the lifting of Switzerland's secrecy laws, favours may be returned sometime in the future.'

I smile, remembering his initial disbelief about corruption.

'There were two addresses on the account. One for statements and one for other correspondence. The second is her address here in Switzerland. That was the connection.'

'Now they have proof that Genillard accepted the bribe from Natasha ... Is it concrete? Is it enough?'

'Yes, Lucie, it is enough. It is clear evidence.'

'Oh, thank God,' I whisper, thinking of JP.

Without thinking, I lean towards Pittet. Relief floods my body.

'Happy new year,' he says, and places his hand on the back of my head, his fingers winding in my hair. My stomach gives a little flip. It's like he wants to kiss me, in celebration perhaps. But I'm not sure, and I stand rigid away from him. He holds my gaze as if nothing out of the ordinary just happened.

'We have to work on getting me out of here,' I continue. 'And as soon as possible. Léon, I cannot let Natasha take JP away.'

Zeinah was right. With so many people being influenced by my mother-in-law, it was only a matter of time before something out of the ordinary appeared on the radar.

'So what's the procedure? Where do we go from here?' I ask, twisting the string on my sweatshirt hood.

'You have to be patient, Lucie, but we will get you out of here. The information is being submitted to the judge, and the case will be brought forward, will be heard earlier than usual due to the injustice of your imprisonment. No one would expect you to stay longer than necessary, but the judge cannot let you go without studying the documents. Though it might only be a matter of days.'

'And when will they arrest her?'

'I ... I don't know. I assumed you would want to wait until you are free. So that you can automatically regain custody of JP.'

'Léon, it is imperative that I get out of here as soon as possible. I don't think I even have a matter of days. I believe JP's grandparents are about to leave the country, to go to Russia, and they are taking my son with them.'

'This they cannot do. Madame Favre is implicated in this crime, this corruption.'

'I know they *shouldn't* do this. There are many things they shouldn't have done. But it seems they have been planning to leave for some time. I've been told that they are applying for Russian citizenship for JP. They'll probably change his name. I don't see how they can be stopped. People come and go through Geneva or Zürich airports daily, or any of the road borders – Basel, Konstanz, Chiasso. A judge's decree might take another age to obtain. I'm sure by the time we have the means to stop them, they will be long gone. Don't miscalculate the ingenuity of my mother-in-law.'

'Lucie, I promise to get onto this straight away. If you cannot be free within a short time, at least I can try to stop this terrible thing happening with your son.'

'Léon, I know I've said this before, but I'm not sure how I am going to be able to pay you for your legal services. I have to be honest. I don't know how much my parents can afford. Even within my marriage to Matt, there was never a great flow of funds ...'

I feel sick mentioning Matt's name. I no longer want to think of him. Don't want to be reminded of him, especially talking to Léon.

'We worry about that later.'

Pittet turns to leave, and as the door opens to the entranceway that will take him out of the building and into freedom, I long to run after him. I feel pathetic, helpless in here. If JP disappears from Switzerland, I would follow him to Russia. How much can I rely on Léon to do the right thing? I put my trust in a young handsome Swiss man before, and look where it got me.

I walk back to my cell. As I enter I stare hard at three of JP's drawings taped on the wall. Clenching my fist, I beat the plaster twice beside the pictures, bringing to mind the thumping on the other side of this wall all those weeks ago when Fatima lived there. I wonder if Zeinah can hear me.

I'm in limbo, helplessly recognising I shouldn't really be here, and knowing that my son could be days, hours, minutes away from being taken from his home.

Chapter 22

'What do you think you have learned from this whole experience? Not being in Hindelbank, but the unfortunate events that brought you here?'

Dagmar and I are sitting outside in the courtyard. It's cool, but we are sheltered from the breeze, sitting on a bench with our backs against the sun-drenched wall of my block. White clouds scud across the blue sky. The hint of an early spring perhaps. Less than twenty-four hours and I will be out of here. Tonight the girls on the floor are throwing a farewell party for me.

'When I first came here, I felt so weak. I kept wondering if I was a dog in my last life. The kind that is beaten repeatedly by its master, and keeps coming back for more love. I waited too long to question the pointlessness of staying with a partner who constantly betrayed me. In retrospect, how did I possibly think that would end? Would I wait until JP was old enough to deal with our broken family and simply walk away?'

'But you were never confident enough to continually challenge him at the time, when you doubted him.'

'It's to do with that old cliché – love is blind. Sometimes when I remember my stupidity, I still blush. Embarrassment, shame, inadequacy, I feel them all. I can imagine what they were all thinking in the village. The others who knew. Those girls who became his string of conquests. What kind of idiot couldn't see what was going on? Couldn't see, or wouldn't see? It has taken me an age to acknowledge that I should never have accepted it. And for too long I was holding on to the idea that I still loved Matt, which in turn made me feel guilty.'

I shake my head, break off a piece of a bread roll I kept from lunch, and throw it towards the sparrows gathered on the gravel. They race to salvage the crumbs, fighting with each other to get the largest morsel. Dagmar shifts on her chair, sits a little straighter.

'Love,' she says, tapping the side of her empty mug with her fingers. It's the first time I notice she's wearing a wedding band, chinking against the ceramic. I wonder briefly what her interpretation of my marriage must seem like. I wonder if she has ever doubted her own partner.

'Even the most reputable psychologist will never be able to sort the love thing out,' she muses.

I reflect briefly on what love now means to me. Not the love a mother has for her son, or that of the child reciprocated. I know that love now more than ever. I mean the love I thought I had with Matt. Passionate love. The dreamy stuff of fairy tales with Prince Charmings and beautiful princesses. Those trapped within its web think there is nothing as blissful. But love is a double-edged sword, so closely linked to that other dark emotion. Hate.

We sit in companionable silence, watching the birds. I will always wonder what Matt's idea of love encapsulated. To be so confident he was doing no harm in his deceit. To be so smooth a pathological liar. His adamant conviction that my mistrust hurt him, rather than the actions he took that were improper. Ask most human beings, they'll sympathise.

'Do you believe there's such a thing as a lying gene? Like the murder gene discovered in a high percentage of murderers?' I ask.

281

'I do indeed. And in our lifetime, I believe that perhaps they will be using such genetic information to support arguments in courts of law. In your case, unfortunately, adultery is not an offence punishable by the state.'

I remember the last fight in our living room.

'If JP has his father's genes, I hope I can instil in him the importance of honesty and integrity. Matt's sister MC has the same genes, and she's okay. I want to be able to show JP that the world is basically a good place, where truth prevails.'

Dagmar nods with a smile at my comment. One day I will explain all this to JP, when he's old enough to pull apart all the information and decide for himself what exactly went wrong. For now, it's finally time for me to mourn the relationship that brought my beautiful shining son into my life.

'There are other people who play an important part in this, Lucie, and you mustn't forget their loyalty to you. That kind of love might be more tangible to you, something you can understand at this stage.'

For some reason I think first of Léon Pittet.

'JP. Yes, his love is unconditional. I know that, thank goodness. And Anne. I could not have done any of this without her. I don't quite know how to thank her.'

'I'm sure you'll find a way. I find it hard to believe that you're still only 26, and you have been through so much.' She pauses. 'What about your other friends? The people you know in the village.'

'We didn't have that many common friends, but there are people at the college, at our local bar, and at the ski school, more acquaintances really. It will be interesting to see whether any of them will take up where we left off. The trouble is, they knew him too. I can't expect people to take sides, and now I'm probably tainted in all their eyes.'

I look through the chain-link fence to the road leading towards the prison, holding on to the thought that tomorrow I will be on that road, heading out. Tomorrow I will fly.

'Yes, they knew him too,' I continue in a more conciliatory tone. 'I don't think I want to face them, to be honest. They must have known what was going on. Would you want a colleague like that? Knowing he could do that to you too? My biggest mistake was to try and normalise JP's family upbringing. I carried on as if nothing had happened. I ended up as part of the lie.'

I pause, and turn my head to the sun as it appears from behind a cloud. The light shines as golden as a Greek beach against the insides of my lids.

Dagmar remains silent. I hope she understands that my ranting is actually a cathartic venting of emotions I haven't been able to vocalise before. A little voice tells me maybe my bitterness will be a concern to her, doubting my ability to walk out of here with peace in my mind. But I think not, I think she believes I'm seeking closure, in whatever way I can.

What she doesn't know, is the dark thing still writhing deep in my conscience.

'Lucie, I believe deep down inside you always blamed yourself …' My heart misses a beat before she continues. 'Which is why you have confused your emotions all this time, mistaken what you call love for a dogged acceptance of the maximum emotion that Matt could offer you. Our sessions have only rendered you human. It seems to me you have finally accepted your situation, without seeking blame or revenge. All human beings have their faults, but we cannot keep kicking ourselves about them. We can't choose where we've come from, but we can choose which path to take from here. You have already used the correct tools to get your son back. You know next time you will not let anyone kick you around. And there will be a next time. You are still so young. Our whole life is a learning process. We never stop. Some of your lessons have been harsher than others.'

Dagmar pauses. 'Have you thought about whether you will stay in the village?'

'I'd like to, but I know how people talk. They think I'm a murderer.'

I swallow. That word. It will sit on me like a tattoo, fading over the years, but never forgotten. People know they should, but they can't take that memory back. I was a dark person in their minds once upon a time. 'Murderer' has permanence to it.

'It won't be long before they're out. Didier will probably only serve a few months,' I continue. 'Natasha, maybe a few more years. I'm still not sure I can live in the same village as them.'

'And have you thought how you will support yourself and your son?'

'I'll use some of the money that has been deposited in my bank account from the Russian Art Council. They had an award scheme for the recovery of the remaining stolen icons. I'll rent a small apartment for us both, and start building a life again.'

I recall my recent correspondence with the Hermitage curator. I had to give back the icon in my possession too, but the reward money is a significant amount. I didn't want to accept the money at first. I considered it the filthy means by which the Favres have lived their deceptive lives, but both Anne and Léon have reminded me that this time the money has come from a good cause, the gratefulness of the museum, and I must think of it as an investment for JP's future.

'If I can stand to stay in the village, I will see if I can get my part-time job back at the college. I don't know who the professor is there now, and many of the students will have changed, but a few will remember me, and I had some good colleagues there who I know will not be sorry that Matt is no longer a member of the faculty with so many affairs with students going on. It's just … if they're still in the village …'

'Maybe your in-laws will themselves find enough humility to find it too difficult to live in the same village with you. Considering the web of lies they wove. And especially that other people now know the truth.'

'Sometimes people don't want to see the truth. They want to hang on to a good story. I don't know if I can be the happy ending of their good story. We'll see. It will be hard on JP, but he's young ...'

'And you're both strong, good people, Lucie.'

I look up at Dagmar and smile. She believes in me.

Jesus, I'm only 26 but I feel like I'm 50. These last months have felt like half a lifetime. But there is a future out there for JP and me, wherever we decide to make our life.

* * *

It's one of those days you want to be outside. And it's the day I simply have to be out. A light breeze carries cherry blossoms from the tree at the back of the prison yard across the garden like flurries of snow. A few ragged clouds scud across the sky, and as I haul my bag towards the gates of the prison, the wind blows my hair across my cheek.

As I pull back the strands from my face, my eyes fill with tears as I see three people walking towards the prison gates from the car park across the road. Anne is holding JP's hand. He sees me, but is reluctant to run forward. The heavy cold bars of the prison gates are still between us. I'm surprised to see Léon Pittet walking beside them. I knew he would be collecting JP from the social service home in Lausanne where he has been for the past few weeks, but I didn't think he would make the journey all the way to Hindelbank with JP and Anne. He's wearing a pair of faded jeans, a polo shirt and a shy smile. The casual outfit ironically makes him look older than his well-tailored suits do.

Dagmar, a few inmates and a handful of the guards have gathered to say goodbye. I turn and smile, resting my eyes briefly on Zeinah, grinning happily for me, and then on Yasmine who has her arms crossed, but wears a soft expression on her face.

She knows deep down, despite the promises, that we will never see each other again.

The guard opens the gate. The chief warden comes to take some documents from Léon, and then the gate clunks closed behind me. I am free.

JP runs then, throwing himself into my arms, and I pick him up and swing him around. He wraps his legs around my hips, clings to me like a barnacle, and will not let me put him down. My bag is crammed with the pictures he has been sending every day from the children's home, along with notes from the foster parents about the activities he has been doing with the other children. For me it was a great halfway house, no longer having to wonder what he is doing at any given moment. One step closer to being with him.

'Anne! Thank you so much! Where's little Monique?'

'François is looking after her at home with Valentin. She's waiting to meet you there, and the boys are ready to welcome you.'

Anne smiles, letting me know I'm always welcome with her.

Léon puts his hand on my back.

'I'm off your case now, Lucie,' he says. 'I won't be billing the hours from now, however many there may be. That's up to you. Anne would like me to drive you all home. So the two of you can … catch up.'

Léon leaves his hand a little longer on my shoulder, and a small frisson causes a pulse to tick on my neck. I open the back door of Anne's car and lift JP into Valentin's car seat. He can climb in himself, but my arms want to keep contact with him for as long as possible. I secure the seat belt, fumbling with the buckle.

It finally hits me that I am free, and I look down at my trembling hands after double-checking JP's belt is secure. I hold my palm in front of my eyes, and JP's smile appears out of focus between my fingers.

These fingers are my tools of precision. They have caressed my baby, painted copies of masterpieces, and clutched the neck of a ceramic vase from Provence. I blink, and can still see the pattern of blue and yellow flowers, hand-painted carefully by an artisan in Cassis. Aimed carefully at the soft part of my husband's temple, the blow may not have killed him, but my intent revisits me now like a shameful fantasy. With JP still in my vision, I know I will continue to protect him, for as long as possible.

The truth hits me like a sledgehammer.

Matt's death was justified. I can say that now. Call it a crime of passion if you like. Through this confusing journey to get myself out of prison to be with my son, and in the fading misrepresentation of love that I discussed with Dagmar yesterday, I now believe Matt deserved what he had coming to him. All that betrayal had to have karmic consequences.

I straighten up and gaze across the field of sprouting green corn, towards the village of Hindelbank and beyond, to the Bernese Plateau and the Alpes Vaudoises.

To a future with my son.

Acknowledgements

The seeds of *The Art of Deception* were sown some years ago by author and actor André Lvov Mikhelson whose escape from Russia as a boy during the revolution inspired parts of the novel. A handful of scenes were written during a crime writers' retreat in the rolling hills of Tuscany a few summers ago, and I thank Meg Gardiner for her tutoring and our intensive writing sessions at The Mill. Thanks to those who have given invaluable feedback at various stages: Antony Dunford, Andy Stafford, Louise Buckley, and members of the International Women's Book Club in Zug. Thanks to my wonderful editor at HQ Digital, Dom Wakeford, for his shrewd honing of my work. For information about prison life at Hindelbank I thank Director Annette Keller, and beg forgiveness for any artistic licence. For advice on Swiss tax law I thank Albert Blattmann. And lastly, as always, thanks to my devoted partner Chris for bouncing plot ideas back and forth during our hikes in the Alps, and inspiring me to keep writing.

Dear Reader,

Thank you so much for purchasing and reading *The Art of Deception*. I hope you have enjoyed the story.

I have incorporated many of the things I love into this novel, including fine art, human diversity and the mountains. Hindelbank Prison is a real penitentiary, the only one exclusively designated for women in Switzerland, situated north of Bern. The setting for the backstory in the novel is based on the Swiss ski resort of Leysin in the Alpes Vaudoises where I spent many years during my twenties, and where I still have life-long friends who are like family to me.

The most important people in an author's career are you, the readers, whether you are a blogger, a reviewer, or someone who simply enjoys a good yarn. Many of you helped make my first novel *Strangers on a Bridge* such a success, and I hope you have enjoyed this second novel. A fellow author once told me that reviews are like a coin in a busker's hat. I'd like to use that analogy and encourage you to leave your review on the platform of your choice. Each of those coins contributes towards an author's bread and butter.

And I hope to bring you many more tales for your enjoyment in the future.

À bientôt!

Louise

Dear Reader,

Thank you so much for taking the time to read this book – we hope you enjoyed it! If you did, we'd be so appreciative if you left a review.

Here at HQ Digital we are dedicated to publishing fiction that will keep you turning the pages into the early hours. We publish a variety of genres, from heartwarming romance, to thrilling crime and sweeping historical fiction.

To find out more about our books, enter competitions and discover exclusive content, please join our community of readers by following us at:

🐦 @HQDigitalUK

f facebook.com/HQDigitalUK

Are you a budding writer? We're also looking for authors to join the HQ Digital family! Please submit your manuscript to:

HQDigital@harpercollins.co.uk.

Hope to hear from you soon!

Turn the page for an extract from another thrilling read
by Louise Mangos, *Strangers on a Bridge* …

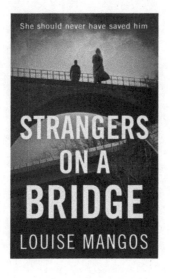

Chapter 1

APRIL

I wouldn't normally exercise on the weekend, but several days of continuous spring rain had hampered my attempts to run by the *Aegerisee* near our home during the week. The lake had brimmed over onto my regular running paths, turbid waters frothy with alpine meltwater. The sun came out that morning, accompanied by a cloudless blue sky I wanted to dive into. Simon knew I was chomping at the bit. He let me go, encouraging me to run for everyone's peace of mind. He would go cycling later with a group of friends when I returned home for domestic duties.

I chose a woodland track from the lowlands near the town of Baar, and planned to run up through the Lorze Gorge beside the river, continuing along the valley to home. A local bus dropped me at the turnoff to the narrow limestone canyon, and I broke into a loping jog along the gravel lane, which dwindled to a packed earthen trail. Sunlight winked through trees fluorescent with new leaf shoots, and the forest canopy at this time of day shaded much of the track. The swollen river gushed at my side. Branches still dripped from days of dampness as the sun dried out the woodlands. I lengthened my stride and breathed in the metallic aroma of sprouting wild garlic. The mundane troubles of juggling family time dissipated, and as I settled into my metronome rhythm, a feeling of peacefulness ensued.

The sun warmed my shoulders as I ran out from the shade of the forest. I focused on a small pine tree growing comically out of the mossy roof shingles of the old Tobel Bridge. Above me, two more bridges connected the widening funnel of the Lorze Gorge at increasingly higher levels, resembling an Escher painting.

Before I entered the dim tunnel of the wooden bridge, I glanced upwards. A flash of movement caught my eye. My glance slid away, and darted back.

A figure stood on the edge of the upper bridge.

In a split second my brain registered the person's stance. I sucked in my breath, squinting to be sure I had seen correctly at such a distance.

Oh, no. Don't. Please, don't.

The figure stood midway between two of the immense concrete pillars rising out of the chasm, his fists clutching the handrail. His body swayed slightly as he looked out across the expanse to the other side of the gorge, the river roaring its white noise hundreds of feet below him. Birdsong trilled near me on the trail, strangely out of place in this alarming situation.

At first I was incredulous. How ridiculous to think this person was going to jump. But that body language, a certain hollowed stiffness to his shoulders and chest, even from a distance, radiated doom. Unsure how to react, but sure I didn't want to observe the worst, I slowed my pace to a walk, and finally stopped.

'*Haallo!*' I yelled over the noise of the river.

My voice took some time to reach him, the echo bouncing back and forth between the canyon walls. Seconds later his head jolted, awoken from his reverie.

'Hey! Hallo!' I called again, holding my arm out straight, palm raised like a marshal ordering traffic to halt at an intersection.

I backtracked a few metres on the trail, away from the shadow of the covered bridge, so he could see me more clearly. A path wove up through the woods on the right, connecting the valley to the route higher up. I abandoned my initial course and ran up the steep slope, having lost sight of the man somewhere above me. At the top I turned onto the pavement and hurried towards the main road onto the bridge, gulping painful breaths of chilly air. My heart pounded with panic and the effort of running up the hill.

The man had been out of my sight for more than a few minutes. I dreaded what I might find on my arrival, scenarios crowding in my mind, along with thoughts of how I might help this person. As I strode onto the bridge, I saw with relief he was still there on the pavement. I was now level with him, and no longer had to strain my neck looking upwards. Fear kept my eyes connected to the lone figure as I approached. If I looked away for even a second, he might leap stealthily over the edge. Holding my gaze on him would hopefully secure him to the bridge.

'Hallo …' I called more softly, my voice drowned by the sound of the rushing water in the Lorze below. I walked steadily along the pavement towards him. Despite my proximity, this time he didn't seem to have heard me.

'*Grüezi*, hallo,' I said again.

With a flick of his head, he leaned back again, bent his knees, and looked ahead.

'No!' The gunshot abruptness of my shout broke his concentration. My voice ricocheted off the concrete wall of the bridge. He stopped mid-sway, eyes wide.

My stomach clenched involuntarily as I glanced down into the gorge, when moments before I had been staring up out of it. I felt foolish, not knowing what to say. It seemed like a different world up here. As I approached within talking distance, I greeted him in my broken German, still breathing heavily.

'Um, good morning … Beautiful, hey?' I swept my arm about me.

What a stupid thing to say. My voice sounded different without the echo of space between us. The words sounded so absurd, and a nervous laugh escaped before I could stop it.

He looked at me angrily, but remained silent, perhaps vaguely surprised that someone had addressed him in a foreign language. Or surprised anyone had talked to him at all in this country where complete strangers rarely struck up a conversation beyond a cursory passing greeting. His cheeks flushed with indignation. I reeled at the wave of visual resentment. Then his eyes settled on my face, and his features softened.

'Do you speak English?' I asked. The man nodded; no smile, no greeting. He still leaned backwards, hands gripping the railing. *Please. Don't. Jump.*

He was a little taller than me, and a few years my senior. Sweat glistened on his brow. His steel-grey hair was raked back on his head as though he had been running his fingers through it repeatedly. His coat flapped open to reveal a smart navy suit, Hugo Boss maybe, and I looked down to the pavement expecting to see a briefcase at his feet. He looked away. I desperately needed him to turn back, keep eye contact. My hand hovered in front of me, wanting to pull the invisible rope joining us.

'I … I'm sorry, but I had this strange feeling you were considering jumping off the bridge.' A nervous laugh bubbled again in my throat, and I hoped my assessment had been false.

'I am,' he said.

Chapter 2

Immeasurable seconds of silence followed the man's admission. My brain shut out external influences. A blink broke the rift in time. Sounds rushed back in – the swishing of an occasional passing vehicle, gushing water in the river below, the persistent tweeting of a bird, like the squeaky wheel of an old shopping trolley.

'Now you've stopped me,' he said. 'This is not good. You should go away. Go away.'

But the daggers in his eyes had retracted. I held his gaze, trying not to blink for fear of losing the connection. Many clichés entered my head. In desperation I chose one to release the tension.

'Can we talk? I know things must be bad. But maybe if you talk it through with someone ...'

I shrugged, unsure how to continue. Perspiration cooled my body, and I shivered. Pulling the sleeves of my running shirt down to my wrists, I rubbed my upper arms. Wary of the abyss at my side, I took a step closer to the man. He didn't speak, but stood upright, and raised his hand as though to push me away. He turned briefly to look into the depths of the gorge, and I grabbed his arm firmly below the elbow, gently applying pressure. His gaze at first fixed on the hand on his arm, then rose again to my face. He studied my furrowed brow, and the forced curve of my smile.

'Please. Let's talk,' I said.

I had no magical formula for this, but I sensed my touch eased the tension in his body. My nails scraped the material of his coat as my grip on his arm tightened. He slumped down to sit on the pavement with his back to the bridge wall. I closed my eyes briefly and puffed air through my lips.

Step one achieved. No jump.

Traffic was sparse on a Sunday. One car slowed a little, but kept going. No one else was curious enough to stop. The regular swish and thump each time a vehicle drove over the concrete slabs echoed between the walls of the bridge. We must have looked like an odd pair. Me dressed in Lycra running pants and a bright-yellow running top, the man in his business attire, now looking a little dishevelled. The laces on his black brogues were undone. I stared at his feet, and wondered if he had intended to remove his shoes before he jumped.

'Can I help?' I asked, crouching down. The man looked at me imploringly, hands flopped over his knees. The strain of anguish had reddened the whites of his eyes, making his irises shine a striking green.

'I don't know,' he said uncertainly.

'Well, let's start with your name,' I said, as though addressing a small child.

'Manfred,' he said.

There was no movement towards the traditional Swiss hand-shake. Still squatting, pins and needles fizzed in my feet. I kept one arm across my thigh, the other balanced on fingertips against the pavement.

'Mine's Alice, and I'm sorry, I don't speak very good German …'

'It's okay,' he said. 'I speak a little English.'

I snorted involuntarily. It was the standard *I speak a little*

298

English introduction I had grown used to over the past few years living in Switzerland, usually made with very few grammatical mistakes. The tension broke, and relief flooded through me. *He would not jump.* I sensed my beatific smile softening my expression. Manfred looked into my eyes and held my gaze intently, absorbing the euphoria.

I turned to sit at his side, blood rushing back to my legs. His gaze followed my movement, a curious glint now in his eyes, and his lips parted slightly, revealing the costly perfection of Swiss orthodontics. Leaning back against the wall, the cold concrete pressed against my sweat-dampened running shirt. I extended my legs, thighs sucking up the chill of the pavement. Our elbows touched and he drew in his knees, preparing to stand. I laid my hand on his arm.

'You must not do this thing. Please …'

He looked at me, tears pooling briefly before he swiped at his eyes with the back of one hand.

'You stopped me.'

'Yes, I stopped you. I don't want you to jump, Manfred.'

'You …' He scrutinised me.

'It's messy,' I said.

Manfred's gaze travelled from my face, looking at the dishevelled hair I knew must be sprouting from its ponytail, down to my legs stretched in front of me.

'Taking your life,' I continued. 'It's messy. Not just the – you know …' I made a rising and dipping movement with my hand. 'Trust me, I've been there.'

'You … wanted to jump?' Curiosity animated Manfred's voice.

'Not jumping, no. God forbid. A failed attempt at overdose. A teenage stupidity after a heartbreak. But I wasn't going anywhere on a dozen paracetamol.'

I'd never told Simon this, and I bit my lip at the admission. I remembered the 'mess' I had caused: a hysterical mother, a bruised oesophagus, a cough that lasted weeks after the stomach pump, embarrassing counselling that all boiled down to adolescent drama.

'Whatever has happened to make you do this, people will always be sad. You will harm more individuals than yourself. Not just physically,' I continued.

Manfred hissed briefly through his teeth. '*Ja, guet*,' he said, the Swiss German 'good' drawn out to two syllables. *Gu-weht*. He stared at a point below my face. I knew he was watching the pulse tick at the base of my throat, the suprasternal notch. The place where Simon often placed his lips. I blushed, and zipped my running shirt up to the collar.

His gaze shifted back to my face. A slip of a smile, and then a frown.

'I cannot live with myself any more. I cannot live with who I am, what I do. What I have done,' he said.

The back of my neck tingled.

'But it doesn't solve the problem for other people,' I interjected. 'It creates more. There must be another way to work out your … your problems. Your life is precious. Your life is sacred and will be special to someone.'

His lips formed a small circle.

'My life is …'

'Precious. Valuable. Prized. A good thing, not to be thrown away,' I reiterated.

He smiled tentatively, siphoning my relief, feeding on my compassion. I felt my euphoria returned to me, delivered on a platter of … what? Gratefulness? No, it was something else.

My mouth went dry.

300

If you enjoyed *The Art of Deception*, then why not try another exhilarating read from HQ Digital?

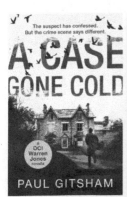

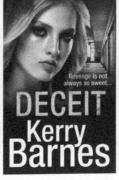

ONE PLACE. MANY STORIES

Bold, innovative and
empowering publishing.

FOLLOW US ON:

@HQStories

ONE PLACE. MANY STORIES

Bold, innovative and
genre-setting publishing.

FOLLOW US ON:

@HQStories